Pirate's Fortune

Supreme Constellations

Book Four

Praise for Gun Brooke's Romance Novels

Fierce Overture

"Gun Brooke creates memorable characters, and Noelle and Helena are no exception. Each woman is "more than meets the eye" as each exhibits depth, fears, and longings. And the sexual tension between them is real, hot, and raw."—*Just About Write*

September Canvas

"In this character-driven story, trust is earned and secrets are uncovered. Deanna and Faythe are fully fleshed out and prove to the reader each has much depth, talent, wit and problem-solving abilities. *September Canvas* is a good read with a thoroughly satisfying conclusion."—*Just About Write*

Sheridan's Fate

"Sheridan's fire and Lark's warm embers are enough to make this book sizzle. Brooke, however, has gone beyond the wonderful emotional explorations of these characters to tell the story of those who, for various reasons, become differently-abled. Whether it is a bullet, an illness, or a problem at birth, many women and men find themselves in Sheridan's situation. Her courage and Lark's gentleness and determination send this romance into a 'must read.'"—*Just About Write*

Coffee Sonata

"In *Coffee Sonata*, the lives of these four women become intertwined. In forming friendships and love, closets and disabilities are discussed, along with differences in age and backgrounds. Love and friendship are areas filled with complexity and nuances. Brooke takes her time to savor the complexities while her main characters savor their excellent cups of coffee. If you enjoy a good love story, a great setting, and wonderful characters, look for *Coffee Sonata* at your favorite gay and lesbian bookstore."—*Family & Friends* magazine

Course of Action

"Brooke's words capture the intensity of their growing relationship. Her prose throughout the book is breathtaking and heart-stopping. Where have you been hiding, Gun Brooke? I, for one, would like to see more romances from this author."—*Independent Gay Writer*

What Reviewers Say About
Gun Brooke's Supreme Constellations Series

Protector of the Realm
Supreme Constellations: Book One

"*Protector of the Realm* has it all; sabotage, corruption, erotic love and exhilarating space fights. Gun Brooke's second novel is forceful with a winning combination of solid characters and a brilliant plot. The book exemplifies her growth as an inventive storyteller and is sure to garner multiple awards in the coming year."—*Just About Write*

"Brooke is an amazing author, and has written in other genres. Never have I read a book where I started at the top of the page and don't know what will happen two paragraphs later… She keeps the excitement going, and the pages turning." —*MegaScene*

By the Author

The Supreme Constellations Series:

Protector of the Realm

Rebel's Quest

Warrior's Valor

Pirate's Fortune

Course of Action

Coffee Sonata

Sheridan's Fate

September Canvas

Fierce Overture

Pirate's Fortune

Supreme Constellations Book Four

by

Gun Brooke

2011

PIRATE'S FORTUNE

ISBN 13: 978-1-60282-563-5

This Trade Paperback Original Is Published By
Bold Strokes Books, Inc.
P.O. Box 249
Valley Falls, NY 12185

First Edition: September 2011

Credits
Editors: Shelley Thrasher and Stacia Seaman
Production Design: Stacia Seaman
Cover Art by Gun Brooke
Cover Design by Sheri (graphicartist2020@hotmail.com)

Acknowledgments

First, I want to express my gratitude to my first readers, Jan and Sam, who between them took on the job of helping me not lose face by missing silly mistakes before submitting the manuscript to BSB. I also want to thank Pol, who allowed me to pick her brilliant mind regarding tactical stuff.

Dr. Shelley Thrasher, my editor—thank you so much for being the perfect match for me. We work so well together and you make the editing phase fun and educational every time.

Radclyffe—aka Len Barot—president of Bold Strokes Books, thank you for providing a fantastic environment within BSB for us authors to grow and evolve. I'm proud to be one of your first authors, and that you still want me around.

Sheri the graphic artist, thank you for collaborating with me on the cover, and for making my 3D art work so well.

Stacia, Cindy, Connie, Sandy, Lori, and all the proofers and copy editors, and other people who work for and with BSB to publish our books—you are all such "fire souls," to translate a Swedish word directly, and I think you deserve tons of praise.

Thank you to my faithful science-fiction-loving readers, who have been with me from the start with this series and kept asking for the next book. Now I end the series with this book, and even if I occasionally go through separation anxiety, I also look forward to taking you with me on a new sci-fi adventure with the next series I have planned.

Also…thank you to those among my friends who are always encouraging and supportive. You know who you are.

Acknowledgments

To Elon.
To Malin and Henrik.
To Joanne.

You are like handprints on my heart.

Prologue

Madisyn, darling, can you hear me?" The male voice sounded familiar, yet somehow alien.

"Mmm." Madisyn's lips and tongue wouldn't obey. Her eyelids felt heavy or, rather, as if they weren't there. "Uh…"

"Calibrating the synapses now." The metallic-sounding male voice changed, became darker and garbled.

"Wha…?" Madisyn stiffened as pins and needles traveled through her system, making every nerve ending burn in agony. "Ah!"

"Too much, Silestian!" A female voice blended with the male. "Reduce the synaptic stimulant."

"Reducing."

The pain slowly dissipated and Madisyn struggled to open her eyes. Everything was a blur. She blinked several times, the movement jerky, numbness taking over as the pain subsided.

"You need to boost the synthesized synaptic fluids, Silestian," the female voice said, her tone sharp.

Silestian? Father? Where was she and how did she get here? Everything was hazy, and she couldn't pinpoint the origin of any of the sounds.

"Just relax, child," the female voice said. "Just your father and I are here. Look at me. Can you see me?"

Slowly the surroundings stopped swaying and the lights stopped searing her eyes. A woman's face came into focus; it was indeed her mother. "Mama."

"Oh, thank the Seers." Lonia Pimm smiled through tears. "She recognizes me. Madisyn, darling, your father is here too. You'll be all right."

"What's wrong…with me?" Madisyn managed to say, her mouth numb as she formed the words. Even her own voice sounded alien.

"You were in an…an accident, but the worst is over. You'll be fine. Won't she, Silestian?"

A man came into view and Madisyn wanted to cry. Her father looked so worried and worn. A dry sob broke free, and Madisyn tried to move her head to hide her feelings. Though she expected medical equipment and hospital staff, she saw her parents' laboratory. Why would she be on a gurney in their laboratory if she'd had an accident?

"Mother?" Madisyn trembled inwardly, or at least she thought she did, as she was still completely numb.

"We will explain everything in time, darling. Just trust me—you will be fine." Lonia kissed her forehead. "We love you more than anything or anyone else, Madisyn. We just couldn't bear to lose you. You will understand later, I promise."

Her mother's words, and waking up in the lab rather than a hospital, sent a flurry of thoughts through Madisyn's fatigued mind. Lonia sounded both regretful and afraid.

Madisyn turned her head the other way, grateful that she wasn't entirely paralyzed. A drape closed off the rest of the laboratory, but a mirror over a sink at the far end made it possible to see behind it. At first Madisyn thought she was seeing one of her parents' prototype androids, but when she tried to look more closely, two things proved her wrong. Her vision changed, and a series of numbers and mathematical signs scrolled along her left field of vision. She blinked confusedly; her eyes had zoomed in on the android in the mirror.

It wasn't an android at all.

"Oh, no." Madisyn wanted to scream, but couldn't. She stared at the reflection, at *herself*, and could only murmur two words, over and over. "Model Eighteen-B? Model Eighteen-B? Model Eighteen-B?"

"For the love of the Seers, Silestian, close the drape." Lonia bent closer to Madisyn. "Listen, darling. Focus on my voice. We had to try, your father and I. We had to. We were losing you."

"You…made me…into…Eighteen-B?"

"You were dying, darling. We had no choice." Lonia was crying now, and Silestian embraced them both.

"My daughter. We couldn't let you go," her father said, his voice barely audible. "And we didn't use Eighteen-B."

"What? What am I? What did you do?" Madisyn tried to sit up, needing to see for herself.

"Easy, child. Easy," Silestian said, holding on to her and helping her to sit propped up against his shoulder.

Madisyn looked down her body. The long, lanky limbs of her nineteen-year-old self had disappeared. Instead, she gazed in horror at the unfamiliar, perfect-looking body of an android. "What…what did you do to me?" Madison asked, hating her strange voice.

"It'll be fine. We'll fine-tune your voice and customize your appearance. I promise, my darling." Lonia had stopped crying and spoke with emphasis. "We couldn't let you die."

"You should've. You should've." Panic rose inside Madisyn and she wanted to lash out physically at them. "I hate you for this. You have to kill me. Stop this…machine…and kill me!" She had to endure their hugs and embraces, but for hours she wept without tears, whispering repeatedly, "You have to kill me. Please kill me. Please. Please."

Chapter One

Admiral Rae Jacelon stood behind the desk in her office, her hands behind her back, gazing at the stars. They appeared as blurry streaks as the Constellation warship moved with unimaginable speed. The *Paesina* had disembarked from the Gamma VI space station eight hours ago, and with Jacelon in command, it headed a convoy of ships flying into intergalactic space.

They planned to engage the Onotharian Empire and liberate Gantharat. Jacelon smiled joylessly. Excited about returning to battle, she wasn't naïve regarding the political intricacies behind the conflict.

Jacelon briefly allowed thoughts of when she had commanded Gamma VI to surface. As a commodore, she had come across a Gantharian fugitive and married her only a few days after they met. Becoming an instant spouse and parent should have been a recipe for failure, especially since the young boy, Armeo, was the heir to the Gantharian throne, with a horde of threatening pursuers trailing him.

The woman accompanying Armeo was destined to care for and protect him. Kellen O'Dal carried the title of Protector of the Realm, an honor that Jacelon now bore through marriage. They had been married almost eighteen months, and Jacelon had never dreamed of finding such love. She thought of Kellen each day when she first woke and right before she fell asleep. She couldn't imagine life without either Kellen or Armeo, yet they were separated again, as Kellen's duties as a lieutenant commander of the Supreme Constellations military forces had sent her on a different mission.

The device indicating that someone was at her door pinged.

"Enter." Jacelon kept her back to them. She was expecting her visitor and was not about to show them any courtesy whatsoever—yet.

"Your guest, Admiral," a male voice rumbled.

"Thank you. Dismissed."

"Aye, ma'am."

Jacelon turned around slowly. The woman on the other side of the desk wore slate-gray coveralls, like all civilians who traveled aboard an SC military vessel. With her dark brown hair held back in a tight, low bun, Weiss Kyakh stood ramrod straight, her deeply set frost green eyes unwavering.

"I take it you haven't changed your mind after boot camp?" Jacelon spoke coolly, making sure her animosity didn't show. Kyakh had facilitated the kidnapping of her mother, Dahlia Jacelon, so it was difficult to treat Kyakh as anything but a criminal.

"I can hardly refuse your *offer*, can I?" Kyakh spoke in a low tone, but sounded confident.

"You need to commit. People's lives are at stake, innocent people who have nothing to do with any of us. The SC covert-operative training facility should've taught you this, and more."

"Oh, I learned a lot. Innocent people don't exist. Everyone has an agenda, and they all have a price."

"Then what's your price?" Jacelon noted the pride in Kyakh's eyes and the defiant angle of her chin.

"My freedom."

"Ah." Jacelon placed her hands on her desk. "You are looking at life in an SC maximum-security prison." Jacelon knew what that meant and was sure Kyakh did too, but she didn't even blink. The MAXSEC prisons were stark buildings erected on several moons throughout SC space. Without an atmosphere, and with a booby-trapped sensor grid surrounding the moons, they were virtually impenetrable and close to escape-proof.

"And if I agree to infiltrate this band of pirates?" Kyakh asked disdainfully. "Your plan is flawed. Anyone who knows me would realize that I wouldn't join a band of thugs when I have access to the best people out there."

"Correction, *had* access. Past tense. We've made sure everybody knows that all your people are either dead or in custody. So far, we've kept the truth about your status a secret. Rumor has it you managed to escape when war broke out and that you're laying low, biding your time somewhere. As for your objectives, trust me, this is no mere band of thugs but a highly motivated and outfitted organization, led by a man called Podmer."

"Podmer?" For some reason, the pirate leader's name got through to Kyakh, who quickly sorted her features back into a look of indifference, but it was too late. Podmer was surely the key to coercing Kyakh to comply.

"Ring a bell?"

"Yes." That one syllable held a universe of emotions.

"He's nearly royalty when it comes to piracy. I would almost think he's been your role model." Jacelon was playing the devil's advocate now.

"Podmer is a cold-blooded murderer. A thug in designer clothes, using designer drugs and traveling in a state-of-the-art ship, but a thug nonetheless." Kyakh spat his name. "I may be a thief, and I have lives on my conscience, I don't deny that…but I use my talents in other ways."

"You kidnap distinguished diplomats, fire on children, and don't care much about collateral damage."

"I do not fire on children!"

"People who work for you did. It was mere coincidence that they hit Ayahliss instead of Armeo!" Jacelon circled the desk and stood within Kyakh's personal space. The other woman didn't flinch, but lowered her gaze after a few moments.

"White turned out to be less than dependable, but she acted against orders."

"You are still accountable!" Jacelon raised her voice marginally.

Kyakh paled. "I'm aware of that."

"Are you all right? My chief medical officer assured me that you were fit for duty."

"Dr. Meyer is very thorough. I'm fine."

"Very well." Jacelon rounded her desk and sat down. "Take a seat. We need to discuss a few things."

Kyakh remained standing for a few seconds, but then complied.

"Podmer has moved up in the world the last two years, and the conflict between Onotharat and the SC is adding to his wealth and, thus, his power. He is running a lucrative arms dealership, with most of the weapons the property of the SC military." Jacelon scrutinized Kyakh's face for an emotional response, but so far she saw none. "We need to know who he's doing business with and how he manages to obtain the weapons. Our last intel suggests that he's planning something elaborate, something that might cause setbacks for the SC. We need someone like you to infiltrate his senior officers' group."

"Why someone like me?"

"You enjoy a certain reputation. You're also like royalty when it comes to space pirates. You would be an asset to any such gang."

"You flatter me," Kyakh said ironically.

"Not even a little bit." Jacelon wasn't in the mood to smile. "You'll be working with our contact aboard Podmer's mother ship. She's been undercover with his band of pirates for more than six months."

"Why can't this person finish the job?"

"She's unable to get close enough to enter his inner circle of senior crewmembers."

"And you expect me to work with such an inept person?" Looking arrogant, Kyakh shrugged. "I don't hold hands during any sort of mission."

Jacelon bit off the exasperated curse that formed on her tongue. "Our agent is not inept. In fact, she's extraordinary and her success rate is a hundred percent."

"Then what's her problem?"

"She's unable to complete her mission only because of one reason. She's a BNSL."

"Oh, for stars and skies, she's an android?" Kyakh flung her hands up.

"She's a one-of-a-kind, highly advanced prototype of a Bio-Neural Synthetic Lifeform."

"And that's supposed to reassure me?"

"Oh, I never figured you for a person who needed reassuring, Kyakh."

"And what if this android malfunctions during a critical phase of the operation?" Cold, and getting colder still, Kyakh's eyes narrowed.

"She won't. She has more fail-safes installed than you and I could even dream of. She was constructed at the Stagmanza University on—"

"On Guild Nation, in its prime capital, Toran Denza." Kyakh sounded reluctantly impressed.

"You seem familiar with the Guild Nation, the newest member of the Supreme Constellations." Jacelon noted how Kyakh immediately schooled her features back into her former disdainful expression.

"My paternal grandmother was born on Guild Nation."

"I see. A good way for you to connect with Madisyn Pimm."

"The android has a *name*?" Kyakh snorted. "This gets better and better."

"I'm glad you think so, since she will be my liaison while you're on your assignment. Madisyn will not know your true status or your sordid past, but she will report anything amiss…with just about anything and everything during your mission. We will provide you with a plausible backstory of how you became a civilian agent for the SC."

"I wouldn't lose any sleep over an android knowing about my past."

"In this case I'm more concerned that it might jeopardize the mission."

"Not that I want to seem dense, or suggest that you are, Admiral, but what's to keep me from making a run for it, once I'm out there on my own?"

"I thought you'd get around to asking that." Pleased, Jacelon couldn't stop from smiling. "You must have heard that we have obtained cloaking ability for our vessels."

"Yes. I even saw the blueprints but didn't have time to outfit the *Viper* with it before—"

"Before you crashed, killing and wounding hundreds of Disians on Corma."

"Yes."

"Well, we can transfer the same cloaking ability to other pieces of technology. You have the same implant under your skin that Ambassador M'Ekar had when he was confined to house arrest, with one clever upgrade."

"You cloaked it?" Kyakh looked dumbfounded, to Jacelon's satisfaction.

"We did. Given your technical skills, you would no doubt easily be able to bypass the poison-inducing feature, if you could find it. But since you won't be able to locate it…" Jacelon shrugged. "If Madisyn Pimm reports anything that suggests you've gone AWOL or betrayed us, I won't hesitate to activate it. This also happens if Madisyn Pimm is taken offline or otherwise destroyed. If something happens to her and you don't report in within twenty-four hours…" Jacelon snapped her fingers. "Click. That's it. The poison will invade your system, and unless you receive an antidote within six hours, you will die. And, oh, I should mention that the formula for this poison is brand new. In fact, you're the lucky first customer."

"I'm thrilled." Kyakh stood rigid at Jacelon's desk. "Guess I was more correct than I realized when I talked about an offer I couldn't refuse."

"Yes. I suppose so."

"All right. I'll carry out your assignment. Then I expect to regain my freedom."

"All the legal documents are ready for your signature, and mine." Jacelon watched as Kyakh meticulously read through the digital files before signing them with a retina scan. She hated this woman for what she'd done to her family, but also reluctantly admitted that Weiss Kyakh somewhat fascinated her. Much like a poisonous spider could be simultaneously beautiful and lethal.

A lot depended on how Kyakh managed to carry out this assignment, and Jacelon could only hope she hadn't made a horrendous mistake by pitting one pirate against another.

Chapter Two

Pimm!" Captain Podmer, tall, burly, and with a bluish-red complexion, roared from his command chair on the bridge. "Return fire!"

"Aye, Captain. Plasma pulse fire," Madisyn Pimm answered calmly while punching in commands at the tactical station. "Direct hit to the Supreme Constellations vessel. Their shields are holding."

"Damn." Podmer gripped the armrests. "Arm the torpedoes."

"Torpedoes armed. Initiating aiming sequence." Madisyn made sure the torpedoes would disable but not destroy the SC ship. She kept scanning the information feed on her computer console. "Torpedoes locked."

"Fire!"

"Targeting their weapons array." The torpedoes hurtled through space in a low arc before they connected with the other ship. "Direct hit," Madisyn said without emotion. "Their shields are failing and their weapons array has sustained damage."

"Hit them again."

"Aye, sir." Madisyn obeyed, and this time the torpedoes crumbled what was left of the SC ship's shields. The protrusion beneath its belly exploded in quickly dying sparks. "The SC ship is rendered defenseless."

"That's what I want to hear." Podmer rose from his chair. "I'd have you blast them to atoms, but I don't want to attract too much attention. We'll have to settle for leaving them helpless." Podmer looked disgruntled. "How far until our rendezvous point, Struyen?" he asked, turning to a young man at the ops station.

"Four hours and thirty minutes, Captain." Lucco Struyen was a transporter brat. Born on a generational transporter ship, he had grown up in space and only rarely set foot planetside. He had joined Podmer's band of pirates as a teenager and quickly proved himself indispensable. Madisyn had caught herself shuddering at the cold expression in his eyes. Something about Struyen made Madisyn never turn her back on him willingly.

"Pimm, you'll be the liaison responsible for our new tactical officer." Podmer favored handing out military ranks to his crew, which suggested that he might have a background in the Fleet. She would have to relay her suspicions to her SC contact at some point, but right now she could focus only on the new double agent she was supposed to work with. Madisyn wasn't sure if she was relieved not to have to carry the entire burden alone aboard the pirate ship *Salaceos* or annoyed at having to bring a new operative up to speed.

"Captain," Struyen said, interrupting before Madisyn could respond, "I don't think Pimm is the best choice, considering she's rather new aboard the *Salaceos*."

"Really?" Podmer squinted at his senior crew. The bridge held five stations, including the captain's command chair. "Are you volunteering your services, taking on this newcomer yourself?"

"I'm always ready." Struyen smiled triumphantly at Madisyn, and she calmly kept an eye on her controls, not revealing how she despised the callous young man. Sometimes not being allowed to show emotions was the hardest thing of all.

"I'm sure you are," Podmer now said slowly, "but I don't think you're ready for someone like Weiss Kyakh."

"Kyakh?" Struyen's voice nearly cracked, which would've amused Madisyn if she hadn't been filled with such contempt for him that she had no room for any other feelings. "But I thought she was killed. Everyone thinks—"

"She was killed on Corma. She was badly hurt, but managed to escape the SC prisoner transport." Podmer grinned. "She laid low for a while, and now she's back and for hire again."

"Have you met her, Captain?" Struyen asked, clearly not about to push the idea that he'd be the liaison anymore.

"No, not personally. Very few of her peers have. Her reputation is solid, but her elusiveness has kept her successful."

"Until Corma." Struyen shrugged.

"True, but the circumstances were very difficult, even for a seasoned pirate." Podmer retook his seat. "Not only was she transporting a high-profile Onotharian prisoner of war, but she was involved with kidnapping some big-shot SC diplomat."

Madisyn had to admit she was curious regarding Weiss Kyakh. Her masked internal sensor implant had received the intel she required to make a positive identification, and she had filed the information in her encrypted memory banks. The SC had outfitted Kyakh with a tailor-made history, making her a dream associate for someone like Podmer.

Madisyn forced her facial expression to remain unreadable as she browsed through the files. Images flickered through her mind of a tall, wiry woman with dark hair and light green eyes, reminding Madisyn of the vast glaciers on the Guild Nation northern pole. What would Kyakh be like in real life? Undoubtedly, she would regard Madisyn with the same standoffish skepticism as everyone else.

"Pimm!"

"Sir?" Chastising herself for allowing her mind to wander, Madisyn focused on her annoyed captain.

"You're relieved. Go prepare your quarters. You're sharing them with Kyakh."

"Aye, Captain." This last piece of information blindsided Madisyn. Her quarters were her only refuge aboard the *Salaceos*. Even after so many years, it still took a huge toll on her to play the part of true BNSL. In her quarters, she could relax and rest. Real BNSL androids needed sustenance to feed their biomatter, such as their artificially grown skin and other tissues. Madisyn required that, but also regular sleep, to rest her human brain. The special features her parents had outfitted her, their prototype, with also entailed small, elaborate internal force fields to hide her secret.

To bunk with Weiss Kyakh, whose backstory indicated that she was as tough as they came, posed considerable danger to Madisyn on a personal level. Madisyn's mother had constantly instilled in her that she could never tell anyone the truth. According to the world, Madisyn had passed away, the victim of a band of space pirates. The official version told the story of how her bereaved parents created the most advanced Bio-Neural Synthetic Life form to date, in her honor.

After her parents were killed, only Madisyn knew the truth.

Madisyn sighed inwardly. She should be used to it, but it was utterly lonely to be the only one who knew that she possessed a human brain and spinal cord.

❖

Weiss Kyakh stalked through the small, run-down space station. Located just outside the Supreme Constellations border, it was a popular stop for traveling scum, occasional shady SC citizens out to strike an illegal deal, as well as deserters and adventurers. She stopped by the window where the store owner, Madame Roja, displayed garments, jewelry, body art, face paint, derma reconstructers, and old-fashioned makeup. Dr. Meyer had done wonders with her scars, but she looked too polished. Weiss needed to look the part of a rough and seasoned fugitive before she joined Podmer and his crew. She browsed the long-lasting body paints and purchased a set and a derma reconstructer.

Back at the tiny quarters, she recolored the part of her hair that had turned white around a scar. She ran the reconstructer over her face, after making sure it was set to sharpen her features, thus erasing the lingering fatigue after her injury. The tired lines had softened her expression, and now she needed to look her normal edgy and unbreakable self.

Once she finished, she sat down and started her computer. Opting to forgo the normal voice-operated feature, she punched in commands, opening the encrypted SC document. She found the file containing the assembled intel regarding Podmer and his band of pirates, and her contact, Madisyn Pimm. Weiss studied the two images, one of Pimm's face and the other a full-body picture. If Jacelon hadn't told her, Weiss would never have known Pimm was artificial. Unruly blond curls framed a soft face, and long black lashes shadowed gentle blue eyes. She was slender but curvaceous, and obviously sculpted to look entirely humanoid. Zooming in on the picture of Pimm's face, Weiss had to admire the engineering behind the artificially grown skin. Complete with pores and small hairs, it was indistinguishable from real skin.

Weiss's subspace communicator, located in her epaulette, beeped softly via the internal audio sensor planted in her ear canal.

"Jacelon to Kyakh, come in." Admiral Rae Jacelon's voice was unmistakable even if some static distorted the signal.

"Kyakh here, Admiral. Go ahead." Weiss placed a hand over her ear so she could hear better.

"Your chip places you aboard the Dasmach space station. Perfect. You will rendezvous with Pimm on the *Salaceos* at approximately 2000 interstellar time tonight."

"Affirmative." Weiss hesitated, not wanting to sound worried or weak while communicating with Jacelon. "I'm concerned that Podmer might have acquired scanning technology capable of detecting the communicator or the chip." She hated having the chip implanted at an unknown location in her body.

"Doubtful." Jacelon spoke curtly. "It's made of an undetectable compound that isn't available on the market yet. It's a closely guarded military secret."

"If you only knew how easily I've obtained 'closely guarded' military secrets over the years, you might be more understanding," Weiss said disdainfully.

"I can only imagine," Jacelon replied. "However, in this case, I don't think it's an exaggeration. The Guild Nation provided the formula only weeks after it was tested for the first time, and rather than putting it through more extensive trials, we decided to analyze its use in the field. The benefit should be obvious."

"So are the downsides."

"I understand that, but you have little choice."

"So I'm chock full of Guild Nation technology and I'm hooking up with a Guild Nation android. Let's hope these people are as good at tech stuff as rumor suggests."

"Report back every two hours during the first twenty-four aboard the *Salaceos*, starting at 2200. If you're unable to talk, use the nonverbal signal. Your reports will be cross-referenced with Madisyn Pimm's."

"Of course. Kyakh out."

They broke the communication, and despite her dislike for the admiral, Weiss felt a little less lonely knowing Jacelon was a mere subspace call away.

❖

Madisyn stood next to the crewman responsible for guarding the gate, keeping her eyes locked on the crowd of people passing across the concourse. She recognized Weiss Kyakh instantly when the tall woman appeared at the end of the corridor. Striding forcefully toward the gate where the *Salaceos* was docked, Kyakh wore a long, black leather-like coat that fanned out behind her like a cape. Her face revealed nothing as she calmly approached them, a set of high-end hover luggage following her.

"Weiss Kyakh," she told Madisyn, and pressed a sensor on the remote control that halted her luggage. "Permission to come aboard."

"Permission granted, Ms. Kyakh. My name is Madisyn Pimm."

"Ms. Pimm." Kyakh nodded politely.

"Call me Pimm or Madisyn, please. I'm not much for titles."

"I'm Weiss."

Madisyn motioned for Weiss to follow her and guided her through the narrow corridors to their quarters. "This isn't very spacious, I'm afraid." She wasn't sure why she was apologizing, since it was hardly her idea to share quarters.

"It's fine." If Weiss disapproved, she didn't let on.

"You can take the left bed."

"You use a bed?" Weiss sounded surprised. "You sleep?"

Madisyn was used to misconceptions and prejudice against her kind. "Yes, of course. I need rest like everyone else, to recharge the batteries." She laughed heartily at Weiss's expression of discomfort. That joke never failed. "I'm kidding. I don't run on batteries. Believe it or not, I digest nutrients to sustain my systems, just like you do."

"Really." Weiss looked doubtful. "All right. I better report to the captain."

"Yes. We're departing in less than an hour. You must meet him before then. His orders."

"Very well." Weiss hoisted the hover luggage up on the bed, then walked out of their quarters. "Lead the way."

"It's a big ship, but crew quarters are tight. Not a priority in our business to be comfortable." Madisyn motioned for Weiss to follow her. "Podmer keeps a good game room, though, for the crew to use."

"I see." Weiss's expression didn't divulge anything as she walked next to Madisyn through the corridors. They used the elevator to reach the bridge.

"Captain. This is Weiss Kyakh." Madisyn stepped aside, letting Podmer assess their new crewmember. Weiss focused on Podmer as she greeted him, making it possible for Madisyn to observe her. As tall as Podmer, Weiss looked twice as lethal as the burly captain. She stood there, wiry and strangely elegant, gazing calmly at him.

"Kyakh! I never thought I'd have the honor." Podmer slapped Weiss's shoulder hard enough to topple a physically weaker person. "You've always headed your own crew."

"Things change."

"Why don't we have a drink in my quarters and discuss your duties?"

"Thank you, but I don't drink."

Podmer seemed taken aback, and Madisyn knew he would regard this as a character flaw, being quite fond of old-fashioned Earth whisky himself. "Nobody's perfect," the captain muttered. "All right. Guess we can postpone our chat, since we're about to depart." He turned to Madisyn. "Pimm. Show Kyakh around and introduce her to the new propulsion system." He didn't wait for Madisyn to respond, but turned back to Weiss. "You'll see why venturing into SC space and hooking up with that disgruntled Guild Nation shipyard technician was worth it." Podmer ordered his helmsman to initiate the undocking procedure.

"Come on," Madisyn said to Weiss. "We have a lot to talk about."

Chapter Three

"I miss you." Kellen regarded her wife, Admiral Rae Jacelon, on the communication screen in her quarters aboard the cruiser ship *Circinus*.

"Oh, Kellen." Rae sighed and her eyes turned a stormy, dark gray. "I'm so sorry, but I won't be able to catch up with you like I thought."

Kellen's heart contracted painfully. "I suspected as much." She tried to not let her disappointment color her voice. "You're a senior member of the war council."

"Not only that. I'm responsible for some of the covert operations that my father claims he can't trust anyone else with." Rae pushed a hand through her short-cropped red hair. "I'm not sure he's right, but a lot is riding on this mission, and handled right, it can help shorten the war."

"I'm sure Ewan wouldn't keep us apart unless it mattered." Kellen was fond of her spouse's parents, and the fact that Admiral Ewan Jacelon outranked them all made it a moot point anyway.

"How's my mother?" Rae asked, a knowing smile forming on her lips. "Has she recovered enough to drive you all crazy yet?"

"Dahlia is doing very well." At first, Kellen had been against her mother-in-law using the journey to Gantharat as convalescence time after her ordeal of being kidnapped. She knew better than to underestimate Dahlia Jacelon and tried to push her concerns aside. Dahlia had surprised everybody aboard the *Circinus*. Captain Jeremiah Todd, Rae's friend and former subordinate on the Gamma VI space station, was in command of their ship and ultimately of the entire convoy of ships heading for Gantharat space. "She's taking every opportunity to go through her physical-therapy routine. Nobody could guess that she went through pure hell in the Disi-Disi jungle on Corma only a few months ago."

"She's a fighter."

"As is her daughter." Kellen touched the screen with a gentle hand, caressing the outline of Rae's jaw. "You look tired."

"I do?" Rae pushed her fingers through her short, fiery red hair again. "I have something slightly unorthodox going on, and if my plan backfires, heads will roll. Probably mine."

"What?" Alarmed, Kellen zoomed in Rae's picture on the communicator screen.

"Figure of speech, darling, but the piracy situation is setting us back so much, something needed to be done."

"I see." Worried at the look of apprehension on Rae's face, which she surmised stemmed from fatigue rather than doubt, Kellen adopted a matter-of-fact tone. "Don't second-guess yourself, Rae. You worked long and hard on this plan, and even if the approach is unusual, it's still by the book." Rae was a stickler for doing things the right way. "Remember, you always tell me that you can get away with breaking big rules, if you make sure your poultry are aligned when it comes to the minor things."

"Poultry?" Rae looked dumbfounded. "Oh. You mean ducks. Ducks in a row."

"As I said." Kellen knew the saying, but Rae loved the humor her getting it wrong brought to their conversation.

"I suppose you're right, darling." Rae blew Kellen a kiss. "You very often are."

"I wish you wouldn't sound so surprised," Kellen said, smiling.

"Ha. I wish. It's more a rule than an exception. Speaking of ruling, how are Reena and Ayahliss?"

"Amereena has buried herself in the Gantharian legal texts, which is a lot, and Ayahliss is focusing on her *gan'thet* training. She's making progress when it comes to technique, but she's still hotheaded and hell-bent on vengeance."

"Not good. She needs to control herself or she'll end up killing innocents. Perhaps it was a mistake to bring her."

"I don't think so." Kellen shook her head. "It was better for her to be with us so I can supervise her training, rather than have her run away and join a pirate ship in order to return." Ayahliss, the orphaned young woman Kellen had come across when liberating Gantharian prisoners, was a strange mix of street-smart resistance fighter, scholar, and martial arts expert. Only Protectors of the Realm, assigned to guard the Gantharian royal family, were trained in the lethal art of gan'thet, but Ayahliss had learned from monks in a secret retreat during the occupation. She had not, unfortunately, learned the equally important self-restraint that having such skills required. Ayahliss was fiercely loyal to her home world and hated the Onotharians more than anything.

"And the vibes we picked up on between her and Reena?"

"They're doing their best to act casual around each other, but the only ones they're fooling are each other." Kellen smiled. Judge Amereena Beqq was twice as old as the twenty-four-year-old Ayahliss, but obviously the intense young woman mesmerized her. "I don't know what will happen between them, if anything."

"I don't mean to gossip, Kellen, but their unresolved emotions could become a security risk."

"Yes. I've thought of that also." Kellen had tried to talk to Ayahliss about Reena Beqq, and in polite but firm terms, Ayahliss had asked Kellen to stay out of her private life and at the same time assured her that Amereena was not interested in her that way. When Kellen tried to determine what Ayahliss meant by "that way," Ayahliss ended the conversation and stalked off. After that, Kellen had merely observed them.

"I miss you," Rae said. "I wish I could go with you."

"I—I dream about you every night." Kellen sighed. "It makes it very painful to wake up alone, without you."

"It sure does." Rae smiled wistfully. "Same time tomorrow, darling?"

"Yes, *henshes*."

"I love you."

"I love you too." Kellen felt a stab of pain in her abdomen when the fleet's logo replaced Rae's elegant features. She resisted the urge to open another communication channel to keep Rae there a little longer. They both needed whatever sleep they could manage. Kellen scowled at the bed beneath the viewport. It looked uninviting, cold, and empty.

❖

The Ruby Red leather suit, a present from Kellen when Ayahliss had mastered her gan'thet skills to a degree that she deserved the traditional Protector combat garment, fit her lean yet muscular body. Ayahliss fought an invisible adversary as she whirled her gan'thet rods around her in the ancient, intricate patterns that she'd practiced so many times that she could do them any hour of the day, even if she was roused in the middle of the night.

She slowed to a deceptively immobile stance, one leg stretched out at a forty-five-degree angle, both arms in defensive positions, holding the rods loosely. A faint sound from the door made her grip the rods tight and whirl through the air while defying gravity. She halted a mere centimeter from the person who'd had the audacity to disturb her session. With the rods crossed before her, the ends surrounding Supreme Court Judge Amereena Beqq's leonine neck, ready to snap it with a mere twist of her wrists, Ayahliss inhaled deeply and took a step back.

"This was unwise of you, Reena," Ayahliss said through clenched teeth. "I was in the zone. I could've killed you."

"That would've been unfortunate." Reena looked calm on the surface, but Ayahliss, who took pride in finding out what every tiny little shift in Reena's expression meant, knew she had more than startled her.

"I'm sorry. I should've realized that nobody aboard the *Circinus* is my enemy." Ayahliss knew she spoke stiffly, but her words were sincere. She idolized the Supreme Constellations citizens who had accepted her and given her a home. In turn, she relied on their judgment when it came to their faith in the SC Fleet and Military Forces. Ayahliss was grateful that the SC had taken on the Onotharian Empire after all the atrocities the Onotharians had committed against Gantharat and its people.

"Apology accepted. I just came by to ask if you would be interested in helping me with some translations. I can read most of the modern Gantharian language, but the old dialects are frustrating. Some words sound like a completely different language, not even related to what your language sounds like today."

"Like the difference between Premoni and your native tongue?"

"Yes. Were you surprised when you found out how many different languages exist within the SC?" Reena smiled.

"I was surprised to find that Earth alone had so many different ones." Ayahliss decided that she was done for tonight and stowed her rods in their special casing. She hardly dared admit to herself that she wanted to walk Reena to her quarters. "And yes, of course I'll help you with the translations."

"Thank you." Reena suddenly looked uncomfortable. "Well, I should go to bed. I mean, to my quarters."

"May I escort you, Reena?" Ayahliss expected Reena to turn down her offer. Reena had been kind and understanding during the times she took care of Ayahliss and Armeo when Rae and Kellen were on a mission, but afterward, something had changed between them.

"Absolutely." Reena smiled broadly, but still seemed ill at ease.

Ayahliss wished she could say something to elicit the tenderness Reena had showed her before. She had spent countless hours awake during their voyage trying to figure out exactly what had altered things between them. Short of asking Reena, which seemed like the definitive humiliation, one she couldn't abide, Ayahliss felt completely lost.

Reena walked briskly through the *Circinus*'s corridors and didn't seem open to conversation. Desperate to receive at least a few personal words, Ayahliss ventured into the private sphere. "May I talk to you about something?"

"Oh. Certainly." Reena's smile turned decidedly nervous, which puzzled and intrigued Ayahliss.

"Kellen doesn't believe I'm ready for this assignment. She doesn't trust my ability to harness my feelings and use them in my combat skills."

"Is she right?"

"Perhaps a little. But I've changed. I've meditated every day and practiced the techniques for entering the state of bliss that the gan'thet masters must conquer."

"You seemed to be in control when you didn't snap my neck off just now." Reena had relaxed again and now jokingly elbowed Ayahliss. "Once you might not have been able to stop yourself, especially if you were upset or excited."

"This was training, not combat. In a combat situation, I may not have the strength to…well, I guess, pull back."

They reached Reena's quarters and she stopped in front of them, scrutinizing Ayahliss. As usual, her blood-red hair hung in wild curls down her back, her black judge's cape emphasizing it. "Kellen isn't the one who really doubts you."

"No?" Had Reena heard someone among the crew express concern regarding her? Plenty of them were probably wary of her talents and her intensity.

"No. *You* are your worst critic. And that's not bad, unless it keeps you from evolving and growing both as a person and as a martial arts master."

"Oh." Warmth, unexpected and curious, filled Ayahliss's chest and spread through her system. "Do you ever doubt me?" she asked before realizing what she meant to say. Groaning inwardly, she wanted to take the pathetic words back.

"No. I have faith in your intentions and also in Kellen's ability to teach as well as to reel you in, if you get ahead of yourself." Reena studied her, but her amber eyes didn't reveal anything. "But I worry about you."

"Worry?" Ayahliss was surprised. "How?"

"You're brave, and you wouldn't hesitate to place yourself in a harmful situation to reach your objective. Kellen is the same way, if a bit more polished, but you warriors…you're far too willing to sacrifice yourself during a conflict."

Feeling criticized, Ayahliss clasped her hands. "And you officers of the court believe in negotiations and diplomacy. That tactic has not gotten the people of Gantharat anywhere in the last twenty-six years!"

Reena's eyes changed from a warm, golden glow to a fiery stare. "Is that how you talk to Dahlia, who could've ended up in the hands of Onotharian agents? She would've died at their hands before she succumbed and revealed anything."

Pain, sharp and all too familiar by now, made Ayahliss step back. She had struggled with this memory ever since kidnappers had snatched Dahlia, a woman she idolized and whose poise she secretly tried to emulate, right before her eyes. The fact that Kellen and Rae had rescued Dahlia and that she had nearly recovered completely was of no consequence.

"You don't have to remind me whose fault it was," Ayahliss managed to say with rigid lips.

"Fault? What are you talking about?"

"I failed Dahlia. The Jacelons have kindly forgiven me, but that doesn't change the facts."

"You nearly died trying to save her!" Reena looked appalled instead of angry now. "Ayahliss, please. Don't." She gripped Ayahliss's shoulders gently, but firmly.

The touch scorched through the gan'thet suit. Part of Ayahliss wanted to give in to the comfort Reena was offering, but her own conflicted emotions forbade it. She stepped back again. "You're right. I spoke without thinking. It's late. I hope you have a good night's sleep."

Ayahliss didn't wait for Reena's reply, simply because she knew how close she had come to throwing herself into the other woman's arms. Reena was stunning and embodied everything Ayahliss admired, but something else lay between them, something Ayahliss didn't fully understand. Her sheltered upbringing hadn't prepared her for social situations and normal family relationships. Dahlia Jacelon had taught her a lot, but nothing of the contradictory emotions that threatened to overpower her when she was around Amereena Beqq.

"Ayahliss, please?" Reena called out.

Ayahliss nearly stopped and turned around, but forced herself to keep walking toward her quarters, located at the other end of the corridor. She slammed her hand against the sensor next to the door, waiting impatiently for the nanosecond it took to verify her biosignature. Inside, she threw the casing with her gan'thet rod on a chair and sank down on her bed.

Hugging herself, she failed to hold back her bitter blue tears, their color indicative of her species. She hated crying, loathed the futility of wasting tears rather than taking action, but right now she couldn't do anything else.

CHAPTER FOUR

Weiss had spent her life after the age of ten on one pirate vessel or another, with one exception: When she was thirteen, she stayed temporarily on an intergalactic space station outside SC territory for three months while the ship she usually resided on was being repaired in a space dock. Weiss managed to persuade her guardian to allow her to attend school on the space station, which old Gaskian grumpily agreed to, after making it clear that he viewed it as a waste of time.

Weiss kept to herself the first couple of days, but on the third day, a girl her age, Toloma, approached her, offering to show her around. Toloma, born and raised on the station, knew every corridor and, more useful than that, every hiding place. They bonded at every level, both space brats, and even if Toloma lived permanently on a station, neither of them had set foot on a planet other than very briefly.

"One day I'll have my own ship and be in charge," Weiss had told Toloma when they hid in their favorite spot in the cargo area. From their vantage point, they could see the bottom of all the moored ships and keep track of all the vessels coming and going. Surrounded by stars and the vastness of space, Weiss loved the impressive view. Even the most beat-up ship looked majestic when it approached the space station, and it wasn't hard to picture herself as captain.

"Can I come with you then?" Toloma asked eagerly. "I've never been *anywhere*, and we could be explorers."

"Sure." Weiss regarded her with affection. She had never had a female friend her own age, and Toloma was the cutest girl she'd ever seen. Petite, with rosy cheeks and black curls falling down her back, she looked like a princess Weiss had once seen in a vid-storybook. Toloma was seasoned yet shy, used to fending off tough pirates aboard the station, but also with a very strict father who was the co-owner and manager. "You and I could take turns being captain," Weiss said generously. "I'm strong, and you're smart, and between us, we'd be unbeatable."

"Oh, Weiss, you're the best." Toloma hugged her. "I don't want you to ever leave. I've never had a friend like you."

Weiss sighed, returning the fierce embrace. "I know. I hate the thought. But listen," she said, pushing Toloma away, "I'll come back. I promise. Once I've found my mother, I'll tell her we must return here so you and I can keep going to school together."

"What if you don't find her?"

"Don't say that!" Weiss sat up, her heart pounding. Her one overshadowing goal was to be reunited with her mother. Nothing in her life would ever be right until that happened. "I will find her. She's looking for me, and I'm looking for her. It's just a matter of time." Breathing hard and fast, she stared at Toloma.

"Oh, Weiss, you'll find her. I know you will." Tears clogged Toloma's voice and she clung to Weiss's hands. "And I know you'll come back."

"I promise. One day soon. You'll see."

❖

Weiss jerked awake in the dark. Her erratic breathing drowning out the low hum of the *Salaceos*'s propulsion system, she fought the emotional onslaught of her dream. It had been so vivid, like a true caption of the months she'd spent on the space station all those years ago. She hadn't allowed herself to think of trusting, sweet Toloma in a long time.

"Weiss? What's wrong?" Madisyn sat up in her bed.

"Nothing." Annoyed that a damn robot witnessed her moment of weakness, Weiss stood and walked toward the bathroom. "I should say 'go back to sleep,' but that's redundant."

"Not really." Madisyn shifted in her bed. "Lights on, twenty-percent luminosity."

Escaping the revealing light, Weiss rinsed her face in the

bathroom, wondering why she felt so self-conscious and defensive around Madisyn. Granted, this android enjoyed sentience status, but as far as she was concerned she was artificial, a glorified robot. Weiss glowered at her own reflection in the mirror. She was pale and her eyes a darker green than normal. Recognizing the storm clouds gathering in her mind, she focused on her breathing and stretched her arms. She was her own worst enemy if she let her temper rule unchallenged. She exhaled slowly, finally, and exited the bathroom.

"Better?" Madisyn sat ramrod straight, her transparent, light blue eyes following Weiss as she crossed the floor.

"I told you I'm fine." Content that she sounded matter-of-fact, Weiss glanced at the chronometer. They didn't have to get ready for their upcoming mission for several hours. After eight days aboard the *Salaceos*, it was time for Weiss to prove herself to Podmer, as well as to Madisyn. Perhaps that's why she was so on edge?

"Yes, you did. It's up to me to judge if I believe you."

"You're not my babysitter." Weiss's annoyance surfaced again. Madisyn's creator was obviously a genius, having created a BSLF that mimicked human behavior with such aplomb. Weiss had read up on the criteria for sentience status and knew that Madisyn had to pass rigorous tests regarding ethics, morals, empathy, and different levels of compassion.

"No, that would suggest that you're a child, which you're obviously not." Madisyn managed to sound sarcastic, as if she thought Weiss was acting like a child anyway.

"We should go back to…hmm, sleep, or whatever you call your resting process."

"Why don't we clear the air while we have time? That might be worthwhile." Madisyn pulled her legs up, crosswise, underneath her. She looked like a girl rather than a no-particular-age android.

"That's not very wise, considering where we are. Who knows who might be listening in?"

"Ah, but I've taken care of that." Madisyn gestured around the room. "When I first started working for Podmer, I made sure I could have my privacy here whenever I needed it."

"Really?" Weiss gestured toward the bulkhead. "If the surveillance in here is off, wouldn't Podmer be suspicious when he scans the crew quarters?"

"I only engage the scrambler when necessary. Random sleep sounds replace the surveillance."

"Very well." Weiss couldn't think of any other reason to refuse. She needed to stay on Madisyn's good side. After all, her reports to Jacelon helped keep the admiral's finger off the trigger to the damn cloaked microchip somewhere in her body. "What do you want to know?"

"Some people are very uncomfortable around synthetics. I've experienced that type of prejudice firsthand since…my birth."

"Birth? I didn't know *synthetics* were actually born. Speaking of that, how old are you?"

"I have been in use for nine years."

"You look younger. I mean, your exterior looks younger."

"I was modeled after my creators' daughter. In her memory."

"Who created you? I heard you're one of a kind."

"Aren't we all?" Madisyn smiled faintly. "Silestian Pimm and his wife Lonia created me and gave me their daughter's name. A band of space pirates killed her when she was twenty years old."

Weiss jerked inwardly, but refused to let her reaction show. Madisyn didn't know how true her cover story was. The Pimms had possibly programmed their own hatred of pirates into their synthetic android. That would jeopardize the whole mission, thus the only way for Weiss to escape, if Madisyn learned she was a true pirate.

"It's not very common for synthetics to obtain sentience status. Was it difficult?" Weiss did her best to sound polite and interested.

"It was. The lengthy tests invade your privacy and push your body near the breaking point." Madisyn sounded almost sad as she spoke. "Silestian Pimm coached me and supported me through the whole process." Madisyn quieted, then gently cleared her throat as if swallowing tears, though Weiss knew that was impossible. "He and his wife lived long enough to celebrate the sentience-status certificate with me."

"What happened to them?"

Madisyn's expression turned cold and Weiss marveled at how human she seemed in every way.

"Like their daughter, they fell prey to pirates," Madisyn said slowly. "So, you see, I'm very motivated to carry out this mission.

Space thugs cut short the life work of the Pimms, who were brilliant. I owe it to them to help mitigate the risk of something like that happening again."

"I see. You have a personal stake in this situation."

"Yes." Madisyn looked evenly at Weiss. "I know you can't tell me everything about yourself. Jacelon made it clear that your true identity must remain classified. It must be hard to impersonate Weiss Kyakh, though. That woman's record speaks for itself."

"It's become second nature by now." Weiss didn't have to act to sound casual and emphasized her words with a shrug.

"I suppose." Madisyn looked slightly uncomfortable. "So. Do you have any questions regarding me that will make our collaboration smoother?"

"So far I've seen you eat, sleep, and more or less act like a humanoid. What about you is different? Do you have any mechanical parts that might break down or something?"

Madisyn took Weiss completely by surprise. Tossing her head back, she burst out laughing, a thoroughly delightful sound that normally would've been contagious. "Oh, that's priceless! No, Weiss, I don't have anything that will corrode, or cogs that might dislodge." Madisyn *giggled,* which didn't make Weiss feel any less stupid for asking. "All jokes aside, Weiss, my system is fully comparable to yours on a molecular level. Unlike your brain, though, mine consists of cultivated gray-matter cells, combined with synthesized spinal liquor. Nanochips travel throughout my central nervous system and communicate with a BIO-CPU, which is located between my spinal column and the cerebellum…and I can see that this is too much information."

"Hey, it's amazing, groundbreaking technology, but you lost me somewhere around synthesized spinal liquor." Weiss regarded Madisyn in the dim light; sitting there dressed in her sleepwear, she looked so young and innocent. Her curly blond hair was disheveled, and her blue eyes glittered as they reflected the light from the star streaks outside the viewport. If the real Madisyn Pimm had lived, she wouldn't have been Weiss's type. Normally, Weiss went for overtly sexy and willing women, not cute, willowy blondes. "All right, I think I understand more now. Thank you for taking the time to explain."

"Some people have problems with BNLFs because they've had

bad experiences with synthetics or androids, and don't distinguish between them and BNLFs like me. I can't be replaced. Only one of me exists, with my unique experiences and memories."

"That may be. Still, you remember only nine years of living as a synthetic android." Weiss winced at her own words. If Madisyn was offended, she didn't let it show.

"And in your book, that isn't much of a life, is it?"

"I didn't say that."

Madisyn's steady gaze made something deep inside Weiss squirm. "Yes, I believe you did." Abruptly she crawled back under the covers and ordered the lights to zero percent. "You are correct. We might as well catch a few more hours' sleep before our mission begins."

Weiss sat in the dark for a few moments before lying down. She doubted she'd be able to sleep.

CHAPTER FIVE

"We're heading for the mines on Nemalima, the secondary moon of the Nema home world." Podmer leaned against the conference table on stocky arms. "Conditions are challenging and we need to work using pressure suits. Even you, right, Pimm?"

"Even I." Madisyn avoided sounding overtly sarcastic, but just barely.

"Nema has kept mines on Nemalima for decades, and they are the sole providers of *davic* crystals in this sector. The davic ores on Nemalima run deep and wide. Their level of purity is rare."

Madisyn knew how much people coveted davic crystals. Ships could run for years when fitted with high-quality crystals, and less than a kilo could power the energy plants that sustained entire planets for months. The Supreme Constellations had tried to negotiate with the Nema home world and find a way to add the naturally volatile Nemastians to the Unification of Planets, but the Nemastians seemed happy as a sovereign planet system in intergalactic space, probably because of their seemingly endless supply of these crystals. If they were to join the SC, they would have to share their best bargaining chip.

"The entrances to the plants on Nemalima are heavily guarded, but we're going to hit them tomorrow and grab their stock of processed davic crystals."

"How are we supposed to get by these 'heavily guarded' gates?" Weiss Kyakh asked disdainfully. "What intel have you gathered? How many heads are we using?"

"Glad you asked," Podmer said with a wolfish grin. "You, Pimm, and two security officers will head up the surprise attack. Once you've created a pathway in, the second team goes in to get the crates. We'll move them with cables hanging from the shuttles. I want twenty crates, minimum."

"Aye, sir," Madisyn murmured, already calculating how to carry out this assignment with as little collateral damage as possible. Mines like these attracted a rough, tough workforce, but that didn't matter. She intended to mitigate any damage to people or property that Podmer and his gang had in mind. She gazed over at Weiss, who was studying the plans and charts displayed on the view-screen table. Frowning, Weiss touched a few controls and zoomed in on a couple of details. What had caught Weiss's eyes?

"Be ready to go at 1100 hours. Pimm, get Kyakh equipped."

"Yes, sir." Madisyn motioned for Weiss to follow her. "Survival pressure gear is stored in the starboard cargo bay."

Weiss nodded briskly and followed her into the corridor. "We need to talk," she mouthed.

"Okay." Madisyn hoped they would be alone for a moment in the cargo bay before the rest of the team showed up to get their gear. The look on Weiss's face bothered her. Perhaps the plan had a serious flaw.

❖

"I doubt this will go as smoothly as Podmer thinks." Weiss scrutinized her helmet and the rest of her jump gear. "Davic crystals are heavy. Their density makes them the hardest crystals within the chartered part of space. If we load as much as he wants, it might prove dicey to return the crew on the same shuttles. Davic crystals can also become unstable if not stored properly."

"We have to limit the amount without it being obvious, then." Madisyn spoke calmly as she ran a quick diagnostic of her helmet.

"Or we risk being left behind."

"Not a very enticing prospect." Tapping in commands on the right side of her helmet, Madisyn nodded as small fiber-lights began to flicker. "I'm the one Podmer elected to lead this mission. I'll make sure we don't overload the shuttle. If those miners are only half as tough as they say they are, I sure don't want to overstay my welcome."

"Good. Neither do I." Weiss fastened the helmet to the snug

pressure suit and made sure the locks snapped in place. She hadn't space-dived in years but hoped her body would remember how.

Madisyn's voice crackled in her helmet headset. "Pimm to Kyakh. You read?"

"Loud and clear. No need to shout, Pimm." Sounding her normal pesky self for the benefit of anyone listening in, Weiss glared over at Madisyn.

"Check your visor readings. You should be able to see your own vital signs as well as those of your teammates." Madisyn snapped a harness to her upper body and attached explosives and other contraptions to it.

"I can see my own, Struyen's, and six others. There are nine of us. Who's missing?"

"I am." Madisyn smiled broadly, her nose crinkling. "Me? Robot, remember?"

"Funny, Pimm." Weiss half smiled before she remembered herself and scowled. "So, how would I know if you…eh, malfunction?"

"Check the second listing to the left on your visor. MP. Those are my readings. Not exactly a heartbeat, but close."

"Ah. Got it." Their exchange pulled at something inside Weiss, but she couldn't afford to be weak around anybody, least of all the woman, no, the *robot* that could end her life with a single unfavorable report.

They took their seats in the first shuttle. Weiss slammed down the safety bar over her shoulders and gripped her plasma-pulse rifle tight. Madisyn did the same across the aisle from her, and now her gaze was indifferent. Weiss felt the familiar tremor as the pilot engaged the propulsion system. The vibrations escalated to a growl, making it easy to envision the sleek craft as a feline predator as it leaped from the shuttle bay of the *Salaceos*. Outside, it hurtled through space toward the pale disc in the distance that was Nemalima, secondary moon of the Nema home world.

❖

Glancing around, Ayahliss regarded the other women at the mess hall table. Would she ever be as composed and accomplished as they were? Across the table from her, Kellen, and Dahlia sat Commander Owena Grey and Commander Leanne D'Artansis. Owena had been

Rae's chief of security when she commanded the Gamma VI space station. Leanne, Owena's wife, was one of the best pilots in the SC fleet.

Owena and Leanne relayed news from Leanne's home world, Corma, where several leaders had stepped down after being charged with corruption. Ayahliss didn't understand the exact circumstances, but it clearly had something to do with Dahlia's kidnapping, which happened before the war broke out. Ayahliss worried that if she tried to participate in the intricate political conversation, she would only embarrass herself. Instead, she focused on the food, utilizing the social skills Dahlia had taught her back on Earth. She had been so disrespectful when she first went to stay with Dahlia and Ewan Jacelon. She had disdained all of Dahlia's attempts to show her these things.

Initially, Ayahliss had focused on protecting Armeo, the young Gantharian prince who symbolized her home planet's freedom. Armeo turned out to be a loving, energetic boy who instantly stole her heart. Still stubborn and with her mindset rooted in the rough years in the Gantharian resistance, Ayahliss relented only when Dahlia told her that knowing how to carry herself in the universe was a skill that, when mastered, could serve her well.

"Nobody listens to someone who sounds like an ill-mannered, petulant child," Dahlia had said, "no matter how just their cause is."

"It should be enough," Ayahliss had replied. "What I say should be more important than how."

"You would think so, but that's not how it works. Presentation is important."

"It seems shallow and like a waste of time." Ayahliss cringed while remembering how scornful she had sounded.

Dahlia had merely laughed. "Oh, my. You sound like my daughter when she was your age. Listen. Being civil and learning how to approach people is not about being shallow. It's about showing respect and talking to people in a way they can relate to—to show them that you're credible by doing what you do *well.* Do you understand, Ayahliss? You will reach your goals so much faster if you learn how things work, and how *people* work. So you see, learning about customs, traditions, and respecting them is also quite smart. Trust me, the cleverest thing of all is to listen before you speak."

Thus, Ayahliss sat quietly between Dahlia and Kellen, absorbing every word but only talking when someone spoke to her. She would be on her own again soon, and she needed to gather as much knowledge as possible before then. It hurt to think about not belonging with the Jacelons, Kellen, and Armeo—and most of all, it pained her that she'd never know what all her confusing feelings regarding Reena might have led to. Her duties as a resistance leader meant she had to remain on Gantharat. Hopefully she would find some of her old comrades, even if they couldn't compare to her new friends. She had never lived with a family before staying with the Jacelons, and it had been both a blessing and a cruelty to have known what it was like. Ayahliss didn't dare allow herself to plunge into the vortex that was her emotional response to Reena.

Eventually, Kellen began to send her curious glances, but Ayahliss did her best to act as if nothing was amiss and finished her dessert.

"Ayahliss. Is everything all right?" Kellen asked when they finally rose, walking out of earshot from the others. "You're being very quiet."

"I'm fine, Kellen. Thank you." The knot in Ayahliss's stomach contradicted her words, but how could she explain something to Kellen that she couldn't even fathom?

"You're not being…yourself." Kellen frowned and maneuvered Ayahliss toward the viewport at the far end of the mess hall. "Are you planning something that will jeopardize both your safety and our mission?"

"I promise I'm not. I would never." Ayahliss meant every word, though she wasn't being entirely truthful. "I give you my word I would never put you, Dahlia…or anyone else on this ship in danger."

"Does this promise include you?" Kellen's eyes, so piercing and cool, didn't waver.

"Sure."

"I want to believe you, but I also know how fiercely loyal you are to Gantharat. Just remember that Armeo counts on seeing you again, so you have to be careful. You have a new family now. You're not just responsible for yourself anymore—"

"I know that!" Anxiety mixed with anger coursed through Ayahliss's veins. "I know." She struggled to sound calmer. "I have obligations."

"Yes, you do, but I don't think you see what I mean." Kellen was not a very tactile person, but now she took Ayahliss's hand. "Listen to me. Rae's parents regard you as something of a daughter, especially Dahlia. Armeo has adopted you emotionally as his older sister. He adores you." Kellen hesitated. "And Amereena has taken you under her wing, it seems…even on a personal level."

"Reena is not pleased with me. I…I yelled at her."

"You did?" Kellen's frown deepened.

"I had to. She doesn't understand." Ayahliss wrapped her arms around herself, but realized how revealing the gesture was and let them fall to her sides instead.

"I need to discuss this subject further with you, Ayahliss, but not now. After our training session tomorrow?"

"You shouldn't have to worry about it, Kellen. Honestly, it was nothing, really." It would be much harder to avoid Kellen's questions than Reena's.

"You know as well as I do that you can't perform the gan'thet satisfactorily if you're not composed mentally. I know what I'm talking about. I've gone into battle far too many times while under too much emotional pressure."

"And you're still here, still fighting."

"Yes, but I'm older and, no offense to the monks, I was trained by classic masters, one of whom was my father."

"That just proves my point." Ayahliss drew a deep trembling breath, unsure if fury or disappointment dominated the emotions welling up inside her. "If you'll excuse me, Kellen, I'll retire to my quarters. I have a training session tomorrow."

"Ayahliss, what—"

"Good night." Ayahliss turned to walk out of the mess hall, nearly stumbling over Dahlia, who stood right behind her.

"Child, what's wrong?" Dahlia tried to grasp Ayahliss's arms. "You're upset."

"I'm fine, Dahlia. I'm sorry. I have to go." Panicking, Ayahliss managed a polite smile before she hurried out of the room. She rushed through the corridors, barely missing several crewmembers. Finally inside her quarters, she pulled off her jacket with unsteady hands. Only when she was dressed in nothing but a tank top and underwear could she breathe. Slowly she cooled off and calmed down.

Punching in commands on a panel in the wall next to the door, she let the small quarters fill with classical Cormanian music. The instruments sounded almost Gantharian, and she felt transported in time and space to the monastery hidden in the mountains. Only the sound of birds and music broke the silence there. The monks chanted several times a day and also played instruments, a skill they passed on to the children in their care.

Ayahliss sat down on the bed, just beneath a viewport, looking at the silvery streaks outside. Traveling this fast made it impossible to see individual star constellations, but they were beautiful anyway. Ayahliss's first deep-space journey had taken her from Gantharat, her home world, to the Supreme Constellations, to Earth, which was like Gantharat in so many ways and so incredibly alien to her in others.

She had tried to fit in, and after her initial anger and resentment, she had gained the trust and the affection of one of Earth's most prominent people, Dahlia Jacelon. Chief Diplomat Dahlia Jacelon, she corrected herself. Dahlia had obviously seen something in Ayahliss. When Rae had treated her with suspicion, Dahlia had instead begun to teach Ayahliss social skills and such superficial things as fashion and table manners. Nothing surprised Ayahliss more than realizing that finding your stride when it came to such mundane matters helped you obtain respect from other people.

"So the surface is more important than what's underneath?" Ayahliss asked Dahlia scornfully, clasping a silly little fork with strong, callused hands.

"Of course not. People tend to scan the surface first, before they even give you the chance to prove yourself, though. If you are impeccable in your exterior, as well as how you carry yourself, you'll find that people will take you more seriously quicker."

"So, what you're saying is, if I learn to use this fork and wipe my mouth like a lady, I won't have to kick someone's teeth in to get them to listen?"

"Ayahliss!" Dahlia stared at her. "Ah. A joke."

"I do have a sense of humor."

"You have yet to prove it."

Ayahliss was about to glare at Dahlia for being so stuck-up when she saw the twinkle in her eyes. "Ah. A joke. An *Earth* joke." She huffed with emphasis.

"You'll do fine, child."

Ayahliss pressed her wrists against her forehead, burying her fingers in her short hair. She tugged at it, welcoming the prickly feeling when she deliberately hurt her scalp.

The door chime buzzed, making her jump. Trembling in the cool air from the ventilation unit, she padded over to the screen. "Who is it?" she asked.

"Reena. I need to talk to you." Amereena Beqq's face and wild red hair filled the screen. "Please."

"All right." Ayahliss didn't bother to put her uniform back on. Instead she donned a thin robe, tying the belt haphazardly. "Enter."

The door opened and Reena walked in, dressed in civilian attire, a soft blue dress with long sleeves. The fabric billowed around her and seemed to change between pale and navy blue depending on the light. Sandals with long, wide silk ribbons tied around her slender calves added an inch or two to her height.

"I assume you've spoken to Kellen." Ayahliss didn't bother making her statement into a question.

"No. Well, yes, but she came to me, not the other way around. I had planned to talk with you tonight anyway, and seeing how worried Kellen was only made me more determined."

"And if I hadn't let you in?" Ayahliss knew she sounded childish, but she didn't care.

"I would've camped on your doorstep. Do I look like someone who gives in once I've made my mind up?"

"No."

"Well, then." Reena's eyes softened. "Are you all right?"

"I'm fine." Sarcastically, Ayahliss motioned toward the door. "There."

"Ayahliss. Please." Evident but indistinguishable emotions made Reena's voice tremble faintly.

"All right." Ayahliss cleared her throat nervously. "All right. I'm...I'm confused."

"Talk to me." Reena looked around, then sat on the small couch. She patted the pillow next to her. "Join me."

Ayahliss sat down slowly. The couch barely seated two, which made their knees touch. Her body suddenly tingly all over, Ayahliss clenched her hands into fists and forced herself to breathe evenly.

"I know you think you failed Dahlia, and something tells me

that you still beat yourself up about Armeo's little stunt at the hotel on Corma."

"You saved the situation. You were there and saw how useless I was."

"I thought we were over that. We talked about it, Ayahliss. You did nothing wrong. You couldn't be expected to physically restrain him if he had made up his mind to go exploring. Instead you stayed with him and made sure nobody got too close."

"But they did. And I nearly broke that woman's arm." Ayahliss felt Reena's hands on her shoulders as Reena shook her gently.

"Good for you. She should've known better than to crowd him. What's done is done. Now we're on our way to do something really important. You know more about this than any other civilian. You're one of our most important subject-matter experts. You and Kellen. And your intel regarding the resistance movement is actually even more accurate than hers, so if we look at it that way…" Reena gestured with her palms up.

"I'm afraid." This wasn't at all what Ayahliss meant to say. Set on keeping up appearances, she dug her nails into her palms.

"Why?" Unbelievably soft, Reena's voice lowered nearly an octave. She took one of Ayahliss's fists between her hands. "Talk to me."

"I'm afraid of what I'll find when we reach Gantharat. I'm afraid that I'll screw up and get people killed. Kellen, Dahlia…you." Ayahliss drew another breath, but there seemed to be very little oxygen in the room. "I'm not an expert. I was just a regular resistance fighter in a small cell, which was ambushed and caught."

"Don't sell yourself short." Reena squeezed Ayahliss's hand firmly. "You're a formidable fighter, and you think fast on your feet. You're beyond brave, and if you're at fault for anything, it's that you're a bit too impulsive and lack self-preservation. The things you believe about yourself are not true. Your own insecurities are playing tricks on you. I also think you really miss Armeo, and you're afraid something will happen to him when you're not there to take care of him."

"He has protection."

"I know. Level-one protection by the best security officers the SC can produce." Reena gently pried Ayahliss's hand open. "There. Relax, Ayahliss. You're like a taut bowstring."

"Bowstring?"

"It's an ancient weapon that launched arrows using a bent branch and a string."

Ayahliss tried to picture such a contraption, but her weary brain could only process the fact that Reena was sitting so close, caressing her hand and lower arm. Was she even aware that she was stroking Ayahliss in this way? Ayahliss didn't intend to draw attention to it, in case Reena stopped. It felt so good—so soothing, comforting, and exhilarating at the same time.

"Better." Reena slid impossibly closer. "You're not quite as pale. Can I dare to hope that you're starting to see things my way?"

"What do you mean?" Did Reena want her to reciprocate the gentle, insistent touch?

"I mean, can you see that you're too hard on yourself?"

"Oh." Ayahliss wasn't sure why her chest stung with utter disappointment. "Perhaps."

"'Perhaps' is a long way from your total conviction earlier." Reena smiled broadly, which made her so beautiful; she looked years younger. She stopped caressing Ayahliss's arm and gazed down at it. "You're so strong, yet so slender. How's that even possible?"

"Gantharians' bodies are denser and have another metabolism than a human."

"I'm Cormanian."

"Same thing. I have difficulty distinguishing between Earth humans and Cormanian humanoids. If it wasn't for your eyes and…eh…your freckles, I couldn't tell."

"Freckles? Oh, you've noticed them, have you? Damn. Here I thought I'd been so clever with the skin rejuvenator and makeup."

"Why?" Why had her observation caused Reena distress?

"Why? To Cormanian women, freckles are a sign of aging. Not something we cherish, exactly. As for my eyes, yes, they're different from those of Earth humans."

"Subtle difference. Your iris is sort of luminescent in the dark, and your pupils are slightly oval-shaped."

"You've paid attention." Reena began to massage Ayahliss's other hand, even though she had already relaxed her fingers.

"I don't think your freckles make you look older. I…I like them. They make you seem approachable. You know. Softer." Ayahliss groaned inwardly. Surely it was Reena's touch that made her say things she normally would suppress.

"Oh." Reena grasped Ayahliss's left hand tight. "Ayahliss. For stars and skies, this is insane." As if she only now realized how little Ayahliss was wearing, her eyes glimmered in the muted light. Slowly she raised her hand and ran a light fingertip along Ayahliss's lower lip.

"Reena." Her mouth suddenly dry, Ayahliss wanted to throw her arms around Reena and hold her close. Instead she pressed against the armrest behind her, trying to put as much distance between them as possible short of standing up. Her legs wouldn't support her right now.

"You're gorgeous. I know you're not for me, but I can't help but see…you. All that you are. Or perhaps all that you let me see. You're an enigma, a mystery, and it hurts that you're not for me to figure out." Reena let go of Ayahliss's hand and looked regretfully at her.

"I know I'm not for you. How could I be? You're amazing, famous, and acquainted with political leaders. You're powerful." Ayahliss tried to demonstrate that she understood and was puzzled at how Reena's eyes darkened and how she suddenly scowled.

"And too old for you."

"Old?" Ayahliss tried to understand where that comment came from. She had taken Reena's comments about Cormanian freckles as a way for her to be evasive, an act. This second remark about age made Ayahliss think it could actually be a sore spot for Reena.

"I'm twice your age."

"What does that matter?" Ayahliss could list a thousand reasons why she was wrong for Reena, but age?

"Normally I wouldn't let it faze me, but—it matters." Speaking with sorrow in her voice, Reena raised one of Ayahliss's hands to her face. She rubbed it gently against her cheek, then turned her head and grazed it with her lips. "Now, please listen to me. I need you to remain focused on this mission. We all have our assignments, and I can't worry about you exploding into dangerous situations."

"I won't endanger anyone." It hurt to speak.

"That's not what I mean. If I can't trust you to act with all the knowledge and discipline Kellen has taught you, I won't be able to concentrate on my own assignment. Don't you understand? I worry about *you*." Reena stood, letting go of Ayahliss's hands. "So many things about this mission are difficult. We'll reach Gantharian space in two days, and a lot of things need to be ready by then. Good night, Ayahliss."

"Reena?" Rushing to her feet, Ayahliss shyly touched Reena's arm. "I know I'm struggling with guilt. I'm not stupid. I need to work through it to be a useful member of this crew, of this mission, but it's just…it's not easy. This is not the only, I mean, the first thing I'm guilty of. I've seen and done a lot in my years in the Gantharian resistance. It took being rescued by Kellen and Rae to make me regard things differently."

"A lot to take in during such a short time, isn't it?" Reena's eyes were warm again as she looked up at Ayahliss. "You're doing much better than you give yourself credit for. If I can make one more wish?"

"Of course." Her heart suddenly pounding, Ayahliss wanted to slide her fingers through the red masses of Reena's hair.

"Don't push Kellen away. Or Dahlia…or me? We all love you and want to help you reach your potential. Just bear with us, all right?"

Oddly disappointed, but also stunned that Reena would use the word "love" the way she had, even if she'd included Kellen and Dahlia, Ayahliss nodded. "I promise. Can I ask a favor in return?"

"Anything."

"Don't—don't give up on me?" Ayahliss held her breath and barely dared meet Reena's eyes.

"Oh, Ayahliss, how could I ever?" Reena flung her arms around Ayahliss's neck and held her close.

Ayahliss acted without thinking, mimicking Reena by wrapping her arms around her and returning the embrace. She had hugged Kellen, Rae, and Dahlia, but none of those times had she ever felt this way. Every hair follicle on her body rose to attention, and the inside of her body seemed to melt into a buttery consistency. She felt hot and cold at the same time, and her heart thundered.

Reena smelled like the red flowers on the meadows beneath the mountains where she grew up, and of something more, something indefinable, yet all Reena. Her long, wild mane of red curls tickled the back of Ayahliss's hands, igniting shivers along her limbs.

"Ayahliss, you need to let go of me. This was unwise. I shouldn't have hugged you. Not like this." Reena spoke fast. "Ayahliss? Let go of me, darling?"

Ayahliss took in the term of endearment more fully than Reena's message. Reena had called her "darling"? Rae called Kellen this all the time. The potential significance was too much. Ayahliss let go of Reena as if she'd burned herself.

"I apologize also. I don't know what happened." Ayahliss tried to smile casually, but failed. "Good night, Reena."

"Good night." Reena left and the doors hissed together behind her.

Ayahliss felt the cool air from the ventilation against her legs and gazed down. Her belt had come undone and her robe was fully open in the front. How long had it been like that? Had she hugged Reena half-naked? No wonder the poor woman looked so flustered. Groaning, but also with a faint smile about how ridiculous the situation was, Ayahliss undressed and slipped into bed. Expecting yet another sleepless night, she was relieved that drowsiness overtook her almost immediately.

Chapter Six

Weiss never understood how some people could enjoy weightlessness as something to do for sheer fun. She hated it, and always had, despite being born in space. As a child aboard a generational ship, she had learned the basics regarding space walks by the age of four. Some of her friends loved it, but she despised not being in control.

"Pull the handle, Weiss. Stay on course." Madisyn's voice crackling in her earpiece startled Weiss back into present time. Cursing under her breath, she tugged at the handle and the fusion pack on her back ignited, propelling her toward the surface of the moon. The slight tug on her body reduced the eerie feeling of nothingness that engulfed her every time she was in weightless conditions.

"Landmark one in sight. Trying to pinpoint landmark two." Weiss spoke sharply as she looked for the third rock formation they needed to triangulate their position. "I see lights two finger-widths from the first landmark."

"I see them too. Might be the crew quarters." Madisyn was not visible to Weiss's left. "I have the third landmark in sight. Stay close."

"On your tail, Pimm." Pressing her hands close to her legs, Weiss followed Madisyn in a narrow spiral toward Nemalima's jagged surface. The landscape appeared increasingly hostile and unforgiving as they got closer. They needed a reasonably smooth surface to land safely, but that hope was futile this time. Weiss didn't like not being the front person, the leader, but Madisyn's superior vision made her the best person for the job. Annoyed, Weiss corrected herself. Madisyn was an individual, not a person.

"Touchdown in forty-five seconds. Brace for impact. Engage radio silence and only acknowledge touchdown with two clicks."

They would have to operate quickly and with as little communication as possible, since the miners possessed an elaborate security system. Podmer had based his plan on the theory that the grid around the mining colony was set to detect vessels, not something as small as a body.

The ground seemed to rush up to meet Weiss, and she engaged the anti-G thrusters to cushion the last of the drop. She hit the ground with her knees bent and staggered sideways, trying to remain on her feet. Not about to do the usual body roll on the sharp rocks, she was relieved when she found her bearings and didn't bounce all over the small canyon. She clicked her communicator sensor twice. Next to her, Madisyn had performed a textbook touchdown and was already scanning their surroundings. Weiss pulled out her own scanner and saw they had landed a bit farther to the south than anticipated, but they could easily make up for it. She made sure the anti-G pack was turned off to conserve energy output.

Following Madisyn, Weiss tried to emulate her long strides, using the moon's low gravity to propel her forward. She hated feeling clumsy and was relieved when she soon found the same rhythm as Madisyn. One crewmember joined them, and to their sides, Struyen and the other five members of their team fanned out in two groups, according to plan. Three hundred meters farther toward the illuminated side of the moon, Madisyn stopped and raised her hand, indicating they should halt. She clicked the communicator twice and Weiss heard two sets of double-clicks moments later. All were in position.

Weiss made sure her plasma-pulse rifle was set to heavy stun and moved carefully behind Madisyn as they approached the site of the security-grid beacon. Madisyn unhooked a small device from her belt and placed it on the ground a few meters from the beacon. They had to render it harmless for the rest of their mission to be successful. Being a Guild Nation BNSL android, she possessed more knowledge regarding technological solutions than any of them.

Madisyn backed up, using her scanner. Her broad smile told Weiss what she needed to know.

"Pimm to team two and three. Beacon is neutralized and sensors are scrambled. We can now forgo radio silence. Set weapons to heavy stun. Move into position."

"Team two advancing." The communicator buzzed to life.

"Team three moving in."

"Affirmative." Madisyn nudged the small device, which was responsible for scrambling the mining company's sensors and projecting false readings, sliding it beneath a rock formation. "Team one moving toward storage area."

Weiss and Struyen joined Madisyn as she hurried along a man-made path among the rocks. Moon dust whirled around their feet and Weiss focused on not stumbling. She pressed the rifle close to her body as she doubled over to stay out of sight of any guards.

"Any life signs?" Weiss asked as they stopped only a few meters from the entrance to the plant.

"None on the outside." Madisyn scanned the area. "I'm reading faint humanoid signatures inside the structures."

"How many?"

"Too soon to tell. When we get inside, I'll be able to perform more accurate readings."

"I don't like this." Podmer was a skilled strategist, but this plan had too many variables. "An army of guards could be in there, waiting to take us out."

"Our intel says there's not." Madisyn shrugged. "Team one in position."

The other two teams echoed her words.

"We need to break through the doors and take care of the people there before we can signal the shuttles. Come on. Team one going in."

They couldn't turn back now. Weiss hoisted her weapon as Madisyn and Struyen ran before her to the large hatch leading into an airlock. Struyen attached yet another device to the lock and punched in a series of commands.

"Stand back, just to be safe." Madisyn pushed Weiss and Struyen to the side and raised her rifle. The lock snapped open and a gush of oxygen escaped as the hatch swung open, making Madisyn sway, but she remained on her feet. "Clear. Let's go. Teams two and three, what's your position?"

"Team two right behind you."

"Team three ready to guard the perimeter."

They rushed into the airlock, and only seconds later, team two joined them. Weiss saw the members of team three take up position outside. Struyen closed the hatch behind them.

Madisyn motioned toward Weiss. "Hit the decompression sensor."

Quickly, Weiss strode over to the opposite hatch and examined the panel. Her heart hammered, but a familiar sense of serenity descended upon her as she engaged the decompression unit. The indicator went from yellow to blue. "We're good to go."

"All right. Remember, we need twenty crates. Weiss, Struyen you're with me. Team two, you get the crates ready. Everybody set?"

"Yes, ma'am."

Weiss nodded at Madisyn, who pushed a sensor to open the inside hatch. It slid to the side and she stared into a vast room lit only by a dim green light. With her weapon ready to fire, Weiss moved in. She made sure the door opening was clear, as well as the walls and ceiling around it. Except for a discreet hissing sound, it was eerily quiet in what seemed to be a warehouse. Team two moved cautiously behind them as she and Madisyn quickly made sure that no guards would surprise them.

Team two began pushing crates onto hover carts, stacking them by the hatch. Weiss in turn couldn't rid herself of the strange sense that things were going too easy. She pulled out her own scanner and walked along the outer wall of the warehouse, making sure nothing would take them by surprise. She turned at the far wall and began moving along the shelf that ran along the middle of the structure. Halfway back to the hatch, Madisyn caught up with her.

"What are you doing? They're nearly done. It's time to—"

"Wait." Weiss stared at her readings, trying to make sense of the information. "Something's wrong."

"What are you talking about?" Madisyn glanced at Weiss's scanner. "*T'shiad!* What the hell is that?" She yanked the reader out of Weiss's hands. "Something is causing this, something that's making smaller and smaller cycles."

"Counting down. It's an explosive device, possibly a plasma charge."

"Damn, how long do we have?" Madisyn began to run toward where team two was loading the crates.

"According to this, less than two minutes." Weiss ran along with her. "Weiss to team three. Get the shuttles over here. We need to move out now. Now!"

"Affirmative."

Weiss pushed the first cart fully loaded with crates of davic crystals through the hatch with the help of one of the others. Madisyn struggled to mount the last of the crates on the second cart. She tore them out of the hands of the two men, shouting at them, "I've got this. Get out of here. Get out now!"

While the two men scrambled through the hatch and into the airlock, Weiss jumped back inside, set on helping Madisyn shove the second cart through the hatch. Halfway through, it stopped and wouldn't budge, and even though Weiss put all her weight behind it.

"It's stuck on something underneath." Madisyn's voice came in short gasps. "Let me see."

"We should just leave it."

"No. Help me." Madisyn knelt on the floor and stuck her head and shoulders underneath the cart. "It's a lever that's come off the hatch. There. It's gone. Come on, let's do this."

Weiss glanced at her scanner, which she'd attached to her wrist. "We don't have enough time."

"All right. Listen. Let's get this out of here and then follow me." Madisyn didn't hesitate as they pressed hard enough against the cart to make it slide through the inside hatch and into the airlock. Madisyn barked her orders to team two and Struyen. "Decompress and get the stuff out of here and hook it onto the shuttles. Weiss and I can't fit in the airlock with you."

"But, Pimm—" Struyen looked shocked, but something sounding like excitement infused his words.

"Follow orders. Go!" Madisyn shouted, and slammed her hand on the sensor that closed the hatch.

"Great." Weiss was furious. "You've just killed us."

❖

"Come on. Faster!" Madisyn ran with long steps along the wall. She turned her head, making sure Weiss was right behind her. "Behind the crates over in the corner."

"I can't believe this." Weiss spoke in short gasps. "We're dead."

"Here. Get down." Madisyn didn't waste time trying to explain, but pushed Weiss in behind the crates. She checked her internal chronometer. Five seconds. Impulsively, she threw herself on top of Weiss, covering her body with her own. "Hold on."

"What—"

The explosion roared through the warehouse and sent crates flying around them. Madisyn wrapped her arms and legs around Weiss. She needed to keep her alive. The turbulence after the explosion lasted only a few seconds, but felt longer. Once she realized it was over, Madisyn tried to move, but several crates that were resting against her back pinned her down.

"Weiss?" Madisyn managed to get a hand in between them to feel Weiss's side through the suit. She pulled up her bio-signature on the visor. A rapid flutter under her fingertips indicated life, and, at the same time, she saw encouraging readings of Weiss's blood pressure and heart rate.

"Madisyn? Damn the stars. My ears are still ringing."

"You're okay." Relieved that her decision hadn't killed Weiss, Madisyn patted her.

"You have to get off me, though. I can hardly breathe."

"Hmm, that might pose a problem. I'm not all that's on top of you. It's me and several crates."

"Struyen to Pimm. What's your status?" His voice reached them via the communicator.

"Pimm here. Weiss and I are alive, but buried under debris. What about the rest of you?"

"We went flying, but the shuttles are here and we're securing the carts. You need to get out of here fast. We've got company."

Naturally. All alarms had to be blaring at the mining headquarters. Madisyn pushed at the crates.

"Ow." Weiss's moan made Madisyn stop instantly.

"Sorry. Let me try to move a little before I push on them. "Pimm to Struyen. Don't wait for us. Get the merchandise out of here. Then, if it's possible, come back for us."

"Pimm—"

"Just do it, Struyen. It's an order."

"We'll be back."

"We'll be here. Pimm out." Madisyn shifted her weight to the left and freed her arm completely. "Hold on, Weiss. I'll try to push the crates off us." She pressed her palm against the floor, next to Weiss's head. Nothing happened and she tried again. "You have to help me, if you can."

"All right." Groaning, Weiss moved her arms up next to her. "Damn, I damaged my left wrist." Weiss sounded more disgusted than in pain.

"Do what you can. You heard Struyen."

"Yeah."

"Come on. Push." Madisyn dug in and used all her superior strength to shift the crates as Weiss did the same. Something moved, and suddenly several crates slid down and crashed to the floor next to them. "Good. Again." After two more attempts, Madisyn was able to move away from Weiss and help her up. She didn't wait to ascertain any damage; it was enough that Weiss could stand.

"I lost my rifle," Weiss said.

"I have mine." Madisyn began moving along the wall, over to a section that had crumbled in the blast. "We don't have to use the door. Let's go." Climbing through the hole, she kept her weapon ready, but nobody had reached that part of the structure yet. In the distance, Madisyn could see the shuttles with the crates hanging from wires. The other teams and Struyen had fastened their harnesses to the wires and were now clinging to the crates on their way back to the mother ship. *Mission accomplished.*

Madisyn saw no obvious path among the rocks and didn't dare use her helmet light. She moved forward as fast as she could and heard an occasional faint curse over her headset. Soon they had put enough distance between themselves and the wrecked warehouse to slow down. They were well within the dark side of the moon, and Madisyn hoped this would make it more difficult for the mining security guards to locate them.

"I—I need to rest." Weiss sounded tormented and dangerously out of breath.

"We can take a minute." Madisyn stopped at a cave-like opening in the black rocks to their left and turned just in time to grab hold of Weiss, who staggered to the side, clutching her arm.

"You're injured."

"My arm. I think it's fractured again." Weiss slowly sat down on a ledge. "It hurts like hell."

Madisyn didn't know Weiss, but she most likely didn't allow small injuries to stop her. If she said her arm hurt, the pain was no doubt excruciating. "I can't get an accurate scan through the suit. I'm sorry."

"Don't worry. I'll be fine if I can just catch my breath."

Madisyn scanned in the direction they had come from. "I read multiple bio-signatures and three spacecraft."

"It won't take them long to pinpoint our location." Weiss leaned back against the rock, cradling her arm.

"We can always hope they think everyone left on the shuttles. If we can set up a scramble field—"

"That would make us invisible for anyone coming to our rescue."

"Only if I failed to embed a marker in the signal." Madisyn dug through one of her side pockets for a disperser. She hooked it up to her scanner and coded it with a signal that would mask them to the Nemalima miners, but not to anyone aboard the *Salaceos*. Madisyn pushed the disperser into the ground, and a pink light began to glow at its tip. "I bought us a little time."

"How little?" Weiss asked shortly.

"Oh, maybe thirty minutes. After that, the energy will start to fade. These small dispersers don't last very long."

"Fine." Weiss sounded like her normal sarcastic self, but as she sat slumped against the rock, protecting her arm like that, Madisyn saw her in a new light.

"I wish I could give you a pain reliever or work you over with the bone knitter."

"I said I'm fine." Weiss pushed away from the rocks. Flinching in obvious pain, she moaned and bent over.

"What did you do?" Madisyn threw herself forward, holding Weiss by the shoulders. "Weiss?"

"It's…nothing. An old injury."

"Looks like something to me." Afraid that Weiss would fall over and injure her arm even more, she helped her sit on the ground, supporting her now-trembling body.

"Don't."

"They'll be here soon. Just hang in there." Madisyn ignored the pained attempt from Weiss to resist her. "Just pretend that I'm a MEDI-droid."

"MEDI-droids are impersonal. And polite."

"Is that your way of saying that I'm too personal and rude?"

Weiss made a sound that sounded like something between a huff and a snort.

Madisyn's inner sensors suddenly gave her a jolt. She looked up and saw a faint light beam farther down the path, behind them. "Shh. I see something." She squinted, adjusting her visor. "Damn it. We have company."

CHAPTER SEVEN

Madisyn handed the scanner over to Weiss and took up position behind a large rock next to the path where the security guards now approached them. "They're about a hundred meters from our position," Madisyn said, hoisting her plasma-pulse weapon. "I have them in my sight, and the plasma-pulse is set to heavy stun. It'll knock them out, but not harm them."

"Can you take them all out?"

"You questioning my marksmanship?" Madisyn didn't turn around, but tried to defuse the tension with humorous sarcasm.

"Wouldn't dream of it." Weiss didn't miss a beat.

"Good. Watch our backs and leave these *drontes* to me." Using the Guild Nation word for clowns, Madisyn took aim, making sure her sight was lined up with her internal processor. The data flickered in her left field of vision, and she automatically adjusted her aim. She couldn't afford to miss. Worst-case scenario, the Nemalima guards would kill them or take them prisoner. The consequences went far beyond blowing their cover. Not only would Madisyn's six months of undercover work be wasted, but if anyone examined her more closely, everything would be over. This fear had been the perfect incentive to keep her from getting caught, or exposed, throughout her career as a secret agent. *Nothing like the fear of being gutted like a fish to keep you sharp.*

"They're closing in," Madisyn whispered, blinking twice to make the lenses in her eyes zoom in. "Anything on sensors from our friends?"

"Nothing so far." Weiss moved the scanner in small circles. "I get a lot of static."

"That's the force field. I placed a filter for it, but it will still impact readings."

Madisyn pressed herself close to the rock, making sure she was out of sight. The force field masked their signatures, but it wasn't foolproof. The Nemalima mining company had obviously upgraded their systems, and they could have gotten their hands on the latest scanning equipment.

"Madisyn. I read two signals. Coordinates five-five-three." Weiss moaned and pushed off the rock behind her. "They're not ours."

"Damn it." Madisyn glanced at the handheld scanner. "You're right. The miners aren't stupid. They've deployed a second team."

"You still have time to take everybody out."

"I'm not so sure." Madisyn shuddered. "Even if I stun the first team, they might have time to alert the others. They could be linked like we are, able to read each other's bio-signatures."

"We—I mean, *I* can't move. Not fast enough to reach a better location." Weiss cleared her throat. "You should move to higher ground. That will make it easier for Podmer's crew to find you."

"We're getting out of here. We have a mission to complete and I can't do it alone."

A stunned silence, then Weiss sighed, sounding exasperated. "What's your plan, then?"

"Give me a second." Thinking fast, Madisyn pulled a filament wire from one of her belt packs. She motioned for Weiss to move farther back among the jagged rocks. "Take cover."

"But—"

"Go on. We don't have much time." Madisyn attached the filament to a small rock and quickly pulled it across the path, back and forth several times. It was hard to hold the filament with the gloves on, but she managed to wind it across the path four times before she ran out of wire. Finding a primer, she attached it and set it to a frequency they could monitor with the scanner.

Quickly, Madisyn followed Weiss in behind the rocks, making sure she could still see the approaching guards.

"What are you doing? A bell shock?"

"Yeah, with a twist." Madisyn took the scanner and set it to the right frequency. "This is going to knock them for a loop, but hopefully not kill anyone." She made sure she had her weapon ready and kept her eyes on the approaching lights. "Team two has almost caught up with us," she murmured. "We may get them all at once, if we're lucky."

Before them, the light from several search-flashes created distorted shadows from the rocks around them. Madisyn nearly held her breath, something she knew was not considered normal for an android of any model.

"Here they come," Weiss murmured, placing a hand on her shoulder. "Not yet."

"I know." Madisyn waited until the first team was practically on top of them and the second only ten or fifteen meters away. "Close your eyes." She punched in the command on the scanner, then shut her own eyes. Through her eyelids, she saw the violent flashes of light, and the ground seemed to vibrate under their feet.

After what seemed like forever, Madisyn opened her eyes and saw two guards lying on the path. She raised her weapon and moved forward to check on team two. It took her a few seconds, but then she saw the outline of two other guards on the path in the other direction, approximately seven meters from her position.

"Well, what do you know? Here come the gilded horsemen." Weiss stood next to Madisyn, glancing at the scanner in her left hand. "Our crew is back for us."

"Good." Madisyn wanted to check on the guards, but knew she didn't have time. She could only pray they hadn't suffered any serious injuries. "I'm turning the beacon up." She entered another set of commands. "Let's move a bit farther up the path."

"All right." Weiss was trembling visibly now. She was limping and protecting her arm, and obviously had just about had enough.

"Lean on me," Madisyn said, and slowed down.

"No need." Curt and standoffish, Weiss dragged herself behind Madisyn.

"If you're going to be able to climb over these guys over here," Madisyn gestured toward the still forms on the path, "you'll have to."

An impatient growl erupted from the speaker in Madisyn's helmet, but Weiss allowed her to wrap one arm around her waist. "Here we go." Madisyn guided Weiss across the unconscious guards, but as they were clearing the second one, he jerked and grabbed Madisyn's left leg.

"Damn! Go on, Weiss." Madisyn gasped at his strong hold on her ankle. Somehow he had a good grip on her foot, perhaps because of the pocket that held her double-bladed laser knife. The thought of the weapon barely registered with Madisyn before it was in the guard's hand. The blade hummed to life, then slashed through her suit. The inner mesh kept it from doing any real damage to her system, but her suit was depressurizing.

Suddenly a boot-clad foot entered Madisyn's field of vision and kicked the laser knife out of the guard's hand. He curled up around his clearly injured hand, but as his communication device wasn't set to their frequency, Madisyn couldn't hear him cry out. Weiss was leaning against Madisyn again.

"Let's get out of here. Struyen is over there." Weiss tugged at the straps holding Madisyn's gear in place on her back. "Snap out of it. Let's go!"

Madisyn's vision blurred and her system was already running diagnostics to mitigate damages. She tried to move and, to her surprise, she was able to even though her movements were jerky and unbalanced. She and Weiss clung to each other like drunks after an extended shore leave among the illegal bars on Carossa Prime, staggering toward the hovering shuttle.

"Struyen to Pimm. Dropping the wire. You have to use the same one. We broke the other three unloading the goods aboard the *Salaceos*."

"Affirmative." Madisyn squinted toward the shuttle's belly, blinking repeatedly. Her entire system was trying to keep her alive, focusing on the loss of pressure. Everything else was on hold, including such simple configurations as her vision.

"Here it comes," Weiss said, reaching for the wire with her good arm. "You have to secure it around us."

"All right."

"And fast," Weiss added, glancing over Madisyn's shoulder. "Two of the guards are closing in."

Madisyn didn't waste any time. She pulled the wire taut around them, virtually strapping them together chest to chest. "Pimm to Struyen. Wire is secured. Get us out of here."

"Let's leave this godforsaken rock," Struyen growled over the com system. "Afraid that you have to dangle for a while, ma'am."

"Negative," Weiss interjected. "Pimm's suit has been compromised. Reel us in."

"We can't." Struyen didn't sound very apologetic. "We were lucky to extend it at all. If we try to reel you in, the wire might sever it."

"Just go." Madisyn wrapped her arms around Weiss and held on tight. Just as she did, plasma-pulse fire lit up the space around them. Turning bright blue for a fraction of a second before the plasma charges dissipated into the nothingness of space, it stung her eyes in a way she'd never experienced. Madisyn had never been severely injured after becoming a sentient BNSL. The fact that her humanoid brain and her spinal cord were intact meant that the pain was as real as if the injured body part had been humanoid as well. Her parents had done their job almost too well, connecting her brain with the bio-neural system that made her superior to most humanoids in strength and endurance. In their effort to create a new, fully functional body for her, they had given her artificially grown human skin and a synthetic peripheral nervous system, and connected every single part of her anatomy, which sometimes made Madisyn curse them.

❖

Weiss felt Madisyn's wiry arms around her and was grateful that she had tucked her fractured arm in between them where it couldn't get tangled in the wire. To her surprise, Madisyn trembled as they were hurled through space underneath Podmer's shuttle. Why would a BNSL tremble? That didn't make sense. Why would any tech designer create an android vulnerable enough to flinch when plasma charges erupted around them? It was a wholly humanoid reaction. Why go for that type of authenticity?

"Madisyn? You all right?"

"I'm fine. How's your arm?"

"Okay. I mean, it will be."

"I have a bone knitter in our quarters. Podmer makes sure we can take care of minor injuries ourselves." Madisyn spoke fast, but her tremors seemed to become less noticeable.

"Go figure. Saves time, I suppose."

"I wonder how we're going to board the *Salaceos* hanging like berries on a vine from this wire." Weiss tried to picture the shuttle landing in the hangar inside the belly of the *Salaceos*. Perhaps the crew could hook them with something and pull them in if they modified the ship's force field.

Plasma singed the space around them again, and Madisyn pressed her forehead against Weiss's shoulder. "I'm sorry. This seems to really screw up my sensors right now. Must be the damage to the suit."

Weiss wasn't comfortable with the close proximity, not only because of her injured arm. The way Madisyn felt against her was entirely too intimate. Weiss had existed without the touch of another person for a very long time, unless she counted SC law-enforcement agents and medical personnel. Out of necessity she had deliberately changed from a pleasure-seeking player to a virtual hermit in a matter of days, two years ago, something that had greatly bothered her crew. Unable to explain it to herself, Weiss had made sure everybody knew the matter was off-topic. The only time she had engaged in physical activities was in hand-to-hand combat training or actual fighting.

She had no use for any of the fortune hunters that had willingly kept her company and been willing to meet her every whim during the previous years. Weiss had gone for voluptuous women back then, and she had kept them well-fed and dressed, with plenty of credits to use in the ports. After several years, Weiss began to realize she couldn't tell their faces apart. One willing body was so like the next, and their conversation, if you could call it that, was of little interest. Weiss didn't miss the hollow physical pleasure; in fact, it was a relief to just be left in peace, to have her quarters to herself and not have to share with the latest sultry pirate groupie.

Weiss looked up and saw the shuttle approach Podmer's ship. Slowing down, they still closed in on the shuttle bay area very fast, and Weiss held her breath as they were tossed against the hull. She fully expected to be crushed, but then she spotted four crewmembers with what looked like large magnetic hooks.

"Pimm. Weiss. We'll get you." A female voice crackled in Weiss's headset. "Hold on. This still might be a painful ride."

"Great." Weiss braced herself, clenching her teeth to block out the pain in her arm.

The sudden stop sent Weiss and Madisyn into a crazy spin. Their bodies meshed together, which sent continual, white-edged pain through Weiss's arm. She thought she heard herself scream, but hoped she was wrong. Madisyn shifted her grip, wrapping her arms and legs tighter around her.

"I'm...sorry..."

Weiss couldn't hear what else Madisyn yelled before they slammed into the deck, tumbling so fast she was sure they would be crushed against the bulkhead. Eventually they lay gasping on the shuttle bay deck. Weiss was close to passing out from the pain but drew a few deep breaths to regain some form of equilibrium.

"Weiss..." Madisyn's low hiss was barely audible. "Talk to me."

"I'll live."

Madisyn snorted and began laughing, only to stop just as suddenly. "Ow."

Pain? An android that experiences pain? That's a first. Weiss rolled away from Madisyn, and helpful hands yanked her to her feet. She could see Struyen exiting the shuttle and walking toward them.

"For stars and skies, I thought you two were toast." Struyen raised an eyebrow at the panting Madisyn. "I see even androids get winded when they can't breathe."

"I'm as reliant on oxygen as you are, and you know it." Madisyn spoke with a steel-enforced voice that made Struyen take half a step back. "I will hand in my report tomorrow. I can tell that we are in mass-distortion drive. Good."

"Yes, Podmer is pleased with the heist even if we ran into a bit of a hassle."

"A bit? Yes." Weiss made sure nothing or nobody touched her arm. "Guess you could say that."

"And Podmer wants me to take the bridge this evening." Struyen looked like he'd been awarded a medal.

"Fantastic. Don't pick up any hitchhikers." Madisyn pulled off her helmet and limped toward the double door leading out into the corridor. "Weiss. Let me help you with the helmet." She pulled it off gently. "This way."

Weiss followed Madisyn to their quarters, suddenly so fatigued she felt like sitting down right there on the deck and falling asleep. By willpower alone, she made her way through the ship.

Once back in their quarters, Madisyn looked wearily at Weiss's arm. "Your arm has been mangled more than once. We really should get you to sickbay. It's just—" She rubbed the back of her neck.

"What?"

"The ship's so-called doctor is such a brute, and not a very good doctor. I mean, if he were a top-notch physician, what the hell would he be doing with this crew?"

"You have a point." Weiss was fading fast and had to sit down. "Either way, I need to get out of this damn suit and so do you. Your leg looks, um, weird."

Madisyn glanced at her deformed leg where the laser knife had made an indentation. "That's going to take some engineering."

"Does it, you know, hurt?"

"In a way, yes. I have nerve endings just like you, even if they're artificial."

"I see." Weiss sat still as Madisyn began to peel off her space suit. She moaned under her breath when Madisyn resolutely used an electric scalpel to cut off the sleeve. She pulled it aside, her hands incredibly gentle, and reached for the bone knitter.

"The skin isn't broken, and the fracture isn't misaligned. You were lucky after all, especially after that tumble we took just now." Madisyn ran the bone knitter several times across Weiss's lower arm. "We need to repeat this procedure tomorrow, but this should stabilize the fracture and help with the pain. If you still need them, I have some pain-relief imbulizers."

"No pain meds."

"You sure?" Madisyn tucked the bone knitter into a drawer. "They would help you sleep."

"I've had enough of such things the last few months." Weiss knew she sounded short and ungrateful. "Now, what about you?"

"I'll tend to my injury now that we're done with yours. I'll be fine."

"Doesn't look like that to me." Weiss studied Madisyn's injury with critical eyes. "If you hadn't worn the mesh-enforced layer in the suit, that guard would've severed your leg."

"But he didn't." Madisyn pushed off the space suit and had turned to walk into the bathroom when Weiss put a hand on her shoulder.

"Let me. Consider it a perfect way to get to know one another."

"What are you talking about?"

"Aw, come on." Weiss motioned for Madisyn to sit and elevate her leg. "This is just the type of thing that will build team spirit."

"You're crazy. Team spirit?"

Weiss pulled the insulating sock off Madisyn's foot. She wasn't sure what to expect, but the perfect toes with toenails like mother-of-pearl weren't it. The foot was pale and cold. Acting automatically, she cupped her hands around Madisyn's foot and rubbed it. "Does this help at all?"

"Uh. Yes." Madisyn drew a trembling breath. "I have my own version of the humanoid blood vessels. They can use a boost, I suppose. Thank you."

"You saved my life back there. Least I can do." Weiss tried to view her actions as a way to soften Madisyn up, to make her lower her guard, but a deep sense of truth insisted that she had other motives.

"If you put it that way."

"Now let's see. Oh, damn, that looks…bad." Weiss stared at the indentation in Madisyn's leg. The skin was stretched thin and pale-pink muscle tissue was bulging on the edges of the crater. "What the hell are you going to do?"

"I have a few tools. You think you could help out?" Madisyn was trembling again.

"Sure. Just give me instructions." Looking up, Weiss could have sworn Madisyn was paler, but that was impossible.

Madisyn directed Weiss to a cabinet where she found a tool kit with the University of Guild Nation's emblem on it. "This?"

"Yes."

Weiss pulled out a set of sinister-looking long, narrow spanners and a small plasma burner that would put the fear of the deities in most humanoids. "All right. Showtime." Weiss tried to smile reassuringly, which only made Madisyn appear more nervous.

"Use the ten-millimeter spanner and a knife. Press down just below my meniscus with the spanner, and make sure to have the magnetic side toward me. Push a syringe in a ninety-degree angle just below. Halfway in, it will start to deflate the swelling in my calf."

Weiss felt utterly clumsy, and the numbness in her fractured arm didn't help her focus. She pushed the syringe in and the coarse needle pierced the pale skin.

"Oh." Madisyn swayed.

"You all right?" Weiss stopped what she was doing.

"Proceed."

"Very well." She kept it up for a while, furtively checking Madisyn's perfect features for any signs of discomfort. After what seemed like a very long time, Madisyn's leg looked normal again.

"There you go. Good as new, sort of." Weiss retracted the syringe. "You can breathe now."

"Thanks." Madisyn gazed up at Weiss with an enigmatic smile that barely curved the corners of her mouth. "As you heard me tell Struyen, I do breathe, and I breathe for the same reason as everybody else. Exhale to rid the system of waste products, inhale to keep a steady oxygen level." She stretched her leg slowly. "Hey, that's fantastic. You're not half-bad around the tools."

"That will have to be our secret."

"Oh, another one. No worries. I'm chock full of secrets these days. One more or less." Madisyn smiled, a thoroughly charming, toothy grin.

And so am I. Weiss studied Madisyn as she walked to the tiny ensuite bathroom, moving stiffly, much like Weiss herself. When the door closed behind her, Weiss sighed deeply, completely unable to figure out why she couldn't take her eyes off Madisyn. *The android.* Sentient, Weiss reminded herself.

Soon Madisyn returned, clean and fresh-smelling. Weiss murmured something she couldn't even decipher and fled to the bathroom, which was so small she barely had room to maneuver. After she engaged the shower chamber and pulled off her undergarments, dirt and grime evaporated from her skin and fell into the recycling drain on the floor. Utilizing sound waves, this method of cleansing was more thorough than an aqua shower, but not half as pleasurable, Weiss thought, suddenly ready to trade just about everything she owned for hot, wet water.

A glance in the mirror showed her as pale but composed, and after pulling on newly replicated underwear, she used the smaller sonic nozzle to clean her teeth. She moved quickly, and unable to justify staying in the bathroom any longer, she returned to their quarters.

Madisyn was sitting on her bed, her eyes half-closed and her arms loosely holding her knees. "Scrambler's on. We have to send our report tomorrow."

"Yes." Weiss crawled into bed and pulled the thin thermo blanket up around her. "Not much to tell. Blew up a moon, practically. Wish you were here."

Madisyn snorted. "Yes, something like that." She closed her eyes briefly. "Switching off scrambler."

Weiss studied Madisyn in the dim light from the stars and their bed lights. She was startled to feel something hot and smoldering warm the lower part of her stomach. Desperate to focus on a single detail in Madisyn's demeanor or appearance that showed she wasn't humanoid, wasn't *real*, all Weiss saw was soft, pale skin, even softer, unruly blond hair, and she remembered the way she'd felt, how she'd trembled during their full-body contact. What was *that* about? The memory of Madisyn's body so close, after years of abstinence, was enough to send a quiet moan over her lips.

"You in pain, Weiss?" Madisyn asked, actually sounding sleepy.

"No. I'm fine. Just tired." Aware that she sounded curt, she turned her back toward Madisyn, which did little good. No matter how hard she closed her eyes, she could still see the pain in Madisyn's eyes as she'd mended her artificial leg. Real pain. *What the hell's going on?*

CHAPTER EIGHT

Amereena stood on the bridge of the *Circinus*, scrutinizing the image of the blue-green planet that grew larger as they approached Gantharat. She knew more of this world's political system than most within the Supreme Constellations. Amereena loved the law and believed in it unconditionally, especially the intricacies of trying to understand an alien world and how its population operated. She still had much to learn but was confident she had enough knowledge to help this diplomatic mission succeed, together with Dahlia Jacelon and the Protector of the Realm.

"Beautiful, isn't it?" Kellen stood next to her, transfixed by the sight of her home planet, so like Earth in many ways. "I can't believe we're about to impact history this way."

"You sound more uncertain than I've ever heard you." Amereena glanced at Kellen, noticing her clasped hands and how she had jutted her chin out.

"So much has changed so fast. I'm trying to figure out how long it has been since Armeo and I fled and ended up in Rae's…eh, the SC's care."

"And what a blessed day it was." Amereena remembered how she'd been called in to determine custody of the young prince, the sole heir to the Gantharian throne. It hadn't been that hard to realize that Kellen, formidable Protector of the Realm, was not about to let anyone else have any influence over her protégé. What was more, the devotion and sense of family between Kellen and Armeo, matched only by the overshadowing love between Kellen and her wife, Rae, was clear.

"If you had not been on our side or, rather, Armeo's side, things could have been very different." Kellen turned and walked toward the conference room.

"It wasn't a hard decision to make." Amereena followed her, nodding to Dahlia Jacelon, who was preparing some documents on her computer. "Last-minute preparations, Diplomat Jacelon?"

"Can't be too careful. I don't like leaving anything to chance."

"Neither does your daughter, nor *this* daughter." Amereena indicated Kellen. "Kellen has provided coordinates to the resistance headquarters, as well as a few other resistance strongholds, where our mission should begin. I've spoken to Captain Todd and the commanding marine officers. They're ready for you to brief them on the last details before we enter cloaked orbit."

"Good." Dahlia spoke shortly, but smiled in passing at Kellen. "Ayahliss?"

"She's cleaning up after another gan'thet session." Kellen shook her head. "Something is eating away at that girl. She's throwing herself into training as if this is the last thing she will do in life."

Amereena flinched. "What?"

"I've tried to talk to her, but she won't let me in. She knows enough of the technique and self-restraint now to earn the right to wear the Ruby Red suit in combat, but something else, something indefinable, concerns me."

"Concern regarding her determination? Or her readiness?" Dahlia asked.

"Neither. I'm worried about how she approaches her training with such abandon." Kellen frowned, looking questioningly at Amereena. "I don't mean to be presumptuous or to pry into anyone's private decisions."

Amereena knew Kellen meant every word. They had become friends and allies, and they both wanted justice for Gantharat and, ultimately, peace in this sector of space. Her feelings for Ayahliss were unexpected and confusing at best, but mostly startling and guilt-inducing.

"I wish I could help by talking to her, but she's not exactly listening to me." Amereena sighed. Ayahliss was evading her. Whenever they ended up in the same location, Ayahliss excused herself with perfect politeness and left. She always had several plausible reasons why she was needed elsewhere, and Amereena tried to ignore the stab of pain that this behavior caused.

"That's what I fear also." Kellen lowered her voice and placed a gentle hand on Amereena's shoulder. "I know it's difficult for you. Ayahliss isn't cruel, only unpolished. She learned even fewer social skills in her upbringing than I did. Rae overlooks this and sees beyond my shortcomings, but it's a lot to ask regarding Ayahliss." Kellen stopped, and a blue sheen in her eyes betrayed the presence of the famous blue Gantharian tears. "I've come to regard her as a younger sister, and I'm afraid she'll throw herself into the fighting and willingly risk her life. I need to convince her that she has everything to live for, and everything to gain, by being cautious and obeying orders." She lifted a corner of her full lips in a half smile. "And, yes, I realize how ironic it is that I'm saying this."

Dahlia closed her computer and joined them. "You've come a long way by being her mentor and by being married."

"Yes. I'd like to think so."

They had to leave the topic as marines and space fleet personnel began to enter and take their seats. Amereena made sure her notes were in order, but half her mind was with Ayahliss. She could easily picture the younger woman's lithe, wiry body, her soft, short hair, and the large dark blue eyes.

"We're here to review the final details before we launch the shuttles and land on the surface." Dahlia's matter-of-fact voice startled Amereena and brought her firmly into the present. "The resistance is ready to join us in our effort to support the Gantharian interim government. Two vessels are accompanying us, having brought back the resistance fighters who have received a clean bill of health from the training camp on Revos Prime."

Dahlia continued to explain the last-minute changes to the troops. Captain Todd took over after a while and eventually dismissed the junior officers. Once they had left, he pulled up new maps of Ganath, Gantharat's capital. "We have established where we need checkpoints once we secure the city and are able to contain the Onotharians still located within their headquarters." Todd looked pointedly at everyone. "With the number of Onotharians living among the indigenous population, we can't relax for a moment. We don't know which side the majority of them will choose to pledge allegiance to."

"In other words, we need to watch our backs," one of the senior officers said.

"Exactly." Todd turned to Kellen. "Any other words before we begin countdown, Protector?"

"I have nothing to add when it comes to the logistics, but I still wish to express my gratitude that you are prepared to fight to free my home world and my people."

Todd closed the meeting and dismissed the other officers, his face stern as he entered some information into his computer.

Kellen turned to Dahlia. "Are Roshan and Andreia with the resistance fighters joining us from Revos Prime?"

"I believe so, yes."

"Excellent. I haven't heard from them in a long time."

"I have to return this to my quarters, but I'll see you in the mess hall." Dahlia gestured at her computer. "I also need to verify some documents, but it won't take long."

"See you there soon." Kellen nodded at Dahlia.

"Who are Roshan and Andreia?" Amereena asked absentmindedly.

"Rae and I encountered them when we returned to Gantharat the second time."

"Oh, of course. The resistance leaders you and Rae helped save." Amereena had read the mission report from the daring rescue of thousands of captured Gantharian resistance fighters. Kellen had allowed herself to be captured and taken to an asteroid prison, where she had met Ayahliss. Amereena took a deep breath. She couldn't afford to let her guard down emotionally now. She was here to offer legal advice and gather information for the diplomatic corps to use in future negotiations, something that would take all her time and energy. Brooding over Ayahliss and what was going on between them was counterproductive.

"Ayahliss should be ready now," Kellen said, inadvertently tapping into Amereena's thoughts. "We're meeting her in the mess hall."

"I'm not hungry, Kellen."

"Or you're not willing to spend time with Ayahliss because of the way she acts around you."

"Kellen, please." Amereena winced. "But you do have a point."

"You care for Ayahliss." Kellen looked unwaveringly at her.

"Of course I do." Trying to sound casual, Amereena heard how she failed. Instead, her voice trembled and she couldn't meet Kellen's eyes any longer. "Damn."

"I'm being intrusive. I apologize." Kellen's gaze softened. She took Amereena's hand between hers. "It just hurts me to see the two of you in pain."

"The two of us." Amereena laughed and could hear how bitter the sound was. "That would suggest there is an 'us,' which there isn't. How could there be?"

"Are you really asking me?"

"No. I guess the question was rhetorical. The answer's obvious."

"Is it?"

"I'm too old for her. She's too young. I'm a high-ranking judge, an officer of the judicial system of the SC. She's destined to become something amazing, maybe even a Protector one day."

"You might have said the same thing about Rae and me not long ago."

Amereena's hand jerked between Kellen's. "Are you suggesting that the situation compares?"

"Yes."

"You don't know that. You can't possibly know—"

"I can make an educated assumption based on personal observations." Kellen held on to Amereena's hand. "Something is tormenting Ayahliss, and it's not only the upcoming fight and all that's at stake for her fellow resistance fighters. Her behavior makes me believe her issues are far more personal in nature."

"For stars and skies, Kellen, you can be relentless when you want to."

"I'm sorry, Amereena. I don't mean to be harsh, and I don't pretend to know what you and Ayahliss should do to solve your personal issues. I do, however, suggest that you try, since going into battle in her current state of mind could be the last thing Ayahliss ever does." Kellen's voice was a few degrees cooler and she let go of Amereena's hand. "I care for you both, but when you and Dahlia are at the negotiating table, Ayahliss will be directly in the line of fire, risking her life."

Feeling herself go pale, Amereena drew a deep breath, ready to swear that life support aboard the ship was failing. "All right. I see. I'll talk to her."

"Thank you."

"Don't thank me yet." Amereena grabbed her computer. "Ayahliss might not listen to me." In fact, she was sure it was futile to even try.

❖

Ayahliss stood outside the mess hall, loathing how cowardly she felt. She had avoided Reena ever since their embrace in her quarters, and now she was perspiring at the mere thought of sharing a very public meal with her. No wonder Reena regarded her as a child, when she acted this way. A mature, self-assured woman would stroll in like she owned the damn ship and act like nothing was amiss. Not long ago, Ayahliss had mistaken being cocky for being confident, but her time with the Jacelons and Kellen had shown her the difference.

Two senior officers passed her and politely kept the doors to the mess hall open for her. Unwilling to draw any attention to herself, she nodded curtly and strode by them. Relieved the noise sheltered her, Ayahliss had lined up to be served when she heard someone say her name.

"We've saved you a seat over there." Dahlia pointed over at the senior officers' corner where Kellen sat next to Reena.

"Thank you." Ayahliss looked bleakly at the food the kitchen staff placed on her tray. It was difficult to judge what kind this was, since being at war had made regular food unavailable for anyone aboard a military vessel. As long as they were involved in an armed conflict, regulations stipulated emergency rations—in this case, something green, something purple, and mostly something beige.

"I know," Dahlia said, and made a wry face, "it actually doesn't taste as bad as it looks. I think this is some sort of goulash."

"You've never served that to me, have you?"

"I'm pretty sure I haven't." Dahlia laughed, which made Kellen and Reena look up and notice them.

"There you are," Reena said slowly, and nudged the chair next to her away from the table.

Ayahliss had hoped to sit next to Kellen, but changed her mind because she would have to endure Reena's gaze throughout the meal. Sitting down, she tried to remain inconspicuous and not participate. This approach seemed to work at first, and she began to relax as she focused on the tasteless meal. The other three talked, but she listened more to how their voices rose and fell, the quality of their timbre and how familiar they were to her now.

"Ayahliss? Are you all right?"

She flinched as she looked up and noticed that she was alone at the table with Reena. How could she have missed Kellen and Dahlia leaving? How long had she been lost in thought?

"Are you all right?" Reena repeated her question, looking truly concerned now. "You're so pale."

"I'm Gantharian." Ayahliss put down her utensils and refused to look at Reena.

"Yes, but even so." Reena spoke softly. "You seemed to be completely lost in thought before. I suppose you're eager to go home."

"Home." Ayahliss tried to think of the last place on Gantharat that she'd considered a home. She had been too small when the monks found her to remember her birth family. The monastery had been a home, but she had always known it was temporary, no matter how caring the monks had been. The emphasis had been on learning, on developing the body and soul. She had sometimes wished to be hugged or to sit on someone's lap, but the monks made it clear that it was highly inappropriate. Was that why she was so drawn to Reena's touch? Was she so starved for physical attention? This didn't make sense, since Dahlia, Rae, and Kellen didn't have this effect on her. Ayahliss shook her head. It was all so confusing.

"Please, darling. Look at me." Reena's frantic whisper and a startling hand on Ayahliss's thigh under the table made her jump. "I'm sorry, but you're scaring me. You seem almost out of it."

"I'm preoccupied. I apologize." Ayahliss could feel Reena's touch through her pants, and the sensation was close to scorching. "I should go to my quarters and make sure I've packed everything."

"I'm done. I was just waiting for you. May I go with you?"

Ayahliss wanted to say no, but it was a lie and she couldn't be rude to Reena like that, especially not in public. "Of course. Thank you."

They returned their trays to the recycler and left the mess hall, both sighing as they exited the noisy room. Reena chuckled and Ayahliss had to smile at their simultaneous reaction.

"Too noisy for my taste, but I guess that's what happens when you cram so many soldiers into one room just before a mission." Reena casually took Ayahliss's arm and kept walking. "I'm glad you're talking to me."

"I..." Ayahliss was about to deny the gentle reproach, but changed her mind. "I'm sorry. I've had a lot on my mind."

"I realize that. I don't want your apology."

"What do you want?" Wincing, Ayahliss wished she wouldn't speak so often before she considered her words.

"I want you to feel free around me. To trust me."

"I do. I mean, I do trust you."

"But you're guarded around me, and I suppose I can hardly blame you for that." Reena sounded and looked sad.

"Reena, don't." Ayahliss's throat swelled into a knot that wouldn't go away. She hated feeling this emotional, but she didn't know how to handle it. "Please."

"Oh, darling." Reena nudged Ayahliss into a corridor and she tried to object.

"This isn't my—"

"No. These are my quarters." Reena opened the door with a quick command and tugged Ayahliss inside. "I can't let you go down to the planet in this state. You need to be able to focus on your assignment, and if I'm responsible for your distress, we have to figure things out."

Ayahliss stood inside the door and looked at the otherwise so stern and powerful judge. Her hair billowed around her shoulders, wild curls like a force of nature in a red cloud. Her austere black trousers and long black shirt, buttoned in the front, couldn't hide the fact that she was curvaceous and utterly feminine.

"I need to know something," Ayahliss blurted out.

"What? What, Ayahliss?" Reena took her hands and pulled her toward the couch beneath the viewport. "Please, tell me."

CHAPTER NINE

The alarm klaxons tore through the sound of running feet in the narrow corridors of the *Salaceos* as Madisyn dashed toward the ladder leading to the bridge on deck one. Logging into her duty station, she glanced over at Weiss, who stood ready at tactical to the right of Podmer in his command chair.

"Target in grid four-eight-one, Captain." Weiss delivered her report in a clipped voice. "We are barely outside SC territory."

"All the better."

Madisyn wondered why the captain of the ship Podmer was pursuing risked being on the wrong side of the border during wartime.

"Move in at full impulse." Podmer drummed his fingers against the armrest of the command chair, the only sign of his excitement.

"Full impulse." At the helm, Struyen tapped in new commands.

"They're powering their distortion drive," Weiss said. "They've detected us."

"Take out their propulsion system," Podmer ordered.

"Aye, sir." Weiss focused on her console. "They're dead in the water, Captain." To everyone else, Madisyn knew Weiss sounded casual, but having glimpsed some of the authentic Weiss, Madisyn detected a tinge of something hollow, desolate.

"Good. Open a communication channel." Podmer glanced at Madisyn.

"Channel open. Go ahead, Captain." Madisyn adjusted the volume.

"SC vessel, this is the *Salaceos*. Stand down weapons and prepare to be boarded." Podmer's thundering voice echoed across the bridge. "I repeat. Stand down and prepare to be boarded."

"Negative, *Salaceos*. This is Captain Rhoridan of the Supreme Constellations vessel *Koenigin*. We are prepared to match your firepower." A stern female voice seemed completely unimpressed, and Weiss had to admire this captain's guts.

"I'm sure you're ready to fire, Rhoridan, but are you really ready to risk your passengers' lives?" Podmer spoke with a slight purr. "Our scans show you harbor more than sixty passengers. I'm pretty sure they've paid good money for a luxurious trip among the stars."

"It beats the alternative. Being assaulted by common thugs is hardly appealing."

"*Koenigin* is locking plasma torpedoes, Captain." Madisyn ran continuous scans of the SC ship.

"Double the charge of our own torpedoes and reroute all auxiliary power to our shields." Podmer leaned back in his command chair, crossing his legs. He looked more like he was enjoying a day at the beach in his favorite sun chair. Madisyn knew he thrived on playing this cat-and-mouse game, but also that his hot-tempered, ill-mannered behavior lurked just beneath the surface.

"Ten seconds, Captain," Madisyn said.

"All hands, brace for impact."

The other ship's torpedoes hit and rocked the *Salaceos* enough for the bridge crew to cling to their seats.

"Report," Podmer barked. He was agitated now, judging by how his veins stood out like a pulsating pattern along his forehead and down along his neck. He could switch moods within the fraction of a second, which disconcerted Madisyn.

"Shields are holding and no damage to the hull." She ran her finger along the list of reports streaming from the different areas of the *Salaceos*.

"Persistent woman," Podmer muttered. His words were clearly not a compliment. "Fire torpedoes."

Weiss punched in commands, and on the large viewscreen, two pale lines showed where the torpedoes pierced the blackness of space between the two ships.

"Direct hits on their port nacelle. Their aft shields are weakening." Madisyn's midsection contracted at the thought of the passengers on the SC ship. What could Podmer possibly want with a luxury cruise vessel like the *Koenigin*?

"Another charge. This time full volley," Podmer said menacingly.

"Sir," Weiss said. "That might irreparably damage her, which would compromise your mission."

"I intend to shut that woman up for good, but you're right. I need to get into her computer system. Fire at the other nacelle. Take it out."

"Firing." Weiss glanced at Madisyn as she obeyed Podmer's orders.

As the new torpedoes hit, the impact made Madisyn's chest constrict as a crater appeared where the port nacelle once was.

"Excellent. Audio again, Pimm."

"Yes, sir."

"Podmer to Rhoridan. Ready to see things my way, perhaps? Life support seems to be a rare commodity on your ship."

"Damn pirate trash. You're locusts, and your opportunistic way of life thrives because of the war effort!" Captain Rhoridan was clearly not ready to surrender. Her voice, filled with contempt, suggested that Podmer would not enjoy an easy victory.

"Your propulsion system is irreparably shot to pieces. You're leaking plasma and oxygen." Podmer hissed now, losing his flamboyant cool demeanor more with every minute. "Prepare to be boarded."

"You keep repeating yourself," Rhoridan snarled. "Show yourself here and our welcome might surprise you."

"Audio off." Podmer rose and slowly turned around. His face dark, he pointed at Madisyn. "Pimm, you're in charge. You and Kyakh take the away team and remove that bitch from the bridge. I want her *head*." Podmer handed over a memory device to Madisyn. "This will compress all the data from their main computer console, which is located on the bridge. Load it on this." He stopped for a moment, then grabbed Weiss's arm. "You're her backup. Nothing must go wrong."

Weiss turned pale since Podmer had squeezed her newly healed fractured arm. She didn't let her pain show, but Madisyn knew how sore it still was.

"Got it." Weiss looked coolly at Madisyn.

"Get going." Podmer resumed his seat in the command chair.

"Aye, Captain." Madisyn tucked the computer stick into her uniform and hurried down the ladder with Weiss right behind her.

Next to the hangar deck, twenty of what Madisyn thought of as the "mercs"—mercenaries of the worst kind who sold their allegiance to people like Podmer—stood waiting, their hard faces revealing nothing in the soft light. The klaxons still blared.

"Computer. Mute klaxons," Weiss said loudly, apparently disliking the repetitive sound as much as Madisyn did. "All right, people, we're going over in our Troop B shuttle."

With Madisyn at the helm, the shuttle lunged through space toward the *Koenigin*. Debris surrounded its aft section, but Madisyn knew they shouldn't count the people aboard the cruise ship out just yet. Nobody traveled these sectors without being aware of the threat of piracy. Even regular passenger transports and luxury cruise liners were heavily armed these days.

Madisyn's operations console lit up. "They're firing. Shields on maximum!"

The shuttle rolled like a ship tossed around in a typhoon. Weiss clung to her harness where she sat next to one of the mercs. Struggling with the helm, Madisyn managed to force the shuttle into a steep climb.

"Where the hell is that coming from? We took out their weapons array," Weiss yelled from behind.

"Sneaky of them, huh?" Madisyn steered the shuttle into a roll. "No matter how they masked this auxiliary array, they sure are making the most of it now." Madisyn used her internal motion sensors and let her hands fly across the console. She rarely used her non-human abilities in the presence of humanoids, as it only served to set her apart from the others even more. Now their lives could depend on how fast she countermanded Rhoridan's attack. "Firing short-distance torpedoes." She tracked the deceptively small missiles as they plunged through space, praying she had programmed them right. She wanted to take out Rhoridan's weapons, but not add to the hull damages.

"Good shot, Madisyn," Weiss called.

Madisyn let the shuttle do a wide berth, then placed herself parallel with the *Koenigin*, which wasn't moving. If the artificial gravity was down, it would be difficult to board.

"Let's move." Weiss motioned for the mercs to unbuckle their harnesses. "We're docking, people."

Madisyn locked the helm and tugged on her combat vest. She

hoisted her plasma-pulse rifle and made sure it was set to heavy stun. The mercenaries were most likely not taking any chances, and if they fired any shots, they would shoot to kill. She hated this part of battle.

Weiss followed suit and was now standing inside the hatch, ready with a shock-grenade. The automated docking sequence aligned their shuttle with one of the outside docking ports, which was a better approach than trying to go via the other ship's shuttle bay, which was sure to be heavily guarded.

"We're through. On my mark." Weiss raised her hand. After a faint, screeching sound their hatches popped open and Weiss tossed the grenade through. The deafening bang startled Madisyn, and she was glad she had time to close her eyes and shield her sensitive lenses. She ran through the hatch after Weiss, directing the men and women behind her in different directions. Pairing up, they had orders to herd anyone they ran into toward the cargo bay.

Just inside the other ship's hatch, three humanoids lay unconscious. Madisyn checked their vital signs quickly, relieved that they seemed all right. With Weiss, she took their sidearms and tucked them into the back of her vest before she put restraints around their hands and ankles and chained them to the bulkhead.

"Waste of time, if you ask me," one of the mercs muttered. "They're going to die when the boss gets rid of them anyway."

"I didn't ask you." Madisyn pushed the burly man out of her way, secretly pleased that her bio-android strength made him bounce against the bulkhead. "Let's get on with it. You two clear decks three and four. Bring everyone to the cargo bay." Madisyn assigned decks to sixteen of the remaining mercs. "You two stand guard here," she said to the last two and mentally prepared herself to climb five decks up. She and Weiss were going to take the bridge and check the officers' quarters.

"Let's go, then." Weiss nodded and hoisted her rifle, and they found the door leading to a round shaft containing a narrow ladder. Madisyn wasn't thrilled about heights, but after she scanned the shaft, she pushed her rifle onto her back and began to climb. She counted the doors while she ascended, keeping an eye on Weiss. The other woman grunted a few times, as if she was in pain. Worried about Weiss's arm, Madisyn forced herself to just keep going. Her protective attitude toward Weiss puzzled her, but she chalked it up to their secret partnership. They *had* to rely on each other.

Eventually they reached the fifth door and Madisyn stopped, allowing Weiss to catch up before she reached for the hatch. "Ready?" she asked quietly. When Weiss nodded grimly, having pulled her sidearm while hanging on to the ladder with her uninjured arm, Madisyn opened it slightly. Nobody fired on them, so she pushed it open enough to slide through. The light in the corridor was dim and faintly red. In the distance, several explosions showed where the mercenaries were herding the passengers and crew toward the cargo bay.

Madisyn glanced at her wrist-sensor. "Four life signs closing in from the stern." She raised her weapon. "We better hurry, or we'll find crewmen willing to die for their captain around every corner all the way to the bridge."

"Go. We need to do this fast and get back to the shuttle." Weiss didn't have to explain. If they left the mercenaries in charge down in the cargo bay for too long, they might have a bloodbath on their hands.

Madisyn hurried through the corridor, her eyes constantly returning to the small sensor on her sleeve. She didn't once glance behind her; instead she had augmented her hearing, another feature she rarely used, since it made it virtually impossible for her to focus in a crowd. Now she needed all her extra abilities, and for once she was grateful that she could easily turn them on at will.

The *Koenigin* was a luxurious cruise ship, with everything from plush carpeting to stylish light fixtures. Madisyn had never considered going on a recreational space cruise, even when her parents were alive. They weren't the kind who went on vacations. Instead they'd been passionate about their work and only traveled for a specific, preferably scientific, purpose. Now she didn't go anywhere unless she was under orders and had a political, military, or criminal investigatory reason for it. She shook her head at the way her mind had wandered, not sure where these thoughts came from, and focused on her task again.

Her sensor beeped quietly, and Madisyn raised her arm, making a fist. She performed a deeper scan, tapping into the information with her inner sensors. She held up her hand again, this time extending four fingers. She moved her hand, signaling that two enemies were hiding in some storage room farther up, and two behind a bulkhead to their right.

Moving stealthily, Madisyn slid forward along the wall. When she glimpsed movement, she curled up and rolled forward. Raising her rifle, she fired twice at the two humanoids behind the bulkhead. She barely grazed the second one and he aimed at her. She fired again, and so did Weiss just behind her. "Damn it," Madisyn muttered, knowing full well they couldn't carry out their original assignment without some collateral damage. Still, these crewmen were only unconscious and would survive, if all went according to her and Weiss's plan. This was the logical approach, and still it broke Madisyn's heart to know that lives could be lost, stolen by the same type of people who'd taken her parents'. And her own.

"Move on," Weiss said harshly. "Madisyn, seal the door ahead."

"On it." Madisyn pulled a small, weapon-like handle from her harness, pressed a sensor, and a barely visible flame shimmered in golden green. Running up to the door, she hurriedly sealed it, fusing the crack in several places. It would take a plasma burner to open it, but it would keep whoever was in there safe and out of the way—and hopefully alive.

They quickly made their way to the bridge and were a few meters from the door when Madisyn's sensor buzzed. "Ten humanoids up ahead, Weiss. Two doors down, to the right."

"The bridge." Weiss spoke darkly.

"Damn it, Weiss." Madisyn stepped to the side, letting Weiss see her readings. "I don't know what the hell Podmer's after, but I sure don't want to kill ten people for him to get his filthy hands on it," she whispered in Weiss's ear.

"I hear you." Weiss closed her eyes briefly. "If we can maneuver Captain Rhiordan into a position where she can remain in control, we can sabotage him."

"And get slammed for it."

"Not necessarily. Podmer was impressed with this woman's attitude even if he'd be hard-pressed to admit it. It wouldn't be a stretch to think he expects serious trouble from her."

"All right. Your call. You take the lead. I have your back." Madisyn put away her sidearm and pulled her rifle forward, hefting it and making sure it was set to heavy stun.

"I believe you do." Weiss kept Madisyn's gaze for a moment, then mimicked her movements, adjusting her plasma-pulse rifle as well.

❖

The door to the bridge was locked, but Madisyn's plasma torch easily took care of that. She cut through the door like a laser knife through paper, and Weiss tossed a shock-grenade inside. The sound nearly deafened her, and she shook her head slightly as she and Madisyn stormed the bridge.

Ten individuals lay on the floor in different states of unconsciousness. Quickly glancing around, Weiss saw a middle-aged woman with short black hair slumped in the captain's chair. She wore a captain's insignia on her golden lapels, and despite her vacant expression, she radiated command.

Madisyn quickly moved around the room, gathering sidearms and rifles from the dazed bridge crew. Some of them tried to get up, and Weiss kept her weapon raised. "Over there. Move!" She nudged the woman she'd identified as the captain. "Rhoridan?"

"Huh?" The woman sat up, blinking rapidly. "What the hell—"

"Get up. Go over to your crew. We've seized this vessel." Weiss and Madisyn made sure the entire bridge crew was neutralized.

"You won't get away with this," Captain Rhoridan said, her voice barely audible. "This is an SC ship."

"Yeah, yeah." Weiss sauntered over and kept them at gunpoint. "Madisyn, I believe that's the console over there."

Madisyn hurried over to the communication console, a sleek-looking metal box attached to the wall. About two meters wide and half a meter tall, it boasted a multitude of sensors and ports. She took the computer stick from her pocket and inserted it into the metal box. At first, the lights stopped flickering and died, and the low hum it emanated quieted as well. A few moments later, though, it woke up again, rebooting itself with a faint crackle.

"Away team, report." Madisyn tugged at her communicator.

One after another, the mercs reported in, all of them successful. Weiss nodded toward Madisyn. "We're on schedule."

Madisyn pressed a sensor on her communicator to allow for long-range communication. "Away team leader to the *Salaceos*. We have secured the bridge and the rest of the ship."

"Good. Carry out your assignment and return. We're picking up two SC border-patrol cruisers. They're an hour away, so don't waste time."

"Aye, Captain." Madisyn walked over to Weiss. "I think we have what we need," she murmured. "Have you tied them up?"

Weiss hadn't wasted any time. While Madisyn collected the required data, Weiss had used her restraints and tied everyone's hands behind their backs. Not only that, she'd linked them all together and attached them to the railing behind the command chairs.

"I don't think they're going anywhere." Weiss brushed off her hands and grabbed her weapon again.

"Computer," Madisyn said, raising her voice. "Transfer all command codes to my voice pattern."

"That will never work." Rhoridan glared at her.

"Command codes encrypted and transferred." The computer's impersonal voice belied the captain's statement.

"Don't worry. You'll hack it eventually." Turning to Weiss, Madisyn motioned with her weapon toward the door. "All right. Let's go."

They ran through the corridors, joined by one pair of mercs after another. When they reached the docking port, Weiss was relieved to see the three people they'd first stumbled upon had regained consciousness.

"Let's go back." Madisyn motioned for the others to return to the shuttle. "Madisyn to Podmer. We're ready to leave."

"Not until Kyakh jettisons the bridge crew." Podmer's slow pronunciation made him sound even more callous and unforgiving.

"Sir?" Weiss stopped in mid-motion, one foot over the bulkhead opening.

"You heard me. It's nothing you haven't done before. Get rid of them."

"We got what we came for. We downloaded the data."

"And now you're going to do as I say and delay the ones who will come after us. They'll know I'm not to be toyed with."

Was he utterly insane, Weiss thought, or merely a megalomaniac? "All right." She shrugged.

"Weiss!" Madisyn gasped behind a bulkhead, out of sight of the others. Her horrified expression made her feelings clear.

"I'll deal with it," Weiss said monotonously. "All I have to do is open the double escape hatches and override the safety subroutines for life support." Weiss strode over to the nearest console. "Won't take me long."

Madisyn shook her head, her eyes dull and expressionless. She pushed her way past Weiss. "Fuck you." The chill in her voice made Weiss cringe, but she knew what she had to do. Her mission was to not blow her cover and to report to Jacelon, and if it meant some sacrifices, that's what she would do.

After having entered a few commands, Weiss opened her communicator again. "Kyakh to Podmer." Pausing briefly, she rested her eyes tiredly on Madisyn, reading horror and contempt in her expression. *I should be used to having people regard me like vermin.* Still, it hurt deeply. "Mission accomplished. It's done."

CHAPTER TEN

Madisyn left the shuttle and strode past Weiss without meeting her eyes. She simply couldn't bear to look at her. Feeling the weight of the computer stick in her inner pocket, like it was blood-soaked, Madisyn wanted to deliver it to Podmer as fast as possible. As she thought of the ten senior officers being hurled out into space, and what that did to a humanoid body, she shivered.

Podmer wasn't on the bridge; instead he was waiting in his ready room. Madisyn pressed a sensor, asked for admittance, and noticed absentmindedly that her hand was trembling. This telltale sign disturbed her more than anything and she made a fist, not quite ready to admit to herself just how shaken she was. She had witnessed many things, some just as bad, while being undercover, so why had this incident affected her so powerfully? Was it because Weiss had ruthlessly murdered the ten people? Weiss, whom she had tended to—saved her life—and was forced to depend on. How could she live with doing something like that? How could she kill innocent beings to avoid blowing her cover?

"Enter." Podmer's cold voice broke her line of thought.

Madisyn stepped inside the ready room, this time too distraught to marvel at Podmer's decorating skills, or lack thereof. Normally Madisyn was fascinated that Podmer could fit so much of his loot into such a confined space. Gemstones, priceless fabrics, rare minerals, Cormanian midnight pearls, and even ancient artwork from Earth fought for space on walls and shelves, and in transparent cabinets. Right now, Madisyn couldn't hand over the computer stick fast enough. She wanted to go to her quarters and get into the shower—or, on second thought, perhaps not. Weiss was bound to be there and she couldn't stand to look at her, much less talk to her. "Here you go, Captain." Madisyn put the hateful stick on the desk between her and Podmer.

"I'm not pleased." Podmer spoke between his teeth, and only now did Madisyn see that bluish veins pulsated at his temples. A sure sign of his volatile temper, as was the way he glared with squinting eyes.

"Our mission is accomplished." Why would Podmer be upset?

"By you, yes. By her, no." Podmer pointed.

She turned her head, completely taken aback at the sight of Weiss propped against the door frame.

"I miscalculated the resourcefulness of that damn captain over there. It happens." Weiss shrugged.

"What the hell are you talking about? It happens?" Podmer got up, his face now bordering on purple. "I gave a direct order, and with your reputation for being ruthless, I didn't think it'd pose a problem. One flip of a switch."

"I did flip a switch. It never occurred to me that they'd escaped their confinement in time to countermand the command I entered."

"When did you know?" Podmer growled, slowly sitting down.

"As soon as we were a few hundred meters from the *Koenigin*. No floating bodies in space."

"No floating bodies? And you didn't say anything?" Madisyn stared at Weiss, her eyes close to tearing up; only her grip of her internal sensors saved her.

"I'm as outraged as you are," Podmer said, misunderstanding her emotional outburst. "Now I look like I'm running from that bitch."

"You got what you came for." Weiss sounded bored. "Don't waste time with appearances. Who gives a damn what anyone thinks?"

Madisyn had to admire Weiss's way of making Podmer shrink, of making him seem petty and even silly. Podmer went from looking purple and mad as hell to seeming flustered. Madisyn had to quickly find a way to not stare in amazement. She had never seen the domineering, even megalomaniac, captain of the *Salaceos* look chastised.

Another part of Madisyn was trying to figure out how Weiss had managed to save the *Koenigin* bridge crew.

"You're dismissed," Podmer muttered and grabbed the computer stick.

"Aye, sir." Madisyn brushed by Weiss, knowing it probably looked like she ran out of the room, which wasn't far from the truth.

She needed time alone in their quarters to just breathe for a minute after being tossed between emotions so fast.

She didn't even get ten seconds before Weiss joined her.

"Are you all right?" Weiss stood inside the door.

"I am." Closing her eyes briefly, Madisyn put the scrambler on. "We can talk." She preferred that they didn't, but she thought Weiss would want to.

"I couldn't tell you. I knew you hated me for what I did, for what you thought I'd done, and I couldn't risk you not being able to keep it together."

"Weiss. Don't. Don't say another word."

"Why not?" Weiss looked nonplussed as she sat down on her bed and began to remove her vest. "I had to do what I did. I couldn't tell you."

"I realize that." Madisyn pressed her palms against the nauseating feeling in her stomach. It didn't help. Not being able to actually throw up sure was a downside to being nauseous.

"Madisyn. You look…ill." Weiss put the vest aside and moved closer. "How's that even possible?"

"I said 'don't talk.' I meant it." Trembling, Madisyn pressed her knuckles against her lips. "Please."

"For stars and skies, what the hell is going on with you?"

"Nothing." To Madisyn's dismay, tears welled up, and she cursed her parents for not foreseeing this, her one weakness, when they saved her life. A BNSL couldn't cry, but placing someone with real emotions within a synthetic body made to mimic almost all body functions of a living person would cause emotions, which would produce the same physical manifestations. If she was lucky, one day she might even throw up. Madisyn's gallows humor didn't help. Her tears ran over and down her cheeks. She tried to stop them with her hands but they forced their way between her fingers.

"You're…you're crying!" Weiss's consternation would have been hilarious if Madisyn's emotional meltdown hadn't caused it.

"Just—shut—up." Madisyn was about to get up and run into the bathroom, but Weiss stopped her, pushing her back onto the bed. She sat down next to Madisyn.

"I've never heard of a BNSL that can cry real tears, not even one as advanced as you." Weiss captured a tear with her fingertip.

Madisyn watched in horror as Weiss tasted the clear liquid. "Weiss—"

"It tastes like the real thing."

"I—I can't talk about this. You can't tell anybody and we won't discuss it."

"We sure as hell will. You're going to tell me what's going on."

"I don't have to tell you anything!" Madisyn pushed Weiss, angry now. Her tears dried quickly. "You put me through hell over there. You made me think you could kill ten innocent people just to stay undercover, thus making me your accomplice. You made me think I was as guilty as you of *murder*." Slamming her palm against Weiss's shoulder, Madisyn was stunned when the other woman didn't do anything to prevent the blow from landing or otherwise defend herself.

"I don't blame you for being angry." Weiss sighed and ran a hand over her face, as if brushing away something nasty. "I was pretty sure I had tied Rhoridan loosely enough for her to free herself and the others, but I couldn't be sure. When Podmer issued his orders, I took a calculated risk. I could've killed them if Rhoridan had been less of a captain than I took her for."

"Gods." Madisyn still trembled.

Of course, Weiss noticed. "Tears. And now adrenaline?"

"Synthetic. All of it." Madisyn spoke hurriedly.

"I don't think so." Weiss took Madisyn's hand. "Your palms are damp. Perspiration? I don't believe anyone, not even a scientist hell-bent on mimicking reality, would come up with synthetic perspiration."

"Sure. For cooling the system. Absolutely."

"Really." Weiss was clearly not buying any of it. "It makes me wonder just how realistic your responses are to other things."

"What do you mean?"

"You're quite temperamental in many ways, especially for a BNSL unit. I've wondered why I find you so damn attractive, since I've never found any android to my liking that way. I wonder how your subroutines would have you react if I kissed you."

"Kiss—what are you talking about? You don't want to kiss me."

"Interesting response. It would've been more logical for a BNSL unit to answer in a more detached, matter-of-fact way. I can think of several more plausible responses. 'I am not programmed for any such action.' 'I am unable to respond in such a manner.' 'Kissing is not within the range of my abilities.'"

"I—I..." Madisyn stopped, her voice barely carrying. She swallowed against an odd sense of dryness in her throat. "All right. We'll talk. I just need to get out of this damn uniform first. I can't stand to wear it anymore right now."

"I second that." Weiss looked relieved. Was it because Madisyn had given in or because they were both getting out of their coveralls? Or perhaps it was the temporary delay regarding what Madisyn might say.

❖

Weiss stepped into the personal cleansing unit and felt the sound waves reverberate around her, removing all outward traces of their mission. Noticing how tight her fists were, she willed her hands to relax. Time and circumstance hadn't allowed her to fill Madisyn in on what she meant to do. Being on the receiving end of Madisyn's outrage and contempt had taken a greater toll on Weiss than she realized. When Madisyn strode by her exiting the shuttle, not even looking at her, Weiss's stomach had twisted into painful knots and she had tried to catch up with Madisyn before she reached the bridge. Now Madisyn knew the truth, but she didn't look as relieved as Weiss had hoped. Something else was wrong, and Weiss couldn't figure out what. She had never been much for utilizing androids, and certainly had never expected an artificial life form, sentient or not, to act the way Madisyn did.

The cleansing unit closed after running its cycle, and though she was clean, she wasn't prepared to leave the bathroom yet. Procrastination wasn't usually one of her vices, but facing Madisyn right now unnerved her, and something told her Madisyn felt the same way.

"Felt," Weiss muttered. "How can she feel anything? Can her circuits or whatever construct feelings out of thin air?" She stared at her reflection. Her olive skin bore traces of scars. Too many, and more than she cared to remember. She pushed her hair, unruly after the shower, haphazardly behind her ears as she followed her trail of thoughts. Feelings were really just chemical with any humanoid, weren't they?

So if a BSNL had circuits or, as in Madisyn's case, artificially grown cells, programmed on a molecular level to perform the same way—surely the outcome would be the same? Matter just as much?

"Oh!" Weiss slammed her palms into the sink. "Hell."

"You all right?" Madisyn softly called out through the door.

"Yeah. Fine. I'm…fine." Weiss had turned to open it when she suddenly remembered being stark naked. Not usually shy or prudish, she muttered a curse and grabbed new underwear from the recycling unit. She programmed her size and extracted a set of comfortable retrospun coveralls. Opening the door, she glanced quickly at Madisyn before she walked over to the food recycler. "I thought I'd be brave and have some artificial Vit-C drink. You want any?"

"Already had some." Madisyn motioned toward an empty cup sitting on a shelf above her bed.

Weiss watched with fake fascination how the recycler poured an opaquely yellow beverage into her mug. Tasting it hesitantly, she grimaced at the vague taste. "I can almost taste the fake oranges."

"I could definitely taste the added chemicals that *mimic* the taste of oranges." Madisyn wrinkled her nose, then winked.

Weiss forgot about her artificial vitamin drink. A BNSL that wrinkled her nose—and winked?

"Weiss?"

"What? Oh. Yes. Chemicals. For sure." Weiss cringed and climbed onto her cot.

"I know I'm repeating myself, but are you all right? I mean, really?"

"Sure. Absolutely." Feeling ridiculous for speaking in a staccato manner, Weiss tried for a smile.

"Oh, for stars and skies, this is ridiculous." Madisyn looked at the viewport, as if searching for support from the surrounding space. "We both know we need to talk and we've digressed and procrastinated long enough."

"Why don't you start?" Weiss realized she was taking the coward's way out, but she was simply out of words.

"I took this particular assignment because I hate pirates, and piracy, more than anything." Madisyn's face was expressionless, but her eyes seemed impossibly black. "They base their existence on murder, theft, and destruction—all because of greed. There's no such thing as 'the noble savage.'" Pulling up her knees, Madisyn curled against her pillows. "And now I can see how your mind is whirling. You're wondering how a damned android can hate anything or anyone."

"You're sentient. Of course you can hate."

"Ha. You know that most people still think sentient androids are little more than glorified robots."

"I'm not most people."

"For sure. You're so credible in your role as Weiss Kyakh, pirate, even I find myself buying into it."

Weiss recoiled at the vehemence behind Madisyn's words. "Go on."

"This is where things get a little weird. I mean, this is where I need to ask you for complete confidentiality."

"I don't gossip," Weiss said tightly.

"No, you don't understand." Madisyn crawled over onto Weiss's bed, placing both hands on her shoulders. "You can't tell anyone. Not even Jacelon. Nobody."

"Oh." Mystified, Weiss felt the warmth of Madisyn's hands against her, through the fabric of her coveralls. Dreading what she might hear, she spoke quickly. "I promise."

"You're sure? There could be a conflict of interest involved."

"I still promise." Against her principles, Weiss vowed not to betray Madisyn's confidence, though she usually tried to avoid pledging her word.

"The real Madisyn Pimm was aboard a transport shuttle when pirates attacked it. She was twenty and traveling toward the Guild Nation home world from Earth when four ships appeared out of nowhere. The pirates killed the captain and the rest of the crew, and all the other passengers. They left Madisyn for dead. When the border patrol ship found them, they rushed her to the Guild Nation. There, her parents had to face the fact that Madisyn's body was too damaged to save. She was dying."

Her chest constricting, Weiss couldn't speak. She leaned back against the bulkhead and easily imagined the horrific scenes that had played out in the shuttle all those years ago.

"However, Madisyn's parents simply couldn't accept losing her."

"So they made you in her image. I've read that in your file. Jacelon let me see it." Weiss raised her hand in an apologetic gesture. "I needed to know who my associate undercover was."

"You still don't know," Madisyn said quietly. "Madisyn didn't die. Her body did and was buried, but her mind, her soul and personality, didn't."

"I can understand that you relate to her—"

"Weiss. I'm Madisyn. I'm her. I survived after my parents placed my brain, m-my spinal cord, into their experimental model. Model Twenty-Two Alpha." Madisyn smiled joylessly. "They had worked on a new model, Eighteen-B, and made her look like me in my honor. How ironic. However, Eighteen-B was not advanced enough to host a humanoid central nervous system. Their secret prototype, another Madisyn look-alike, was."

"You're not serious." Weiss couldn't believe it. "All of your system registers as fully synthetic."

"Yes. My parents devised ways for me to mask my human brain and central nervous system against scans." Madisyn grasped Weiss's hands in hers. "They broke the law by doing that."

"I bet they did. The Guild Nation has some of the strictest laws when it comes to their scientific community." Weiss let her eyes roam across the perfect face of the woman in front of her. Could she be telling the truth?

"I can prove it." Madisyn spoke dispassionately. "Here. Scan me." She handed a small medical scanner to Weiss.

Her fingers not entirely steady, Weiss did as Madisyn asked. At first, the only readings were those of a bio-neural synthetic android. Artificially grown tissues were sometimes hard to distinguish from human with the naked eye, but a scanner easily found the markers. Then the scanner beeped and Weiss read evidence of human tissue. Nerve endings, neural pathways, gray and white matter, and synaptic energy. Granted, the spinal fluid was artificial, but Madisyn's brain, cerebellum, prolonged marrow, and spinal column were humanoid. "Oh, hell."

"Yes." Madisyn was shivering now.

"You have a humanoid brain." Weiss knew she was repeating herself. "A wholly humanoid brain...but how can you prove that it's the real Madisyn's brain?"

"Good question. I can't. I mean, back on the Guild Nation home world I could easily do it with a genetic scan, but here, on this godforsaken ship, I can't. I have no reason to lie. I am who I say I am." Tears formed at the corners of Madisyn's eyes. "See? A crying *robot.* What a joke, huh?"

"Madisyn." Weiss couldn't begin to imagine what it would be like to wake up and find herself turned into an android. A freak show in the making. "Many people I know have artificial spare parts. I do too."

"An arm. A leg. Intestines that need replacing. Hearts, lungs, glands. Sure. But I bet you don't know anyone with more than twenty percent spare parts." Madisyn spat the last words.

"Touché." Weiss shook her head. "What did you…how did you react when you came to?"

"I begged them over and over and over to kill me." Madisyn laughed bitterly. "I begged them to turn me off, to end it. They refused."

"Gods, no wonder you loathe pirates." Weiss felt herself go pale.

"Oh, no, that's not why." Madisyn's soft voice betrayed such a profound hatred that it shook Weiss to the core.

"No?"

"No. Once my parents convinced me that life was worth preserving, even if I had to lead a clandestine existence as a sentient android, I concluded that they were right. Life is worth preserving."

"At any cost?" Weiss wasn't sure.

"In retrospect. Yes." Madisyn shrugged, a simple, jerky twitch of her shoulders. "I lived with my parents, learned from them, and we worked at the university."

"What happened? Why this hatred for pirates if it wasn't for what they did to you?"

"I lost the only ones in my life who knew who I really was." Madisyn looked at Weiss with emotionless eyes. "Five years ago pirates jettisoned my parents, and everyone else aboard their shuttle, into space."

Chapter Eleven

Ayahliss barely kept from rushing out of Reena's quarters. Perhaps unaware of what she was doing, Reena regarded her with professional, inquisitive eyes, something that made Ayahliss cringe. It was like being on the defender's bench. Reena was obviously worried about her, but Ayahliss didn't know, or understand, *why*.

"Please, Ayahliss?" Reena's gaze shifted from being judging to soft and genuinely concerned.

"Judge Beqq," Ayahliss began, trying to put a little distance between them by using Reena's title.

"Judge?" Reena scowled.

"I'm getting too close." Ayahliss swallowed repeatedly, knowing she was certainly out of her element. "I'm not used to this. I'm barely used to being friends with anyone, I mean, really friends. I've had comrades in arms, and the monks were my parental figures, sort of, but this…friendship thing, this family thing Dahlia has introduced me to, it's confusing."

"And I confuse you too?"

"You terrify me."

Reena tossed her head back, making her wild red curls tumble freely around her shoulders, and laughed, a not entirely happy sound. "I terrify you?" Shaking her head, Reena moved swiftly and unexpectedly, and Ayahliss found herself pinned to the corner between the couch's arm and backrest. "You do more than that. Don't you see?"

Ayahliss did. She hadn't until then, but now she did, with Reena hovering over her, looking like a forest creature from a fairy tale with her vivid colors and untamed expression.

"I just can't stay away from you, which really is too bad, because I'm too old for you and you are an innocent."

"Innocent?" Ayahliss didn't understand. Surely Reena was aware of her past? "I'm hardly an innocent."

"Oh, but you are. I don't mean in a legal sense. I'm sure you've broken more than one law working for the Gantharian resistance." Reena ran the back of her hand down Ayahliss's neck. "I mean like this. How many times have you been close to a lover?"

A lover? Ayahliss drew a trembling breath. "Never." Her body felt molten, liquid. Hot.

"As I said. Innocent." Reena brushed her lips along Ayahliss's cheek. "I know you had other priorities, but I wonder why you haven't explored this part of yourself."

"I've been busy going on missions for the resistance." Ayahliss didn't know why she felt so defensive.

"That's just it. I've found that being in and around danger makes for increased sexual desire."

"Is that what this is?"

"Oh, darling, this is so much more." The tenderness in Reena's eyes seemed to emphasize the ferocity of how she pressed herself against Ayahliss.

"Then show me." Not sure where the courage to play this game Reena's way came from, Ayahliss took firm hold of her waist and held Reena in place. "You seem determined to make your point, so make it."

❖

"Ayahliss." Reena inhaled the clean scent of the young woman beneath her. "I can understand why you'd see it that way. I promise you, I'm not trying to make a point. You make it sound like I'm trying to win an argument. I'm not."

"Aren't you?" Ayahliss gasped for air. "Aren't you trying to prove you can win?"

"Win what?" Bewildered at the anguish she detected behind Ayahliss's brave words, Reena cupped her chin. "If I'm trying to win anything, it's only your affection. Your loving affection."

Ayahliss blinked, a slow dip of long blue-black lashes over eyes nearly the same color. "Affection?"

"Yes." Reena tried for a self-deprecating smile. "I desire you, your physical affection as well." She slipped one hand around Ayahliss's neck and felt dampness at her hairline. Caressing the smooth skin, Reena reveled in how Ayahliss's expression changed. She had suspected that Ayahliss was governed by her emotions, and this confirmed it. No doubt Ayahliss felt trapped by their mutual attraction, and now that Reena had her physically cornered, she was beginning to give in to her impulses.

A small internal voice whispered that this wasn't fair to Ayahliss, that Reena was manipulating her for her own carnal pleasure. *It's not true! I love her!* Reena furiously pulled Ayahliss into her arms as she answered her internal saboteur. Holding her breath, she stopped moving, shocked by her revelation. The unspoken words had sneaked up on her, and now that she'd thought them, in a sense professed to loving Ayahliss, if only to herself, she couldn't go back.

"Reena?" Ayahliss looked up from where Reena held her tucked into her shoulder.

"Oh, sweet soul, I have you." The desire was still there, red hot, but she also felt an overshadowing tenderness. Reena caressed Ayahliss's hair and looked into those amazing eyes. "May…may I kiss you?"

"Yes." Ayahliss closed her eyes slowly as Reena lowered her head and covered Ayahliss's lips with her own. The sweetness and the scorching heat intoxicated her. Reena was as gentle as possible, given that she had wanted this woman ever since she had come to her and Armeo's rescue on Corma months ago. Now she parted Ayahliss's lips and slipped her tongue inside her mouth.

Ayahliss moaned and threw her arms around Reena's neck. She clung to Reena, digging her fingers into the red curls. "Reena…"

"Sweet soul." Reena ran her lips down her neck, startled when Ayahliss whimpered and shifted next to her. Suddenly, Reena was on her back on the couch, Ayahliss on top of her. Her clothes were being torn and pushed to the side as Ayahliss seemed to blindly fight for access.

"Ayahliss. Please." Reena had herself to blame. She had disregarded Ayahliss's tormented state of mind and only managed to add fuel to the flames. Ayahliss was just trying to extinguish them as best as she knew how. Reena was turned on and afraid, but not for her own sake. For Ayahliss's. "Listen to me, darling. Listen." Lowering her voice, Reena tried to reach Ayahliss, who in turn was close to her goal of undressing Reena. "Ayahliss?"

"This it?" Ayahliss growled and nibbled her way across Reena's chest. "This is what you wanted, right?"

"Yes. And no." Passive now, Reena sensed her treacherous body give in to the heated caresses, and when Ayahliss reached naked skin, Reena knew it wouldn't take much for her to climax. "Don't…don't be angry with me, Ayahliss?" Searing, pulsating heat coursed through Reena, and when Ayahliss touched her breasts, she cried out and arched, shameless in her state of arousal. Still, a part of her was unable to give in to the fire raging in her belly and her limbs. She took hold of Ayahliss's arms and shook her. "Ayahliss, *please*."

Suddenly still, hardly breathing, Ayahliss lay on top of her, her face buried in Reena's hair. Reena waited a few moments, trying to prepare for the harsh words she was sure were bubbling to the surface within the volatile young woman in her arms.

"Reena?"

Ayahliss's tear-drenched voice cut Reena to the core. She hugged Ayahliss fiercely, not caring that she was almost naked after Ayahliss's frenzied caresses.

"Sweet soul. I have you." Reena echoed her words of only minutes ago. "Come here. See? Touch me. I need your hands. I need you to keep me warm. You're so beautiful, inside and out. I can't bear the thought of you getting hurt when we deploy."

Ayahliss raised her head and looked into Reena's eyes. "You do? Need me? My touch?"

"Everything about you," Reena said, her voice husky. "Everything. Your soul. Your gorgeous body. Your brilliant mind. Your passion."

"I hurt you."

"Right now? No." *I hurt* you. *I pushed* you. "I'm sorry. I went too far." Reena ran her thumb across Ayahliss's lower lip. "It was wrong."

"What if it was?" Ayahliss spoke quietly and trembled, a faint reverberating tremor that traveled over to Reena. "What if it was wrong? Now you have to make it right."

"I don't understand."

"You say it was wrong, and you aroused me to a point where I nearly ended up hurting you. I still ache for you and I don't know what to do about it. You have to make it right again." Ayahliss's tone was tinged with despair, yet she also sounded calm and accepting.

Reena tried to understand. "I aroused you?"

"Yes." The word was little more than a whimper.

"And it scares you?"

"Yes."

"Why?" Reena whispered, gently framing Ayahliss's face with her hands.

"Because I need to be with you. Be right for you. *H'rea deasavh*, I burn, and I don't know how to stop it, or what to do about it!"

"Gods, Ayahliss." Horrified at the torment emanating from Ayahliss, Reena disregarded her own nudity and wrapped her arms and legs around her. "Come here. Listen. You don't need to do anything. I've pushed you too far, too fast. I let my own fears rule because the thought of you going into battle, of you being in danger when you go planetside…it ripped away my ability to think clearly. Ayahliss, sweet soul, please, tell me what you need. I promise you, anything you need is fine. You haven't done anything wrong."

"I tore your clothes. I was violent. Again. Kellen…she…I obviously haven't learned a thing." Ayahliss tried to get up, but Reena knew that if she let her go now, something would break between them irreparably. She held on, thinking desperately of something to say, or do, that might reach Ayahliss.

"Don't go. I need you. I don't give a damn about the clothes. I need you to stay. Please." Reena pulled Ayahliss closer. "I need you to kiss me. Your lips against mine…I've never felt anything like it. You steal my breath away and I've dreamed of you, of us, like this."

"Of me?" Ayahliss froze, but stopped trying to get up. "How, I mean, I don't understand what you see in me. You're so amazing, and you're powerful. Famous, even."

"Fame and power don't warm my heart, or my bed." Reena cringed at her words, but Ayahliss smiled shyly.

"So you're saying, despite being hung up on the age difference, you find me exciting enough to warm your bed?" Ayahliss raised an eyebrow, but relaxed against Reena.

"Gods, no, I didn't mean for it to sound like that." Reena groaned. "I just wanted to make you understand how lonely it can be, power and reputation be damned."

"I was being facetious." Ayahliss pushed Reena's hair to the side, exposing her breasts in the process. "Oh."

"I haven't really asked you if you find women attractive." Reena ignored a sudden urge to cover her bare skin.

"No, you haven't." Ayahliss studied Reena slowly, her eyes roaming across the abundant hair, her face, and down her torso. "I mean, I hadn't really thought about attraction in a sexual or a romantic sense until I met you. When we talked aboard the court ship, when you took care of me and Armeo, I was stunned, and confused, at how I felt."

"And how was that?"

"I wanted to kiss you. I wanted to touch you. Like this." Ayahliss caressed Reena's long, curly locks. She gently ran her fingers through them, held them against her cheek.

"Oh, sweet soul." Reena blinked against the burning tears. "Kiss me?"

Not saying anything, Ayahliss lowered herself onto Reena, this time slowly, deliberately, and pressed her lips against hers. Reena kept her mouth closed to begin with, but after a while that wasn't enough. She didn't want to rush Ayahliss, but she needed more. Slowly, she opened her mouth, letting her tongue dart into Ayahliss's, teasing her.

"Mmm." Humming, Ayahliss followed Reena's lead. She slipped her tongue into Reena's mouth, and when Reena softly sucked it farther in, the tremors started again. Reena stroked Ayahliss's back, over and over, as the deep, probing kiss seemed to go on forever. Eventually they parted, both panting for air. Reena, who until now had considered herself too cynical and blasé for romance, was astounded that a mere kiss could affect her so.

"Reena." Ayahliss slid sideways off Reena, and the cool air in her quarters made her skin pucker. "You are so beautiful. I apologize. I bruised you." She covered Reena's right breast with her hand. "Does it hurt?"

"What? No. Of course not. You didn't hurt me. I bruise easily, and it's normal that lovers leave marks on each other in the heat of the moment."

"Lovers?" Ayahliss's voice caught. "We're lovers?"

"Not yet."

"But we will be?"

"If you want to." Reena couldn't believe how weak Ayahliss made her feel. And afraid.

"I still don't quite understand, but I want to be your lover, Reena. I want to be with you and…" Ayahliss pressed her body close to Reena's, rubbing against her with a disarmingly innocent expression of desire and confusion. "I ache inside for you."

"Then let me help you." Promising herself that this was all that would happen tonight, Reena tenderly pulled Ayahliss onto her shoulder. She pushed her hand in between them, cupping Ayahliss's sex gently, on the outside of her clothes. The telltale gasp proved she had found the origin of Ayahliss's ache. "Tell me if you want me to stop, but I think I know how to help you, sweet soul." Reena rubbed Ayahliss's hot center and the faint undulations were encouraging. "That's it, darling." Soon Ayahliss was trembling and whimpering against her.

"It burns. It's getting worse," Ayahliss whispered. "Oh, I can't stand it. I don't know what to do."

The mere fact that Ayahliss felt inept was probably part of her true torment. Reena hadn't planned to take it further, but Ayahliss needed more. Deftly, Reena slipped her fingers through the opening in the front of Ayahliss's coveralls. The underwear was made of thin non-woven cotton Reena pushed aside and out of the way. When she discovered a sparse tuft of hair and drenched, swollen folds, Reena was shocked at her own reaction.

She was ignited, and moisture flooded her. "You're so wet and ready," she said in a strained voice. Moaning, she let one finger glide into the wetness, careful not to penetrate Ayahliss. She wasn't sure about Gantharian women's physiology, or how painful a first insertion might be. Wanting nothing but pleasure for Ayahliss, she was relieved to find a swollen and, as it turned out, very sensitive clitoris. Reena felt her own respond immediately as she caressed around Ayahliss's sex, and the sobbing moans and whimpers, so sexy and innocent, made Reena clench her teeth.

"Reena. I need to touch you too." Gasping, Ayahliss ran a shaking hand along Reena's stomach.

"Are you sure?"

"Yes!" The frenzy in Ayahliss's response made Reena think perhaps this felt too one-sided to her.

"Give me your hand."

Ayahliss readily complied.

"Just apply pressure here, and maybe rub a little." For some reason, these instructions made Reena's cheeks burn as she placed Ayahliss's hand between her own legs, on the outside of her trousers. "Ah…like so, yes."

"Hot." Ayahliss rubbed against Reena with her body and her hand in unison.

Reena wondered if she might even climax before Ayahliss. Having her arms full of an amorous, aroused Gantharian warrior, so beautiful, so brilliant in her own way, how could she resist?

"Reena!" Startled blue-black eyes bored into Reena's, then closed as Ayahliss's orgasm drenched Reena's fingers. The slick folds rhythmically fluttered and added pressure between her legs; Reena climaxed too.

"Oh!" Reena wrapped her free arm around Ayahliss and held her tight as they crashed through the unbearable sweetness together. Wave after wave, the much-needed release took the last of her breath. Eventually, Reena got her breathing under control and found that Ayahliss had somehow managed to reverse their positions. As it turned out, lying with her head on Ayahliss's shoulder was quite wonderful and just where she wanted to be.

"That was fantastic, and so unexpected." Ayahliss's formal words would've been amusing if she hadn't sounded so reverent and loving.

"I agree. 'Unexpected' is the word."

"I felt your climax as much as my own." Ayahliss yawned. "I apologize."

"Just close your eyes. Soon enough we have to get up, but not yet."

"Good." Ayahliss settled against the pillows and the armrest. "You rest also."

"I will." Reena knew she wouldn't sleep. She intended to lie here and watch this stunningly beautiful woman and revel in the strong sensations that had taken hold of her. So many feelings, and so strong. Like love. Love? Reena had to close her eyes hard for a moment to not flinch and disturb Ayahliss. Love was dangerous in an armed conflict. If a person thought too much about love and matters of the heart, she lost her focus. She would not be able to do her job if she worried about such things. Still, as much as Reena nudged at the concept of love to remove it from her mind, it lingered. Eventually she gave in and, with a deep sigh, she had to surrender completely and admit it to herself. She was deeply and irrevocably in love with Ayahliss, Gantharian Protector in training and resistance fighter.

CHAPTER TWELVE

Weiss would always remember how cold she felt when Madisyn's words struck her like a fist below her ribs. She gasped and recoiled, as if putting more distance between them would make it easier. Twice, pirates had destroyed Madisyn's life. Weiss didn't dare examine why this cruelty hit her so hard, when she had been the one delivering blows and robbing people of their possessions for so long. Granted, she had never indulged in random or gratuitous violence, but she had impacted people's lives in similar ways.

Madisyn looked at her with dry, indifferent eyes, but the tremors in her hands revealed how affected she was. Slender, with her unruly blond hair, she was beautiful, something Weiss had credited to her inventors. Now that she knew Madisyn was made to look like her own organic body, the synthetic one seemed less artificial.

"I don't know what to say," Weiss murmured. Part of her was sick inside, and another part wanted to slide over and hold Madisyn tight. This uncharacteristic impulse made her feel even more ill at ease.

"Not much to say. This is my life. I've made it my business to fight piracy in any way I can. Right now, it serves my purpose to work for SC intelligence, but if I find it doesn't, I'll resign and do it some other way."

"I see." Wetting her dry lips, Weiss tried to avert her eyes, to give herself some respite from her ache when she met Madisyn's gaze. It was impossible.

"I lost my mother much the same way when I was ten." Shocked at her own revelation, Weiss tried to clench her teeth around her words, take them back.

"What?"

"I was raised on a generational ship. We were heading toward SC space when pirates attacked. The ship was destroyed and a few of us captured. I was separated from my mother." Breathing shallowly, Weiss fought the pain beneath her ribs. "I looked for her for more than ten years."

"Why did you stop? Did you find her?" A faint hope shone in Madisyn's eyes.

"No. The pirates, who kept me, finally told me. She died along with everybody else among the bridge crew. I don't know why I was so shocked at the time. Guess hope truly lingers." Weiss blinked repeatedly. "I don't compare this to your trauma. You suffered so much more and I can understand your hatred."

"At least I had my parents well into adulthood."

"And afterward, you were alone." Weiss hurt even more for the lonely, deprived Madisyn than for her own loss, which amazed her. She had focused on her own pain, her own perpetual anger and entitlement, for so long. Now this young woman, her heart-wrenching fate, tore at Weiss's armor.

"You know, one of the worst things about losing my parents is that nobody touches me. No hugs, no embraces, even though they never dared touch me in public. Nothing. As for sex—forget it." Madisyn laughed again, and the sound was strangely sorrowful.

Weiss couldn't remember when someone had last hugged her. The only physical contact she'd had in ages was during hand-to-hand combat. Once she'd sought pleasure in any space port without thinking twice about it, but that was a long time ago.

"Would you?" Madisyn startled Weiss by rising on her knees.

"Would I what?"

"Hug me? I mean, if I asked you as a friend, would you give me a hug?" Madisyn's eyes now burned a bright blue.

"Ah. Sure." Though this wasn't a good idea, Weiss shifted and sat down next to Madisyn. She placed her hands on Madisyn's shoulders with dread in her heart and no air in her lungs. To her surprise, Madisyn softly moved into her touch, curling up next to her. Weiss wrapped her arms around Madisyn's shivering body, and suddenly it wasn't hard at all. It felt strangely natural to embrace her, even rock her a little.

❖

Madisyn's heart thundered. Artificial components primarily governed her synthetic physiology, but her brain still overrode them. Now, being this close to another person, and being held, threatened to overload all her senses. Weiss's normal aura of feline grace and deadliness had turned into something entirely different. The comforting embrace had started out awkward, and Madisyn regretted it for half a second before it began to feel so damn good. She snuggled closer and Weiss held her wonderfully tight.

"Thank you." Madisyn knew it sounded silly, strange even, to be so grateful. She inhaled Weiss's clean scent, tinged with something crisp and citric. Occasionally, strangers might seem attracted to her because her looks deceived them initially, but not once they pegged her as a BSNL, no matter how sentient and with legalized rights and obligations. Cynically, Madisyn had found that some men and women might even consider a brief sexual encounter, but they might as well have turned to an insentient android to scratch such an itch.

Now Madisyn realized her life might be pure hell from that moment on. Having gone without physical contact for so long, she had learned to live without it. Weiss's embrace brought all the memories back, though Weiss's touch made her feel entirely different than her parents'.

"I'm sorry." Weiss spoke so quietly, only Madisyn's enhanced hearing detected her words.

"What?" Pulling back, Madisyn looked up at the angular features of Weiss's face, her eyes a dark, glimmering green. Heavy eyelids kept Madisyn from reading their convoluted expression, but the faint tremors in Weiss's arms worried her. "What's wrong?"

"Nothing. Just that…I'm not used to, uh, hugging either." Weiss actually squirmed, looking ill at ease.

"You can let go." Madisyn tried to lighten the mood by winking.

"Ah. That's just it. Don't think so. It feels too good."

"Oh, Weiss. We're such a pair, aren't we?" Madisyn cringed at what she'd just said. "I don't mean we're a pair, exactly, but—"

"I understand what you mean."

"I'm afraid." The words were out before Madisyn could stop them. She pressed her forehead against Weiss's shoulder.

"Why? Of what?"

"Oh, Weiss." Madisyn refused to meet her gaze. "I could get used to this. Proximity. Being held."

Weiss sat very still, her arms still locked around Madisyn. At first, Madisyn thought her needy words might go unanswered, but Weiss gently cleared her throat. "Nothing says we can't repeat this, if required. In private."

"Of course." A careful sense of joy spread through Madisyn, and she tipped her head back, letting her usual smile easily form on her lips. "What kind of rough, tough, mean-spirited pirates would we portray if we kept snuggling in public?" She gently kissed Weiss's cheek. "Thank you."

Weiss nearly stole her breath by wrapping her in a fierce hug. "Don't thank me. You're not the only one with needs."

Something stirred inside Madisyn's lower abdomen. A heavy sort of sweetness that sent warm waves down to her thighs made her whimper.

"Madi?" Weiss cupped Madisyn's cheek and tipped her head back.

"Weiss…" Nearly drunk with her unexpected surge of arousal, Madisyn blinked slowly.

"What's wrong?" Frowning, Weiss pushed Madisyn's hair from her face, and the tender gesture soothed the fire coursing through her veins. Weiss's callused hands felt so good, better than anything Madisyn had ever dreamed of, and her somewhat clumsy touch was endearing. Something told her she better not relay that thought to Weiss.

"I'm fine. I mean, I'm all right." Madisyn stole one last lungful of Weiss's scent and committed the feel of her warmth to memory before pulling back. "Guess it got the better of me. I mean, talking about my past."

"Can't say I blame you." Weiss fidgeted before pushing her hands deep into her pockets. "We need to get some sleep."

"Yes. Absolutely." Madisyn hesitated, not sure how to say what was on her mind. "I'm glad we talked. I'm glad you know. It's been very lonely."

Weiss drew a deep, not entirely steady, breath. "For stars and skies, Madisyn. Lonely doesn't cover it, does it?"

"Guess not."

"I'm sorry. I didn't mean to yell. I just wish—" Weiss dragged a hand through her hair, for once loose and not tied back in her usual austere manner.

"Yes?"

"I wish I wasn't so damn inept at situations such as these." Frustration only made Weiss seem more approachable, and Madisyn barely resisted hinting for another embrace.

"Hey, you and me both." Madison gave a one-shoulder shrug. "Today was hard on both of us, but you saved the *Koenigin*'s bridge crew."

"And you gave away your secret. That took more courage." Weiss had a look of longing, something Madisyn tried to not read too much into.

"Time to sleep." Madisyn pulled back the blanket and crawled into bed. The thermo-blanket wrapped around her in another sort of embrace. She closed her eyes and thought of Weiss and how it felt when she held her and brushed her hair back. *She called me Madi.* The sudden memory of the unexpected nickname made Madisyn relax and sink farther into her pillow.

❖

Weiss listened to Madisyn's breathing while she tried to fall asleep herself. She had no idea what had just happened. Aloof and used to being regarded as aggressive and terrifying, she knew Madisyn had claimed a spot inside her frozen heart that had been vacant for many years. Not since she was a very young girl could Weiss remember such tenderness.

The sense of protection that Madisyn evoked in her could prove to be dangerous to her plans. They weren't far from the asteroid belt where she had hidden her wealth over the years. The caverns on the asteroid held enough poisonous gases and materials to warrant heavy-duty survival gear, which kept people away if they ventured onto the hostile surface. Consisting mostly of Dahraxian noble ores, the most sought-after metal in the known part of the galaxy, it would allow her to live in luxury for the rest of her life, once she could retrieve it and then disappear.

A soft sigh, followed by an even softer whimper, distracted Weiss, and she frowned at the spike of tenderness that shot through her. Certain it actually did some damage inside, she imagined it nicking her heart, leaving it to slowly bleed with every beat.

"Damn," she whispered. Her plan was dangerous, but not very complicated. Waiting until the *Salaceos* was close enough, disabling the alarm system and the cloaked chip inside her, stealing a shuttle, and leaving quietly. Now it was complicated, and that complication was called Madisyn Pimm. How could she just go and leave her behind in the midst of the people she hated—and feared—the most?

CHAPTER THIRTEEN

Kellen straddled the hover bike, donned the black helmet, and motioned for Ayahliss to sit behind her. Next to them, several SC marines did the same, carefully hidden behind the large forest located between them and Ganath, Gantharat's capital.

Gazing around her, Kellen made sure her unit was ready to move out. They would have to, in order to use the faint moonlight to their advantage. Martial law had been part of the Gantharians' existence since the occupation began more than twenty-five years ago, and being caught out past curfew meant incarceration in an asteroid prison.

Everybody had mounted their hover bikes, which the resistance had delivered to the small forest path. It had been eerie to find the twenty-some bikes abandoned in the woods, but Kellen's scans had showed no signs of an ambush and no tinkering with the bikes.

As she signaled for the others to start their bikes and follow her, she inhaled the familiar sweetness of the Gantharian fall air. It felt magical to be back and yet, in a strange way, also alien. She had been part of the SC military and lived on several SC worlds since she had fled her home world with Armeo. Caring for the young prince, marrying Rae, and changing not only her own life, but that of her fellow Gantharians had forever altered her existence.

The winding forest path widened as they neared the capital. The resistance fighters had meticulously mapped the forest and regularly updated the system of their hover bikes to be able to use stealth mode. This was also an illegal feature, from an Onotharian point of view. Nobody was allowed to move undetected by scanners, but this didn't stop the Gantharian scientists from coming up with new and improved systems to beat the tyrants.

The forest became less dense and Kellen slowed down, the nearly soundless machine barely purring faintly under her. Ayahliss shifted in her seat and readied her double-nozzled sidearm.

"Not much farther now," Kellen murmured in her earpiece. "Be ready."

"Ready." Ayahliss's voice was low and emotionless.

Kellen pressed the sensor that increased the bike's speed as they turned a sharp corner, coming upon a low, dark building. Evenly dispersed poles created a force field around it, which shimmered faintly in the dark. Kellen forced the bike closer, taking the curve almost lying down, and Ayahliss held to her shoulder as she took aim with the weapon the SC's finest engineers had provided.

Four poles exploded in quick succession, sending a shower of sparks several meters up, illuminating the woods. The marines careened through the disabled force field just behind Kellen and Ayahliss. Two Onotharian guards came running around the corner, firing plasma-pulse weapons. Ayahliss raised her sidearm again.

"No! Shoot to stun." Kellen yanked her own weapon free from her harness as she slid the bike to a stop and stunned the closest guard. "They might be Gantharians."

"Traitors," Ayahliss spat, but used her smaller sidearm to stun the other guard, who had frozen at the sight of the crowd.

"Blast the doors open. We need to get to the weapons and sensor-grid projectors."

"On it." Ayahliss jumped off the bike and ran toward the doors, firing repeatedly with her double-barreled blaster.

"We have company, Protector." The closest marine showed her his scanner readings. "At least fifty of them."

"And they should be ours, but let's make sure." Kellen pulled her plasma-pulse rifle from her back. Switching on the monitor on top of it, she adjusted it to night vision. "Send ten marines into the building with Ayahliss. I'll meet the newcomers with a few of your troops." Kellen didn't like parting with Ayahliss but knew she was trained to handle herself better than any of the marines. "Keep comm channels open."

"Affirmative, Protector."

Kellen cast one last glance at the now-open structure and saw marines disappear with Ayahliss into the building. Checking her monitor again, she spotted the approaching crowd moving fast along two different paths. Their speed indicated they were resistance fighters, familiar with the paths of the deep forest.

She ran between the trees, six marines behind her, and soon she could make out shadows and hear the approaching hover bikes. She motioned to the marines to stay hidden and stepped into the path, forcing the lead bike to come to a rapid halt. The rider forced the bike to rise on its rear pad, much like a spooked *maesha*.

"What the hell…?" The rider jumped off the bike and reached for a weapon. "Identify yourself."

"Roshan." Relief flooded Kellen when she recognized her old comrade-in-arms. This woman had once brought Kellen's father home after Onotharian forces had killed him. Roshan O'Landha, resistance leader, had fought alongside her father, and later they'd belonged to the same resistance cell. Roshan had found out Kellen was the last protector of the realm only recently, when Kellen and Rae had rescued several thousand freedom fighters.

"Kellen!" Roshan hit a sensor, placing the hover bike on standby. "Oh, Gods, I can't believe it."

"I see you brought backup." Kellen nodded at the thirty-some bikes behind Roshan. "Andreia?"

"Right here." An agile woman approached after lowering her bike to the ground and stepping off. "It's good to see you, Protector."

Kellen stepped closer, making sure nobody else was within earshot. "Likewise, *Boyoda*." Very few people knew that Andreia M'Aldovar, Onotharian by birth and Gantharian by heart, was the mythical resistance leader with the call sign Boyoda. When Kellen and Rae had evacuated the resistance fighters to Revos Prime, Andreia had assumed another identity, to keep her true one hidden. After living a double existence as resistance leader and Onotharian poster child for the occupation, she had a price on her head from both camps. "I wasn't aware that you had arrived from Revos Prime already."

"We knew the Onotharians would be waiting, so we leaked false information to everybody. We've actually been back fifteen days, enough to get organized and coordinate with headquarters." Roshan glanced behind Kellen. "I see from the lights over there that you've managed to get into the structure."

"I brought some new technology. We managed to take out the sensors with two shots," Kellen explained. "Hitch a ride back there? The sooner we get out of here, the better."

"Sure." They mounted the bike and hurried back after Kellen gave a signal to the marines to return to their vehicles as well.

Ayahliss came toward them, her eyes glimmering. "Protector, we have found—Paladin!" She used Roshan's call sign, smiling broadly. "O'Daybo," she greeted Andreia, her smile fading a little. It had hit Ayahliss hard to learn that their most revered resistance leader was an Onotharian.

"Ayahliss." Roshan embraced the flustered young woman. "Good to see you."

"And you." The affectionate greeting seemed to take Ayahliss aback. "Protector, we have disabled most of the surveillance grid for the inner city of Ganath. In the core of the city, the Onotharians are virtually blind and deaf. We've also located the main weapons storage within the facility."

"Excellent. Better than we thought. It's time to move the interim government inside the main structures and create a stronghold. We also need to focus a big part of our forces on the transmitting networks, to get the message out." Kellen looked around. "We're going to start something tonight that we've worked a long time to achieve. As we speak, diplomats and officers of the court are moving in, so we need to work fast."

"I can hardly believe it," Andreia said softly, her voice trembling. "It's been so long."

Roshan placed an arm around her shoulders. "It certainly has."

"Protector? Ma'am? We've removed the weaponry and loaded it on the hover carts." The marine captain pointed toward four carts behind the hover bikes closest to the door opening.

"Excellent, now we just have—" A sharp signal interrupted Kellen and she yanked her communicator from her shoulder. Concerned, she realized the incoming message was from the diplomatic security detail. "Kellen O'Dal here. Go ahead."

"Protector. We're taking heavy fire and have been cut off from the main part of the detail." A young marine was obviously running, gasping as he spoke.

"The diplomats?" Kellen forced down the icy sensation burning her throat.

"They're with us. We're trying to keep them safe while our unit is engaging the enemy."

"Ping your coordinates with the scramble-beacon. We're not far away."

The marine transmitted his coordinates, and Roshan and Andreia brought up a digital map of the city.

"We have your location, Corporal. Keep your head down and the diplomats safe until we get there." *Pray he does.* Kellen shoved the weapons into her harness and jumped onto her hover bike. Turning her head, she looked into the dark blue fire of Ayahliss's eyes.

"Reena? Dahlia?" Ayahliss spoke without inflection.

"Under attack. Let's go." Kellen pulled the bike into a steep climb, grateful for the powerful engine. As her SC unit moved out, followed by the resistance fighters, she kept up an inner mantra: *Be safe. Please, be safe.*

❖

Reena wiped the dust from her eyes, squinting through the long strands of her hair that had dislodged from its severe bun. Next to her, Dahlia kept low behind the overturned hover car.

"You're bleeding," Dahlia said, pointing to Reena's forehead.

"Oh." Reena looked at her fingertips where bloodstains confirmed Dahlia's words. "It's not bad."

"Where the hell did they come from?" Dahlia peered over the edge of the car. The air around them was damp and held the special burned smell of plasma-pulse weapons fire. She quickly moved back down onto her knees when more firing erupted. "Damn. You'd think that a double security detail would be enough."

To their left, a marine flew backward through the air. He ended up on his back, his body twitching violently before it became very still.

"For stars and skies!" Dahlia threw herself forward, but Reena managed to grab her and pin her to the ground.

"He's in the line of fire," she yelled. "Stay down, or he'll have sacrificed his life for nothing."

Dahlia tried to free herself for a few moments, pushing at Reena. She eventually relaxed, her eyes never leaving the wounded young man. "Can't we try to pull him over here?"

"Wait." Reena impatiently pushed her hair back and watched the other marines lay down cover fire as two of them ran with one other injured soldier hanging listless between them. "All right. Hurry." She and Dahlia crawled over to the marine. Afraid to even raise her head, Reena fumbled blindly for the man's harness and grabbed it. She dared a glance and saw that Dahlia had a steady grip on his belt. "Pull."

Dust collected in Reena's eyes and nose as she crawled and yanked at the harness. The unconscious—or dead—man was so heavy, her shoulders felt like she was ripping them from their socket. Grunting, she dug the heels of her shoes in, and together she and Dahlia dragged the soldier behind the vehicle.

"Is…he breathing?" Dahlia crouched on all fours, barely audible above the noise.

"Let's see." Blinking at the sting in her eyes, Reena carefully opened the visor of his helmet. He was clearly of Imidestrian origin, his green-yellow eyes half-open and his lips white. "Oh, this isn't good." Reena would have to risk removing his helmet to administer CPR. She told herself that if his neck was injured, they had already aggravated the injury by yanking him to safety. Unclasping the lock, she carefully slid it off and, listening, she realized he wasn't moving any air.

"I'll do compressions." Her words curt, Dahlia knelt next to the soldier.

"All right." Reena wiped some blood off the man's face and yanked the med kit off his belt. Not about to wait until she got the portable ventilator out, she manually breathed a few times into his lungs. Dahlia compressed his rib cage five times, then attached the ventilator to his mouth and nose. Pressing it down, she knew it would supply the exact amount of oxygen needed to prevent further damage to his brain.

"Judge Beqq!" Another soldier, the major in charge of their security detail, crawled up to them, his eyes narrow. "We have called for backup." He regarded their efforts. "As long as you stay behind the armored hover car, you're protected. I'll see if I can send someone back here to help with Sergeant Lisht."

"Just keep the enemy at bay until backup gets here," Reena said and pressed the mask firmer around Lisht's face. "He's not breathing."

"Pulse?" the major asked.

"Wait." Dahlia pressed her fingers at Lisht's neck. "None so far."

"No more heroics. We're here for your mission." The major pushed himself back and crawled around the vehicle. Reena looked up just in time to see his body go rigid and almost hover, only to fall sideways against the scorched metal. "Gods!" Reena ducked as more dirt sprayed their way. "We're in big trouble."

"I'll say." Dahlia was out of breath, but kept working on Lisht. "Keep going with the mask."

"Aye, ma'am." Reena disregarded the tightness in her chest and pushed the ventilator back onto Lisht's face. Suddenly the young man coughed and moaned into the mask. Removing it, Reena saw him blink against the dust in the air.

"Easy." Dahlia ceased the compressions. "You're injured. Lie still."

Because of pain or Dahlia's authoritative voice, Lisht remained on his back. Reena switched to oxygen only and let the mask rest on his face.

"The team?" Lisht asked after greedily drawing a few breaths.

"Under heavy fire. Your major is down."

"Then I'm it." Pushing onto his side, Lisht tried to sit up.

"I think not." Reena eased him back down as he lost all color. "Your team is holding our position, and backup is coming—" Alarmed by a roaring sound, Reena glanced up. It was hard to make anything out, but the sky seemed filled with large projectiles.

"Are those hover bikes?" Dahlia rubbed her eyes. "And are they ours?"

"Guess we'll find out really quick." Several of the shadows touched down farther away. The firing increased, and Reena saw blue-tinted plasma charges directed toward the enemy.

"Ours." She sighed in relief. "Hear that, Lisht? Backup's here."

"I…hear…" His voice was weak, and Reena looked down only to discover a substance darkening the ground around him. "Damn it, he's hemorrhaging." Desperate to find the source of his wound, she slid her hands underneath his jacket. "Where's it coming from?"

"I don't know." Dahlia pushed her hands underneath him. "I can't…oh…damn." She sank down on her knees, her hands hanging bloody at her side. "It's his entire back. It's one big wound and he's bleeding out."

"No. Oh, Gods." Reena blinked as futile tears burned behind her eyes.

"Reena!" The sound of fast feet hammered against the ground and Ayahliss threw herself down next to them. "There's so much blood."

"Not mine. His." Numb, Reena motioned toward Lisht. "We tried to save him." Reena found herself engulfed by Ayahliss's strong arms, and for a moment she allowed herself to gain strength from the embrace. "I'm all right. Really." She looked up and saw Kellen kneeling next to a somber Dahlia. "Glad you're here."

"We need to get you to safety. We have a new hovercraft waiting for you. The Onotharians are already pulling back." Kellen peered around the wreckage.

Reena squeezed Ayahliss's hand quickly and stood on wobbly legs. Her clothes were torn, and only now did she feel the pain from the cuts and bruises that covered her legs and arms.

"You're bleeding." Ayahliss trembled as she carefully separated the torn fabric of Reena's coverall. Her body armor had protected her from the worst of the attack, but it didn't extend to her legs.

"It's not so bad." Annoyingly dizzy, Reena tried to focus as the sky darkened even more. The last thing she heard was Ayahliss's frantic voice.

Chapter Fourteen

Madisyn moved and snapped open her eyes when a warm weight hindered her movement. Their quarters were still dark; the automatic light had yet to go to twenty percent illumination. Cautiously, Madisyn turned her head and felt a soft puff of air as someone exhaled right next to her cheek. What the…? Weiss?

Afraid to move, Madisyn tried to get her bearings. She was in her bed, and Weiss was in her bed. She let her eidetic memory scan what had transpired last night. She had told Weiss everything. Her secret was no longer that, a secret. One other living being knew that she was humanoid in all the ways that really mattered. Someone knew, and not just anyone. Weiss knew.

Weiss shifted next to her and wrapped a strong arm around Madisyn's waist. Unable to completely mute a soft gasp, Madisyn raised a hand to clasp her mouth. Instantly, Weiss took hold of her wrist and held her firmly.

"Who—?" Weiss pushed herself up on her elbow and Madisyn could see her eyes glimmer in the faint light from the surrounding stars.

"Weiss. It's me. Madisyn."

"Madisyn. Oh. Of course." Weiss held her for a moment longer before she suddenly seemed to realize it. "Oh, sorry. Did I hurt you?"

"No, but what are you doing here?"

"What do you mean?" Weiss rubbed her face.

"In my bed."

Madisyn could feel how rigid Weiss became at the question.

"You were dreaming. Last night, as we were falling asleep, you kept moaning and whimpering." Weiss, sounding calmer and more assured, propped her head up against one hand and placed the other one just above Madisyn's midsection.

Could Weiss feel the fluttering sensation inside her? Despite her ability to control her body's reactions, Madisyn was unable to stop her heart from pounding and her skin from creating goose bumps as her hair follicles rose in unison. "I never whimper," she said. *I hope.*

"Well, you did last night, and I figured since I more or less forced your secret out of you, I should be the one who provided some, well, I guess, comfort."

Madisyn couldn't help but smile. Weiss was hardly the touchy-feely type, at least not while in character as rough and mean pirate. Obviously she had a softer side that could manifest itself when least expected. Slowly relaxing, Madisyn exhaled and turned on her side to face Weiss. "Thank you."

"What for?"

"For caring enough to not let me ride out the nightmares by myself. I do get them sometimes, and since my parents were killed, I've always had to face them alone. If I had nightmares last night, I don't even remember them. Perhaps you prevented the worst of the images. You have no idea what a relief that is."

"Ah. That's all right. You kept me awake anyway." Weiss gave a wry smile. "Then again, you kept me awake just as much when I moved over here."

"I did? How is that?" Madisyn tried to gauge Weiss's expression, barely visible. "Lights, ten percent."

A dim light lit up their quarters. Madisyn blinked as she saw a faint pink hue on Weiss's cheekbones.

"You really have to ask?" Her voice sardonic, Weiss raised one eyebrow.

"Sure. If I stopped having a nightmare, why would I keep you awake, unless I had cold feet or something?" Madisyn wiggled her toes. They felt warm as usual, nothing wrong with her inner thermostat.

"Stars and skies, woman, are you really that dense?" Weiss shook her head. "I haven't shared anyone's bed in a long time, and here you are—soft, beautiful, warm, and squirming against me."

"I do *not* squirm!" The ridiculous objection left Madisyn's lips before she could stop it. "I mean, even if I did, why would you have any problems with that? I know very well that someone like you would never find me even remotely attractive."

"What do *you* mean, someone like me?" Her eyes frosty slits of green, Weiss still kept her arm across Madisyn.

"You've been all over the known universe and then some, according to our boss. You're experienced and, even if I'm not, I can tell that you're used to the finer things in life. I'm sure that translates to…to companions."

"True. I used to enjoy the company of temporary lovers, preferably young women who knew and abided by the rules." Weiss spoke darkly, and her grip around Madisyn's waist tightened. "And, trust me, none of them had soft curly blond hair, pale unpainted skin, and baby blue eyes."

"No? What were they like?" Madison asked hurriedly. Perhaps it wasn't polite to ask, but she needed to deflect the attention from herself.

"What were they like?" Weiss guffawed. "Often curvaceous, experienced, elegant, sometimes bordering on sleazy. Knew what they wanted. Knew what I wanted."

"What did you want?"

"Sex. Release tension. Some distraction. Some fun." Shrugging, Weiss slid her hand slowly up Madisyn's abdomen. "And you, who lost so much so young. Where do you find release? Or some fun?"

"I don't. I'm a robot, remember?" Madisyn knew she sounded bitter, but if she gave in to the multitude of emotions Weiss's hand created, she didn't know where she would end.

"You're not. You're a humanoid girl from Guild Nation, a brilliant scientist, a family girl who suffered trauma that would've left pretty much everyone else out of her mind."

"I was out of my mind for a while." Madisyn sobbed, only once and very quietly, but Weiss bent down immediately and brushed her lips against her forehead.

"You're brave, dedicated, and passionate. You risk everything for your cause. So you see, these women in my past, a long time ago by now, were nothing like you. They can't compare even for a second. You shame them all in every way."

"Except in the way you wanted them." Madisyn cursed her tongue for speaking before she engaged her logic.

"What do you mean?"

"You're trying to be nice. I appreciate it, but I don't need your pity. I've found my way of life, my purpose, and it's enough."

"So, let me see if I understand you correctly," Weiss said slowly, not removing her maddening hand from the side of Madisyn's chest. "You are content to be an undercover agent, fighting piracy, and you aren't missing the touch between friends or lovers, because you never experienced it. You also feel inferior toward women who are well versed in the art of making love. That about it?"

"I don't feel inferior to anybody!" Madisyn knew it was a lie, but she would never admit it, especially not to Weiss.

"Don't you?" Weiss moved her hand and lightly cupped Madisyn's right breast. "I'm fairly sure I'm the first who has touched you this way. I might be wrong, but the way you feel under my hand, I don't think I am."

"Even so, there's more to life than sex. There are far more important things. Like…like…" Tears of fury rose behind her eyelids as the words became trapped inside her.

"Don't cry." Weiss slid her hand up to frame Madisyn's face. "You don't have to worry."

"Why would I worry? You said it yourself. I'm not your type."

"That's not what I said, exactly." Weiss rubbed her thumb across Madisyn's eyebrows. "What I said was, you're not like any of those women in my past. You're so much more. You outshine them, and your courage and compassion make you someone I've never come across before. You're a real person. A whole person." She dipped her head and brushed her lips against Madisyn's.

Forgetting to breathe, Madisyn could hardly believe that somebody, Weiss of all people, was kissing her. She was torn between wanting to pull away and craving to throw her arms around Weiss. Madisyn was certain her body wasn't built to handle such conflicting emotion.

"Kiss me back." It wasn't an order, nor was it a request. It sounded like the most natural statement in the world, like Weiss had longed to kiss her and now simply had to.

"What if I—I make a mistake?"

"You won't. I promise you. You won't." Weiss pulled Madisyn half on top of her.

Unable to resist, Madisyn lowered her head toward Weiss. "Computer, lights out." The sudden darkness was a blessing until Madisyn realized that she had to feel her way as her optical nerve adjusted.

"Yes. Just like that." Weiss's voice deepened. "Just relax."

Madisyn trembled uncontrollably as she pressed her lips against Weiss's. They were so warm, soft, and alluring; she couldn't repress a moan as she sank into a full-body embrace. She parted her lips because she had a deep need to taste Weiss. She might never get another chance to do this.

"Mmm, Madi..." Weiss rolled them over, ending up on top. She rested on her elbows and nibbled Madisyn's lips, intermittently soothing the teasing nips with soft, gentle kisses. Madisyn arched her back, her body reacting as if someone had poured burning plasma on it. She had never explored her BNSL body's preparedness for sexual encounters. Her natural shyness had kept her from discussing the matter with her parents, but now she realized what her mother had meant when she said, "The Twenty-Two Alpha is fully functional; it will serve you well." What an understatement. Cringing slightly, Madisyn accepted Weiss's tongue into her mouth and felt for the first time the physical manifestations of arousal. She assumed the wetness between her legs was normal, as was the way her nipples pebbled into sharp points, chafing against her sleep shirt.

Weiss had her arms around Madisyn and pushed her hands up underneath the shirt, stroking her back slowly. Madisyn whimpered and pushed her hands into Weiss's hair, which hung loose against her cheeks. Reveling in how it wound itself around her fingers, as if to keep her close, Madisyn returned Weiss's kisses with trust and passion.

"Madisyn?" Weiss murmured against her lips. "This is...getting out of hand."

Madisyn didn't want to listen. She needed more of these feelings, more of the amazing sensation of being held like she was the only woman in the universe—Madisyn flinched and pushed back. "All right! Let go. Let go of me." She shivered now as panic began to set in. It was ridiculous to fantasize like this, to pretend even for a second that she would ever be important to anyone.

"There, you're fine. See. No hands." Weiss moved back. "Lights on ten—"

"No. No lights." Madisyn hardly recognized her own voice, raw and intense. "I need a moment. Please."

"Hey, Madi, don't." Weiss gently gripped Madisyn's hands. "You're fine. It was a kiss, that's all. A kiss."

"Sure. Absolutely." Why was she so damn short of breath? "You're right." Just a kiss, true, but it was her first.

They sat in silence as Madisyn struggled to find her bearings. She used every technique her enhanced system possessed to stymie the raging synthetic hormones, mildly cursing her brilliant parents for creating a body such as this, even equipped to indulge in sex if the need arose. For stars and skies, it certainly had. How was she supposed to work side by side with Weiss now that she knew what it felt like to be held by her, kissed by her?

The automatic illumination switched the light on at twenty percent and a computerized voice stated the stellar time. Madisyn pushed her shoulders back and for the first time met Weiss's steady gaze. Was there something new there, something different? Quite sure it was wishful thinking, Madisyn couldn't disregard the fullness of Weiss's usually narrow lips. She had done that. Her kisses had made them look like that. Somehow this realization alleviated the lingering feeling of awkwardness. Madisyn swung her legs over the edge of the bed.

Perhaps she should merely regard this experience as nothing but an extraordinary start of an ordinary day among the worst scum of outer space. If nothing else, it took her mind off any potential regrets about letting Weiss in on her most guarded secret.

❖

Ayahliss studied Reena as they sat down to have breakfast. Soon she would join the team that guarded the diplomats, but for now it was only the two of them. Ayahliss scrutinized Reena's forehead, which didn't even show a scar.

Shuddering at the memory of the deep gash that had bled all over Reena's face, Ayahliss gripped the mug of coffee tighter. She had thought for several tormenting seconds that Reena was mortally wounded. Not sure where her strength had come from, she had carried Reena aboard the MEDEVAC shuttle. The medics pushed her out of the way, which put her self-control to the test. Only the fact that they acted in Reena's best interest made her step back and observe as they treated her.

"We have half an hour before we're due in the shuttle bay." Reena looked up, her eyes warming as she regarded Ayahliss. "Don't," she said softly.

"Don't what?" Ayahliss said, stalling.

"Don't look at me like you don't expect to see me ever again. Kellen and Captain Todd have made sure that we'll have twice as many security officers with us when the negotiations take place."

"I want to go with you."

"You have your own assignment with the resistance fighters. If anyone should be concerned, it's me. You're doing far more dangerous things than I." Reena clearly meant to keep the mood light, but she had a haunted expression as she took Ayahliss's hand.

"I will use caution," Ayahliss vowed quietly.

"I will hold you to it." Reena sounded just as serious. "You are important to me, Ayahliss. I…I cannot lose you."

Ayahliss felt like tiny icicles she never knew about melted inside, creating a flood of tears that she simply couldn't allow herself to shed. She held on tight to Reena's hand. "I fear for you. I fear losing you. I can't even imagine never knowing what caring for you would be like." Ayahliss held her breath, knowing full well she was being presumptuous.

"That's just it. We both need to be careful. We have to make sure we're alive and well, and ready to come back to each other. I know it's early yet, but war leaves you with a huge magnifying lens when looking at your life and what matters." Reena caressed the back of Ayahliss's hand with her thumb. "You know you matter to me—more than I can say."

Ayahliss gasped, and even if she somewhere was aware of the other people in the mess hall, she saw only Reena. The cascading, wild red hair, her long lashes shadowing the brilliance of her eyes, and most of all, the untamed exuberance that seemed to endlessly call to Ayahliss.

"I never expected this. I mean, to feel this way." Ayahliss clung to Reena's hand. "You understand?"

"I do. When we have the opportunity to be alone again, I will share in great detail just how well I understand." Her eyes twinkling, Reena smiled, a thoroughly naughty and infectious smile. "I look forward to it."

"So do I."

They finished their meal, and outside in the corridor they walked their separate ways: Reena to her quarters to gather her documents, Ayahliss to hers to assemble her gear. This could be the last time they saw each other, but Ayahliss deliberately shook off the feeling. Instead, she promised herself that next time she and Reena were alone together, she would confess her love.

CHAPTER FIFTEEN

"We are ready to dock with the *Ondamann* in five minutes, Captain," said the *Salaceos*'s helmsman.

"Cloak still operative." Madisyn kept her eyes on the readings.

"Unless we want them to start firing from sheer embarrassment that we sneaked up on them like this, I suggest we decloak now," Weiss said, her voice dry. "Onotharians spook easily."

Podmer frowned in Weiss's direction. "I never said this was an Onotharian ship."

"Please." Weiss gestured dismissively. "The name? The configuration? Pretty obvious."

"Ha." Podmer cleared his throat. "Pimm, you heard your buddy. Decloak."

"Aye, Captain." Madisyn punched in the command that switched off the cloaking feature. *Buddy?* She had a flashback of how she had awoken that morning with Weiss tucked in close behind her. The sensation had been more alien to Madisyn than any new-world life form, and she remembered how she had pressed against Weiss, reveling in the sensation of her slender body.

"The *Ondamann* is hailing us, Captain." Struyen manned the ops station, his eyes narrow and contemptuous as he glanced up. He had always kept his distance from Madisyn, and the way he looked at Weiss suggested he was more than wary of her. Perhaps since she could take him down with one hand tied behind her back.

"On screen." Podmer stood, adjusting his jacket. "This is Podmer of the space vessel *Salaceos*."

"Lix M'Ossar. Welcome to the Volice asteroid belt. You are, however, quite late, and we need to put our plans in motion instantly." A diminutive man, his voice as crisp as his exterior, came into view, all decked out in white.

"Our apologies. We had to calibrate our system to allow for the magnetic disturbance within the belt."

"Most successfully. We didn't expect you to be able to use your cloaking device." His voice dry, M'Ossar seemed reluctantly impressed. "Elect your most trusted associates and report to our conference room."

"I'll be right there."

Madisyn could see that Podmer didn't appreciate the obvious order. Admiral Jacelon wanted the specs for each Onotharian ship they ran into so, scanning the ship, she used the algorithm she had written for moments like this. If the other ship had sensed her scan, it would have been a very unfortunate situation. Now Madisyn piggybacked on the cloaking device she had just shut down, though not entirely. This way the beam was virtually undetectable and could easily be mistaken for normal background space noise, especially this close to a magnetized asteroid belt.

"Weiss, Struyen, you're with me. Pimm, you have the bridge. Keep an eye on these fools. They possess great wealth, but also the habit of wanting a lot for a little. Be prepared to lock on to their weapons array."

"Yes, sir." Madisyn took the command chair as the other three left the bridge. Junior bridge officers took Weiss's and her stations. Madisyn knew better than to turn her head and look at Weiss, but she augmented her hearing temporarily, which was enough to hear a few fading words in the elevator.

"Onotharians are famous for playing it safe, and in this situation it's a matter of stunning first and asking questions later." Podmer laughed, a joyless sound. "Keep your weapons on stun, but your backup piece on a lethal pulse setting."

Affirming murmurs suggested Weiss and Struyen followed orders.

"Any last-minute ideas, Weiss?"

"We won't be able to sneak any weapons by them." Weiss sounded calm. "How's your combat hand-to-hand training, Struyen?"

"As good as anything you throw at me." Struyen's voice was thin, but abrasive.

"It's not me you have to worry about." Smooth and patient, Weiss's voice began to fade, getting out of reach. "I need to know you can fight."

"I can…"

It was impossible for Madisyn to strain her hearing any more. She knew firsthand that Weiss's close-combat skills were impeccable. As for Struyen, like so many other pirates, he relied on his weapons. Any potential fighting would most likely rest on Weiss's shoulders.

Weiss walked behind Podmer through the vast corridors of the *Ondamann*. The Onotharians' preference for gilded ornaments and their affinity for decorating even their warships were evident throughout the craft. Even the bulkheads shimmered in iridescent blue. Huffing under her breath, Weiss lengthened her stride, secretly pleased that Struyen had problems keeping an even pace with her and the much-taller Podmer.

The Onotharian guards, dressed in battle gear as if they expected to be placed on a hostile planet at any moment, stomped evenly in front of them as they escorted them to the conference room. Weiss had counted twelve guards, six in the front and six behind them, which she found still more proof of Onotharian overkill.

Eventually, they reached a conference room big enough to host a hundred people. Podmer stepped inside, and Weiss let Struyen elbow his way in ahead of her. Two other guards moved up and scanned them. The procedure took long enough to make Podmer growl impatiently, but eventually one of the guards asked them to sit down.

Weiss took in her surroundings, reluctantly impressed by the size of the large screens along the left wall. A multitude of small viewports ran along the opposite side, where Weiss could barely spot the *Salaceos* if she leaned forward.

"Attention! General M'Aldovar present." The Onotharian guards stood straight as rods, their eyes rigidly directed forward.

M'Aldovar? The familiar name puzzled Weiss. Where had she heard it before?

A dark-haired man, handsome and young-looking for his impressive rank, entered. He rode in a hover chair, a hissing sound revealing that he was hooked up to an oxygenizer, and placed himself at the head of the long table.

"I'm General Trax M'Aldovar," the man said, his voice low and clearly strained. Faint traces of scarring just above his tall collar suggested that his neck had once been injured.

"I'm Podmer. This is Weiss Kyakh and Lucco Struyen, two of my senior crewmembers."

"Weiss Kyakh. I see." M'Aldovar nodded slowly. "Your reputation precedes you."

"General." Weiss didn't let on whether the general's recognition pleased her or not, but merely nodded politely.

Podmer and M'Aldovar began to discuss what they had stolen on the Nemalima moon and the data Podmer had confiscated aboard the *Koenigin*. Weiss listened to the two men with a meticulously bored facial expression, knowing this was something Madisyn would need to report back to Jacelon.

"And you let the ship resume course toward SC space?" The general raised his voice for the first time, giving it a raspy, startling sound. "Are you insane?"

"We meant to jettison her bridge crew—" Podmer tried to explain.

"Meant to?" M'Aldovar's strained outrage sounded more menacing than if he had actually been able to yell at them.

"General, even if they got word back to the SC, they haven't had enough time for a new vessel to deliver the altered command codes." Podmer pushed his hand forward in an apologetic manner.

"That is the only thing that redeems you, Podmer." M'Aldovar glanced over at Weiss. "And why has someone of your reputation hooked up with someone like him?"

"A free ride well out of SC territory."

M'Aldovar laughed, a horrifying hissing sound that reminded Weiss of a Torrvordian lizard that had bitten her as a child. It had made that exact sound just before it sank its fangs into her arm. She'd been five, but the memory was vivid enough for her to recognize the lizard's look in M'Aldovar's eyes. *Wait. Wait a damn minute.*

M'Aldovar? Weiss recalled the extensive background material from her SC operative training. Trax M'Aldovar was the name of the man who had nearly killed Jacelon the first time she'd gone with her spouse to Gantharat. Instead, Kellen O'Dal had killed him. Or so everybody assumed. Unless this was an imposter, Trax M'Aldovar, formerly of the Onotharian Clandestine Service, was now a general of the very same. And with a strong motive for revenge.

"Good point." M'Aldovar returned his attention to Podmer. "I need the davic crystals and the intel. Deliver them and—"

"Half now. Half when we get paid." Podmer inflated his chest. Lowering his chin, he looked at M'Aldovar as if he was measuring his true power.

"What?" M'Aldovar looked more puzzled than angry.

"Half now, half later. Standard procedure."

"All right." The general dragged out the words as if really contemplating them. "All of the data, half the crystals." He spoke gently, gasping against the oxygenizer in an increasing speed.

"Sir, please." One of the guards, who Weiss now saw boasted a senior physician's badge, stepped up next to M'Aldovar. "Remember how we practiced this. Nice and slow."

"Damn it." M'Aldovar bit down around the last word fast enough to make the other man jump. "Leave me alone." He clasped his right hand around the armrest, the other lying rigid around a contraption that probably kept the hand from shriveling up completely.

"You listen to me, Podmer. I don't intend to waste what little oxygen I have on you. You will deliver the crystals and hand over the data according to our initial terms." M'Aldovar glared at Podmer, and Weiss thought that the way his amber eyes sparkled, they should burn a hole in him.

"That's not—"

"That's how it will be." M'Aldovar could obviously use his voice well despite being short of breath. His low growl impressed even Weiss, who had stared down more men than she cared to remember. "It's either that, or you will sit there with useless intel and crystals you won't be able to move."

"Fine," Podmer said. "This is not how I conduct business, but very well." He managed to make it sound like he was doing a friend a favor, but Weiss could see from the small drops of perspiration around his temples that he was shaken. She assumed this was a first for the pompous pirate.

"Excellent," M'Aldovar said smoothly. "My associate—M'Ossar, here—will tend to the details. Once he has verified that you've fulfilled your end of the arrangement, you will receive payment in full." M'Aldovar gestured toward a sparsely built man standing just behind him.

"All right." Podmer rose, his complexion blotchy. "Weiss can handle it. I have other things that need my attention." If he intended to insult M'Aldovar, he failed. The Onotharian seemed indifferent.

"Very well. Good-bye." M'Aldovar turned the hover chair and left the conference room.

Weiss sighed. Podmer had been humiliated, and he would take it out on the crew or anyone within his field of vision.

"Shall we, Ms. Kyakh?" M'Ossar asked, interrupting Weiss's thoughts.

"By all means." Weiss opened the small case on her belt and pulled out the chip holding the data they'd stolen from the *Koenigin*. Madisyn had sent word to Jacelon regarding the attack on the cruise ship, but they hadn't heard back. They had to go through with Podmer's deal, hoping that Jacelon would have enough time to get new intel to the troops heading for Gantharat. If not, the convoys could find themselves in the hands of the Onotharians, who would anticipate and countermand every one of their moves.

M'Ossar scanned the chip carefully, handling it with long, wiry fingers as if it were an explosive device ready to go off if not treated like Volocuvian crystalline droplets. "It seems accurate," M'Ossar said in his low, dry tone. "Now, the crystals."

"Well, what do you know, I didn't bring them with me." Weiss found the man annoying enough to warrant tossing him out an airlock.

"We must arrange for you to deliver them instantly. General M'Aldovar does not appreciate any delays."

"The general will have to accept the fact that moving them will take at least as long as a shuttle trip back and forth."

"I suggest I take a shuttle from our ship to yours. I need to verify the crystals' purity and oversee the transport myself."

"Very well. See you later, then."

"Good-bye." The thin man nodded curtly and left the room.

Escorted by two guards, Weiss returned to the shuttle bay. Once there, she realized Podmer had left without her. She cursed loudly enough for the guards to grip their weapons tighter. "Kyakh to the *Salaceos*. Come in." She yanked at her communicator.

"*Salaceos* here," Madisyn replied. "I have already sent a shuttle for you. It should be there in a few minutes."

"Thank you. I don't exactly feel like hanging around any longer than necessary."

"I hear you." Madisyn's voice calmed Weiss enough for her to stop pacing.

"Prepare the crystals to be moved at once to the *Ondamann*'s shuttle docks. A crewmember from this ship will oversee the procedure. No mistakes."

"Got it." Madisyn gently cleared her throat. "See you when you get back."

"Yes. Weiss out."

Madisyn signed off and Weiss gazed around the shuttle bay. It held an impressive array of shuttles, ranging from small two-seat fighter vessels to large cargo/troop transporters. She might as well send Jacelon this new intel, together with the fact the man everyone thought the Protector of the Realm had killed was very much alive and holding even more power than before.

"Your shuttle is cleared to dock. This way." One of the guards motioned for Weiss to follow them to an airlock. For a second, Weiss wondered if this was a trick, but then chastised herself. If they wanted to eliminate her, they could just shoot her. Who would stop them? She stepped into the airlock and saw it connected to a *Salaceos* shuttle. Entering the small ship, she strapped herself in behind the pilot.

"Get us back to the *Salaceos* fast." Weiss couldn't explain her sense of urgency.

"Aye, ma'am." The shuttle made a wide pass around the *Ondamann* before approaching Podmer's ship. The asteroid belt shimmered like a precious stone necklace in the light of the distant sun. Her loot, her whole future, was hidden on one of those asteroids. It had always been her prime goal to one day be free and start a new life far away from the SC and its surrounding sectors. Now she wasn't so sure. In fact, she wasn't sure at all.

❖

"We won't get another chance like this."

Madisyn stopped halfway to the shuttle bay. Podmer was on his way back and had requested she meet him when he returned. Already from a distance she heard Struyen from behind a door leading into a storage room. The vehemence in his voice made her stop just inside, automatically using her augmented hearing as she made sure she was out of sight if anyone stepped out.

"How do we do it?"

Madisyn recognized the voice of another male senior crewmember. He was one of Struyen's buddies; she had seen them work out together many times in the gym.

"We're going to start shipping those goods over to the other ship soon. A lot can go wrong during such operations." The ugly snicker in Struyen's voice made Madisyn want to hit the door sensor and throttle him. She forced herself to remain still, determined to hear the rest.

"Ah. You mean, like an airlock accident?" a third voice said, sounding considerably younger than the other two. Madisyn guessed it belonged to Lemo, a rather new recruit to the *Salaceos*, a young man who seemed to hero-worship Struyen and his followers. With increasing dread Madisyn realized that Struyen had quite a large entourage, judging by how many flocked around him in the mess hall and the gym.

"An airlock accident is too mundane," Struyen said. "We need to be more creative than that. She's no fool, you know, and neither is Pimm. If Podmer gets word that we intentionally got rid of his new star, we can expect the same treatment. It has to be completely random and believable."

Madisyn gripped a ledge in the bulkhead. She knew who they were talking about. It was clear that Struyen disliked Weiss, but this was totally unexpected. Madisyn's first thought was to alert Podmer, but without proof, all she would accomplish was to reveal to Struyen that she knew about their plans.

"Either way, it has to happen quickly." Struyen sounded impatient. "Podmer is handing over the goods once he's back aboard."

"What about an accident with the loading droid? Wouldn't that be poetic justice?" another voice said. "I mean, after she and Pimm are all cozy in their quarters, what if she became a little personal with yet another machine?"

Madisyn heard the shuffle of feet and ran down the corridor. She had barely entered the stairwell before the door opened behind her. She hurried down the two decks to the shuttle bay area. No, she couldn't tell Podmer, not yet. She needed to talk with Weiss and figure out a way to keep her safe. As if their mission wasn't difficult enough.

CHAPTER SIXTEEN

Reena gazed up at the ceiling of the ancient Gantharian structure. Long, wide stairs made of something resembling white marble, worn down by the centuries, led up to vast columns. Inside, the ceiling walls were at least ten meters tall, and the ceiling was made of something blue and softly glimmering. Reena had been to the most beautiful and impressive courthouses within the SC, but she had to admit, this example of early Gantharian architecture was right up there with any of them. She saw four tall wooden doors, adorned with brass-like rivets and boasting massive square handles, at the far wall. The structure was abandoned and its imposing entrance had been nailed shut. Instead, the resistance showed the SC representatives in through a small hidden door.

"Judge Beqq," a female voice said, interrupting Reena's admiration. "Welcome to Gantharat. This is a big day. My name is Vimra O'Sianto." A woman with long, chalk-white hair bowed politely, her arms crossed over her chest. She wore a long, blue robe, and her blue-tinted skin tone and crystal-clear, nearly translucent blue eyes indicated her Gantharian descent.

"Judge O'Sianto, the honor is mine." Reena returned the greeting, bowing with her arms crossed. "This is indeed a great day. For us to be able to meet like this is a miracle. We could hardly see any signs of Onotharian presence in Ganath, once we managed to press through the ambush."

"I was not surprised, but still very afraid for you and your delegation, when I heard of the attack." Judge O'Sianto shook her head. "I hope no lives were lost."

"On both sides, I'm afraid." Reena thought of the young man who'd died while protecting them. They had worked tirelessly on him and the other wounded for over an hour, medics, diplomats, and soldiers alike, until a rescue team could reach them from the *Circinus*.

"I am sorry to learn of this. I have long waited for this moment, for the beginning of Gantharat's liberation, but that does not mean I wish for any Onotharian lives to be lost either. Those young men and women are following the direct orders of the Onotharian authorities."

"Perhaps. But they are still the enemy, let's not forget that." Dahlia joined them together with Kellen and Owena.

"Judge O'Sianto, this is Diplomat Dahlia Jacelon, of the Supreme Constellations, and Kellen O'Dal—"

"Protector. I am honored." Judge O'Sianto bowed deeply. "Our prince's survival, and yours, was the miracle we needed to find the strength to fight." She bowed also toward Dahlia. "Welcome, Diplomat." She politely acknowledged Owena with a nod.

"Thank you." Dahlia looked around the large hallway. "Where is Ayahliss? Oh, here she comes with Andreia and Roshan." She returned her focus to O'Sianto. "Where do we hold the meeting? Time is of the essence. My daughter, Admiral Jacelon, your other Protector, has sent intel that we need to work out the agreement right now, or we might lose our window of opportunity. She is in combat as we speak."

Reena thought she saw a faint twitch at the corners of Kellen's mouth. Kellen would sacrifice anything to keep her protégé safe, but the thought of Rae being in danger was distressing even for someone as stoic as Kellen.

"I have the interim government assembled behind the second door from the left." Judge O'Sianto motioned for them to join her. "Your guards will remain here, yes?"

"Yes." Kellen turned to the twelve marines and Ayahliss. "My tactical chief will make sure they don't let anyone else through. Owena, at the first sign of trouble, don't hesitate to alert the *Circinus* and initiate immediate evacuation of the dignitaries."

"Aye, Protector." Owena hoisted her rifle. "We've got it covered."

"I know." Kellen merely quirked an eyebrow, turning her head. "Ayahliss?"

"By the book, Protector," Ayahliss answered smartly.

Reena wanted to say something, anything, to Ayahliss before they entered, but this was the worst of times to get personal. Still, the proud stance of the tall, stunning young woman who held her heart induced a multitude of emotions in Reena, and she wished she had time to exchange a few words. Ayahliss chose that moment to gaze directly at her, and the barely noticeable look of recognition showed that she had read some of Reena's emotions in her eyes.

"Please, follow me," Judge O'Sianto said, and began to walk toward the wooden doors. The other women, except Ayahliss, followed her. Just as she stepped through the doorway to the vast chambers inside, Reena turned and looked again at Ayahliss. *We've come this far. We're so close. Please, be safe.*

❖

"Evasive pattern, Delta-blue." Jacelon gripped the armrests of the captain's chair hard, grateful for the harness holding her in place as the *Paesina* momentarily lost inertial dampeners. The space ship spiraled through the oncoming fire from the Onotharian cruisers and assault craft.

Jacelon had carefully placed the ships belonging to her strike force in a semicircle around the Onotharian force's base on a small, uninhabited planet halfway between SC space and Gantharat. If she took them out, the negotiations would become something entirely different, as this was the spearhead of the Onotharian force. Her intelligence reports proved that the Onotharians had impressive spacecraft, but their space force was small and could not match the SC unification of nations' combined strength.

Choosing to captain the lead vessel herself, she was confident that her good friend Alex de Vies would monitor their effort from the command central. Jacelon could have chosen to do this, but sitting back was too much for her to handle, knowing that Kellen was deployed, doing her part.

"Admiral, we have three new contacts on our port bow." Her lieutenant at ops spoke fast. "Two cruisers and a freighter."

"Fire on their weapons array. Make them count."

"Aye, ma'am." The tactical officer's hands flew across the controls in intricate patterns. "Their shields are down at forty percent. The freighter's weapons are down."

"Take us in underneath the *Darga*. We need to neutralize the two cruisers hammering at her. She can't take much more." Jacelon kept her eyes on the Cormanian freighter, surrounded by a swarm of assault craft and two Onotharian ships that laid down fire continuously. If they penetrated the shields around the *Darga*'s propulsion system, the vessel would explode and the two hundred crewmembers would be lost.

The *Paesina*'s helmsman pushed her through the small gap underneath the *Darga*. In a daring maneuver, while belly up against the *Darga*, Jacelon gave the order to fire. "Plasma fire, full volley."

This neutralized most of the assault craft. Jacelon saw them tumble through space, two colliding with each other in a cloud of scattering debris. Suddenly, the *Paesina* rolled under her feet again, this time even more violently than before. Behind Jacelon a console burst into flames, quickly extinguished by the automatic system.

"Report," she barked, pushing her hair out of her face.

"Direct hit to the port engine. Not sure how, but they penetrated the shields. Must be a multiple hit, ma'am."

"Casualties?"

To her left, Lt. Gosch, her next in command on the *Paesina*, quickly checked. "Two bad plasma burns in engineering. Minor injuries on decks four, six, and seven." He looked up, behind them. "You all right there, Ensign?"

"Yes…no, not really." A faint thud made Jacelon turn around too, and she saw that the young woman behind them had fallen, the left side of her face red and swollen.

"Damn it." Reacting fast, Jacelon disengaged the clasp to the harness and hurried to the ensign's side. Kneeling, she felt for a pulse. Faint and thready, it fluttered under her fingertips. "We need a med team."

"On it, ma'am," the ops officer replied quickly. "They're on their way."

"I need someone to monitor her until they get her. She's in bad shape."

"Allow me, Admiral." The lieutenant commander from engineering, a Guild Nation woman in her forties, quickly kneeled next to the ensign.

"Sia, please. Can you hear me?" The pain and barely contained panic in her voice told Jacelon that these two shared a personal relationship. This wasn't her business, but it brought back memories. Once, she had been the one critically injured, and Kellen had prayed at her side for days. "Help will be here soon." She squeezed the engineer's shoulder before returning to her chair. Pressing her lips together, she strapped herself back in.

"What's our situation?"

"The *Los'Hesos* and the *Untasta* are making great progress and have almost immobilized or taken out their part of the grid." The tactical officer hesitated. "We lost the *Weoman*."

"Damn." Jacelon checked her console, studying the pattern of ships around her. She saw several Onotharian cruisers move in one direction and followed their trajectory on her computer. Something cold coursed through her heart, oozing into her bloodstream, when she realized they were going for her father's and Alex's freighter. They must've figured out where the orders originated.

"Set a course to grid sixteen, one-six-five-five," she said, her voice emotionless. "Ready plasma-pulse torpedoes, antimatter capped."

"Ma'am?" the tactical officer said. "Antimatter capped?"

"I know, Lieutenant. You heard me. We have no time to waste." The antimatter caps were rarely used, due to the risk of radiation. In combat, when ships were operating with failing shields, using such caps risked contamination. They were still legal only in situations like these.

The *Paesina*'s helmsman pushed her through space, skillfully avoiding the direct fire from more distant ships and the constant smaller shots fired from assault craft. Rolling her, he managed to put them just within range of the ships heading toward the command central vessel.

"Fire full-spread torpedoes on my mark." Jacelon watched the fast ships plunge against her father's ship, swallowing the bile that rose in her throat. No time for any weakness, physical or otherwise. "Ready… mark."

Green-tinted, the missiles pierced the space around them, and within a few seconds they reached the cluster of ships. Impressive explosions tore through them and ripped them to pieces, and even though the *Paesina* kept a safe distance, her front still rose like a nervous thoroughbred horse from the shockwave.

"What about the command vessel?" Jacelon squinted, trying to make out ships through the debris and dust spreading throughout the area around them.

"Took a tumble, but no casualties," the ops officer replied.

"Good." Thank the stars.

A high-pitched tone seared Jacelon's eardrums. She pressed her hands over them, knowing full well what it meant. "All hands brace for impact. Incoming cloaked missile." Damn Onotharians and their love for everything cloaked.

The tone turned into a low growl, which seemed to reverberate through the ship like a large predator was swallowing it.

"Reroute all auxiliary power to shields!" Jacelon yelled.

"Shields not holding, Admiral."

Closing her eyes as the thunderous sound grew, Jacelon drew a deep breath and held it. *Kellen. I'm so sorry, Kellen.*

❖

Kellen sat mostly quiet, listening to the men and women of her home world and the distinguished diplomats and legal experts of the SC discuss the interim government and what was needed to set Gantharat up for success. Eventually, when the parties had managed to reach some agreements and draft an initial document, she spoke up.

"Let us not forget the reinstatement of the prince," she said calmly. "I have yet to hear you plan how that will take place."

"We will of course welcome Prince Armeo back as he is entitled to be. A parade. Yes, of course, but not until we have rebuilt his home, the castle." A man at the far end of the rectangular table smiled. "He is but a boy still, there is yet time."

"I disagree," Kellen said. "Prince Armeo is the rightful heir to the throne. The O'Saral Royales have always governed Gantharat as a democracy."

"We haven't had a monarch in more than twenty-five years—"

"Because the Onotharians murdered everybody except their youngest daughter's son." Kellen stood slowly. "Is it my imagination, or are you reluctant to reinstate the royal family? You bow before me like I am something special, yet you seem indifferent to welcome back the young boy whom the people love and worship. Not just because of his heritage, but because of his courage and warm heart."

"You misunderstand, Protector." Another man rose. "Gantharat is heading for a new future after years of oppression. We are not sure if going back to the old ways of a monarchy is in Gantharat's best interest."

"You may have been oppressed, but that doesn't mean you can disregard the law, once the oppression is eliminated." Kellen towered over the sitting men and women, daring them to contradict her. "The law clearly states that any surviving member of the O'Sarals is the rightful heir to the throne. In case they are too young to govern, his Protectors will do so for him until he is of age."

"Ah. You are aspiring to gain some political power yourself, Protector?" the first man burst out, his tone still polite, yet offensive.

"I only aspire to serve my home world. If it means assisting Prince Armeo in performing his duties, so be it. If it means guarding these negotiations with his and Gantharat's best interest at heart, I will do that. Until a Gantharian government votes to abolish the monarchy and repeats this vote after yet another public election, the law is in effect."

"The Protector is correct," Vimra O'Sianto said calmly. "Prince Armeo is our legal leader, and his Protectors make it possible for him to rule by proxy."

"I concur," Amereena Beqq said.

"From a diplomatic point of view, I advise not to cause any upheaval by provoking monarchy-loyal Gantharians, which I judge is the majority." Dahlia spoke with a firm, convincing tone. "They have waited long for their freedom, and just as long for their beloved royal family and its protectors. One has become the symbol for the others, and vice versa. If you pull the O'Sarals from the equation, you're making it virtually impossible for this process to succeed."

Kellen looked gratefully at her mother-in-law. Dahlia's strong voice, her innate authority, spoke of the matter at hand and made it all clear and reasonable.

"Very well." The first man who'd spoken up sat down, a huff in his voice.

"I think we have reached as far as we ever could have hoped for today. I do not think we should risk being out after curfew. The

Onotharians are fewer in numbers and focus on skirmishes with the resistance, but if they knew of our meeting, or found us gathered like this, especially after dark…" Vimra O'Sianto spread her hands in a gesture both familiar and alien to Kellen. She hadn't prayed in a long time, but the gestures and murmured words came naturally to her after all.

After the prayer the participants began to leave one by one. Some had their own guards; others merely disappeared into the night. When it was time for them all to leave, she received a comm signal from the *Circinus*.

"Todd to O'Dal. Come in."

"O'Dal here." Kellen answered quickly, stepping away from the others.

"Kellen, please report back to the ship immediately."

Jeremiah Todd never used her given name when they were on duty. Something was wrong.

"What is this about, Captain?"

"Kellen, please."

"Tell me." Kellen was not about to give in. Cold shivers were already tumbling down her spine.

"Kellen, it's Rae. Cloaked missiles attacked the *Paesina*."

"And the ship?" Kellen found it nearly impossible to breathe. She drew in air, but it seemed empty of oxygen.

"Destroyed."

"Jeremiah…" Her voice was unrecognizable, and suddenly Kellen felt strong arms around her. Owena stood next to her, one arm around her waist, the other around Dahlia.

"Is it Rae? What about Ewan?" Dahlia spoke tersely and her eyes betrayed nothing yet.

"Diplo—Dahlia? Jeremiah here. We don't know your daughter's status. They've lost contact with her and the others aboard the *Paesina*. Admiral Ewan Jacelon is safe. He is heading the search for the crewmembers. Several escape pods have been sighted drifting in the debris field."

"I have to go back." Kellen was ready to return to the ship instantly and turn it around. If not the whole ship, she was not beyond stealing a shuttle and heading back.

"Kellen. Kellen!" Amereena Beqq shook her arm gently. "Let them do their job searching. We need to do this. It's what every single person who is part of this war effort subscribes to and is ready to risk their lives for. Come on, Kellen. Let's get you back to the ship so you can find out all the details as soon as we get more word. You too, Dahlia."

"Very well." Kellen straightened up, unable to face anyone. She would break down if she glimpsed any of the sympathy she felt surrounding her. "Let's go."

Kellen strode to where they had left their hover cars and jumped inside the nearest one. She waited impatiently as Owena supervised two marines who were scanning the vehicle for signs of sabotage.

"Please be all right," Kellen murmured. Glancing at Dahlia sitting slumped, looking nearly broken, in a chair behind her, Kellen took her hand. "They're going to find her and she's going to be all right."

"Kellen. I can't lose her."

Oh, stars and skies, neither can I. I can't live without her. How could I?

CHAPTER SEVENTEEN

Weiss, listen to me. He's up to something. It has nothing to do with any of us blowing our cover. It has everything to do with the fact that he's jealous of you and fears that Podmer relies more and more on you for the important assignments." Madisyn gestured emphatically where she stood in their quarters. Distraught, almost panicky, she looked expectantly at Weiss.

"I really don't think you need to worry. I'm not afraid of Struyen." Weiss tried to reassure Madisyn without sounding condescending.

"It's not just him!" Now frustration and anger had entered Madisyn's tone, and she had begun to tap her foot. "Didn't you hear me? Struyen was talking about you with at least three other people. You can bet that these four in turn have loyal buddies among the crew."

"They all fear Podmer."

"Maybe not enough." Suddenly subdued, Madisyn sat down on her bed. "I just don't understand why you can't see the danger. Not only are we on a dangerous mission, but now it's become personal."

Weiss flinched. Stars and skies, it already was, and not because of Struyen.

"Madisyn, please, trust me when I say that I'm used to taking care of myself. I've done that all my life."

"I'm sure you have, but that was before...before..." Madisyn looked down at her fists.

"Before what?"

"Before there was a war." It was obvious Madisyn had meant to say something else. "This is such an intense situation, us constantly having to keep our guard up. Having someone with a personal agenda breathing down your neck might distract you."

"I don't distract easily." *And I lie so well.*

"You're pretty confident in your super-humanoid strengths and abilities, aren't you?" Madisyn was starting to look angry.

"Hey, I appreciate that you worry about me. I really do. I just want you to realize that it's not necessary."

"And if it was me? Let's say Struyen had found out the truth about me and was getting ready to either expose me or disable me." Madisyn glowered at Weiss.

The thought made the knots in Weiss's stomach turn to ice. "I'd kill him before he even got that far," she said, her voice flat.

"But you'd be concerned."

"Of course I would. You—" Not seeing the trap until she stepped right into it, Weiss sighed deeply. "All right. All right. I understand why you worry. What do you want me to do?"

"You have to leave the *Salaceos*. Have Jacelon pull you out." Madisyn pressed her lips together, but it was obvious they were trembling.

"Leave? I can't do that." Not until the words were out did Weiss realize how true they were.

"Sure you can. You can tell Jacelon you've been compromised. I can carry on the last part if you give me a detailed description of what was said during the meeting with the Onotharians."

"I can't leave. I *won't* leave you." Weiss moved closer and sat down opposite Madisyn, taking her clenched hands in hers. "That's not negotiable."

"Why not?"

"I had planned to leave, but now I realize how impossible it would be for me to abandon you among these thugs. You hate them, and you have good reason to. In fact, you have good reason to hate *me*."

"What are you talking about?" Madisyn frowned, relaxing her hands and turning them inside Weiss's grip, palm against palm, "Why would I hate you?"

Her heart hammering, Weiss tried to figure out a way to explain that wouldn't turn Madisyn against her forever. "You know how everybody has heard of Weiss Kyakh aboard this ship."

"Yes, that was a brilliant stunt on Jacelon's part."

"No stunt." The words made Weiss's throat hurt. "I *am* Weiss Kyakh."

"What? Well, of course, but—"

"Listen to me. Jacelon drafted me into doing this mission after she captured me."

"What are you talking about? I know your fake backstory says you're this big-shot mercenary. It's part of the plan, the ruse to make you part of Podmer's inner circle." Madisyn had begun to shiver, and Weiss knew she was beginning to backtrack every conversation they'd had, everything Jacelon had told her.

"We didn't fabricate a background," Weiss said hollowly. "I'm Weiss Kyakh. Until a while back, I ran my own operation, offering my talents for anyone with enough wealth to pay me." Simultaneously filled with dread and relief, she tried to hold on to Madisyn's hands. "I actually was part of a mission to help an Onotharian dignitary escape and helped him kidnap Jacelon's mother."

"You're crazy. Why would you say something like this? Why would Jacelon place her mother's kidnapper in a situation where she could easily escape and—" Madisyn stopped talking for a moment. She seemed to be holding her breath before she finally spoke. "You couldn't, could you? They had to have something, a chip perhaps, inserted in you. And that's why I received an order to keep a close eye on you. I figured they needed me to keep you safe." A joyless laughter erupted from Madisyn and only stopped as she pressed her hand over her mouth.

"I had a chip. I disabled it." Weiss's tongue felt like a wad of cotton in her mouth. "So I could leave. I'd planned to."

"What's keeping you?" Madisyn pushed Weiss's hands away, scooting backward on her bed, out of reach.

"You. You're keeping me. I could never leave you."

"That's just perfect. A thug offering to keep me safe from other thugs." A single, deep sob shook her body.

"I know. I'm all you hate, all you despise." Weiss felt as if her heart was ripped out and shredded between her ribs. "The facts remain. Even if you probably think Struyen wants to get rid of me, I'm not going anywhere."

"You disabled your chip, I'm not sure how, but I suspect it has to do with that time when I found you passed out on the floor. And, oh, stars, I was an idiot. How I worried." Madisyn pushed her fingers into her blond curls and tugged at them. "I just can't believe I didn't see this. I just don't understand. You said pirates killed your mother. Was that a lie too?"

"No. That was all true."

"How the hell can you become as despicable, as hateful, as the people that killed your own mother? How can you be so cold?" Madisyn's voice escalated until it broke.

"It was all I knew. I lived with pirates from age ten until I was old enough to create my own future. By the time I learned what happened to my mother, I didn't *care*. I was angry, I was cynical, and I had nothing to live for. I knew only one route to being safe—creating my own wealth. I started small and planned big. Nobody would ever be in a position to hurt me again, to *use* me again. Nobody."

"So you became the user. The abuser."

"Better than to have it done to you."

"And then Jacelon captured you, and now she's using you." Madisyn laughed joylessly.

"Yes."

"You must hate that. And everything, and everybody here. Damn, I'm more naïve than I thought. That'll teach me to be so trusting."

"Jacelon needed the job done."

"And when we're done?"

"You won't have to see me again. I'll be very far away."

Madisyn's face was all angles and her lips a fine line. "I don't care where. Just keep your distance from now on."

"Don't beat yourself up about not knowing who I am. How could you know? We fed you a story."

"You're forgetting something. I do know about *pirates*," Madisyn spat. "First I knew the ones who killed the girl I was and forced my grief-stricken parents to turn me into a freak. Then I knew what the pirates did to my parents years later. So I would say I know plenty."

"You're right. You do know far too much about piracy from the victim's angle." Weiss could have tried to justify herself, saying she had never deliberately or directly gone after civilians, which was true in a sense. Her past actions had resulted in major collateral damage, so she was responsible for the loss of life among innocent civilians. Suddenly she was back in the Disian village on Corma, where her spacecraft had crashed in a residential area, killing and injuring countless people. The stench of burning wood and melted metal, and the sound of panicked voices screaming for help made her gasp and slump back on her bed against the pillow.

"I wish you would leave." The words came slowly, but with emphasis, as Madisyn pushed at her covers. She slid in between her sheets and pulled them up to her chin. "I wish you would just follow through with your plans to double-cross Jacelon and *disappear.*"

"I can't. I will see this mission through, because I refuse to abandon you to fend for yourself among these people. Once we're done, when we have enough intel to send back to the admiral, we'll both leave. I'll personally escort you back to Guild Nation, and if you still don't want me around…then I'll leave."

"I don't understand why you're suddenly so adamant about staying. You were obviously dead set on stealing away just a day or two ago. I won't tell you again. I don't need you."

Sheer raw pain made Weiss feel like her head would implode. "I know. And I won't tell you again. I'm not budging no matter how many times you tell me to. Lights out." She couldn't bear to see the hatred and hurt on Madisyn's face a moment longer. "I wish…" Weiss stopped herself, mortified at how close she was to making a complete and utter fool of herself. Madisyn loathed her and everything she stood for. *Had* stood for. So much had changed, and the Weiss that would have easily thrown someone like Madisyn to the wolves seemed to have vanished.

"What do you wish?" Madisyn sounded gruff in a way Weiss wouldn't have thought possible only moments ago.

"Nothing." Weiss pulled her own covers close around her. She was suddenly cold all the way through. "Just that things were…different."

❖

Madisyn lay awake for a long time. She could hear the rustling of bed linen as Weiss tossed and turned. Trying to understand the implications of what Weiss had told her, she knew sleep would be a rare commodity that night. Weiss Kyakh was really the pirate and mercenary that the doctored file Jacelon had sent her implied. Madisyn remembered being quite impressed with such a well-constructed background. What a fool she'd been, and how gullible. No doubt, Weiss had laughed at her naiveté.

Weiss was someone Madisyn had come to rely on, to trust, and—yes, care about. Knowing that love would never be for her, Madisyn had come close to nourishing hope for at least some physical closeness. Weiss never acted like Madisyn's biosynthetic makeup was an issue. Given that Weiss was obviously skilled at deception on a large scale, of course she must have wanted to lull Madisyn into believing that she cared for her. Now Weiss was trying to sell her the idea that she had lost her mother, in the same way Madisyn had lost her parents. This only served to twist the laser knife and cut off any chance of acceptance and sympathy on Madisyn's part. Clearly, Weiss saw this mission as a way to escape from a life sentence in an SC prison. Stars and skies, she'd kidnapped the mother of an admiral. Madisyn remembered something about Jacelon's mother being a diplomat and her father a high-ranking senior officer. That would give anyone a free pass to an off-world, MAXSEC prison even in a humane society like the SC.

Madisyn buried her face in her pillow, desperate not to cry. One thing her biosynthetic body didn't do well was tears. Every teardrop caused physical discomfort, and if she gave in to her sorrow now, she would cry half the night. Weiss wasn't worth it. She was a lying, murdering, backstabbing pirate. She was right too. Madisyn did hate pirates, and her, more than anything.

Suddenly raising her head off her pillow, Madisyn sharpened her hearing further. Had that been a sob or a moan coming from Weiss? Hardly. If it had been, it was only meant to manipulate her.

An annoying inner voice tried to ask what motive Weiss would have to stay with her and finish the assignment. In doing so, she risked being exposed. Struyen and his cohorts could go after her, and if they were compromised, she would be killed. It didn't make sense unless she really did care, despite her sordid past. Recoiling, Madisyn shied away from such a thought. Pirates didn't care about anything but getting their grubby hands on other people's wealth and power. Weiss most likely saw an advantage in this mission, a way of turning the tables on the SC and Podmer so she'd gain all the profits.

Another deep sigh from Weiss's bed made Madisyn turn her back and pull one pillow on top of her head. She turned her hearing down to its lowest setting and pressed the pillow tight to her ear. Perhaps if she cut out any sound from a clearly distraught Weiss, she might be able to catch some sleep. Something inside her, something weak, or perhaps merely far too soft, suggested that she reach out to Weiss.

Madisyn immediately slammed this embryo of a notion. She had to find her way back to the way things were before Weiss Kyakh stepped aboard the *Salaceos*. Until then, Madisyn had done well and lived a fulfilling life as a successful operative for the Guild Nation and the SC. She ignored the little voice that said it might have been easier in many ways, but it was also far, far lonelier.

Chapter Eighteen

Kellen strode through the corridors of the *Circinus*, the heels of her tall black boots hammering against the plating. She forced her fear, all-encompassing and overwhelming, into a small corner of her mind, where she had constructed a mental door, and locked it. The news from the battle that had cost Rae her ship, and, stars forbid, her life, were still sketchy. After Kellen spent most of her night on the bridge with Jeremiah Todd and Dahlia, waiting to hear one way or the other, the ship's physician had finally forced her to try for an hour's sleep.

At first, Kellen reacted with anger and resentment, but when Ayahliss and Dahlia promised to go with her, said that all she had to do was rest on the couch in Dahlia's quarters, she relented. Dahlia was obviously nearing complete exhaustion and wouldn't rest unless she did.

Ayahliss and Reena ended up joining them, and all four of them took turns sleeping for about an hour each. Curled up in two armchairs and on the couch, covered in SC-issued blankets, they had murmured among themselves and rested as best they could.

Jeremiah paged them just as Kellen was ready to return to the bridge. He had news from Ewan Jacelon. Quickly rousing Dahlia, Kellen asked Ayahliss and Reena to escort Dahlia to the bridge. Kellen had to go right away or she might lose what little calm she still possessed.

Entering the conference room right next to the bridge, she saw her father-in-law's bruised and battered face on the viewscreen.

"Kellen," he said, his bloodshot eyes brightening marginally as he saw her. "Dahlia?"

"She'll be right here." Kellen swallowed something bitter and swollen in her throat. "Rae?"

"Still no word." Ewan stroked a hand across his face. "There's so much debris, and the released antimatter—"

"Antimatter?" Kellen's blood chilled until her fingers seemed numb. "Someone used antimatter in the battle?"

"Yes. Rae fired antimatter-capped missiles in order to keep the command central vessel safe." Ewan's expression changed, his eyes fastening on something behind Kellen. "Dahlia. I…" His voice failed him.

"I heard. Antimatter." Dahlia stopped next to Kellen, placing an arm around her waist for support, or perhaps to offer support. Behind them, Ayahliss and Reena stood quietly waiting. "Are you all right, Ewan?"

"Yes. A few bruises."

"Have you been seen?"

"Not yet. No time." Ewan's short-cropped words told Kellen not to debate his decision to not see a physician yet. "Fortunately we have recovered sixty-five percent of the crew and have monitored more life signs in escape pods."

"What about the *Paesina*?"

"Debris. Some larger parts, but nothing that sustains life support."

"Oh, Gods." Dahlia's fingers pinched Kellen's side.

"One larger escape pod from the *Paesina*'s infirmary is intact. We heard from Dr. Gemma Meyer. She's unharmed and they are being towed to a rescue vessel as we speak."

"Gemma. That's great news." Kellen liked the CMO she'd known since the day Rae took her into custody at the Gamma VI space station. "Sensors?" Kellen struggled to keep the door to her fear firmly locked.

"Another promising thing. We are reading scattered life signs pretty much everywhere around the blast site."

"Rae can be one of them." Dahlia sounded like she was praying. "She's resourceful. Fast."

Kellen drew a trembling breath. She also knew that Rae would give her own life to save another's. She would surrender her deep-space survival suit to a junior crewmember, just because she'd consider it the right thing to do.

"That's right, Dahlia," Ewan said, his eyes kind and sorrowful. "I'll get back to the bridge and see what's happened. I'll relay news to you as soon as I know anything."

"Thank you. The moment you hear something." Dahlia shuddered. "Please."

"The moment."

The image of Ewan flickered and turned into the SC Unification of Planets crest.

"Kellen. Kellen?" Dahlia shook Kellen's arm gently. "We have to keep working as well, or we'll drive ourselves crazy."

"I concur. I need to work off some…energy, before the next meeting. I'll be in the gym and then I'll meet you planetside. This time, I've arranged for the security detail to be twice as large as the other day."

"Yes, Protector," Dahlia said with a wan smile. "I don't blame you for using extra caution. We do seem to have a knack for getting into slimy circumstances, don't we?"

"We do." The understatement made Kellen smile, very faintly and only because she knew this was what Dahlia hoped for and needed. "Ayahliss, will you spar with me?"

"Of course." Ayahliss bowed politely, as custom dictated.

"I'll meet you at the gym."

Going by her now-empty quarters, Kellen changed into her Ruby Red gan'thet leather suit. She pulled her hair down, the familiar movements somehow calming as she arranged her long, blond hair in a tight whip of a braid. She tied the leather ribbon so tight it pulled at her hairline, but the small discomfort only seemed to add a tiny sense of normalcy.

Kellen tucked the gan'thet rods under her arm and left her quarters. Halfway to the lift, she wondered if it was her outfit or her expression that made ensigns and crewmen practically become one with the bulkhead as she passed. She rode the lift down to deck four where the gyms were located. She was just warming up when Ayahliss walked inside. Also dressed in a Ruby Red suit, she looked confident and expectant.

"Warm up," Kellen said, and began a series of solo exercises. She whirled through the air, one leg stretched out in front of her, the other bent. She landed, agile as a feline, and twirled on her toes while crouching. Using the muscles in her calves, she pushed from the floor and rolled to her left, producing her rods in a lethal cross. She repeated the two exercises until she could execute them perfectly.

"I'm ready, Protector." Ayahliss stood in a respectful position, baring the inside of her wrists as she held out her rods.

Kellen approached her, inspecting the suit and the rods, and eventually Ayahliss's expression. "Good. Let's start with the *veya mo'desh* pattern."

"Veya mo'desh pattern? That is for beginners." Ayahliss looked disdainful.

"Beginners or not, let's go."

Kellen assumed the position that characterized veya mo'desh: the left rod in an offensive pose just above her head, the right diagonally in front of her chest. Planting her feet with one leg bent and the other extended behind her, she shifted her weight until she was ready. Ayahliss mimicked her pose, her eyes shimmering.

"Gajesta!" Kellen called out, her voice dark. *Fight!* The ancient battle cry echoed in the gym as well as in Kellen's head. She moved fast, with Ayahliss following lithely as she pressed forward. She jumped and gained momentum as she quickly sidestepped Ayahliss and hooked one rod behind her knee. She went down in a roll, avoided Ayahliss's rods by a hair, and came up behind her to her left. Ayahliss pivoted, her leg sweeping just above Kellen's knees, which gave Kellen the chance to use her rods to trap her left leg.

The furious growl from Ayahliss when she hit the mat made Kellen release a feral smile. She pounced onto Ayahliss, straddling her chest and locking her arms with her knees and crossing the rods over her neck. *"Syuve!" Surrender!*

"No." Ayahliss tried several gan'thet patterns to throw Kellen off, but when Kellen merely tightened the hold with her rods and frowned warningly, she relented, lowering her rods at her side. "Syuve."

"Good. Again." Kellen jumped up, and for the next thirty minutes, she relentlessly pushed through a rigorous training session that had them both drenched in sweat and gasping for air. Heading for the showers and recyclers, Ayahliss looked cautious rather than furious at having been defeated nine times out of ten.

"Yes?" Kellen said when Ayahliss looked hesitantly at her.

"Vanquished them all, Kellen?" Her eyes glazing over, Ayahliss resiliently did not acknowledge the tears that formed at the corners of her eyes.

"What are you talking about?"

"Your demons. Your fear. Your anger." Ayahliss raised her chin. "Any or all."

"You're not making sense—"

"Yes, I am. Rae is missing and you plow a new ditch in the gym mat with me. I haven't seen that look in your eyes since Dahlia was missing. This is even worse. Don't shut us out, Kellen."

"I'm not shutting anyone out." Kellen felt her back go rigid enough to crack at the slightest touch.

"Perhaps you don't see it that way, but you are."

"And if I am?" Kellen snapped. "I have to function. I have to carry on with the program that will fortify the Gantharian interim government and keep Gantharat free in the future. There are treaties, contracts, laws, rules, regulations—"

"And Rae."

Kellen felt like a plasma-pulse burst had hit her. "H'rea deasavh! Yes. Of course there is Rae. And Armeo. I haven't even told him yet. I…can't."

Ayahliss pushed off her Ruby Red suit in one flowing movement and entered a cleansing tube. "You shouldn't tell him anything until we know. You're doing the right thing."

Kellen followed Ayahliss's example and stood in the cleansing tube until the humming sound began to claw at her taut nerve strings. She turned the setting to anti-static, relieved when her hair settled in soft tresses along her back. Outside, Ayahliss waited, half-dressed already. During the silence, Kellen programmed a new SC uniform at the recycler and ran her precious Ruby Red through for cleansing only. She fastened the harness and belt harder than usual, as if she needed the tightness to hold her body and soul together. If only she could do something about her shattering heart.

CHAPTER NINETEEN

The debris field was dense with what was left of fifteen disintegrated spaceships. The light from the distant sun glimmered in jagged metal parts, making it difficult to focus. Even short-range sensor readings came back inconclusive as the antimatter corrupted the data.

Jacelon moaned and shifted in the pilot's seat. She was still partially in her survival space suit, its lime green sleeves tied around her waist. The makeshift bandage underneath them had begun to seep, and she cursed the fact that the wound was too deep for a layman to try a derma fuser.

Jacelon glanced behind her on the floor, concerned if she had restrained the enemy enough. Facing the instruments again, she tried getting the sensors online, worried for her crew, especially the two young ensigns she'd pulled with her as she'd been the last to leave the bridge. She had more or less dragged them by the collar, as they seemed overcome with debilitating fear, and ordered them into their survival gear. Pushing them to the airlock, she didn't have time to decompress properly; she simply opened the hatch and hurled them into space.

Behind them, the *Paesina* rolled and shook when secondary explosions tore through her. The cloaked missile had hit her belly, which made it possible to evacuate the upper decks, but now the consequence of the weapon was obvious. *Paesina* was in her death throes and Jacelon could do nothing to save her. She floated in space, among debris and fighting aircraft. Her communicator only produced white noise, no matter which frequency she tried. An emergency beacon was automatically set to go off on her survival suit, transmitting her coordinates, but it would take a while before anyone found them. A human body was very small in the vastness of space.

Jacelon gasped as a large object, part of the hull of a ship, hurtled toward her. It hit her midsection despite her effort to curl up, separating her from the others. A searing pain spread all over her abdomen, and she moaned as she hugged herself. Afraid that it had torn her suit, Jacelon checked the readings on the small computer on her left sleeve; to her relief, the suit was intact. Still moving away from her former position because of the momentum from the collision, she tried to locate the others.

Jacelon kept checking her computer as she floated through space. She couldn't do anything to stop or slow down. The pain in her side became a slow throb, but she was bleeding. She could feel blood seep around the wound in her suit.

Suddenly she stopped, her entire body flattened against the hull of a small vessel, also drifting. She fumbled for something to hold on to. Small ridges along the hull allowed her to do so, and she dragged herself along it. She searched for an airlock, and only when she had slid all along the side of the ship did she realize it was an Onotharian shuttle.

Not about to panic, Jacelon knew this was her chance. If the ship was drifting, that meant the crew was injured or dead, or the ship was irreparably damaged, and she was about to find out.

The airlock was half-open, and Jacelon squeezed inside, mindful to not tear her suit. She pushed the sensor that would normally close the hatch, but nothing happened. Groaning, she pushed the manual lever. The pain in her abdomen increased exponentially when she tugged at the handle, but the hatch closed and a rewarding thud meant it was locked into place. Fortunately the subroutines for repressurizing the airlock were not compromised. Jacelon still kept her survival suit on as she checked her computer. Cautiously she opened the hatch leading into the shuttle. Relieved that the shuttle's life-support system was operating normally, she peered inside. She was unarmed and had no idea what to expect.

Two Onotharians lay on the floor, seemingly unconscious, and one other was slumped at the helm in the front. Removing her helmet, Jacelon looked for something to restrain the Onotharians with, in case they woke up.

Eventually she cut through their own belts with their laser knives, fastening each one around their hands and ankles behind their backs. It was impossible to move the large man from the helm. Jacelon merely pushed him onto the ops station and rolled him onto the floor between it and the chair. She had disarmed all of them and kept their sidearms on her lap as she sat in the pilot's seat. She figured she could keep an eye on the unconscious man on the floor and control him.

Jacelon pushed the survival suit down, quickly examining her injury. Now when she was in a place with gravity, blood was slowly seeping down her legs, saturating her uniform. Not about to waste time, she rolled the sleeves tight and tied them around her. She winced as the pain spiked and took deep trembling breaths. Turning toward the console, she ran a short diagnostic, grateful she knew enough Onotharian to operate the computer. She was surprised to find the shuttle fully functional and initiated the startup sequence. Moving very slowly, she steered the shuttle back to where she had become separated from the two ensigns just after the blast.

Sensors were hard to read, but eventually she picked up two life signs twelve hundred meters ahead. She maximized the magnification on the small screen embedded in the viewport and saw the two figures clasped together, drifting.

"Admiral Jacelon to any SC officers and personnel, come in." She tried her communicator again. "Admiral Jacelon here. Respond."

"Ensign…berg here. Drifting in grid…three-three-" The young voice was husky and the connection kept breaking up.

"I have you in my vision, Ensign. Is that you, Hallberg?"

"Aye, ma'am." The relief in his voice was evident.

"I'm coming in with an Onotharian shuttle. I'll try to come to a full stop close to you. What's your status?"

"I'm here with Dgobdo, Admiral…unconscious…ding onto…"

"You're breaking up, Hallberg. Perhaps I'll hear you better as I approach. Hang on. Keep an open comm channel." Jacelon steered the shuttle cautiously and as slowly as possible, between debris and wreckage. She saw bodies, in SC uniforms and Onotharian, floating dead without their survival gear. Her jaws worked and she willed herself to relax her facial muscles. A few minutes later, she tried talking with Ensign Hallberg again. "Jacelon to Hallberg. Do you see the shuttle yet?"

"Yes, ma'am, I think so. A sleek Onotharian shuttle is approaching on a trajectory five degrees to my right."

"Good. That's me, Hallberg." Relieved that the sound was better, Jacelon debated sending out a distress call, but hesitated, since long-distance communication could still be compromised. She might attract help from Onotharians rather than her own people. The SC had won this fight, and they were performing a grid search for survivors. Jacelon knew the SC vessels might fire on this Onotharian ship rather than render assistance, as they might suspect an ambush. Nobody would put it past the Onotharians to fake a distress call. "I see your beacon on short-range sensors now."

Jacelon began to slow the shuttle, squinting through the debris for the lime green suits. The scattered parts of what had been hulls and decks slammed against the Onotharian shuttle, and she realized she was still going too fast. She set the controls to reverse the engines. Outside, two small green dots appeared and grew quickly.

"I see you, Hallberg."

"Good. I'm not doing too well, Admiral. Dgobdo is…I think he's dying, ma'am."

"I'm almost there, Hallberg. Stay focused. Listen to me. Have you attached Dgobdo's harness to yours?"

"Affirmative."

"This shuttle seems to have a rescue arm. I'll deploy it once I'm close enough." Jacelon maneuvered the shuttle into position and punched in the command for the arm to move out. Deceptively thin, it emerged from underneath the airlock she'd entered through. She had a good view of where to steer the arm from a visual sensor at its end. She extended it toward Hallberg and Dgobdo, gradually, to not knock them farther away. When she was almost there, one of the green figures reached out and grabbed it.

"Good, Hallberg. Now attach your harness to the arm, if you can."

"Just pull us in, Admiral. I have a good grip. I don't dare let go."

"All right. Let me know if you start to slip."

"Aye, ma'am."

Painstakingly slow, when she wanted only to hurry up, Jacelon pulled the two men toward the Onotharian shuttle. Beads of sweat broke out on her forehead and upper lip. She also experienced shivers, which wasn't a good sign. If she was already running a fever, her injuries were worse than she initially thought. She didn't dare take her eyes away from the monitor and the controls. In a moment she would have Hallberg and Dgobdo safely aboard, and then she would attend better to her wounds.

"Nearly there, Admiral." Hallberg's voice sounded clearer. "Another three meters to go."

"Good." Jacelon pulled them in to the hull and heard the faint thud as the arm folded into its slot. The hissing sound of the airlock recompressing meant she could finally relax. She stood, suddenly light-headed and unsteady, and held on to the bulkhead as she walked over to the hatch. When the readings stated it was safe, she pulled the lever and opened it. Inside, one man, Dgobdo, was lying on his back, his helmet still on. Next to him, Hallberg sat and removed his helmet. "Good to see you again, Ensign."

"Admiral. Thank you for coming back for us."

"Anytime. How's he doing?" She motioned at Dgobdo.

"Not sure, ma'am."

"We need to get him inside. Can you help me move him over the threshold?" Jacelon had no way of knowing what lifting Dgobdo would do to her injuries, but they had to try.

Together, they hauled the listless ensign into the shuttle.

"Admiral? These are Onotharians." Hallberg looked shocked, pointing at the three unconscious men.

"Yes. I found them this way. Not sure what knocked them out. They haven't moved since I got aboard."

"We need to secure the third one over by the helm." Hallberg pulled off his harness with a grimace of pain. "Here, you can use this…" He slumped back, losing consciousness.

"Hallberg? Hallberg? Oh, damn!" Jacelon took the harness and made sure Hallberg was comfortable next to Dgobdo before she tied the third Onotharian's arms and legs together behind his back. "There."

Her vision fading, Jacelon barely made it back to the pilot's seat. She closed her eyes and rubbed her temples. She couldn't allow herself to pass out now. She had to keep searching for her crewmembers, unless the rescue ships took one look at her and blew her out of the water. This thought made her pull herself together.

She was going to have to reconfigure the shuttle's identity, make it look obvious that it was under SC control. Pushing her hair behind her ears, Jacelon began to enter commands, hoping it wouldn't take the search-and-rescue units long to find them. Her time was running out, and if she loosened the makeshift bandage, she might lose what little blood pressure she had. *I'm trying, Kellen. I'm really trying.*

CHAPTER TWENTY

Weiss supervised the transportation of the ore from the mezzanine, careful not to attract attention by staring openly at Madisyn. They had barely talked the last two days, and Weiss didn't like how torn up she was about the entire situation. She, who had turned cutting her losses into a fine art, was now lovesick like a youngster, devastated after Madisyn's rejection. What was she thinking? She wasn't exactly a good catch.

Madisyn had begun to blossom under her attention. Madisyn, who never thought anyone would ever find her desirable if they knew the whole truth about her, had to feel so betrayed. Well, it wasn't Weiss's idea to keep her true identity from her. She stalked along the mezzanine, cursing Jacelon for putting her in this position. Why couldn't that damn woman just have sent her to a maximum-security prison?

"Kyakh! Over here!" Struyen broke her miserable train of thought. "We could use an additional pair of hands."

"You can manage," Weiss shouted back. "Podmer made me supervisor."

"Ah, come on. You're just too fancy, too good to do honest work, aren't you?"

Weiss couldn't believe her ears. She started laughing, which made Struyen turn dark red with rage.

"What the hell's so damn funny?" he hissed.

"A pirate claiming he's doing honest work." More laughter erupted and Weiss had to wipe at the corners of her eyes. "That's rich." She could see several other crewmen who found it amusing, but who also knew better than to laugh out loud at Struyen.

"You won't be laughing much longer," Struyen said in a dark voice. "And once Podmer sees who he really can rely on—"

"Yeah, yeah, get back to what you were doing, Struyen, and quit wasting time." Weiss knew she was antagonizing the man even more, but it felt good. Right now, she didn't care very much what happened to her, and the only reason she hadn't stolen the shuttle and taken off to lick her wounds was her feelings for Madisyn. She was still determined not to leave Madisyn alone with these idiots. Whether she liked it or not, Madisyn would have to put up with Weiss keeping her safe.

"Everything going well?" Podmer said from behind, startling her.

"Yes, Captain." Weiss nodded down at the crewmembers hauling the ore onto small sledges. "Are we going to use shuttles, or…?"

"No, we're going to dock the ships, well into the asteroid ring."

"Ah, that will make it virtually impossible for any patrols to spot us on sensors."

"Exactly." Podmer smiled, looking pleased. "I admit that M'Aldovar character unsettled me, but he's paying twice the going rate for davic crystals, so I'm not really complaining."

"Twice, eh? Good. Will that mean any bonus for us, sir?" It would be in her character to be greedy, she thought.

"At least for some of the senior crew." Podmer shrugged and adjusted his immaculately tailored jacket. "Looking to set some aside so you can get back to being your own boss again, Kyakh?"

"Something like that, sir."

"Can't blame you. Once you've captained your own ship, it's not easy to take orders from someone else. You've been quite good about it. I appreciate how you've cooperated."

"Thank you. I'm all for making some extra credits."

"And so you will if this goes smoothly." Podmer placed a fat hand on her shoulder and Weiss had to use all her willpower not to break his wrist. "Let me know once you have it all ready to go."

"Aye, Captain."

He strode down the mezzanine and out through the door leading to the corridor. Weiss followed his figure with narrowing eyes. She loathed the man and the way he treated his crew. She was just as ruthless as he was, but she had kept a tight ship, with clear and just treatment of her crew. They had, with few exceptions, respected her, even liked her.

Weiss glanced down and saw that the men would be ready in a few hours. She didn't have much time. She had to contact Jacelon about this transaction. If an Onotharian general was so adamant about this ore, it wasn't hard to figure out that the SC needed to know. Madisyn might have contacted Jacelon already, but Weiss was sure Madisyn hadn't told Jacelon that she was aware of Weiss's true background. Sighing deeply, Weiss knew she might as well be up front about that too. But she wouldn't tell Jacelon that she had disabled the chip. If Jacelon found out about that, she might extract Weiss immediately, and who would look out for Madisyn?

Weiss pulled out a small device from her inner pocket. Having taken all night to construct it from parts she'd come across over the weeks aboard the *Salaceos*, she had managed to mirror the settings from Madisyn's computer, including the encrypted transmission software. It would need something to boost it with, and fortunately she was standing next to a vast piece of bulkhead that would serve well as an amplifier.

Placing the device on the wall, Weiss pulled an adhesive from another pocket and attached it. She put in Madisyn's password, something it hadn't taken her very long to memorize, and hoped for a signal. She kept a wary eye on the men and women working six meters below her. No one was paying any attention to her, but she needed to make sure and be quick.

"Weiss Kyakh for Admiral Jacelon, emergency-emergency-emergency, over."

Static hummed and she tried again. "Weiss Kyakh here for Admiral Jacelon, emergency, over."

Static mixed with waves of whistling made Weiss worry that someone might overhear. Still below, crewmembers hollered to each other and made even more noise. So far, nobody looked up at her.

"Weiss Kyakh for Admiral Jace—"

"Admiral Jacelon here. Who is this?" a gruff male voice responded, making Weiss flinch.

"I need to talk to Admiral Rae Jacelon." Weiss's head reeled. A male admiral Jacelon. That had to be Jacelon's father. Dahlia Jacelon's husband. Oh, stars and skies, the husband of her latest kidnap victim. Wonderful.

"Who is this?" The man offered no explanations.

"Admiral Jacelon, my name is Weiss Kyakh, and your daughter sent me on a mission."

"Kyakh." The contempt was obvious, but he didn't cut the connection. "Go on."

"I have important information. It's vital that you put her through."

"It's impossible. You have to give your information to me."

Weiss hesitated. Surely Jacelon's father, an SC officer with even higher rank than his daughter, would be able to do something about Podmer's plans.

"All right, sir. I'm currently aboard the *Salaceos*, a ship belonging to—"

"Podmer. Yes, I know the background. Go on."

"All right. He is about to trade davic crystal and intel obtained by attacking the SC cruise ship *Koenigin* to the Onotharians. To a General Trax M'Aldovar."

"Did—did you say *Trax* M'Aldovar?" Ewan Jacelon sounded incredulous. "Impossible. My daughter-in-law killed him."

"Severely disabled him, yes, Admiral, and he relies on a ventilator to breathe, as well as a hover chair for moving around, but I guarantee, Trax M'Aldovar survived."

"This is bad news." Ewan Jacelon's voice was cold and flat. "Where is your position?"

"Transmitting that as we speak, Admiral." Weiss sent the grid readings. "Just inside the Gantharat system, as you can tell. A dense asteroid belt around an uninhabited planet."

"All right. I will relay your information to the team we have deployed closest to you."

"I need further orders on how to proceed, since this transaction is going down now, and for all I know, M'Aldovar might disappear as soon as the crystals are in his possession."

"He must be stopped at all cost, Kyakh. I repeat. Stop him by any means necessary."

"Aye, sir." Weiss flinched as a sound over by the door startled her. "Got to go, Admiral. Kyakh out." She snatched the device from the bulkhead and tucked it inside her jacket. Two of Struyen's buddies entered, sauntering toward her with sly grins on their faces.

"Hey, Kyakh." The taller of the two, clearly of Onotharian descent, his eyes narrowly placed and with an unpleasant yellow tone to them, raised his hand.

"What are you doing up here?" Kyakh spoke quietly, something any member of her own crew would have recognized as a warning sign.

"Just enjoying the view," the other pirate replied, eyeing her with blatant desire.

"Get back to your duty stations. You are both needed in the cargo bay." Even and cool, Weiss's obvious lack of dismay or fear seemed to get through to the taller man.

"Why don't we enjoy the view—together?" the second pirate said, and pulled out something resembling a martial arts baton. "My friend Shafas here and I have something to discuss with you."

"Struyen isn't going to take the fall for you when I report you to the captain." Weiss leaned against the bulkhead and crossed one leg over the other, scrutinizing her nails with deliberate indifference. "You'll only make total fools of yourself." She made sure she kept an eye on the baton. "Shafas, I know these morons have you convinced, but think about it. Who is Struyen's best friend among the two of you? Who will most likely be the one left to our captain's less-than-amiable nature?"

"Holta?" Shafas turned to his friend. "Perhaps—"

"Shut up," Holta replied, clearly angry now. He shifted his grip around the baton, back and forth. "That goes for you too, Kyakh."

"Really." Weiss kept her casual position, but every muscle in her body was ready to launch. "Use your head, Shafas."

"Holta?"

"I said, shut *up*!" Holta leaped toward Weiss, his baton raised.

Weiss quickly moved her bent leg in behind her, to brace for impact as she rolled with the onslaught. Holta was shorter but had more bulk, and the only thing she believed would work was to absorb the energy of his assault. She threw herself backward, gripping his lapels. His body flew across hers, slamming into the railing. Weiss felt Holta grab her harness and pull her toward him. Slamming her hand up from underneath his, she broke his hold and rolled to a crouching position. Shafas, panic in his eyes, ran toward her. Not having any time to think, Weiss grabbed the railing with both hands and pulled hard. Both her feet left the floor and plunged into Shafas's abdomen. He staggered backward and fell, hitting his head against the bulkhead with a resounding thud.

"You bitch!" Holta was back on his feet, and before Weiss had time to regain her balance, he slammed into her, one arm around her waist, one with a painful grip of her hair. He smelled of sweat and some vile tobacco, and the grunting he made closer to her ear sickened her even more. Driving her knee up, she made contact with his testicles. The air left his lungs rapidly, and Weiss didn't give him time to even think of recuperating. She repeated the maneuver, and when she felt his grip of her hair loosen, she drove her fist sideways into his windpipe.

Squeaking now rather than roaring, Holta clawed at her face, and she wasn't fast enough to pull away in time. The burning sensation of his nails breaking her skin made her furious. Until now she had fought like she always did, cold and detached, but that all changed. Weiss pushed Holta away from her, able to gain momentum in her blows. With quick jabs at his temples and his gut, she finished him off with a well-aimed uppercut. He followed Shafas as he stumbled over his unconscious friend's legs. Cross-eyed, he lay there, blood oozing from his mouth.

"Kyakh to Podmer." Kyakh spoke into her communicator.

"Podmer here. All done?"

"Negative, sir." Kyakh leaned against the railing, looking down at the men and women hauling the davic crystals. "Struyen's cronies, Holta and Shafas, just attacked me. Apparently Struyen sees me as a contender for the throne and sent his friends to do his dirty work. Wish someone had told him I'm not interested in either your position or your ship. All I want is what credits I have coming."

"What the hell's that idiot up to now? I'll deal with it."

"You better send someone to take these fools to sickbay. I'm on my lunch break. Kyakh out." Weiss carefully touched her cheek as she stepped over the two semiconscious men. Blood soaked her fingers and she grimaced at the pain. "Nothing that Madisyn's derma fuser can't fix."

People that she met stared at her face, but Weiss didn't allow any questions. She strode to her quarters and headed directly for the bathroom. Tugging at the med kit, she was about to start the derma fuser when a voice from the doorway interrupted her.

"If you use that without the cleanser first, especially since someone's dirty nails did that, you'll get an infection." Madisyn stood just inside the door, her arms folded across her chest.

"Oh. All right." Suddenly feeling weak, Weiss looked at her reflection in the mirror. "How did you know?"

"I was in Podmer's office when you paged him."

"I see." Weiss looked in the med kit for a cleanser rod, but couldn't find any.

"Oh, for stars and skies, let me do it." Madisyn pushed Weiss away from the sink and made her sit on a small stool. "Let's clean you up."

Weiss closed her eyes as Madisyn gently washed her face. After that, the hum of a cleanser rod made her skin tingle. The darker, louder buzz of the derma fuser made her flinch. She had a sudden flashback to when she had been confined to sickbay in a strange spaceship, missing her mother more than anything. The constant treatments of the burns on her legs had hurt, but not half as bad as futilely asking for her mother every day.

"Weiss? Weiss?" Madisyn frowned, cupping Weiss's cheek as she performed the fusing. "Why are you crying? Am I hurting you?"

"No, no. Got something in my eyes." Furious at herself, Weiss blinked away the treacherous tears. She focused on her breathing, inhaling and exhaling in exact seconds, a technique that had proved useful and efficient many times. Madisyn's hands were warm, and the concern in her eyes was evident even if Madisyn clearly still hated everything about her.

"At least the Struyen situation should work out one way or the other now that you've beat the hell out of his cohorts." Madisyn placed the instruments back in the kit. "It'll be interesting to see what Podmer decides to do."

"Yes." Rising on surprisingly wobbly legs, Weiss headed for her bed. She had to lie down for just a few minutes. Judging from the throbbing pain around her chest, her ribs were bruised, perhaps even cracked. She refused to tell Madisyn. It was torture to be physically near her, and to undress and have her touch her naked skin would be unbearable. Weiss also knew she would have to figure out a way to get in touch with Ewan Jacelon. There had been something more in his voice, something beyond the shock of finding out the man who nearly killed his daughter was still alive. Yawning, Weiss couldn't resist the urge to close her eyes. Just for a moment.

Chapter Twenty-one

The diplomatic team had made great progress after the eight-hour marathon negotiation. Amereena and Dahlia had between them managed to unite old political adversaries among the Gantharian resistance. No group or sub-group had a flawless past, and even though all of them fought to regain their freedom, they went about it in different ways. Kellen had never doubted what her duty was, or which path to choose.

First it was all about Tereya, and then Tereya's son, Armeo. Now she was more fragmented when it came to her duty and her future. Armeo was still her first priority, but after him came Rae, their family and friends, the SC and her commission in its military force. Kellen had not contributed to her full potential during the meeting. Her thoughts returned constantly to Rae, trying to transmit her love by sheer willpower. Kellen tried to convince herself that if anybody could beat impossible odds, it was her wife. Rae loved her and Armeo, who she regarded as the son of her heart, and she would do anything humanly possible—and impossible—to return to them.

Still, war was war, and brutality and death did not discriminate. Kellen had received word that the *Paesina* was only charred space debris, and even if a lot of her crew had been rescued from escape pods, some even from floating freely in space, there was still no sign of any of its bridge crew, including Rae.

Relieved that the meeting was over, Kellen walked ahead of the others to the shuttle that would take them back to the *Circinus*. She strode across the landing pad and waited impatiently while she made sure Dahlia and Amereena walked aboard together with Owena and Leanne.

"Protector, ma'am, there's an incoming subspace message for you." A nervous ensign stood in the opening to the navigational niche. "You can use my console. It is a secure transmission."

"Thank you, Ensign." Kellen exchanged a glance with Dahlia. "I'll let you know if it's about Rae. Instantly."

"Yes, please." Dahlia slumped into her seat, looking pale.

Leanne sat down next to her, offering a bottle of water. "Here. You've been without fluids and food far too long, Diplomat Jacelon."

"Thank you, Leanne." Dahlia gripped the bottle with trembling fingers.

Knowing Dahlia was in good hands, Kellen slipped into the navigational niche and closed the door behind her. She punched in her ID code and responded to the transmission.

"Commander Kellen O'Dal here on a secure channel. Go ahead."

"Kellen, it's Ewan." Her father-in-law sounded gruff, and his use of their first names turned her midsection into a river of ice water.

"Ewan, I hear you loud and clear." That was all she could do: answer correctly by the book.

"Good. Good. I still have no news of Rae," he said quickly, as if to get that part out of the way. "This is not about her at all, I'm afraid."

Confused, Kellen rubbed her stinging eyes. "Go on."

"I don't know how much Rae told you about the undercover operation she ran in the sectors between the SC border and the Gantharat system?"

"She sent Weiss Kyakh as a double agent to some pirate gang. That's all I know."

"Yes. I heard from Kyakh six hours ago." Ewan sighed. "She's aboard a ship, the *Salaceos*, run by a thug named Podmer. Her contact onboard is a sentient BNSL, Madisyn Pimm. Normally, Pimm's the one that reports in, but as things are, Kyakh broke protocol and tried to reach Rae. Her page was automatically forwarded to me when…when Rae wasn't available."

"What did she want?" Kellen did not trust Weiss Kyakh for a second, but something in Ewan's voice made her think that worse people than the woman who had kidnapped Dahlia were out there.

"Trax M'Aldovar is alive."

"Ewan..." Kellen's heartbeat became louder as it seemed to thunder somewhere just below her throat.

"I know. I didn't believe her at first. She claims he is about to purchase davic crystals from Podmer, who in turn stole them from the Nemalima moon."

"I killed him." Emotionless, Kellen stared out through the viewport as the shuttle took off.

"You apparently injured him severely. He is completely paralyzed and depending on a ventilator to breathe. Sounds to me like you snapped his neck, but somehow they managed to save him. Something tells me he's kept this a secret even from his own family, or we would've heard about it via his sister."

Kellen knew that Andreia M'Aldovar, also known as Boyoda, the leader of the resistance movement on Gantharat, would never keep such a thing from them. This would not be easy for her to hear.

"What are my orders, sir?" Kellen was trembling, and the only way to keep from shattering was to remain formal.

"I am transmitting their coordinates. They are not far from your location and I need you to assemble a strike force and take M'Aldovar out. We can't allow him to take these crystals to Onotharat. The Onotharians are weakened due to an energy crisis, and if they get their hands on such an enormous shipment of crystals, they'll be able to keep this war going for decades. Not to mention power their weapons factories and research facilities. I'm sending units from the SC as well, but you have a better chance." Ewan lowered his voice and sounded even closer. "Kellen. You report only to me when it comes to this mission. You have my authority to use what resources you require, including manpower. Assemble your best crew and take him out. Kill him again, as it were."

The gallows humor wasn't lost on Kellen. "It will be my pleasure, Ewan," she said darkly and knew just how feral her smile was.

"All right. Move out ASAP, Protector."

"Aye, sir. Kellen out." She sat motionless for the few minutes it took for Ewan's documents to load onto her computer. Flashbacks from the fight she had engaged in with Trax M'Aldovar mixed with images of Rae, bleeding profusely from a wound in her neck.

Desperate to shake them, Kellen stood and returned to the others. Dahlia's head snapped up, her eyes dark with worry.

"It wasn't about Rae. There's still no news. It was Ewan. I have a new mission."

"What is it?"

"It involves going back into space." Kellen made sure the doors were closed to the junior officers' section of the shuttle. "I'm glad we got so much done today. I need to use Ayahliss, Leanne, Owena, Roshan, and Andreia. Additionally, I'll require a strike-force unit."

"This sounds bad." Dahlia stood, pressing her palms together. "What can Amereena and I do?"

"Keep up the negotiations. Stay safe with the reinforced security detail. Pave the way for peace." Kellen walked up to Dahlia, carefully taking her hands. "We will find Rae, and I will return with Ayahliss and the others after this mission. I know the thought of losing everyone plagues you right now, but I won't let that happen."

"Do you promise, Kellen? I love you like a daughter and…if Rae…you, Armeo, and Ayahliss—"

"Hush. Don't. Rae is resourceful. She's strong. She's every bit as stubborn and determined to survive as you were in the Disi-Disi jungle. She will return, and so will Ayahliss and I. Have faith in that."

"All right. Yes, of course." Dahlia hugged Kellen tight. "Will you be able to remain in contact?"

"Yes. I will report continuously to Ewan."

Dahlia looked relieved as she kissed Kellen's cheek and let her go. "Good." She visibly pulled herself together and took her seat.

Turning to Owen, Kellen said, "Gear up and I will see you, Leanne, Roshan, and Andreia at the shuttle bay at 2000 hours. Ayahliss will also accompany us. I will brief you once we are en route."

"Aye, Protector," Owena said solemnly. Her dark eyes did not waver, and Kellen knew she and Leanne would go into battle with her with the same abandon as always.

Swallowing against a burning sensation in the back of her throat, Kellen tried to wrap her mind around what awaited them as she sat down and attached her seat harness. She would have to reach the resistance headquarters planetside where Ayahliss, Roshan, and Andreia were part of the planning. They had so much to do and simply no time to do it all. Staring out into space through the small viewport by her seat, she allowed thoughts of Rae to surface. How would she be able to focus on her mission when all she wanted was to turn the *Circinus* to her wife's last known coordinates? It infuriated and pained her not to be part of the search-and-rescue detail. Kellen wanted to be there and search, grid by grid, herself.

She leaned her head back and closed her eyes briefly. She could make it through this only by focusing on what Rae would want her to do. Rae most certainly wanted Trax M'Aldovar incarcerated or dead. This man had hurt them both, several times, and knowing he was alive, though severely incapacitated, infuriated her. Pouring all her fears for Rae's situation into her hatred for the man who had nearly killed Rae, Kellen tightened her fists. She intended to kill him once and for all. He would live only long enough to know who his perpetual nemesis was, and she would show him no pardon, no mercy.

A small voice inside asked her how she could wear her Ruby Red gan'thet suit with honors if she killed a defenseless man, a quadriplegic, according to Kyakh. Pushing the disturbing thoughts away, she willed herself to think of Armeo, Rae, and their family and friends, trying to calm down. As the shuttle docked with the *Circinus*, she knew her efforts to think of loved ones only upset her even more.

❖

Jacelon moved slowly through the shuttle, glancing only briefly at the Onotharians. They were secured, tied up twice, just to be sure. One was conscious, but clearly affected by his head wound; he hardly stirred.

Her midsection burned and a worrisome internal throbbing ache weakened her with each passing hour. She surmised she was bleeding, and only a specialized tissue fuser wielded by a physician could help her. Jacelon reached the two men lying on the floor at the far back of the Onotharian shuttle.

"How are you doing, Ensign?"

"I'm all right, Admiral," the young man said between clenched teeth, clearly trying to be brave when facing his commanding officer. "Dgobdo is worse off. He hasn't moved since I pulled him inside."

"Have you managed to examine him?"

"I have. His left eye isn't responding as it should when I shine a light on it."

"Damn." Jacelon wanted to growl. Dgobdo probably had a subdural hematoma, a bleeding between the brain and the skull. She looked at the unconscious man. His complexion was gray and his carotid pulse was slow and barely noticeable.

"What can we do for him, ma'am?" Ensign Hallberg placed an unsteady hand on Dgobdo's forehead, as if trying to heal him through a physical connection.

"Other than keeping him comfortable, which you're already doing, his only hope is that we run into the search-and-rescue vessels."

"They'll assume we're Onotharian."

"Not if I can help it." Pushing herself back on her feet, Jacelon groaned at the pain in her belly, now more piercing than throbbing.

"Admiral?" Hallberg looked at her with increasing concern. "You're injured."

"I'll be fine. Take care of Dgobdo, Hallberg." She saw him hesitate and struggled to not sway. "Do I have to make that an order, Ensign?"

"No, ma'am." Hallberg didn't look convinced. "Just let me know if I can do anything. Anything at all."

Jacelon sighed. "Thank you." She limped up to the helm and continued her scans. Her thoughts went to Kellen, with reluctance, since she knew well of the excruciating pain that would pierce her when she did. Kellen's mission was dangerous enough as it was. Worrying about her meant Kellen could lose focus, which could be disastrous.

Jacelon blinked against the dryness of her eyes. The information on the screen before her became garbled, and she gently rubbed her eyes, afraid of missing something. Trying a technique that had sustained her before when she and Kellen had been forced apart by their different missions, she inhaled deeply and held her breath. Trying to recall Kellen's own scent, something clean, like citrus and leather, Jacelon remembered how Kellen's embrace made her feel. Kellen's strong, loving arms, her full breasts and wiry frame, and the plump, pink lips and the way Kellen's kisses tasted… Jacelon released the air from her lungs. There it was, that magical feeling that only Kellen could instill in her.

With renewed effort, Jacelon returned to her scans. Nothing would stand between her and Kellen. She would find a way to signal for help, and fast, because the agonizing pain in her stomach and the increasing weakness that made her cling to the controls told her time was running out.

CHAPTER TWENTY-TWO

Madisyn regarded the sleeping woman on the other bed. She had to wake her up, but she wished she could just remain here, exploring every feature of Weiss's face, every curve of her lithe body. Madisyn couldn't remember ever being so emotionally conflicted. It was easier when everybody perceived her to be an impersonal android, little more than a glorified machine. With Weiss, that was impossible. Weiss had proved to her that she was indeed a real person, completely functional when it came to emotions as well as sexual desire and arousal.

Before Weiss confessed to a long career in piracy and being a mercenary, Madisyn had felt they were becoming closer, like friends, but also something more. It had shocked her to her depths but also became an unexpected beacon in the darkness that was her personal life. Madisyn had never expected to find true friendship or, the Seers forgive her, romantic love.

The night Weiss held her and they kissed, Madisyn began to glimpse the possibility of experiencing what had so far only been part of very secretive dreams at night. When Weiss confessed to her background, to really being who everybody aboard the *Salaceos* thought she was—Weiss Kyakh, pirate and mercenary, really nothing more than a common thief—something within Madisyn died. She had built her hopes up, despite vowing to herself a long time ago never to do that.

Madisyn hugged herself, a faint moan escaping her lips. Looking at Weiss like this, when she appeared relaxed with softened features and an innocent expression, was almost surreal. Her lips slightly parted and one hand turned palm up against her cheek, Weiss appeared ten or fifteen years younger.

Madisyn glanced at the chronometer on her arm. She couldn't put if off any longer.

"Weiss? Weiss. You've got to wake up. We've got to go."

Weiss stirred, but only rolled on her side and muttered something inaudible.

"Weiss!" Madisyn steeled herself and shook Weiss's shoulder. "It's time."

Weiss was awake and clearly in battle mode before Madisyn had finished the last word. Moving with a feline grace, Weiss flung one arm up defensively and grasped Madisyn's neck with her free hand.

"Stop it. It's me!" Madisyn used her own training instinctively. She shoved her arms up, crosswise, knocking herself free.

"For the love of—" Weiss eyes were narrow slits as she glowered at Madisyn. "What the hell are you doing?"

"Waking you up." Madisyn pushed herself away from Weiss, resisting an overwhelming urge to smooth the tousled hair from the stunningly chiseled face. "We're due on the bridge. We're having company."

"Oh, yeah? Don't tell me. M'Aldovar."

"The very same."

"Damn it, what changed his plan? He never meant to come aboard."

"I don't know." Madisyn rose and put on a black vest over her coverall, tightening the clasps with jerky movements. "I sent a subspace alert to the admiral, but it might be too late for them to move back into position."

"If it is, we'll just have to figure things out ourselves. Bad enough I couldn't get out of handing over the computer chip to them. We need to figure out a way to keep them from getting their hands on the crystals. Having them would enable them to replenish their fleet. It would be disastrous."

"I agree. I will report."

"Why don't you remain behind here in our quarters and do that. I'll go to the bridge."

"And if anyone asks for me?"

"You're performing a security scan of your systems." Weiss

shrugged. "You took quite a hit, just like I did, when we crashed onto the shuttle bay deck after our *Nemalima* adventure."

"True. A robot can only take so much." Madisyn had to smile at her own irony.

"Yes." Weiss stunned her by briefly touching her jaw with her fingertips. "A screw coming loose and that's pretty much it."

"Oh, you!" Madisyn snorted. "I'll repay you for 'screw,' just you wait."

"I look forward to it."

Suddenly, Madisyn realized that they'd slipped into flirtatious mode again, like before she knew who Weiss really was. Taken aback, she recoiled, uncertain how she could have forgotten, even for a second, that to her, Weiss was just as much the enemy as Podmer and his crew.

Weiss's eyes lost their sparkle and she swiftly tied her hair back in its usual austere fashion. She donned a similar vest as Madisyn's. "All right. I'm out of here. See you later. Let me know if Rae Jacelon is back."

"I will." Madisyn watched Weiss stride out of their quarters and heard her steps fade down the corridor. "Oh, damn. I just don't know what to do." She sat down with her head in her hands for a few moments, trying to regain her composure. *Pull yourself together, Pimm. Don't let anyone see you with your guard down.*

Adjusting her inner sensors, she began paging Jacelon. When a male voice responded, Madisyn began to worry. What was going on? After Admiral Ewan Jacelon provided her with information regarding the latest turn of events, Madisyn fought to not be overcome. No matter how impersonal Jacelon senior sounded, this was his child missing in action.

"Sir, I have something important to report as well." Madisyn spoke quickly. "Trax M'Aldovar is going to be aboard the *Salaceos* shortly. I don't know the exact time frame, but within a few hours, approximately."

"Good job, Ms. Pimm." Jacelon senior spoke curtly. "We have a task force on a direct trajectory for your sector. You're only hours away from the Gantharian system. Using your internal beacon, I can pinpoint your exact position."

"Who is in command of the task force, sir? I will need a call name."

"Kellen O'Dal is in command. She's also known as the Protector of the Realm."

It all made sense, Madisyn thought when her whirling mind began to calm down. The protector was famous, and the news of her marrying a human woman from Earth—and a high-ranking military person—had reached Guild Nation even before it was a member of the Supreme Constellations. "Your daughter-in-law, I believe, sir."

"Correct. She is heading a formidable team and has a unit of twenty-four marines at her disposal, as well as twenty assault craft. You will be able to identify her cruiser by these markings and this configuration."

More data streamed to Madisyn's internal sensor, and she blinked at the faint pain. She had never disclosed to anyone that using her artificial senses this way hurt physically, and she would not do so now. Clenching her teeth and closing her eyes, she breathed evenly. It was just a matter of letting the data stream run its course for only seconds.

"Affirmative, sir," Madisyn said when she had all the required data. "I will report back as soon as we have a new development." She hesitated, straightening her vest to occupy her hands. "And sir…I pray your daughter is found in good health, Admiral. I respect and admire her greatly."

"Thank you. She is quite impressed with you, Ms. Pimm."

"I will do my best to live up to her expectations. The Seers are with her."

"Jacelon out."

Madisyn left the quarters, knowing that the upcoming hours would have great impact on the conflict, and she and Weiss, despite their differences and the private hurt, were in the middle of it all. There was no margin for error. If M'Aldovar left with the crystals, he would make sure the Onotharian ships kept running for years. Without the crystals, the SC had a chance to wear them out. Onotharat was a depleted society resource-wise, and with a corrupt and despotic ruler that the average Onotharian must loathe. Madisyn was not a political expert, but even she knew that such a society toppled easily because it had no foundation among the people.

Hurrying toward the bridge, she caught herself smiling faintly at Weiss's comment about the screw. When her assignment was over she would actually miss having someone who knew, who even had the audacity to joke with her about it. And not just someone. Weiss.

❖

Jacelon slumped sideways at the helm of the Onotharian shuttle. Inside her survival suit, her clothes were rigid from her slow-trickling, coagulating blood. She kept tightening the makeshift pressure bandage, but she wasn't kidding herself. She didn't have very long. The darkening edges at her outer field of vision proved that she would soon lose consciousness, and when that happened, the game was over for her and the young ensigns behind her.

The thought of the young men, her crew, her responsibility, made her force herself upright. A new gush of blood, this time more than a mere trickle, warmed her side. "For stars and skies, where are the damn search-and-rescue ships?" Jacelon scanned the debris, but found no new life signs and certainly no SC ships. "How can that be?" she muttered. "Don't they know what happened here? Surely they must know."

At first the small light at the left lower corner of the viewport looked like debris gleaming in the light of a distant star. As it grew in size, Jacelon clutched the helm computer console tightly. Soon the light became two, then three and four. Eventually, she counted ten small flickering lights. A grid search. They were performing a grid search.

Relief turned to concern. She was inside an Onotharian shuttle, and if anybody hated the Onotharians, the medics and search-and-rescue personnel, who had to clean up the mess after the battle, were at the top of the list. No SC soldier was ever expected to shoot first and ask questions later, but it did happen when tempers ran high, and she was sure—having once, as a junior lieutenant, been part of such a team—every crewmember on the approaching ships was ready to throttle, shoot, and laser-blade the first Onotharian they came across.

Jacelon had to figure out a way to confirm her identity before they turned the shuttle into space dust. Every SC citizen possessed an ID code, worn in a chip under their skin. So did Jacelon, but hers was outfitted with a military prefix, which, when scanned, allowed SC authorities to identify her and the enemy to come up blank.

She formed a bold idea. If it worked, she would think it was worth the pain. If it didn't—at least she'd tried. The young men behind her were worth any pain she would experience. Pain was only a vague description. Agony would be a better word for what she meant to do. Excruciating agony.

Jacelon pulled out a small laser-bladed knife and rolled up the sleeve of her uniform jacket. Aiming dead center between her wrist and elbow on the inside of her arm, she bit hard into her lip as she pressed the sensor, engaging the cauterizing feature. She glanced up at the viewport and saw the lights coming closer with each passing heartbeat.

It was time. She couldn't hold back a whimper as she began to cut.

❖

Kellen stood on the bridge of the cruiser *Noma III*, unable to sit down because her nerves were wound so taut. Fueled by the hatred of a man who had wronged and wounded her loved ones, whom she hated with every fiber of her being, she kept her eyes on the viewscreen.

"Kellen?" A soft voice next to her made her flinch and she whipped her head sideways, glaring at the person daring to disturb her thoughts. "Hey, it's just me." Roshan O'Landha raised her hands, palms forward. "Stand down, Protector."

"I apologize. I was lost in thought."

"I could tell, and I'm sorry I startled you. You have a lot on your mind, yet you need to brief us as we're approaching our coordinates."

"I will, I—"

"We have an incoming SC official subspace message, Commander O'Dal." Owena, manning tactical and ops, said.

"Audio." Kellen waited impatiently until Owena nodded for her to go ahead. "This is Commander Kellen O'Dal, on the cruiser *Noma*."

"Commander, Admiral Ewan Jacelon. I have new information for you and your team. I was just briefed by our agent aboard the *Salaceos* that they are expecting Trax M'Aldovar as Podmer's guest within the next two hours. This band of space pirates has a cargo of davic crystals for him. Our agent estimated in an earlier report that they stole approximately seven thousand two hundred crystals."

"That won't happen." Kellen knew she sounded harsh. "If the Onotharians get their hands on them—"

"I know, Kellen." Ewan sounded stern. "I trust you to deal with the situation. Take him out. Stop the deal from taking place. If necessary, eliminate the *Salaceos*."

"We have operatives on that ship, sir."

"One is the mercenary that kidnapped Dahlia, the other one is a BNSL android." The dismissive tone in Ewan's voice made certain that he thought of them as expendable.

"That may be," Kellen insisted, although she harbored as much disdain for Weiss Kyakh as Ewan and Rae did. "We must still take appropriate measures to ensure their rescue if possible. It is what Rae would do." She held her breath while waiting for her father-in-law to explode.

"Of course, you're right." Ewan sounded pressured, but calmer.

"The BNSL android is sentient. Kyakh may be there because of coercion, but she does work for the SC at present."

"Yes, yes." Ewan cleared his throat. "We don't have any news of Rae yet. I know this is as torturous for you as it is for her mother and me, perhaps even more since you are in the field and need to stay focused. You don't have the luxury of dwelling on it."

"That is actually a blessing. I…" Kellen gazed around her and saw nothing but sympathy from the people who were her comrades in arms and her friends. "I am all right. I will complete the mission. You have to promise me to page me as soon as you know. No matter what."

"Very well, Kellen. I have transmitted the *Salaceos*'s coordinates. The asteroid belt near them is emitting some interesting signals, so be on your guard, Kellen."

"Affirmative, Admiral."

"Be safe. Jacelon out."

"Commander D'Artansis." Kellen took a second to collect herself. "Change our course to the coordinates transmitted from SC headquarters."

"Aye, ma'am." Leanne punched in the command, and the *Noma* rumbled beneath Kellen's feet. She was one of the new powerful models, outfitted with the latest modified propulsion system, capable of traveling three times as fast as a tachyon mass drive, which was illegal due to pollution issues. This cruiser also had a cloaking system, which made them invisible to sensors and the naked eye. Now the Noma pierced space like a projectile, black and sleek, with twenty assault craft in her belly.

Kellen sat down in the captain's chair, gripping the armrests. She would make sure Trax M'Aldovar never saw the light of day and Onotharat wouldn't obtain the crystals. Once that was done, she intended to find Rae.

Nothing and nobody could stop her.

CHAPTER TWENTY-THREE

Weiss stood rigid next to Podmer, about to greet the Onotharian general as his hover chair exited the airlock. His shuttle had docked with the *Salaceos* only moments ago, and Weiss wondered why he found it necessary to meet again so soon. He had coerced Podmer into going along with his terms, and the crystals were ready for transfer. He obviously wanted something else enough to risk another meeting with Podmer, whom he clearly despised.

Trax M'Aldovar managed to look intimidating and powerful despite the fact he could move only his head. He hovered high enough off the deck to not have to gaze up at anyone. Weiss knew the psychological impact of such tactics and that this man left nothing to chance. His amber gaze, almost a sulfur yellow, rested on each one of the greeting party before he spoke in the raspy voice Weiss remembered.

"No need for all this commotion. I want this done quickly. Podmer, where can I examine the item?"

"I have yet to concede to—"

"Podmer, if you expect to get paid for the crystals, you will follow my directions. I've got a war to win, and I can't be bothered with squabbling with pirates."

"You still find us useful to supply you with merchandise," Weiss heard herself say, unable to prevent her words. This pompous man personified everything she disliked in another humanoid. She had come across many like him in her life, and she had to date put every single one in their place.

"Kyakh, I would find your insolence amusing if I wasn't pressed for time and in no spirit to banter. Not even with a beautiful *diate'sh* like you."

Weiss recognized an Onotharian insult when she heard one. She forced herself to remain calm and disdainful. "I have never made my living by selling my body to anyone, M'Aldovar, but I can imagine why someone like you would be limited to knowing only such unfortunate women."

A vein began to throb visibly at M'Aldovar's left temple. "Hold your tongue, Kyakh, or I might just give the order to have it removed."

"Why don't we head over to the mess hall?" Podmer interrupted, clearly eager to forestall any more insults or threats from either of them.

"Will you present the piece of technology there?"

"Absolutely. For the right price, anything is negotiable." Podmer smiled jovially. "I'm sure we'll see eye to eye."

"Oh, yes, I'm certain we will." M'Aldovar's irony was obviously lost on Podmer, who strode through the corridor. Weiss wanted to grab him by the arm and demand an explanation, and also point out the fact that the Onotharian general was a lying, murderous bastard, which of course would have been a moot point, as Podmer was exactly that too.

The mess hall had been rearranged to impress a dignitary. Smaller tables had been folded into the deck; only the large captain's table in the center remained, set with gilded obsidian plates and glasses. Weiss raised her eyebrows when she saw the bright white retrospun linen tablecloth. *How domestic, Podmer.*

"Take a seat—" Podmer stopped himself, but too late. "My apologies." He turned furious eyes on the mess hall boy waiting next to the door leading to the galley. "Remove a chair immediately. No, not that one, you fool. The one over by the viewport, for our guest." Podmer, now with a volatile red creeping up his large cheeks, tossed the thin young man aside and dragged the chair out of M'Aldovar's way himself. "Get back into the kitchen and then bring us drinks."

Weiss had to cough to mask her laughter when she could actually *see* on Podmer's face how it dawned on him that he had no clue how M'Aldovar was supposed to handle drinking. Podmer's eyes fluttered back and forth between M'Aldovar and his security detail. Weiss would have given most of her stashed loot to see one of those hard-nosed, rough men try to feed their general.

"Do not panic, Podmer," M'Aldovar said with a sigh. "My hover chair takes care of everything. By all means, bring us drinks. Make mine a double, no matter what it is." He looked like he needed it, from sheer exasperation.

"Oh, good. I mean, yes. Of course." Podmer reissued the order to the mess hall boy, who scurried off, probably grateful to be out of reach of his captain.

"So," M'Aldovar said, and maneuvered his chair into the vacated space, "is the BNSL going to join us?"

Weiss snapped her head up, staring at first M'Aldovar, then Podmer. The fact that the Onotharian general spoke of Madisyn in that manner set her inner alarm klaxons blaring. Why would he call a member of Podmer's crew "the BNSL," and why would he be interested in whether Madisyn joined them?

"I thought we'd negotiate first," Podmer said merrily, pouring the drinks as the boy returned from the galley. He formed his lips into a broad smile, but his eyes were guarded as they skimmed by Weiss.

"What, exactly, are we negotiating about?" Weiss asked, making sure she sounded bored and not overly interested.

"That which turned out to be your main attraction." M'Aldovar laughed, a chilling, hissing sound. "I understand this android is one of a kind."

"And you know this how?" Weiss pressed on.

"Kyakh!" Podmer slammed his hand, palm down, into the table, making the obsidian glasses jump.

"Now, now, it's no secret that your other crewmember, Lucco Struyen has been most informative. Very helpful." M'Aldovar laughed again. "Pour my drink, Ensign. This calls for a toast."

One of his security detail officers stepped up and lifted the glass in front of M'Aldovar. He pressed a sensor on the hover chair and an opening on the top of the backrest emerged. Reluctantly fascinated, Weiss watched as the ensign simply poured the drink into the opening and closed the lid. Another opening to M'Aldovar's left produced a narrow transparent tube, which wiggled through the air close to his lips. Bending his neck slightly, M'Aldovar let his gaze travel between them. "Here's to Onotharian supremacy." He didn't wait for them to respond, but drank from the tube. His broad, stiff grin was one of the ugliest expressions Weiss had seen. Even she, who took pride in never being jaded, could feel the stirring of nausea at the apparent madness in his eyes.

"Supremacy," Podmer finally echoed, and drank. Weiss couldn't make herself sip the strong *valasai* wine. Normally, she had no problem handling alcohol, but if she took a sip now, she would end up spitting it across the table.

"So, back to business. The cute little BNSL. Unlike our previous negotiation, you can pretty much name your price. She's unique."

Only the fact Weiss was holding on to the seat of her chair made it possible for her to remain sitting.

"You want to buy Madisyn Pimm?" Podmer blinked. "She's a sentient being and member of my crew. A *valued* member."

"She is a robot. State of the art and one of a kind, as I understand it, but still—just another piece of technology." M'Aldovar pursed his full lips, which created an extraordinarily lascivious expression.

"You heard Podmer. Pimm is sentient. She is part of his senior staff." Kyakh was so furious, and at the same time so deeply afraid that she was halfway out of her chair.

"A sensitive topic, Kyakh? Have a special liking for androids and robots?" M'Aldovar's hissing laughter made him turn dark red. He shook his head at the ensign who took a step toward him.

"I have no interest in Pimm, but any good crew has to remain loyal to each other, or its operations are doomed." Weiss turned her attention to Podmer. "Like you should point out to that loose-lipped Struyen. He's been nothing but trouble. If you don't—"

"You don't lecture me." It was Podmer's turn to change color. "I decide what goes on aboard the *Salaceos*."

"That's right, Podmer. You tell her." M'Aldovar seemed genuinely amused. "Tell her who's in charge."

"And you will sit idly by and sell a member of your crew into slavery."

"What do you care?" Podmer drank the rest of his valasai wine. "Can you tell me that?"

"I'm just looking out for myself. If you can do that to Pimm, who's been with you much longer, how do I know you won't do something similar to me?" Her heart beating so fast that it actually hurt her ribs,

Weiss thought fast. "What if you decide to hand me back to the SC if they give you enough reimbursement? Both Pimm and I risked our damn necks for you, and though I know you're nothing but a murdering thief, when I had my own ship, I would never have sacrificed one of my own." She spat the last words with all the contempt she could muster.

"This isn't your ship, is it?" Podmer wasn't red anymore. He was pale. "I know your reputation, so that is why you're still sitting there and not bleeding all over sickbay. You should be able to fathom that there is a *difference* between you and Pimm. You're royalty when it comes to our business. Pimm is really not much more than what the general says—an android, though advanced."

"So you're saying you're going to side with me against Struyen?" Weiss scowled.

"Struyen has overstepped his authority. I realize that." His voice calmer now, Podmer pushed against the table with both hands and stood. "He will be reprimanded."

"Will he pay restitution?" It was important that Podmer and M'Aldovar only saw her concern as personal greed, or they might start wondering just why she cared about Madisyn.

"He will forfeit half his part to you. You will outrank him."

"Fine. As long as you're not going against your word," Weiss said, her voice low, with a warning growl.

"No, no. Why would I do that? I'm here," Podmer gestured at the table, "ready to make a profitable deal. Since you're here, you must realize I trust you, and I need you to help me. I don't want Pimm to find a way to self-destruct if she catches wind of this."

Oh, stars and skies, he was planning to do it. He was going to sell Madisyn to this megalomaniac. Weiss sat down again, assuming a mildly interested expression. "I can perhaps be of help. For a price."

"Of course," M'Aldovar hissed. "For a price."

Podmer laughed and had the boy pour more valasai wine. "Now we're on the right track. We just have to plan this carefully so Pimm doesn't become suspicious."

"Leave that to me," Weiss said, nothing but dread and cold winter in her heart. "I'll keep an eye on her."

CHAPTER TWENTY-FOUR

Madisyn shifted restlessly in the captain's chair. She kept an eye on all sensor readings, fully aware of the newly appointed ensign's limitations as the young woman nervously punched in commands for diagnostics over at the ops station. Struyen was confined to quarters, pending Podmer's ruling of his fate. This ought to be reassuring, but Madisyn couldn't shake the feeling that she was missing something. Struyen and his cohorts were dealt with, so far, but M'Aldovar's presence aboard the *Salaceos* had made the ship hum in a way that seemed foreboding.

She flinched as her internal sensors received a muted signal, manifesting itself as a tone only audible to her through her inner ear. Knowing this meant the SC was trying to reach her, Madisyn locked her gaze on the viewscreen on the far wall and accessed her biosynthetic transmission array. She rarely used this feature, since the transparent images projected on her retina gave her motion sickness. But this was clearly an emergency, and she couldn't shake her feeling of impending disaster.

Cursing the fact that she couldn't leave the bridge, Madisyn let the information from the SC scroll past her eyes. To her surprise, it wasn't the dense intel she had expected, but a mere text message in real time.

From the SC cruiser *Noma*:
Commander Kellen O'Dal – Protector of the Realm

En route to your last known coordinates. Objective is to apprehend/eliminate individual known as Trax M'Aldovar. Do not

> permit said individual to escape. Use deadly force if no other option.
>
> Update required regarding current coordinates, crew manifest, weapons array, shields configuration.

Madisyn made her exterior remain indifferent. The protector and her unit were closing in. They were going to get here and seize M'Aldovar, Podmer, and the rest of these murdering bastards. As she thought of how satisfying that would feel, she slid her gaze over to the young ensign. This girl, skinny, with big dark eyes, was not exactly what came to mind when thinking of Podmer's usual menagerie of thugs. She looked like she was *trying* to be part of this crew rather than actually be a member. Madisyn vowed to make sure this kid was not bundled up with the rest of the gang.

Focusing on the message, Madisyn took a deep breath and transmitted as much tactical information as she could. Once she was done, she could feel the chill of perspiration on her back, which startled her, as that had never happened. Madisyn had never heard of any BNSL that produced sweat. What would be the point? Was something going on with her bioneural physique? Was she evolving or self-destructing?

"Podmer to Pimm. Report."

"Pimm here." Madisyn pushed her shoulder back and gripped the armrests. "We are holding our position just inside the asteroid belt. Nothing on long-range sensors, no anomalies. All is well, sir."

"Good. Let the helmsman have the bridge. We need you in the cargo bay."

"Cargo bay, sir?" Madisyn stalled. She didn't like the sound of this. What was going on?

"You heard me, Pimm. Our guest requires some additional information, and you're the one person around here who can retain all of it without a hassle. Kyakh will meet you there."

Relieved to hear this, and also that she'd had time to send the protector all the information, Madisyn stood. "Very well. I'll be there in a few minutes. Pimm out."

After turning the bridge over to the helmsman, Madisyn headed toward the cargo bay. Something was probably amiss with the crystals. Frowning, she turned a corner and stopped just before running into Weiss.

"What…? I was going to meet you and the others in—what are you doing?" Madisyn tried to regain her balance as Weiss pulled her in the opposite direction. "Weiss, what the hell's going on?"

"We don't have much time. We have to get to the shuttle I prepared. Don't argue. Just trust me." Dragging Madisyn behind her, she headed toward the aft sections. "Come on. Hurry!"

"All right." Finally realizing the panic paired with anger she saw in Weiss was for her, Madisyn ran faster. They rounded the corner just as voices revealed that someone was approaching from the opposite direction, Weiss slammed the sensor and opened the door to the shuttle bay, then repeated the maneuver on the inside.

"Over there. Shuttle six." Weiss pushed Madisyn ahead of her.

"So this is how you planned your getaway."

"Yes. Lucky I did."

"Why? Why is it lucky? What's going on?"

"Not now. Later." Weiss pulled the lever and opened the hatch at the back of the shuttle. Inside, stale air rushed toward them.

"Good, nobody's been here." Weiss removed a filament wire from inside the hatch. I'm going to have to shoot our way out of here if there's a code on the door."

"But we can't just leave. I had a text-only message from the SC, from Commander O'Dal. They're on an intercept course heading here to apprehend M'Aldovar. They are using my signal as their beacon. I just sent them the latest information." If she left the ship, the absence of her readings might confuse matters. "I don't know why you're panicking. Talk to me."

"There's no time. Trust me, we have to get out of here *now*."

"I wish you'd tell me—"

"Hush." Suddenly pale, Weiss held up her hand. "Quick, adjust your sensors. Is someone heading here, toward the shuttle bay?"

Madisyn squinted and recalibrated her sensors. "Yes. Several individuals are on the move in the corridors, plus some sort of vehicle."

"Damn!" Weiss hands trembled as she pressed them against her forehead. "Think, think!"

"Y-you're frightening me." Madisyn wasn't concerned about her own safety as much as Weiss's obvious distress. "Please."

"We won't make it. We don't have time to blast out of here. I'm going to have to think of something else." Weiss lowered her hands, suddenly looking older, her eyes nearly black in her pale face. "Madi, listen. Do you trust me?"

Madisyn meant to say "No, why would I trust a pirate," but something in Weiss's demeanor, in her eyes, snuffed out any such contempt. Sensing that her life depended on her answer, she nodded slowly. "Yes. I trust you."

"We don't have much time. I need you to act shocked and kick and scream when I give you the sign, all right? I can't save you if you don't do as I say. Please, Madi."

"Kick and scream?" Madisyn shivered. "I can do that." Everything seemed as nightmarish as her worst dreams, and still here she was, awake in the cold shuttle bay with the woman she should hate, but didn't.

"Good. It's going to get scary before it gets better."

"Hey, Weiss, I'm an operative like you—" Madisyn scowled at Weiss, at a total loss what Weiss was going on about. Only the fact Weiss looked so incredibly distraught kept her listening to the woman she'd sworn to hate and despise.

"I know you are. You're better at all of that than I am, but trust me, in *this*, I'm better than you. I won't let him take you."

"Weiss?"

"I—I really care about you, Madi. I didn't plan to, and I didn't want to, but I do. I have no friends, no family, but if I did, I'd swear on their life that I'll keep you safe." She stiffened. "They're here. I'm so sorry, Madisyn. So very sorry." Her hands moved swiftly, pivoting Madisyn into her. She bent and kissed Madisyn hard for long seconds.

Madisyn's heart beat uncontrollably, only to plummet when Weiss pushed her away and spun her around. Madisyn sensed quick, hard hands sliding restraints over her hands and onto her wrists.

"Sir? Captain? Here she is!" Weiss bellowed while dragging the stunned Madisyn with her. "I caught the little android trying to sneak away."

"Weiss, what the hell are you doing? Let me go!" Madisyn stumbled out of the shuttle as Weiss unceremoniously shoved her. "Weiss, what is going on? Oh!" She stumbled and fell onto her knees.

"So she did suspect something," Podmer's voice boomed above

Madisyn. "Well, good thing you caught her. M'Aldovar is in the corridor, eager to lay eyes on his latest purchase."

Purchase? Madisyn's head spun. "What the hell are you doing? Weiss, you're supposed to be my friend."

"Friend? Me being friends with a glorified robot? I think not." Weiss spoke with cold contempt and dragged Madisyn to her feet. "Let's go say hello to your new master." She looked intently at Madisyn, and at the same time, she made soft little soothing circles on Madisyn's arms. Remembering Weiss's words about kicking and screaming, Madisyn did just that.

"Let go of me, you treacherous bitch!" She threw herself against Weiss, who caught her and pressed her close.

"What a wildcat, eh, Podmer?" Weiss grinned. "Let's go. You're going to really like your new owner. He may be immobilized, but he's all charm and personality."

❖

Ayahliss sat by the viewport in the small mess hall aboard the *Noma*. Unlike the *Circinus*, this cruiser was only sparsely equipped for comfort. The *Circinus* had several decks meant to host civilians, with all the amenities that went along with it. The *Noma* looked barren in comparison, but Ayahliss couldn't care less where she kept her eyes on the stars streaking by as they traveled toward the pirates' last known position.

"May I join you?" A soft voice interrupted Ayahliss's thoughts.

Ayahliss looked up and saw the woman she had sworn allegiance to when she knew her only as the resistance leader Boyoda. Ayahliss didn't even know she was a woman back then. "Ma'am. Of course." Ayahliss had fought long to fathom that the legendary Boyoda was Andreia M'Aldovar, an Onotharian politician, born and raised on Gantharat. She was also the sister of the feared Trax M'Aldovar, whom everybody on Gantharat had a legitimate reason to hate.

"Are you all right, Ayahliss?" Andreia sipped the warm beverage she'd brought. "Can I bring you a mug of Cormanian coffee? This stuff is truly addictive."

"Oh. Thank you, but I already had some." Quite awestruck that

Boyoda would offer, Ayahliss shifted to face her. "And thank you for asking. I'm fine."

"Good. I saw you sitting here, looking a bit lonely. You worry about Judge Beqq and Diplomat Jacelon. And the admiral."

"Yes." Ayahliss blinked away a sudden burning sensation behind her eyelids, refusing to cry in front of her. "I do. I owe them my life."

"So do I." A shadow in Andreia's eyes reminded Ayahliss that this woman had her own sorrows to deal with.

"Are you all right, ma'am?" Ayahliss asked carefully.

"Please, none of that 'ma'am' stuff. I'm a civilian, like you. In fact, I imagine it won't be long until you join the protectors as a full member. Call me Andreia."

"Thank you." Ayahliss wasn't so sure about qualifying for the full title as protector, but didn't argue. "I'm sorry that our mission involves your brother."

"Oh, Ayahliss." Andreia surprised her by reaching for her hand. "I said good-bye to my brother many years ago, long before we believed he was killed. This man the Onotharians apparently promoted to general is a stranger to me."

"Still, if you're faced with having to fire upon him or his ship?" Ayahliss squeezed Andreia's hand.

"Yes, darling, that's something I've thought of as well," Roshan O'Landha's alto voice interjected. She sat down next to Andreia and put her arm around her shoulders.

"I'm glad you asked so we get this out of the way, once and for all." Andreia softly kissed Roshan's cheek. "If I'm face-to-face with my brother and I have no other option than to fire, there's really only one thing I can see myself doing." She turned her eyes, flat and emotionless, on Ayahliss. "Pull the trigger."

Chapter Twenty-five

We can't tell you much more, Admiral, at this point, other than her resilience could make all the difference. Your daughter's previous injuries, the ones she sustained on Gantharat in particular, have compromised her ability to bounce back from this one."

Was that Gemma Meyer? Jacelon tried to open her eyes, but found it impossible. Voices had come and gone around her for a while now, and she wondered dazedly how they could fit all those people inside the Onotharian shuttlecraft.

"So, you're telling me nothing more can be done?" Ewan Jacelon sounded as brusque and abrupt as Jacelon had ever heard him. *Father?*

"By no means am I saying that," Dr. Meyer stated. "While we're doing our job keeping her alive, she has to do hers. A blood loss into her abdomen that continued for several days has weakened her. This, combined with a nasty infection that turned septic, exacerbated her old injury to her carotid artery."

"Why isn't she conscious yet?"

"We're not keeping her sedated, sir. That said, we're not happy with giving her any drugs to wake her up either. I think she will stay unconscious, or in a deep sleep, for as long as her body needs it."

"This sounds all very non-scientific to me," Ewan muttered.

"Far from it. We have cleared her infection. She's no longer in sepsis. We used the derma fusers and deep-tissue fusers to heal the perforation to her bowels and skin. Please, sir, just give her some time."

"All right, all right." A deep sigh followed, and Jacelon felt a large male hand take hers. The familiar touch was so gratifying, she was sure she'd be able to open her eyes and look up at her father, but her eyelids seemed glued together.

"I can't imagine what you went through, daughter," Ewan said, squeezing her hand. "You saved those young men and the damn Onotharians too. If you hadn't infused the bioneural circuitry with your own DNA, the rescue ship might've blown you out of the sky." He cleared his throat. "I'm so glad they didn't. So very grateful."

Jacelon felt a single tear dislodge from the corner of her right eye and run along her temple and into her hair. She needed to move, to wake up properly and tell her father she was all right. More than that, she needed to hear about Kellen—where she was, if she was all right too.

"Dr. Meyer! She moved. She moved her fingers," Ewan bellowed.

"It could be a reflex, sir—"

"No, it's not. Look, she's opening her eyes."

Jacelon blinked at the blinding light above her. "Father? Where are we?"

"Oh, Gods, Rae." Ewan leaned over her and blocked out the painful brightness. "Child. You scared us."

"I'm okay." Rae tried to sit up, but strong hands pushed her back against the pillows. "Where are we?"

"Not so fast, Admiral." Dr. Meyer ran a scanner across her face, the sides of her head, and down her body. "You're not out of the woods yet, even if being awake and alert is better than unconscious. To answer your question, you're aboard the new flagship, the Supreme Constellations *Brilliance*."

"*Brilliance*?" Jacelon groaned as Dr. Meyer prodded her sore side. "Hey, no need to be a brute about it."

"I'm barely touching you." Dr. Meyer smiled at Jacelon, who only now realized how haggard her chief medical officer looked.

"Thank you, Gemma." Jacelon turned her head to look at her father. "Kellen? Mother? Armeo?"

"Your mother is being very successful, paving the way for an interim government on Gantharat. Armeo is thriving at his boarding school with Dorinda. Kellen is on assignment."

"On Gantharat?"

"No. She's heading an operation rendezvousing with Pimm and Kyakh to apprehend Trax M'Aldovar." Ewan looked carefully down at her.

"Trax—what?" Surely this was all the damn drugs talking? Jacelon squinted at her father, trying to judge if he was being facetious. *"Trax M'Aldovar?"*

"Seems the news of his death was slightly exaggerated. Not even his sister knew, for heaven's sake. He's some sort of clandestine service general, and he's meeting with these pirates you have undercover."

"So he's the one after the davic crystals?" It all started to make sense now. "Have you briefed Pimm?"

"I've talked to both Pimm and Kyakh."

"When is it all going down?" Jacelon shifted in bed, wincing at the soreness in every joint of her body.

"I have been monitoring the subspace channels. Pimm and Kyakh are running a little late reporting in. Kellen's cruiser is approximately an hour away."

"All right." Jacelon had to do something. "Now, listen to me, Dad, and don't argue. You have to get me over to your ready room. If you have to roll me in on a gurney, I don't care. I have to know what's going on. I know Pimm, I know Kyakh, God help me, and if I can't fight the good fight in space, I can certainly do so in your office."

"Oh, Rae, I can't—"

"Sir. I will send my best specialist with your daughter to your ready room, if that's all right with you." Gemma stood next to the bed.

"You sure, Doctor?" Ewan frowned.

"She's going to be a major pain here, nagging us until we give in out of sheer exhaustion." Gemma winked at Jacelon. "I know her well, unfortunately."

"Thanks." Jacelon slumped back again. "I confess, I'm too weak to hold a mug of Cormanian coffee, but I have to be there. This is my family we're talking about. Like it or not, it's also about the man who nearly killed me, and the people of Gantharat. I'm a protector, and I need to do my job every way possible."

"I'll arrange for a hover recliner, Admiral." Gemma stepped away, leaving them alone.

"Rae, you make a father so proud and so fearful sometimes."

"Have you told her I'm alive?"

"I haven't had the chance. The *Noma* wasn't reachable when I received news of your recovery. I will notify Kellen as soon as—"

"No. Let me do it. If she hears my voice, it won't be so bad."

"All right." Ewan kissed her forehead before straightening, every bit the senior admiral now. "I will return to the bridge and get a subspace command post set up for you in my ready room. Report to me there ASAP."

"Aye, sir." Jacelon watched him stride out of the room and closed her eyes briefly as she took the opportunity to rest before going back to work. She had no idea which day it was or what time, or exactly where she was. She turned her head and saw only stars through the viewport. "Kellen." Just whispering her name helped gather her strength.

When Gemma returned with more medication, she didn't even object. An orderly lifted her over to the hover recliner and strapped her in. Normally, this would have infuriated and shocked Jacelon, but if he hadn't done so, she would've slumped to the side and ended up in a most undignified heap.

"I know you would rather pilot this yourself, Admiral, but the corridors are crammed with soldiers and different dignitaries and I don't want any more casualties, so let Dr. Vephes handle the control, all right?"

"No problem. I can't exactly see where I'm going from this position. As this is the new flagship, and I'm not familiar with the specs, I don't even *know* where I'm going."

"Good." Gemma raised her eyebrows, clearly suspicious of Jacelon's cooperativeness. "Dr. Vephes is in charge of your health while you're in your father's ready room. When it comes to your physical well-being, what he says, goes. I don't want to hear anything else, or I'll come up there and hover you back here myself."

"I hear you. I do." Jacelon fought the urge to pout at the strict orders. "Good thing we go back a long time, Gemma, or I could've misconstrued that."

"Ha." Gemma's eyes softened. "Just don't exert yourself too much, Rae. We didn't save you from the debris field to have you kill yourself on the bridge. Kellen would never forgive either of us."

"I know." *And I can think of little else.*

❖

"We are less than an hour away from the coordinates in Pimm's latest transmission. I am trying to find her inner beacon on sensors. No luck so far." Commander Owena Grey looked up from her work console. "I suggest we enter from these coordinates," she said, pointing at the viewscreen. "The sun will be behind us, which will make it easier to mask our trail while still cloaked."

"Sounds good." Kellen spoke shortly. "I agree. Helm? Current speed?"

Leanne rattled off the information. "Adjusting the course to the new coordinates."

The doors behind them hissed open and Roshan and Andreia entered with Ayahliss. Kellen had expected Andreia to perhaps opt out of this mission, as they intended to apprehend—or kill—her brother. However, Andreia had always defined herself as a Gantharian citizen first and regarded herself as an Onotharian only from a DNA point of view. She had fought alongside the Gantharian people she loved and identified with for so many years now. Kellen had no doubts about Andreia's allegiance, even if she hadn't hated Trax with a passion. You certainly didn't choose the family you were born into.

"We are receiving a subspace message from the SC," Owena said. "Audio and video."

"On screen." The big viewscreen flickered, and when Rae's face appeared, Kellen gasped out loud.

"Kellen. I'm safe." It was Rae—her face and her voice. Kellen stood on shaky legs.

"Rae."

"I know I look like hell, and it was a close call. I am safe, though. I promise. I'm in my father's ready room, working from my bedside. I'm here to render any assistance I can in your effort to take Trax M'Aldovar out."

"Rae…" Kellen felt as if her brain had short-circuited. All she could do was stare at her wife—the dark gray stormy eyes, the tired lines around them and on her forehead, the slight dryness of her lips. "You are alive."

"Yes, Kellen."

"They found you."

"They did." Rae's eyes welled up, and she blinked several times. "I see you have all of our closest friends there." She raised a limp hand and waved. "Here's my father now."

"Kellen? She really is all right. Not very strong yet, but they have dealt with the issues—"

"What issues?" Kellen asked, her fears reappearing.

"Dad! I told you—"

"What issues?" Kellen walked closer to the screen.

Ewan listed Rae's injuries and what had been done, apparently not caring that everybody on the bridge heard. "And as she was stuck aboard an Onotharian shuttle, she cut her arm, drew blood, and infused human DNA into the shuttle's bioneural circuitry. How's that for ingenuity?"

Kellen was impressed. She had never heard of such a tactic. "And that made the SC stop long enough to ask questions before firing."

"Yes. The rescue ship had already raised shields when the readings came in," Ewan said. "When they saw human DNA on their readings, they deepened their scans and found more human bio-signatures inside. Rae saved two ensigns and ultimately also three Onotharians, who are now POWs in a much nicer prison than would have been the case if the opposite had occurred."

Kellen had not taken her eyes off Rae while Ewan spoke. "Does Dahlia know? Armeo?"

"I have sent a message via one of our courier ships, and I expect to hear from Dahlia any moment. She's been in lockdown several times due to minor attacks by the Onotharians, but neither she nor Judge Beqq is that easily intimidated. They are doing fine."

"Armeo?" Kellen reminded Ewan.

"He never knew Rae was missing. Didn't see the point."

"Good." Relieved, Kellen closed her eyes briefly. "Rae, we're going after Trax M'Aldovar."

"So I heard."

"Kyakh and Pimm have him aboard the *Salaceos* as we speak."

"I have to tell you, Kellen, I don't have a good feeling about that."

"You think there is a risk Kyakh would use this as a way to escape the hold the SC has on her?"

"I don't think she would," Ewan said slowly. "When she called in her report to Rae and found me instead, she didn't strike me as someone about to bail. Admittedly, I don't know the woman, but she took a big leap of faith when she reached out to me. She seemed genuinely concerned."

"I'm not gullible when it comes to someone like Kyakh," Rae said huskily, "but I wouldn't sell her short either. I could be way off there, but I think she's developed a reluctant friendship with Pimm."

"The sentient BNSL. Interesting." Kellen made a mental note of this, sensing it might become important. "We will be within range in less than twenty minutes. I will request radio silence until we are in position within the asteroid belt. Until I contact you, please use text-only messaging, please."

"Understood." Rae lifted her hand briefly. "Be safe, Kellen. All of you."

"We will. Stay strong, Rae. Kellen out."

Kellen sat down in the captain's chair, her knees impossibly weak all of a sudden.

"Fantastic news, Kellen," Leanne said, beaming, from the helm.

"Thank you. Yes." Kellen took another deep breath. "As you heard, we are now operating under radio silence. Adjust cloak to highest setting. We cannot have even the slightest blip on their sensors, or we lose the advantage of a surprise attack."

"Cloak harmonics set to heavy." Owena pushed at the sensors before her. "We are invisible."

Good. Trax had better have enjoyed the last few days, because he was not going to have many more. Kellen drew her upper lip back in a feral grin. "Good hunting, everybody."

CHAPTER TWENTY-SIX

Weiss had never felt more enraged or nauseous. She regarded the spectacle in the cargo bay with a careful look of indifference when all she really wanted was to yank Madisyn out of their claws and run.

Podmer had paraded Madisyn in front of M'Aldovar like she was a prize-winning Gantharian *maesha.* He had not been able to make her display any of her "features," but listed them proudly to the immobilized man.

"She's not bad-looking either, if you're going for the wholesome, slender type." Podmer leered. "Still, I have to warn you, some of my guys tried to have her concede to servicing them when she first came aboard, and though she is an android, she is also sentient with a strong will of her own. Nobody could get her to comply."

"Some would say that's getting the best of both worlds. I'm sure our scientists can reconfigure her, if need be," M'Aldovar said absentmindedly. He looked Madisyn over again. "I don't suppose I should ask her to strip so I can make sure she's as stunning as her exterior suggests."

"Honestly, I wouldn't try that before you have her, what did you say, reconfigured?" Podmer gave another belly laugh. "She's a handful."

"Sounds good to me." M'Aldovar signaled with his eyes to his officers. "Pay the man."

Podmer rubbed his hands as the Onotharians arranged the payment. As they focused on this important task, Weiss dared to look at Madisyn. She stood straight, her hands cuffed and her feet in restraints that allowed only for very short steps. Lifting her gaze to Madisyn's face, she saw no emotion in her features, but her eyes burned with clear hatred. Weiss's heart constricted painfully. Had Madisyn not understood? When she followed Weiss's orders to kick and scream while being captured, Weiss had thought Madi knew they had to stall until a moment presented itself to act upon.

Madisyn now met her eyes dead-on, and the chill they induced traveled throughout Weiss's body. She tried to convey her feelings, but nothing changed in Madisyn's demeanor to suggest she understood.

"I need someone familiar with her physique to accompany us back to my ship," M'Aldovar demanded. "I need to know the specifics regarding her sustenance and so on. If I don't familiarize myself with these facts, she might try to self-destruct without me realizing it."

"Good idea." Podmer agreed willingly. "Kyakh here has shared quarters with Pimm ever since she joined our crew. Have you observed enough to assist General M'Aldovar, Kyakh?" Podmer looked at her as if to dare her to contradict him.

Seeing this as a godsend opportunity to work out an escape, Weiss smiled lopsidedly. "As boring as this droid is, on a personal level, I can safely say that I know what she eats, when she needs sleep, and what diagnostics she runs on a regular basis."

"Excellent. You heard the man, go with them to their ship and install Pimm." Podmer walked up to Madisyn and looked down at her with something mimicking remorse. "Sorry. No hard feelings. Just good business. For you, it should make little difference, really. It will be interesting for you to see another part of space."

Weiss was shocked to hear Podmer talk to Madisyn as if selling her like a slave was a mere career change with new prospects for her. Weiss held her breath as Madisyn's eyes narrowed.

"You unimaginable fool." Madisyn's voice was low but carried clearly throughout the cargo bay. "I never did give you much credit. I saw you as a vain, not so very intelligent thug, and I think that was overstating things. Clearly, you're just as dumb as you look. I pity you." Madisyn turned to M'Aldovar. "Shall we go, then? What are we waiting for?"

Podmer's face was now dark, a sure sign that he was like a high-yield explosive ready to go. "Ungrateful damn droid," he growled. "Get her out of my sight!"

"I'll take care of her." Before anyone else had a chance to react, Weiss lifted Madisyn and hoisted her over her shoulder. "Come on then." She led the way to the airlock. Not daring to show with the slightest caress that she was on Madisyn's side, Weiss let her dangle in such an undignified position, even M'Aldovar's officers smiled faintly.

Aboard M'Aldovar's shuttle, Weiss strapped Madisyn into the seat farthest back and sat down next to her, attaching another harness to herself. M'Aldovar required a lot of assistance as the officers adjusted his hover chair and made sure it was safely locked into place.

"Madi. Please," Weiss whispered. "I'm going to get you out of this." She tried not to move her lips in case they were under video surveillance unawares.

"Don't talk to me." Madisyn spoke quietly, but not as low as Weiss deemed necessary.

"Madi. I'm trying to figure out a way to escape with you. Please trust me."

"Why?"

"Gods, woman, surely you've figured it out by now." Blinking at the stinging sensation behind her burning eyes, Weiss had to use all her motivation and strength not to shout. "I'm doing this, despite my reputation and my past, because *I love you*, damn it!" Startled at her own confession, Weiss kept her eyes forward, scrutinizing the Onotharians as they worked around M'Aldovar and began the launch process.

"What?" Madisyn said, her voice small.

"You heard me." Weiss's lips felt stiff and dry.

"But—"

"Shh. Here they come."

The officers made sure they were strapped in, and one of them checked Madisyn's shackles. When he was done, he let his fingers run through her hair, only to yank his hand back when she growled at him and bared her even, small teeth.

"She always this feral?" the officer asked Weiss. "She'll need some serious modification to be of use to the general."

"Yeah, he might regret ever buying this wildcat," Weiss said.

"There's more than one way to break someone in. A damn droid shouldn't be too hard," the young officer said with contempt.

"Exactly." Weiss smiled, knowing full well just how feral she could look. "In the meantime, my best tip is to keep your distance.

She can sever a finger just as easily as a laser knife. I've seen her in action."

"Really?" The Onotharian ensign took a step back, which delighted Weiss. "All right. We're about to take off. Remain seated. This close to the asteroid belt, it can be a bit bumpy."

"Understood."

The young man left and Weiss heard Madisyn exhale. "Thank you."

"Try not to move your lips when talking. Something tells me that a paranoid man like M'Aldovar has surveillance everywhere. Whisper and keep your lips still if you can."

"All right." Madisyn shifted in her seat. "Did you really mean it?"

"You can laugh or ridicule me later. Yes."

"Why would I ridicule you?"

"Just my luck, huh, to fall for someone who hates me."

"I—I don't hate you, Weiss."

Weiss began to tremble. "What? But you do. You hate anything to do with pirates and mercenaries." It was so tempting to turn her head to try to read the truth in Madisyn's eyes. This might be their undoing, so Weiss closed her eyes almost completely, leaving only a slit big enough to keep an eye on the Onotharians.

"I do. I do hate them. Just…not you."

"Why?"

"Because you've changed."

"Not that much. I'm still the person who kidnapped Dahlia Jacelon and helped M'Ekar to escape. Several people were killed on Corma because of that."

"I didn't say you don't have a lot to atone for. You do. And you are. You're here, obviously trying to save me, risking your own life in the process. You could've left a long time ago, obviously. You're here." Madisyn sounded like she was trying to convince Weiss as well as comfort and encourage herself at the same time.

"Yes, I am, and I'm not going anywhere without you. We're going to get out of this, Madi."

"I like for you to call me that. You're the only one that ever has." Madisyn's voice caught. "If you can't get me away from him, I will remember it."

"Stop it. Stop." Furious at the thought of failure, Weiss curled her toes inside her boots and dug her nails into her palms to regain self-control. "You're returning to SC space with me. You said it yourself. The protector is hunting M'Aldovar, and from what I know of her, failure is not an option. We just have to make sure we're ready when it happens."

"All right. Guess I'm just afraid."

"Nothing wrong with that. This is a dangerous situation on a far more personal level." Weiss would have given anything to wrap Madisyn up in her arms and hold her tight, protect her from everything that frightened her. Being brutally honest with herself, Weiss was just as much in need of such an embrace. She feared she might screw up and lose what window of opportunity the protector's imminent attack might provide.

"Are you afraid?" Madisyn could clearly read minds.

"Not of them, but for you, yes. Of you, in a way, yes."

"What do you mean, of me?"

"I've never loved anyone since I lost my mother. This was very inconvenient."

A soundless laugh from Madisyn startled Weiss, who opened her eyes fully to make sure nobody heard. "Stop laughing!"

"Sorry, but it sounded kind of funny." Madisyn raised her hands and wiped at her eyes.

"How amusing that I can provide some comic relief." Rigid, Weiss retook her position with her arms folded and her eyes half-closed.

"It's not funny. It's sad, really." Suddenly filled with sympathy, Madisyn's whispers soothed Weiss like nothing else ever had. "I think you are on your path of atonement. As am I."

"You? You have nothing to atone for. You're the victim in all this."

"Yes, and I've lived and breathed like an avenging victim ever since my parents died. That's not what they wanted for me. Instead of continuing their work, our work, at the university, I joined the Guild Nation Intelligence Forces as a way to cope, to fight back."

"And I joined the enemy, the pirates, for the very same reason."

They sat in silence for several minutes. Weiss saw images from her childhood flicker through her mind. She hadn't allowed those memories to surface for a long time. When the vision of her mother remained, she wanted to press her wrists against her eyelids and pry the memory of the soft-spoken woman out of her brain. Quicinda Kyakhsehn had done nothing but love and care for her daughter as she worked as a chef aboard a generational ship heading for the SC.

When pirates attacked, it had seemed that the seasoned leaders aboard had everything under control. Herding the children to a shelter deep inside the belly of the vast ship, every one among the four thousand crewmembers knew exactly what to do. But they had no way of knowing that they had come across a new breed of ruthless pirates. This well-organized band dealt just as much in the trafficking of humanoids as illegal drugs, and even humanoid organs.

"Weiss?" Madisyn nudged her carefully. "Weiss. Wipe your cheeks."

"What?" Hastily Weiss felt her cheeks, mortified at the wet traces of tears. *For stars and skies...*

"Are we slowing down?" Madisyn's voice trembled.

"Seems so."

"Weiss?" Madisyn pressed harder into the seat and began to breathe faster. Her eyes darted back and forth between M'Aldovar and Weiss.

"I won't leave you. I promise. No matter what happens, I *won't* leave you, Madi."

"You really do love me?"

"Desperately." Weiss never thought she'd profess to love, certainly not to a complex, unique woman in mortal danger.

"I trust you. If you say you'll get me out of this, I know you will, or die trying." Sounding surer than Weiss felt, Madisyn's words drilled into Weiss's soul. Could it be true that Madisyn didn't hate her as much as before? Weiss gripped the armrests as M'Aldovar's shuttle momentarily lost inertial dampeners. A whining sound showed that the helmsman had engaged the brakes and was about to enter the Onotharians' shuttle bay. Sick at the thought of what might happen to Madisyn now, Weiss steeled herself. Without finesse, the shuttle came to a sudden halt, tossing them against the harness and bouncing them off the backrest.

"Weiss?"

"Yes?"

Madisyn drew a deep, trembling breath. "Whatever happens, don't blow our cover. The mission—"

"Comes first. Sure." Weiss wasn't sure at all. Her rebellious side insisted on making Madisyn her first priority, but her feelings for Madisyn caused an irrational urge to make her proud.

The Onotharian officers came toward them. Yanking Madisyn free from the harness with hard hands, they motioned for Weiss to follow them.

"She can't walk like that," Weiss reminded them, gesturing toward Madisyn's shackles. "Either you have to free her feet, or I will carry her."

The men looked indecisively at each other.

"All right. I don't think M'Aldovar wants his new prize possession to be bruised or dented, so I'll just carry her, all right?" Weiss scooped up Madisyn, one arm under her knees, one around her back. "Hold on to me," she whispered.

Madisyn clung to Weiss and hid her face against her neck. Weiss was about to remind Madisyn that this was perhaps not the ideal way to convince the Onotharians they were indifferent to each other, but she didn't have the heart to push Madisyn away.

"This way," one of the officers said darkly. "The general wants her stored in cargo bay seven."

Stored? What the hell... Weiss followed the officers out of the shuttle bay and into a corridor. Holding Madisyn close, she memorized the layout of the ship as they made their way to the cargo bay.

Bay seven turned out to be a sparsely lit, barren storage facility that held what looked like advanced technical equipment. A medical bed, surrounded by large pieces of technology, took up half of the space. On the other side stood a huge cylindrical container, filled up to fifty centimeters with a green substance. Weiss grew increasingly concerned when one of the Onotharian officers began to punch commands into its computer console. She carefully lowered Madisyn to the floor and supported her as she stood.

A small hatch swung open on the glass cylinder.

"Tuck her right in."

"What the hell is that thing?" Weiss held on to Madisyn.

"Just storage. This way, the oxygenized plasma fluid will maintain her in pristine condition until the general has use for her. It will recalibrate her to extract anything that makes her a security risk."

"Plasma fluid? Are you insane?" Weiss backed up, pulling Madisyn with her. "She'll drown in there!"

"Drown? No, no. She's got synthetic lungs, right? This will infuse the oxygen through her skin and into her system. It'll be unpleasant at first, but she'll live."

"This was not part of the deal. You don't know anything about this type of BNSL," Weiss said, frantic now. "Your general may have bought her, but that doesn't mean he can kill her. She's *sentient*, you idiots."

"She's an android. Onotharat doesn't legally recognize sentience in machines. Get her over here."

The men approached them, and Weiss backed up farther.

"Please," Madisyn said. "She's right. I might not survive in the damn thing, and if I don't, you will have to explain to your boss how you killed something he paid a lot for."

This stopped them for a moment, but then the highest-ranking continued toward them. "It's the general's explicit order to use the plasma chamber. If there's a mishap, I'm sure our best scientists can do something about it. General M'Aldovar moves in the highest circles among the Onotharian chairmen, politicians, and scientists. You see how he is? Well, he was actually dead for several hours. His survival is a testament to Onotharian superiority."

"Or bad taste," Madisyn hissed.

"An android with a sense of humor," the Onotharian officer said, smiling mockingly. "Priceless." He motioned with his fingers in the air. "Get her over here."

"Never." Weiss produced a small sidearm with a flick of her wrist. "I'm taking her back."

"You and who else, and how?" The ensign laughed.

"I can start by firing on either of you." Perspiration broke out on Weiss's back. She knew they were trapped and she needed to stall for as long as she could. Kellen O'Dal was on her way, and if she could keep the men occupied until she was ready to strike—

"I wouldn't recommend it."

"That wouldn't stop me. This might look insignificant, but as you know, the Guild Nation has a few tricks up their sleeves as well, from a scientific point of view."

"So you're going to fire on three of us with one weapon before we manage to return fire?" The ensign laughed again.

His eyes shifted, and something in them as he looked behind Weiss alerted her. She began to turn her head, holding on tight to Madisyn, when pain suddenly exploded behind her eyes. The last thing she heard was Madisyn screaming her name.

Chapter Twenty-seven

Kellen stood over the vast sensor grid table in the cartography room, her eyes locked on the small illuminated outline of the *Salaceos* and the Onotharian *g'shedo*-category vessel. The *Salaceos* was located just inside the asteroid belt, and the Onotharian ship was barely visible where it hid well within the belt. Only the Guild Nation's enhanced sensors made it possible to distinguish between the midsize ship and the mineral-based rocks.

Scanning again for Madisyn Pimm's internal beacon, as well as Kyakh's cloaked implant, she found only a faint trace of Pimm's signal. Concerned, Kellen double-checked the coordinates. Pimm was clearly aboard the Onotharian ship. Where was Kyakh? Had she escaped, was she dead, or had she disabled the chip? Logic suggested that Kyakh had done the latter *and* escaped, but for some reason, Ewan Jacelon had faith in her.

What was it about this woman that made first Rae and then her father give her the benefit of the doubt? Rae had defended her decision by pointing out that Kyakh had the cloaked chip in place. Kellen knew that, given enough time and offering enough credits, Kyakh could possibly disable it, or find someone who could. She had disabled M'Ekar's chip once, after all. If she was able to locate the damn thing, it wouldn't take her long to destroy it.

So, if Rae's and Ewan's hunches were correct and if Kyakh was still there, which ship would she be on? Kellen figured Kyakh would probably find a way to join her fellow undercover agent. Nobody had ever questioned Kyakh's sense of loyalty. The survivors from her ship that went down in the Disi-Disi forest on Corma had all testified to her qualities as a captain. She had never left a crewmember behind, and she treated everybody with fairness, though she terrified most of them.

Kellen rapped her fingertips against the grid table. She was beginning to form a plan, and she needed to run it by her team. Pimm could be aboard the Onotharian ship for several reasons, but the fact that she had not responded to the subspace signal they'd sent to her internal sensor concerned her. So far, Pimm had stayed in touch regularly and always responded to hails. The possibility that Pimm might be disabled or fatally damaged chilled Kellen. Many people regarded sentient androids as nothing more than a political ploy, but in her mind, a life was a life, regardless of the origin.

"We're ready, Kellen," Owena said from the door leading to the bridge. "Leanne reported reaching our position a minute ago and our cloak is firmly in place. Shields are at a hundred percent and all systems are at peak performance."

"Good." Kellen pointed at the grid table. "This is the Onotharian ship. We need to move in closer so we can surprise them. I want the assault craft ready to launch and the cloaking-capable shuttle to spearhead the operation."

"The marines are ready, as are the fighter pilots."

"Thank you. We need to locate Kyakh. Her internal chip isn't registering, which leads me to think she might have disabled it."

"Ah, she could be long gone if that's the case."

"I don't know why I feel so sure she isn't. Perhaps Ewan's and Rae's view of her has rubbed off on me."

"I thought Rae hated her for what she did to Ayahliss and Dahlia?" Owena followed Kellen's fingers as she traced a trajectory on the grid table.

"She did, at first. But even she reluctantly admired Kyakh. Rae can appreciate proficiency in anyone, even an enemy."

"Guess that's hereditary. Dahlia tended to and protected Ambassador M'Ekar, whom she loathed, in the Disi-Disi jungle and ended up saving his life."

"Thus sending him back to 'that mosquito-infested hell of a planet,' to quote M'Ekar." Owena pursed her lips. "So justice was served, and as far as I know, he's still there."

"She saw something in him there, when circumstances changed," Kellen maintained. "Something more humane that turned him into a *person*, not merely a force out to hurt her or someone in her family. I think that's the same reason she convinced Rae that Kyakh was more than a ruthless mercenary."

"And that's why you think Kyakh has suddenly become loyal to the SC?" Owena looked doubtful.

"Or to Madisyn Pimm." Kellen pulled on the harness that came with the Ruby Red suit and attached her rods to her left hip. She double-checked her sidearm before attaching it to her right hip. "Either way, we need to consider the possibility that either Pimm or Kyakh or both is on M'Aldovar's ship."

"Assuming it *is* him and that he is aboard this ship," Owena said kindly.

"He is. I can sense it."

Owena didn't comment on Kellen's uncharacteristic statement. Normally not prone to relying on what humans called a sixth sense, Kellen couldn't explain why she was certain Trax M'Aldovar was aboard. And soon he would be hers. Hers to put in a cage…or to end his life, again.

"Let's go," Kellen said, grabbing a handheld computer. She downloaded the information from the table to it and snapped it onto her belt. "We have a score to settle."

❖

"So you care for that abomination."

Weiss jerked at the raspy, harsh voice. Something wheezed, and the piercing light on the other side of her closed eyelids was painful enough for her to hesitate to open them.

"Admittedly, she is rather attractive, but lowering yourself to copulating with a machine is nothing short of a disgrace. If we were on Onotharat, I'd have you arrested."

"Who's there?" Weiss tried to sit up, but winced at the pain in her head and the back of her neck. She blinked at the light, trying to focus on the outline of a man. Her head hurt with each resurfacing memory as she stared at Trax M'Aldovar where he sat strapped into his hover chair. "Where is Madisyn?"

"The android is kept where she is rendered harmless. She's quite safe."

"Oh, Gods, you've put her in that damn container. That cylinder! She'll drown!" Aghast, Weiss disregarded her own physical comfort and sat up. Someone had put her on a cot in what looked like a holding cell. Blinking diodes outlined the opening and M'Aldovar sat in his chair on the other side. Weiss hesitantly pushed her hand through the opening, but wasn't surprised when a shock traveled up her arm, followed her neck, and hurt her earlobe. *A damn force field.* This technology, under development mainly on Guild Nation, was in its infant stages as far as Weiss knew. The Onotharians seemed to have figured it out, or obtained it—likely stolen it—from someone.

"Very brave of you, hiding behind a tech solution like that," she taunted M'Aldovar. "You're afraid of Madisyn, so you stick her in a cylinder filled with goo. You're afraid of me, so you erect a force field between us. If I didn't know better, I'd say you were afraid of strong women, period."

"Shut up! If you value your life, don't speak another word," M'Aldovar croaked, and began to cough. "I'll dismantle that mockery of a woman before I ever let the two of you see each other. I can tell you're fond of her, and it's downright sick. Unnatural."

"She's more real than you ever were or ever will be," Weiss said slowly, backing up to sit down on the cot. "She's kind and sweet, and she cares about people and ideals. You're nothing but a sociopath with political power and connections. You've been defeated before, and you will be again."

"By whom?" M'Aldovar sneered.

"By—"

Emergency klaxons began to blare and the light switched to a red hue. Weiss heard voices shout in Onotharian over the comm system.

"What the hell…?" M'Aldovar pivoted his chair and drove up to the two men guarding the door. "Find out."

"Yes, General." The men grabbed their communicators and followed orders.

"As I said," Weiss stated calmly, "this is just the beginning—of the end."

"You!" Twirling with his chair, M'Aldovar glared at her, his stare as acidic as if it truly could burn her skin. "You don't speak."

"Try to stop me." Weiss was taking a calculated risk that the force field could withstand plasma-pulse weapons and such. "Why don't you wheel that chair of yours in here and stop me. Must be really annoying, not to mention frustrating, to have a mere woman talk back like this. A woman has defeated you before, so the rumors have it. Didn't a woman put you in that chair? Robbed you of your future, in a sense?"

"A woman made the mistake of thinking she killed me," M'Aldovar hissed. "She left me for dead, but I fooled her. I fooled them all. I rose in the ranks faster than anyone my age and outsmarted any of the others who had intact bodies. What use is a perfect body if you don't have the brains to go with it?"

"True, true," Weiss said, making sure she sounded sickly sweet. "And what does it matter that you have to rely on the assistance of others for every single thing in life? That's no big deal, is it?" Weiss would've loathed mocking any other person's misfortune, or their pain or injuries. This man, however, had taken Madisyn and tucked her in a damn glass tube. As if *she* hadn't suffered enough at the hands of callous, greedy, power-hungry individuals.

A whistling sound, all too familiar, drowned out the roar Weiss's words forced out of M'Aldovar. An explosion rocked the ship, nearly tossing Weiss onto the floor. M'Aldovar's chair rolled forward despite his attempts to stop it with voice commands, and its front hit the force field. A cascade of sparks showered him and he cursed out loud. Clearly, he had some sensation left in his skin, Weiss thought maliciously. Another explosion sent the ship hurtling, and the inertial dampeners went offline momentarily. Weiss didn't wait. She kicked the wall and let the weightlessness carry her toward the opening. Hoping M'Aldovar had done serious damage to the field, she made sure her boots would take the brunt of the force.

The air around her crackled as she floated through the opening, and when she was clear of it, the inertial dampeners came online and she landed with a thud on her bottom on the floor. M'Aldovar's chair had risen a few centimeters off the floor level and now bounced down as well.

Glancing over by the door, Weiss saw that the guards were still carrying out their orders of finding out what was going on. It wasn't hard to guess. Kellen O'Dal and her unit had arrived. For the first time since she'd disabled the chip in her abdomen, Weiss cursed herself for doing so. Kellen couldn't know that she was aboard this ship. *Madisyn!* Perhaps the protector had scanned for Madisyn's internal sensor and found her?

Weiss headed for the door, not sure which deck she was on. Outside, she saw markings in the darkened corridor, but they were Onotharian and she understood only enough of the language to curse at someone.

Madisyn was in one of the cargo bays on the lower decks, and that's what mattered. Weiss yanked open one door after another, trying to find a staircase or a lift. If Kellen intended to blow this ship into space dust, Weiss needed to find Madisyn, get her out of the cylinder, and somehow make contact. Weiss moaned as her headache escalated almost beyond control when she began to run toward the end of the corridor. The ship rocked from more explosions, and the inertial dampeners went offline again, causing her to slam into the bulkhead. She didn't care about the pain. Clawing her way along the wall, Weiss only cared about finding Madisyn, and she was running out of time.

CHAPTER TWENTY-EIGHT

"So good to see you, Reena." Ayahliss looked hungrily at the computer screen on the wall of her small unit. Reena in fact looked fatigued, with dark circles beneath her eyes. She revealed a new vulnerability, something Ayahliss wondered if she normally let anyone see.

"Sweet soul, I miss you." Reena pushed her thick hair out of her face. "I know you haven't been gone long, but the fact that you are on yet another dangerous mission…"

"I will be very careful." Ayahliss wanted to touch Reena's pale cheeks on the screen and tightened her fists under the desk. "Kellen's plan is sound."

"I know you will, and I know it is." Looking frustrated, Reena rested her head in her hand, slumping sideways. "Stars and skies, I'm not helping at all, am I? I'm sorry."

Ayahliss was ready to jump through the screen and hold Reena close. She had never felt protective in her life until she met Armeo, and now her urge extended past the Jacelons and Kellen to Reena. This feeling held so many dimensions and was so new; she could only let it unravel on its own since she had no idea how else to handle it. She did, however, have to prevent this weary sense of guilt written across Reena's beautiful face.

"You don't have to be sorry, Reena," Ayahliss said, now actually touching the base of the screen. "This is exactly what I need to hear. Don't you see?"

"What?"

"I need to know that you are with me in your heart." Reena sat up and leaned closer to the screen. "This will be dangerous, and it hurts me to worry you, but I've never had such a strong motivation to return in one piece. I used to think it was important to return so I could fight another day. This is different."

"Tell me how, Ayahliss." Reena cleared her voice.

"I will go into battle focusing on returning in one piece." Ayahliss lowered her eyes for a moment, her stomach fluttering madly. "To you."

"Ayahliss." Reena's face softened and her eyes suddenly glowed with such emotion they calmed the tremors in Ayahliss's belly. "Nothing, *nothing* is more important to me than your safe return. You have to come back."

"When you return to the *Circinus*, I wish you'd consider staying with me in my quarters. I don't want to miss another moment with you."

Ayahliss was certain she must've misunderstood. "Stay with you? Like moving in?" Her throat constricted.

"Yes. Just think about it, Ayahliss. I care so deeply for you. For so long, I have devoted my life to my work—it's been my passion. This is such a fantastic change. I think of you all the time, and though I'll probably always be career-oriented, my center of gravity has changed."

"Because of me?" Ayahliss didn't know where she found the courage to ask.

"Certainly because of you. I tried to tell you I'm too old for you, but you ignored that. I thought perhaps I could be your mentor, a guide to the Supreme Constellations society, and yes, I have dipped into both of these roles, but I've just scratched the surface."

"It took me a long time to understand why I was so nervous and unsure around you." Ayahliss wanted her to understand that she wasn't the only one harboring doubts and fears. "You seemed unattainable, out of my league, but I've tried to change my point of view. We are humanoids, age be damned, and status too, right?"

Reena laughed, a breathless sound, and Ayahliss thought she could find a trace of surprise beneath it.

"You're so right, sweet soul," Reena said, her eyes glittering now. They seemed to have lost most of their tired, forlorn expression, and

Ayahliss mapped every feature despite already knowing every square millimeter of her. "Promise me again that you'll be safe."

"I do. I promise. I won't take foolhardy risks. You and I have a lot to talk about, and I can't wait to—to hold you again." Ayahliss fiddled with the computer console, restless and desperately needing to latch onto something since Reena was so far away. "You must promise the same thing," she added, suddenly acutely aware that no part of space in this sector was especially safe.

"I give you my word. Dahlia and I have to go planetside to Gantharat before you return. I think Kellen made Dahlia give her word on that one, since this wasn't our original plan."

"Good idea. She needs to stay focused on the mission as well. If Kellen had to worry about Dahlia—again—she might be less able to concentrate."

"Yes." Reena sat silent for a moment, gazing at Ayahliss's face. "I can't look at you enough. I know how you taste and smell, which drives me crazy when I can't reach out and hold you."

"I feel just like that!"

"Isn't that fortunate?" Tenderly, Reena slid her fingertips along the screen. Since every pixel of the screen contained the imagizer, Reena's gentle movement seemed to be a reflection in a mirror. Instead she was the amazing, stunning woman who insisted Ayahliss resided in her heart.

Ayahliss had to let Reena know just how important she was. She swallowed repeatedly, thinking about the words that would convey the truth without actually going too far. To speak of love like this, via an impersonal computer screen, felt wrong. Reena spoke of affection and attraction, but neither of them had openly voiced the words of love. Still, this had to be what scorched her heart and singed her soul. Reena called her "sweet soul," a term of endearment Ayahliss had never heard her use toward anyone else.

"I'll talk with you soon, Reena," Ayahliss finally managed to say. "In the meantime, remember that you're so very important to me. Without you, my heart will be like a desert."

"I understand. I really do." Reena caressed the screen again. "When you get back and we're together again, I'll show you just how much."

Ayahliss loved how Reena's voice deepened and her eyes darkened. "I look forward to it."

❖

"Ayahliss, you're with me in shuttle one with the first team. Owena, you're heading up the second team in shuttle two. Roshan, Andreia, you're in charge of team three. Leanne, you have the bridge here on the *Noma*." Kellen relayed orders in a short, clipped voice. "We will take up the rear of the squadron of assault craft. When I give the order, we will board the Onotharian ship. Any questions?"

A chorus of "no, ma'am" echoed through the shuttle bay.

"Excellent." Kellen looked at her senior crew. "I expect you all to use caution and, also, to leave M'Aldovar to me."

Again, the response was affirmative.

"All right." Kellen relaxed marginally. "Remember, we might have two agents in there. You know what they look like. May the stars bless us with success."

She entered the shuttle, her senses heightened. She was able to reach this level through meditation, but when facing battle, it seemed to happen by itself. Her skin tingled, her vision sharpened, and she heard things a normal humanoid couldn't possibly hear.

Ayahliss took her seat next to Kellen, her young face stark and with the same focus. Kellen knew that Ayahliss had talked at great length with Judge Beqq and then meditated. She now stared straight ahead, her eyes a pale blue.

As the shuttle departed, Kellen rose and pulled up the blueprint of the stealth-scans she'd performed of the Onotharian ship. It wasn't as accurate as an open scan, but enough to give them an idea of the vessel's layout. Connecting to the other shuttles, Kellen used a secure subspace signal to communicate her voice and the blueprint.

"Kellen O'Dal to shuttles two and three. These are the latest scans of the Onotharian ship. Familiarize yourself with the closest route to your objective. We have the element of surprise, but that won't last. Once they know we're aboard, we cannot waver. All plasma-pulse weapons set to heavy stun. If you find yourself in a perilous situation, use deadly force. I repeat what I stressed earlier: Trax M'Aldovar is mine. Do not engage him. Any questions?"

"Everything crystal clear, Protector," Roshan O'Landha said over the comm link.

"No questions, ma'am," Owena said smartly.

"Very well. We have three minutes before we reach their position. So far, they are busy defending themselves against our assault craft, which will continue to attack when we go inside to keep as many of them as possible busy. Do not decloak until you are inside their shuttle bay. Once I learn their shields are failing, I will give the order."

Another set of "yes, ma'am" came through the speaker system.

"Good hunting, everybody. Be safe. Kellen O'Dal out."

Kellen moved back to her seat and pulled her helmet on. She strapped back in and gripped her weapon. The Ruby Red suit protected her against any piercing objects, but not plasma-pulse discharges. She had relented, thinking of Rae, and wore a protective vest on top of it. Not how her revered ancestors carried out their assignment, but things had changed.

Looking up, she saw the Onotharian ship through the viewport in the front of the shuttle. It wasn't the biggest in the Onotharian armada, but it was big enough. According to scans, approximately a hundred and twenty-some crewmembers were aboard. It could have been worse. Some Onotharian ships carried more than five thousand.

"Thirty seconds to touchdown, ma'am," the pilot said.

"Affirmative." Not about to waste time, Kellen stood, holding on to one of the straps dangling from the ceiling, meant for that purpose. "Kellen O'Dal to shuttles two and three. Fifteen seconds to go. Onotharian shields are failing. Ten seconds. Five."

Shuttle one skidded in through the opening that led to the shuttle bay. Kellen watched the monitors and saw the other two shuttles follow. As they halted at the far end of the shuttle bay, Kellen pressed the sensor to open the back hatch. The marines accompanying her team moved out, securing the area outside. Kellen followed with Ayahliss next to her.

To her left, marines fired and she swung, her rifle tucked hard against her shoulder. Three Onotharians ran toward them, moving fast and zigzagging. She fired on the first one, sending him flying. Her rifle, set on heavy stun, then found the second one, and before she could fire again, Ayahliss's weapon found the third.

"We need to start a floor-to-floor sweep," Kellen called out when it seemed they had cleared the shuttle bay. "Remember, look for our agents, Kyakh and Pimm, as well as M'Aldovar."

The marines divided themselves up into teams of three, heading for the door leading to the main corridor. They were at the very bottom of the ship and needed to move up deck by deck very quickly or they might be cut off from the rest of it.

"Ayahliss, as they perform the sweep, you and I need to advance faster. We can't risk the Onotharians barricading themselves and jumping to distortion drive."

"I'm right with you." Ayahliss hefted her rifle, her eyes feral. She glanced at her scanner, which was attached to her sleeve. "No life signs from the corridor other than our marines."

"Good. Let's go." Kellen signaled to the other team leaders that she and Ayahliss were heading out. Roshan returned the wave and motioned for Andreia to follow her toward the aft of the ship. The cargo bays were of special interest for the Gantharians, since they often held medical technology as well as weapons.

The corridor was dimly lit, the bulkhead and deck plating made of a dark gray alloy that seemed to swallow much of the light. Kellen moved past the marines who were conscientiously doing their door-to-door search.

At the end of the corridor, a narrow ladder led up through a tube. Kellen wasn't about to get stuck in a lift, so the ladder seemed the smart way to go. She peered up, weapon raised, but the tube looked empty as far as she could see.

"Let's go. This is our best bet," she said to Ayahliss. "Make sure nobody sneaks up behind us."

"Will do."

Kellen placed her rifle in the holder on her back and pulled out her wristband sidearm instead. Attaching it to her right wrist, she merely had to flex her muscles in a certain pattern to fire a round of heavy stun plasma-pulse charges. She climbed the ladder, her strong legs moving like pistons as she counted each deck she passed.

The Onotharian ship consisted of twenty-four decks, with the shuttle bay located on deck six. The bridge, as customary on most spaceships, took up most of deck one, together with ready rooms, conference rooms, and something that looked like a private mess hall on the blueprints. Probably for the captain and distinguished passengers.

At deck twelve, Kellen stopped again to scan, as did Ayahliss. She saw movement by approximately twenty-five crewmembers, but no indication that any one of them used a hover chair. Instead, they seemed to be scurrying in all directions. The marines' sporadic, unsynchronized attacks clearly had them panicking. *Caught with your trousers around your ankles, aren't you?* Kellen felt a joyless smile curve her lips.

"Let's keep going. So far, no sign of M'Aldovar."

One good thing about climbing the agonizing ladder was that they were out of the worst of the alarm klaxons. Blaring alarms drove Kellen insane within seconds.

Three more decks up, she stared at her scanner. "Ayahliss, please tell me you see the same thing I do."

Ayahliss moved her scanner in small circles. "One male Onotharian, in a hover chair of some sort." Ayahliss smiled broadly, her white teeth glimmering in the muted light. "And what do you know, Protector, doesn't it look like he's all alone, the poor thing."

"It sure does." Kellen had to smile at Ayahliss's gleeful tone. "The corridor isn't as crowded as some of the ones we've passed, which might explain why they're panicking. They haven't found him yet." She squinted at the scanner. "What is that room? So many force fields… Ayahliss, it has to be the brig."

"And what would someone like him be doing in the brig?" Ayahliss sucked her lower lip in. "My first guess would be—to gloat. My second—to interrogate."

"I imagine both." Kellen let her sidearm stay on her wrist as she pulled her rifle from the harness. She raised it as she opened the door to the corridor. At first it seemed abandoned, but then she heard rapid footfalls. She aimed and sent the first two crewmen flying with her heavy stun charge. Soon, she and Ayahliss had a pile of downed Onotharians.

"Come on, I think that's it for now," Kellen called, and ran toward the other end of the corridor. "Brig is this way."

In only seconds they reached the big double door leading into the brig. Just as Kellen was about to hit the sensor that opened it, Ayahliss yanked at her arm.

"What's up?" Kellen snapped her head toward Ayahliss.

"Something's weird."

"Weird?"

"In there. Something's not right, and I can't make out what it is… oh. Oh, Gods."

"What's wrong?" Alarmed, Kellen stepped closer to Ayahliss and gazed down at her scanner. "What the hell?" Kellen rarely cursed, but being around Rae had shown her when it was appropriate to use colorful words, and this was one of them. "Is he weightless?"

"I believe he is." The glee was back in Ayahliss's expression. "For some reason, they've managed to contain the loss of inertial dampeners to the brig, and somehow I don't think they realize that he's in there. My scanner is suggesting two unconscious individuals floating at the far wall. I don't understand what happened in there, but if we open the door without erecting a force field or reinstalling artificial gravity, we'll have a problem."

"Yes, I agree." Kellen wasn't sure of the exact nature of such a problem, but she'd heard stories about small, but deadly vortices forming, as well as bulkheads being ripped to shreds. She wasn't about to risk any possible danger when so many of her crew were aboard this ship. "Let's find out where the controls are. We need to fix this and get him out and back to the shuttle."

"So far we don't have any unwelcome company heading our way. This must be an unpopular deck, with the brig and everything."

"Good." Kellen began to remove plating from the bulkhead, exposing wiring, pipes, and hidden technology. "This reminds me of one more reason why I hate Onotharian ships. So many components, it's ridiculous." She plucked her technical scanner from her belt and ran it along the vast circuit board. "Here. This should be it. Short-circuited. I think we're responsible."

"Breaks my heart." Ayahliss grinned. "Can you bypass it?"

"I believe so. Isn't it useful to be a former resistance fighter?"

"Yes. All the little habits and skills you pick up." Ayahliss passed tools to Kellen and frequently scanned the corridor.

"Perhaps I managed—"

A large thud from the brig interrupted Kellen. She turned to Ayahliss, surprised. "Guess that takes the guessing out of the game."

"I'd say." Ayahliss raised her rifle.

"Careful." Kellen mimicked Ayahliss's movements and directed her aim at the door. She pressed the sensor to open it but nothing happened.

Kellen tried again, this time holding the sensor down longer.

Slowly, agonizingly so, the door slid open. A tremor under their feet proved the assault craft was still doing its job creating diversions. Kellen peered inside. Everything not attached to the bulkhead or deck was scattered all over the large space. Obviously this was the brig, with six holding cells within sight, and, Kellen estimated, another six behind those. In the center of the brig lay a bulky item. A hover chair. Gripping her weapon tighter, Kellen squinted through the dusty debris. Where was M'Aldovar?

CHAPTER TWENTY-NINE

The cargo bay was dark, with only a greenish light coming from the far end. Life support must have failed at some point; the bulkhead was damp with condensation and the temperature low.

Weiss disregarded the stabbing pain in her joints and midsection. She had been tossed around several times on her way back here, when the Protector's ships were firing against M'Aldovar. Limping, she made her way over to the area where she had left Madisyn.

The glass cylinder was half full with the green oxygenized plasma fluid. Inside, hovering due to some insidious Onotharian technology, Madisyn hung suspended, unconscious. Her head bent back at nearly an impossible angle, she seemed already dead, as the greenish light illuminated her from underneath.

"Madi." Weiss looked at all the controls. She had no idea which one opened the cylinder. What if Madisyn died because she did it the wrong way? Her heart beating so fast she feared it might dislodge, Weiss climbed up on the dais of the cylinder, grabbing the bar casing with one hand and touching the glass with the other. It was oddly warm, probably because of the disgusting green goo. It rose around Madisyn's hovering body, and Weiss didn't have long to think of a way to open the cylinder. She hit the glass with her palm, over and over. "Madi! Madisyn! Can you hear me?"

Weiss saw no indication that Madisyn was conscious, only a faint sheen on her biosynthetic skin, which had to be condensation. Surely Madi wasn't able to perspire? Weiss tried not to think about what kind of pain or agony it would take to make an android sweat.

Jumping off the dais, Weiss headed over to the massive computer console. Next to it stood a sinister-looking examination table, white non-woven sheets haphazardly thrown across it. Gods, she hoped they hadn't strapped her to that thing. Madi!

The Onotharian computer was fortunately not as hard to decipher as she had assumed. The symbols were close enough to Gantharian and Revosian for Weiss to interpret them. This was, however, not the same as knowing which cycle or command to use. She let her finger travel down the scrolling list of features, frowning at some, her anger rising at Onotharians in general and M'Aldovar in particular.

A ping from the cylinder startled her. Looking up, she saw the oxygenized plasma fluid begin to bubble, and in a moment of terror, Weiss imagined it actually boiling Madisyn. The green fluid now reached Madi's lower chest. Turning back to the console, Weiss punched in a few diagnostic commands. The computer obediently ran them and promptly told her everything was running at peak performance. Relieved, Weiss dared to use a few of the simpler commands. At first nothing happened, and she added a generic command for empty or vacate. She glanced over at Madisyn. The green fluid had stopped bubbling, which was a promising sign.

Another set of commands initiated a gurgling sound from the glass cylinder. Weiss clenched her hands and kept them ready to use the abort code if this didn't go well. The green fluid wasn't bubbling anymore, but instead seemed to shift a little, back and forth. Suddenly a low rumble quickly turned into a veritable roar.

"No!" Weiss winced at the sight of the green fluid levels rising at an alarming rate. If she wasn't able to stop it, it would be above Madisyn's head within half a minute. Looking around, about to panic, Weiss saw a half-closed cabinet behind the cylinder. She flung the door open. Inside it were Onotharian plasma blasters. Thank the stars!

Grabbing a rifle, Weiss unhooked the safety and placed it against her shoulder as she turned back to the glass cylinder. The green fluid now covered Madisyn to her chin. Weiss couldn't lose any more time. Aiming twenty centimeters above Madisyn's head, she fired.

The glass shattered and flew in all directions around the dais. Oxygenized plasma fluid cascaded in a green tidal wave. At the last moment, Weiss clung to the console in order to remain on her feet. Horrible images of the broken glass cutting Madisyn made Weiss cry out in despair.

"Madisyn!" She drew new air. "Madisyn!"

The floor was slippery from the green fluid, and nearly impossible to navigate. Cursing her slipping feet, Weiss gave up and fell onto all fours, crawling through the goo. She cut herself on the sharp edges of the shattered glass, but now she could see a still form at the base of the dais. Sobbing from anger and frustration, she crawled over to Madisyn and gently lifted her over the broken sides of the cylinder. It didn't look like she had been seriously cut, although it was hard to see as she was covered in the fluid.

Weiss tore her collar from her jacket in one violent tug and used it to wipe Madisyn's face. It didn't look like she was breathing. Perhaps Madisyn didn't always have to? Cursing at how little she knew about Madisyn's configuration, she tried to move toward the door with her precious burden. No matter how she tried, she couldn't stay upright and carry Madisyn simultaneously.

"I'm sorry, Madi, I'm sorry. I'm really trying." Weiss's voice shocked her. She couldn't remember sounding so raw or feeling so distraught, not since her mother was killed. The woman in her arms had sacrificed everything for this cause of hers against piracy, against people like Weiss. Now all Weiss wanted was for Madisyn to have a real life with friends, work, and family. To never be alone again. She hugged Madisyn tight to her chest, willing life back into her cold, limp body, but it didn't help.

"That's Kyakh," someone said in Gantharian. Two women stood inside the door, plasma-pulse weapons raised but not directed at her.

"Help me. She's not breathing." Weiss eased toward them, making sure she kept Madisyn away from the sharp glass. Her knees and shins burned, but she didn't care.

"Let me take her. This is Pimm, right?" The tall blond woman bent down and lifted Madisyn from Weiss's arms as if she were a child. "I'm Roshan O'Landha, Gantharian resistance, deputized SC officer."

"Weiss Kyakh. Mercenary."

The other woman, smaller and with dark hair, bent down and extended her hand. "Not today, Weiss. I'm Andreia M'Aldovar, resistance leader, and I say today you're as much a freedom fighter as we are." She tugged Weiss to her feet and winced as she glanced down at her legs. "You need medical assistance. We have to get them back to the shuttle, Ro."

Weiss looked down and saw that her coverall was torn into shreds and blood was oozing down her legs. Oddly enough it didn't hurt. Yet.

"I'm not the one who needs it the most. We need to get Madisyn to a doctor, or an engineer, damn it, I don't know." Weiss limped over to Roshan. "She—she's breathing."

"She is. I'm not saying she doesn't need care, but I think you had her breathing sooner than you thought. Can you walk?" Roshan nodded at Weiss's legs.

"Yes." Weiss hoisted the weapon she'd found in the cabinet. "I'll have to make do with this. Are we far from the shuttle bay?"

"Two decks down, but we'll get there." Andreia tugged her arm. "Lean on me. If we run into the enemy, you can hold your own, I know, but for now, conserve your energy and use my strength."

"I—yes, ma'am." Weiss hated how submissive she sounded all of a sudden, but something about Andreia M'Aldovar didn't allow for any smart-ass responses or refusals. She placed her arm around Andreia's shoulders and was actually grateful for the support as the pain in her shins returned. To keep her mind off it, she asked the question that had been on her mind since their makeshift introductions. "You said 'M'Aldovar.' Are you related to the bastard who did this to Madisyn?"

"My brother," Andreia said. "And no, we're not related where our values and ideals are concerned. I'm Gantharian, heart and soul. He's Onotharian leadership at its worst. And just so you know, I had no idea he was alive. I don't even think our parents realize it."

"There's one in every family." Weiss focused on their conversation so she could keep walking and disregard the increasing pain. "Guess I'm the one in mine."

"Looks like you're trying to do the right thing now. There is such a thing as redemption." Andreia took a firmer grip around Weiss's waist, grabbing her belt.

"Some things can never fall into that category. I haven't led what you'd call an honorable life. These last months, even while working against the Onotharian oppressors, all I did was plot how to escape and get to my stash." The self-loathing was like bile in Weiss's throat as she glanced over at Madisyn, who lay limp in Roshan's arms. "Madi trusted me. She didn't know the truth. She thought I was an undercover agent with a fake background. Now she hates me."

"But you don't share her animosity?" Her voice soft, Andreia didn't sound judgmental.

"No. Madisyn Pimm is a fantastic, brave individual, who was prepared to sacrifice herself for the sake of this mission. She was ready to die aboard this damn ship, at the hands of a deeply disturbed megalomaniac." Weiss felt no remorse for her words about Andreia's brother.

"Once she comes to, she'll know that you saved her. That *you* risked your life in order to save hers. I know she's a sentient android, but not a lot of people would do what you did. It says a lot about her, and even more about you." Roshan spoke matter-of-factly, but kindly. Suddenly she stopped, pressing her back against the wall. She held on tighter to Madisyn. "We've got company."

Weiss and Andreia took aim with their weapons, ready to fire. Not sure she would be able to remain on her feet much longer, Weiss swore to herself she would go down fighting.

"It's Kellen and Ayahliss!" Andreia sounded relieved. "And—oh, Gods. It's him."

Trax M'Aldovar's hover chair traveled along the corridor, flanked by two striking blond women. She recognized both of them, although the younger of them, Ayahliss, had clearly grown up some in the months since one of Weiss's crewmembers had fired upon her at a space station. That, together with the fact that Weiss had kidnapped Dahlia Jacelon, made Weiss wary. The other one was Kellen O'Dal, the protector of the realm. Tall, blond, and wearing her red suit, she had an imposing charisma. She wouldn't cut Weiss any slack, and Weiss didn't expect her to.

"Good to see you, Kellen," Roshan said. "Where did you find him?" Her eyes turned bitter cold when she shifted her gaze to Trax.

"Believe it or not, in the brig, in weightless condition. He's unconscious." Kellen smiled joylessly as she motioned toward the slumped figure. "His vital signs are acceptable." She looked from Weiss over to Madisyn. "I see you found Kyakh and Pimm. Is Pimm all right?"

"No, she's been exposed to an unknown substance in some sort of chamber. Kyakh is badly hurt. We have to get them to the shuttles." Andreia pulled at Weiss. "You're pale."

"I'm all right." The corridor was flickering and spinning around Weiss. She tried to focus on putting one foot in front of another, counting the steps as they all made their way to the shuttle bay.

"How did you get him out of a weightless environment?" Roshan asked Kellen.

"I used old-fashioned techniques that we learned in the movement," Kellen said, her full lips curving into a smile. "Like fusing wires and adjusting manifolds with a well-aimed sidearm."

"I see." Roshan chuckled. "You know my advice. 'When all else fails, go low-tech.'"

"Indeed I do."

Kyakh knew she was in trouble when she began to experience tunnel vision. A humming tone sung in her ears and her legs slowly seemed to turn to jelly. She tried to warn Andreia, but her tongue wouldn't work. She heard, rather than felt, the pain in her kneecap when her right leg gave way. Andreia held on to her, but she hit her temple against the bulkhead as she went down. The last thing she knew before everything became blissfully black was how incredibly tired she was. The last word from her lips was "Madisyn."

CHAPTER THIRTY

"This is unbelievable. A complete shock, if you ask me. I've never come across anything like this in my career."

Madisyn wanted to identify the woman speaking close to her, but she was simply too fatigued. In fact, she couldn't move anything. Slowly, panic started to build and flashbacks from how she'd woken up and found herself transplanted into an android washed over her.

"I'm so glad the *Brilliance* made it to this part of space. This is where the nucleus of the war is fought, and both Rae and I felt we needed to be here," a dark male voice said. "This young woman has certainly sacrificed above and beyond."

"Examining her, I'd say she's sacrificed even more than that," the female voice said compassionately. "At first I had engineers work on her, then my best physician, while I worked on Kyakh and M'Aldovar."

M'Aldovar? That scum was here? And where was he? Madisyn tried to remember a ship named the *Brilliance*, but her tired brain wouldn't focus. Suddenly the image of Weiss floated to the surface. The last she remembered was how frantic Weiss had been when M'Aldovar had ordered Madisyn into the glass cylinder. They had hit her and dragged her off somewhere. What if they tortured her? Killed her?

A movement close by helped stymie the panic. Someone tucked in a blanket or a sheet around her with gentle hands.

"It didn't take them long to find discrepancies. Lieutenant Commander Dakke quickly informed me that this girl needed a physician more than an engineer, since her brain and spinal column are entirely humanoid."

"What the hell are you talking about?" the male voice asked.

Madisyn gasped. They had scanned her when she was unconscious and unable to suppress any of the markers in her system. Slowly she managed to open her eyes, blinking at the two uniform-clad people. The man was an SC admiral, and the woman held the rank of commander.

"Admiral Jacelon?" Madisyn whispered hoarsely.

"That's right, Ms. Pimm. Welcome back." Admiral Ewan Jacelon smiled down at her. "You gave us first a scare and then a shock. We now know the full magnitude of your sacrifice. You're not a sentient android, you're humanoid."

"Some would call me a freak." Madisyn didn't mean to sound bitter. She meant it as a factual statement.

"I would call it an amazing recovery from a brave and lonely soul."

"Weiss…please, Admiral. Where's Weiss?" Madisyn tried to sit up, but firm hands held her down by gently pressing her shoulders.

"I'm Doctor Gemma Meyer, CMO aboard the Supreme Constellations vessel *Brilliance*," the woman said. "You have quite a way to go before we can allow you to get out of bed. We're restoring some of your skin, and your pulmonary system also needs repairs. We've started a regeneration cycle to create the type of tissue you require, but until we're ready to transplant, you need to remain very still."

"If you don't tell me where Weiss is, I'm getting off this damn bed!" Drawing shallow, painful breaths, Madisyn forced her upper body up onto her elbows.

"Weiss Kyakh is undergoing treatment in our surgery theater," Dr. Meyer said. "She's rather banged up and needs a lot of reconstructive surgery. We have SC's best plastic surgeons and vascular surgeons aboard."

"Vascular? How bad are her injuries?" Weakly, Madisyn relaxed against the pillows. "Did they torture her?" The thought was excruciating.

"Nobody tortured her. She sustained bad cuts to her arms and legs when she rescued you from the oxygenizing glass chamber. She had to fire upon it to get you out," Admiral Jacelon said. "There was a lot of broken glass, according to our people."

"And the Onotharian? M'Aldovar?" Relief paired with awe made it difficult to speak.

"Alive. Barely." A muscle in Admiral Jacelon's jaw twitched and he had unmistakable hatred in his eyes. This man clearly loathed M'Aldovar, who had nearly killed his daughter.

"And Admiral Jacelon? Your daughter?"

"You ask a lot of questions, but that's good. Means you care and that you're well enough to care." Admiral Jacelon held up his hand as if to forestall any more impatient words. "Rae is on her feet again, thank you."

"Good." As if knowing that the ones she had worked with were all right or expected to recover allowed her to relax, Madisyn slumped sideways. "Pain." Her head hurt, and, somehow, the strange sensation of being short of breath seemed hurtful too.

"We're adding more pain relief through your intravenous line." Dr. Meyer pressed a sensor on a console next to the bed. Within seconds, the discomfort and pain lessened.

"Wh-when can I see Weiss? Got to tell her…" Madisyn yawned.

"As soon as it's possible. You're both too injured right now and need rest." Dr. Meyer leaned over Madisyn and met her gaze straight-on. "Trust me. If we see any significant signs of improvement or if either of you takes a turn for the worse, I promise to let the other one know. You and Weiss obviously care greatly for each other. I had to sedate her because she was ready to jump off the bed and force herself in here."

"She's my colleague. She had my back."

"She sure did."

"I'll return for a bedside debrief when Dr. Meyer says it's possible."

The two officers left, and Madisyn was grateful to close her eyes again. She needed to gather her thoughts. M'Aldovar's cohorts had forced her into the cold glass chamber. The green fluid had stung her skin, which had startled her. Certainly, she had experienced pain before, but this was a searing sensation, like being burned.

At this point, Madisyn recalled Weiss going crazy on the outside, struggling against the two Onotharian security officers. Madisyn winced as she remembered every little detail as to how Weiss had received several blows to the head and her abdomen. The last thing Madisyn saw before she lost consciousness was Weiss falling over, her knees unable to support her. Instead the chamber had made her hover, the green fluid rising around her. Madisyn had been certain she would die in there and never be able to tell Weiss how much she cared for her after all.

Madisyn's eyes snapped open. It was true. She did care for Weiss. No matter her past, Weiss had proved irrevocably that she was capable of bravery and honorable actions. *I'd love her anyway.* Love? Madisyn tried the word in her head, not about to say it out loud. Love Weiss Kyakh, who said she loved Madisyn back. Was it possible that Weiss could really love her? Since Madisyn felt the same, perhaps they had a chance?

Thinking that the medication might be making her reason like this, Madisyn let her eyes close again and allowed sleep to take her. They couldn't resolve anything here and now. She could only hope to find Weiss feeling stronger and healthier the next time she woke up.

They had a lot to discuss.

Chapter Thirty-one

Kellen stepped through the docking tube that linked the *Circinus* with the *Brilliance* and strode through the corridors, not about to waste any time. Crewmembers moved out of her way, some actually pressing their backs against the bulkhead.

Next to her, Owena and Leanne lengthened their stride to keep up.

"The admiral said she was all right, Kellen," Leanne said. "She even said she's able to resume light duty."

"I know. I heard her."

"But you need to see for yourself," Owena said. "I understand. If it was Leanne…" She shuddered.

Kellen knew their friends were concerned about Rae, but she was past concern. Rae was her life, the one who gave her purpose beyond her duties as protector and guardian for Armeo. When she secretly feared that Rae might never be found, or that she was dead, Kellen struggled to find a reason to continue. Her joy in life was interwoven with Rae and what they shared, and now Kellen couldn't wait a moment longer to see her. She didn't know just how fast the *Brilliance* was, and when she'd returned to the *Circinus* in her shuttle, Kellen's knees had nearly given out when an ensign informed her she had a personal message waiting, and then Rae's beloved face filled the screen.

Unable to do anything but stare at Rae for several moments, Kellen found her mouth curiously dry and her eyes just the opposite. Rae didn't have the same reaction.

"Darling…" She launched into a detailed explanation of how she'd made it to Kellen's location in record time.

Kellen didn't really care how. She just sat there and enjoyed the husky voice of the woman she loved, grateful she sounded like her usual self. Still, now that she was about to see her face-to-face, the dryness was back in her mouth and her abdomen was in knots.

"We're supposed to meet Ayahliss in your father's ready room," Leanne said kindly. "Why don't we see you and Rae later?"

"All right. Thank you." Grateful for her friends' understanding, Kellen parted ways with them by one of the hubs of this enormous vessel. Consisting of forty-two decks and with a crew manifest of 3,800, it was the latest among five of its kind, each one more elaborate than and technologically superior to its predecessor.

Standing at the orientation board at the hub, she tried to pinpoint Rae's location but couldn't see anything designated the admirals' quarters.

"Hello, Kellen. I shouldn't have used an unofficial name for the section of my quarters."

Kellen spun around. "Rae!" She was staring again, but couldn't stop. They stood among the busy crewmembers aboard the *Brilliance* and took each other in. Rae looked thinner, with deeper lines around the eyes. She was still pale and her red hair in sharp contrast to her complexion. But the fire was present in her eyes and, most important, so was the love.

"For stars and skies, you're so beautiful," Rae said, sounding short of breath. "I've missed you."

"And I you." Kellen wanted to wrap her arms around Rae and kiss her, but this crowded junction wasn't the right place for such a display. "Can we go back to your quarters?"

"*Our* quarters. Yes, the sooner the better." Rae smiled her trademark little curve of one corner of her mouth, and surprised Kellen by taking her arm and tucking it in against her. Only then did Kellen realize how badly Rae was trembling.

Their quarters were located on deck four, where the only other occupants were the *Brilliance*'s captain and guests of the same rank or higher. Kellen vaguely noticed the impressive size and expanse of the rooms before she pulled Rae into her arms.

"I was so afraid," she managed to say.

"Me too." Rae clung to Kellen, her arms around her neck. "At times I thought nobody would ever find us, and if they did, it would be too late. Then I got here and found that you were on a very dangerous mission, and…I know it sounds utterly unprofessional, but I feared we were jinxing it. You know, pushing it too much and asking for too much good fortune."

"Asking who?" Kellen tried to follow Rae's reasoning.

"Deities. Lady Luck. The Seers of Guild Nation. The Gods of Gantharat. Whoever you pray to in times of deep trouble."

"They don't get much deeper than this, I agree with that. Still, it is hardly asking for too much when you want only for the people you love to remain safe during wartime."

"You're right, of course. Perhaps I'm struggling with this notion that I don't deserve this much happiness." Rae buried her face in Kellen's shoulder. "Either way, I'm so happy to be back in your arms."

"Oh, Rae." Kellen hugged her closer, tears flowing. "I would never have stopped looking for you, but in my darkest moments, when they couldn't find you, I feared the worst."

"I know you did. I've done so myself where you've been concerned, several times. I know how devastatingly frightening it can be."

"Yes." Kellen couldn't get enough of the feelings that having Rae in her arms evoked. She nuzzled Rae's neck and kissed her way along her jawline to her lips. Rae kissed her back with fervor, her lips open and inviting.

"Mmm. I love you, Kellen. So very much."

"I love you too." Deepening the kisses, Kellen changed from being upset and distraught to serene and excited. Before loving Rae, she would never have thought it possible to feel this way. Kellen pulled Rae with her onto the couch and settled in with her on her lap.

Rae put her arms around Kellen's neck and hugged her. "I was determined to return to you. I couldn't think about anything else, but I was afraid I wouldn't. When I developed a fever, my mind played out scenarios of how the SC authorities notified you, Armeo, and my parents of my death. For a moment I thought they were real and I frightened myself by calling out, 'No, no, I'm here.' I think I scared the living daylights out of Ensign Hallberg." Rae chuckled, but the tremors traveling from her to Kellen spoke of the horror she'd experienced aboard the Onotharian shuttle.

"You're here now. I'm here now. This was a long separation, with very dangerous assignments. No wonder our nerves are frayed." Kellen caressed Rae's back with long, soothing movements. She needed the touch, the feel of her, as much as Rae needed the comfort. Appalled at how she could detect Rae's ribs and vertebrae, she held her gentler than she normally would.

"I won't break. I may be on the scrawny side right now, but I won't come to pieces if you hug me closer. I really need closer." Rae placed a trail of soft kisses along Kellen's neck. "I love how you hold me, how you make me feel. I always have."

"Yes. I know what you mean. Long before I knew I loved you, I loved how you held me. You used to infuriate me, and I certainly didn't trust you, but when you touched me…" Kellen caught Rae's lips with her mouth. "Mmm, when you touched me, I forgot all about that."

"You drove me crazy with your mere presence." Rae smiled against Kellen's lips. "I had never met a more intense, cutthroat person. I remember calling you a loose cannon, and I wasn't the only one. The fact that my father, whom I didn't exactly have an easygoing relationship with, saw your greatness before I did confused me even more."

"My greatness?" Kellen returned the smile. "That's stretching it, isn't it?"

"No. You're great. As a protector. As a guardian. As a representative of your people. But mostly, you're great for me. You helped bring me close to my parents. You made me aware of how I missed having a family. You brought a child into my life. You brought me love. How can all of that not be great?"

Kellen couldn't see for the new tears that welled up instantly. *"Ilenshes,"* she said, her voice broken. "I never realized you saw things, me, that way. I thought you loved me despite the mayhem I brought to your life. A life you nearly lost because of me."

"You saved my life."

"And you saved *me*." Kellen pressed her wet cheeks into Rae's hair. "You took me in and gave me a chance, and married me. Before you, all I could hope for was to be as good a guardian for Armeo as possible, and to hide him from the Onotharians. I never dared to dream he'd be able to reclaim his throne, or that we could free my world. You, your family, and the people you know, and our friends, have made it possible."

"My darling." Rae cupped Kellen's cheeks. "You hold my heart."

"So do you." Kellen kissed Rae's palm. "My protector."

❖

Ayahliss knew Owena and Leanne meant well by checking on her, as did Ewan. Still on a strange high after helping Kellen apprehend M'Aldovar, Ayahliss didn't know how to lose the jitters. She excused herself half an hour into the impromptu debriefing and stepped outside. The corridor bustled with purpose-filled SC soldiers and officials, and Ayahliss had never felt more out of place.

Unable to return to the others, she began to walk—up one corridor, down another. Eventually she stopped noticing the faces of the people she met or passed. She used her steps as meditation, trying to calm down with techniques Kellen had shown her. Once they had found the unconscious M'Aldovar, a strangely anticlimactic surprise, and managed to place him back into his hover chair quickly enough to save his life, Ayahliss had felt out of sorts.

She had been prepared to fight, to explode in a glorious discharge of energy. Something cataclysmic that would be appropriate after her training and qualifying for the Ruby Red suit. When that didn't happen, the emptiness paired with a strange onset of nerves made her slip back into a familiar feeling of depression.

"Jacelon to Ayahliss." Ewan's voice over her communicator brought her out of her hypnotized frame of mind.

"Ayahliss here. Go ahead, sir."

"Please report to shuttle bay six."

"Very well. On my way. Ayahliss out." She wanted to ask why, but knew not to question admirals, not even one in the family. A quick glance at an orientation board showed she was actually four decks directly above shuttle bay six.

The bay was, if possible, even more crowded, as several more shuttles had arrived. Certain that Ewan wanted her to fetch something, she looked around for someone to ask.

"Ayahliss. Oh, Gods."

Whirling around, Ayahliss stared at Reena where she stood dressed entirely in black, down to her long cape. She kept her wild hair back with a brass hair band, and she was pulling a hover bag behind her, no doubt filled with legal pads and documents.

"Reena." Ayahliss raised her hand, but, suddenly feeling drained, she let it fall. "You—I didn't expect to see you aboard the *Brilliance*." Her lips felt stiff and her voice was just as rigid.

"We're back to update the military leaders on our progress. I think you'll be very proud of Dahlia. She's accomplished a lot in a very short time."

"As have you"

"I'm not a diplomat. I'm all about the law." Reena smiled with a tired look in her eyes. "I've got six hours before I give my briefing. I need to find my quarters and—"

"I'll help you." Suddenly energized, and with a new sense of purpose, Ayahliss stepped up and took the handle of the hover luggage from Reena. "I've walked all over this big tin can of a ship, and I know where the brass stays."

"Brass?" Reena looked startled. "Guess I'm brass, then." She glanced down at her handheld computer. "Deck four, quarters Sig0811."

"This way." Ayahliss wanted to offer her arm for support, but knew it wasn't appropriate aboard a military vessel. Nor did she want to make anyone who didn't know Reena think she was weak. "My quarters are on deck five, which is a great honor. I believe they're just beneath yours."

"Have you had time to think about what we discussed?"

"No. Yes. I mean, I was afraid you might have spoken out of concern and then had second thoughts." Ayahliss kept her gaze forward, too nervous to look at Reena.

"I most certainly haven't." Reena sounded quite affronted, which was oddly heartwarming.

"Really?" Ayahliss spoke fast, tripping over her words. "I mean, Owena and Leanne are my neighbors. Of course Andreia and Roshan are on the same deck as you. All the quarters here are luxurious compared to the ones aboard the *Noma*."

"Given Andreia is Boyoda, that makes sense, I suppose." Reena still didn't look pleased. "Nothing has changed. I still want you to stay with me."

Reena's assertive words made it impossible for Ayahliss to say anything. She walked in silence next to Reena to the lift, which took them to the fourth deck. "Take a right," Ayahliss finally said as they stepped off. "Looks like it's the fourth on the left. Use your communicator as your key."

Reena pulled her communicator from her lapel and held it against the sensor, which opened the door with a soft hiss. "Efficient." She stepped inside and looked around. "Look, this is huge. We'll have plenty of space." Reena suddenly blushed. "If you still want to, that is. I'm taking a lot for granted."

Ayahliss stepped inside and pressed the sensor to close the door. "No. You're not."

"I'm being pushy and selfish." Reena pushed her cape off and tugged the band from her hair, sending it flying in wild curls. "Coming back here, I thought of little else but getting to you as soon as possible. I've been wrapped up in the negotiations, and during the meetings, I deliberately forced every thought of you out of my mind, or I couldn't have focused at all. As soon as I was on my own time, and especially aboard the shuttle heading for the *Brilliance*, all the thoughts and feelings rushed back with a vengeance."

"A vengeance? That sounds pretty bad," Ayahliss said, trying to pass it off as a joke.

"Poor word choice. I'm sorry." Reena gestured helplessly, palms up. "I feel dusty and unattractive as hell. I need a shower."

"On this ship you can even take an aqua shower."

"Really?" Reena's face brightened. "That might transform me in more ways than one. Care to join me?" Her eyes widened. "Oh, Gods, I can't believe I said that."

"You mean it?" Ayahliss whispered. The images in her mind made her feel warmer, heavier.

"Yes. Did I offend you?"

"No. And yes."

"What?" Reena looked up at Ayahliss with alarm as she stepped closer. "No, yes, what?"

"No, you didn't offend me and, yes, I'd like to join you."

"I can't believe I actually invited you to take a shower, but you know what? I'm glad I did. I don't want to be away from you, even to wash up."

Pulling her black cape off, Reena looked like an enchanted mythical creature. Ayahliss wondered, for the millionth time, what

Reena saw in her, who had seen little else but violence and fighting for the last several years.

"Computer. Unless there is an emergency, administer privacy lock on door and communicator. Code Beqq-Sig0811." Reena motioned for Ayahliss to do the same. "Good. No unnecessary disturbances. Come with me, beautiful Ayahliss," Reena murmured, her glimmering eyes half-closed. She took Ayahliss by the hand and pulled her toward the bedroom and into the ensuite. "May I undress you?"

Trembling now, but more exhilarated than she'd ever been, Ayahliss simply nodded.

CHAPTER THIRTY-TWO

Reena had known she had to follow her feelings as soon as she saw Ayahliss in the shuttle bay. She had paged both Jacelon admirals to let them know she and Dahlia had made it safely to the *Brilliance*. Ewan Jacelon had asked his wife to join him in his quarters and offered to send Ayahliss to escort Reena to hers, as it was on another deck.

Reena had accepted.

Now, standing outside the blessed aqua shower, she couldn't take her eyes off Ayahliss. Tall and blond, with a dangerous look in those icy-blue eyes, Ayahliss had a statuesque appearance, which her blue skin tone emphasized.

"How do I unclasp this thing?" Reena pointed at the Ruby Red suit. "It looks like it was painted on."

"Fortunately not." Ayahliss raised her arms and pressed a sensor on her neck. Kellen's Ruby Red suit was made of traditional, natural leather, but Ayahliss's was replicated and made from a leather-like material that looked identical. The suit lost cohesion and slid down a few centimeters before it got stuck on her elbows and breasts. "Like so."

"Like so, eh?" Reena pushed the suit off Ayahliss's arms. It now hung from her hips, where her weapons belt prevented it from slipping farther. "Ah, another challenge." Reena examined the belt and pressed the buckle in the front. Nothing happened. She licked her lips and turned the buckle an entire rev. This proved successful and Reena couldn't hold back a triumphant grin. "Now the boots. More buckles.

Sweet soul, this is draining my patience." Pressing the many sensors on the tall red boots, she unfastened them and pulled them off.

Once she had removed the Ruby Red suit, she took a long look at Ayahliss, wanting to become reacquainted. Ayahliss had clearly gone through a lot since they parted, and for some reason seemed to be brimming with pent-up energy. Reena didn't want to pry and was also fairly sure she would hear all that had happened aboard the Onotharian ship during the debriefings.

Now all that was important was right here in the luxurious bathroom with her. Reena pushed off her tunic and stepped out of her trousers. The black shoes went the same way, and soon she and Ayahliss were equally undressed.

"May I continue?" Reena asked. "I won't do anything you're not comfortable with."

"Yes. I mean, yes, please continue." Ayahliss's voice had suddenly deepened, as had her breathing. Deep and fast.

"Very well." Reena first turned to the control panel for the aqua shower. "Computer, aqua shower, medium spray, forty degrees Celsius." She then slipped her hands under Ayahliss's non-woven camisole. Her skin was like damp silk. Reena tugged the camisole over Ayahliss's head and tossed it into the recycler. Broad shoulders, small firm breasts with dark reddish-blue nipples that puckered before her eyes—Reena's mouth watered. Still, she knew they were supposed to shower and forced herself to merely push Ayahliss's briefs down off her hips. "There. Get in. I'll be right there." She nudged Ayahliss gently into the shower tube. Undressing quickly, she didn't take her eyes off her stunning body. Naked, Reena stepped into the spray of water next to Ayahliss and moaned as the hot water hit her sore shoulders. Sitting at a negotiating table wasn't the cushy job some people thought. It drained both the body and the mind.

"I want to wash your hair," Ayahliss said, surprising Reena. "It's something I've dreamed of doing."

"By all means." Reena closed her eyes when Ayahliss pulled her close under the cascading water. Strong, gentle hands rubbed sweet-smelling hair cleanser along her long curls, massaging them gently. Touched that Ayahliss would know not to clump them all together in one big mess, which would be damn near impossible to untangle, Reena groaned at having her scalp massaged.

She let the water rinse the cleanser from her hair, then felt Ayahliss's hands on her back, sliding a bar of old-fashioned soap against her skin. The feeling was so exquisite, she had to hold on to the grab bar next to the shelf where all the luxurious cleansing supplies sat.

"The label says oat-and-honey soap," Ayahliss said. "It has a nice scent, even if I don't know what an oat is."

"A sort of grain," Reena said dreamily. "Grows on Earth."

"Ah. I see. Hence the roughness of the texture." Ayahliss pulled the soap up and down Reena's back, and the scrubbing inflamed every nerve ending.

"I feel it."

Suddenly kneeling, Ayahliss washed Reena's legs. Having Ayahliss's head so close made Reena blush again. The warmness of her cheeks far surpassed the feeling of the hot water and, unable to hide her reaction, Reena looked down at Ayahliss.

"Feel good?" Ayahliss ran soapy hands along Reena's legs. The inside of her thighs seemed to especially interest Ayahliss, who turned the washing into caressing with a few strokes. Just as Reena was ready to spread her legs for a more intimate touch, Ayahliss rose from the floor. Standing in front of Reena, she took another type of soap and dutifully read the label.

"This one is made from samona oil and...how do you pronounce this? *Galloianti*?"

"I-I believe you're right." Samona oil was a well-known rehydrating soap that left the skin completely rejuvenated. Galloianti was a Cormanian herb Reena had never tried.

Ayahliss slid the new soap up and down Reena's abdomen, stroking her at the same time. She avoided her breasts a few times, but then washed them with slow, circular movements. At first, Reena thought that Ayahliss's touch had caused her puckering nipples to tingle. It took her a few moments to understand that the galloianti was a strong stimulant. Her nipples buzzed and begged to be fondled. Reena whimpered and wrapped her arms around Ayahliss's waist, rubbing her breasts against her smooth skin.

"That soap is something else," Reena muttered. "And *you* are driving me crazy."

"I am?" Ayahliss's eyes twinkled, but there was still something dark and intense in her features.

"Yes. You do. You know you do."

Ayahliss suddenly pulled them both under the spray of water. "Computer. Rinse cycle and then instant drying sequence."

The spray widened and soaked them completely. Ayahliss gently pressed the excess water from Reena's long hair, then a warm gush hit them from all directions. Apparently, the soap's effect wouldn't rinse off easily, nor would the arousal Ayahliss's presence induced.

"Ayahliss!" Reena exclaimed as Ayahliss lifted her and carried her out of the shower tube, through the ensuite, and into the bedroom. She placed Reena on the bed.

"Computer. Lights at seven percent. Play classic Gantharian music."

Reena thought she was dreaming. She was supposed to be the seasoned lover here, and now Ayahliss was acting like she was well versed in the art of seduction. Had Ayahliss been studying for this, much like she had to become a protector?

"Ayahliss…I love you." Reena gasped at her own words. She hadn't meant to blurt out the truth like that, but she couldn't take it back—not that she wanted to. If Ayahliss didn't reciprocate, Reena still wanted her to know that someone did love her, no matter what.

"Reena?" Round-eyed, Ayahliss sat back on her heels for a moment. "You love me?"

"I do. I have, ever since you and Armeo got into trouble and I had to bail you out."

"For months?" Blinking, Ayahliss put her hand over her mouth. "And here I thought it was just me. Reena, my heart is beating so fast." She moved the hand to her stomach. "You know, at first I couldn't even grasp that you were physically attracted to me."

Reena's heart slowed down. *Of course*. "It's all right," she whispered. "It's enough for me to know I love you. To know that *you* know."

"That's not what I meant." Ayahliss took Reena by the shoulders and buried her face in her abundant locks. "I've loved you just as long. When you spent so much time with me on the court ship orbiting Corma, I fell in love with you. I couldn't believe it at first, and I didn't recognize the emotion since I'd never been in love. In a way, I'm very inexperienced, and in other ways, I possess knowledge few people my age do."

"Come here." Reena threw her arms around Ayahliss. Letting herself fall onto the pillows, she reveled in the sensation of having Ayahliss fall on top of her. "I love you so much. Please, my sweet Ayahliss. Make love to me?"

"Gladly," Ayahliss said with a smile. She pushed herself between Reena's legs, probing her sex gently.

"Touch me. My breasts. Everything." Grunting, Reena arched as Ayahliss closed her lips around a steel-hard nipple. Ayahliss's tongue, probably meant to be soothing, inflamed her further, and Reena wrapped her arms and legs around her.

Ayahliss seemed to know just what to do. She pressed her fingers into Reena, filling her as Reena had once done to her. The sensation was pure fire, and when Ayahliss grazed her cluster of nerve endings, Reena cried out.

"Ayahliss!"

"I'm here. I'm yours, Reena. I've always been yours."

"Yes. Yes." Undulating, Reena knew she wouldn't last long. She clenched her inner muscles around Ayahliss's fingers and rode the passion harder and harder. A ravine opened up, and trusting that Ayahliss would catch her, Reena threw herself into it. The pleasure that seared her skin made her come repeatedly. Surprised at her own keening sound, Reena clung to Ayahliss, thirsty for her kisses. Finally, their mouths met and Reena drank from Ayahliss's lips.

Once she was temporarily sated, Reena rolled Ayahliss onto her back. "Hello, lover."

"Hello." Ayahliss was already trembling, clearly on the verge of her own release.

"I'm going to taste you now, sweet soul." Reena bent and began kissing her way down Ayahliss's abdomen. "Mmm. Just what I thought. Delicious."

"Reena?"

"Yes?" Reena murmured against Ayahliss's satiny skin.

"Will I lose you? I can't." Ayahliss didn't sound pitiful or pathetic, only insecure.

"Trust in me, sweet soul," Reena said as she devoured Ayahliss. "No matter what happens, I won't let you go." She found Ayahliss's silky, wet folds and parted them with her lips. She intended to show Ayahliss how much she meant to her by making beautiful, passionate love to her. Figuring out the logistics in their very different lives would be a challenge, but they would make it happen.

Kissing and licking, Reena carried Ayahliss gently into the same ravine she had just visited. As Ayahliss writhed beneath her, Reena hummed happily against the silken tissues. Once Ayahliss slumped back onto the pillows, Reena slid up along her and held her gently.

"Reena—" Ayahliss began to cry. No heavy sobs, no drama, just quiet tears as the last of the tension seemed to leave her system. "I—I love you."

"And I love you." Reena pulled a retrospun wool blanket up around them, as the conditioned air in their quarters cooled their damp bodies far too quickly. "Rest, darling. I'll be here when you wake up."

Reena curled up and made sure they were both comfortable. Who could've guessed that she would fall for someone like Ayahliss? Who was she kidding? As soon as she saw Ayahliss, she knew. *Stars and skies, help me, but I knew.*

Reena kissed the top of Ayahliss's head. Certain she wouldn't sleep, she spent the next four hours merely gazing at the woman she loved.

CHAPTER THIRTY-THREE

Trax M'Aldovar had never hated his disability or his hover chair more. Confined to the machine, he was forced to let it breathe for him, transport him, and perform other necessary functions too humiliating to even think about. Now, facing this veritable tribunal of Supreme Constellations officials and officers, he wished he could have, at least, been able to stand and tower above them. What good was it to be almost two meters tall if you had to cower in a chair like some geriatric idiot?

"Trax M'Aldovar—"

"*General* M'Aldovar." Trax, scornful, was in charge of his vocal cords. "I do not recognize this assembly as a legitimate force in this part of space. You have no jurisdiction here."

"On the contrary," a woman with long, flaming locks said. "When the Onotharian Empire declared war on the Supreme Constellations Unification of Planets, laws of war went into effect. Within the battlefield, this assembly does indeed have jurisdiction."

"I don't know where you studied law, but—"

"At the best universities throughout the SC and intergalactic space. I'm Judge Amereena Beqq."

"Charming." Trax bit off the word abruptly.

"*General* M'Aldovar," said a man Trax had earlier identified from the dossier he had read so many times: Admiral Ewan Jacelon, Kellen O'Dal's father-in-law. To his left sat his wife, Dahlia, who held the most redundant position of all, in Trax's eyes. Diplomacy. What a waste.

"You know some of us, you've probably heard of others." Ewan Jacelon rose and stood in the center of the room. "The *Brilliance* has set a course for Corma, where you will be held as a prisoner of war until you can be tried for your war crimes and other criminal actions."

"You cannot do this!" Trax wanted to throttle the self-righteous man with his paralyzed hands.

"Before we confine you to the prisoners' hospital section, we have arranged this informal meeting, since some individuals have issues to address." Admiral Jacelon nodded to the guard at the door. "Let them in."

Trax drummed his fingers inwardly, a sign of impatience that he sometimes indulged in.

Shocked, Trax stared at the first one to enter. "Andreia? What the hell are you doing aboard this ship? An *SC* ship! And where have you been?" His sister had been missing in action since the resistance kidnapped her during an event that their parents concocted. According to rumor, the thugs had beaten Andreia beyond recognition, and when his parents, famous Onotharian politicians, meant to disclose this outrage, the resistance fighters kidnapped her. She had been presumed dead and a national day of mourning had been proclaimed.

But here she was, looking healthier and more energetic than ever. Most disturbing, next to her stood a tall Gantharian woman with her arm protectively around Andreia's waist. It was…Andreia's friend from university, Roshan O'Landha, entrepreneur and collaborator. Trax moaned. Clearly this woman had fooled everybody. She had endured this rumor and the hatred of her countrymen for more than twenty years, and obviously worked in the resistance the whole time.

Trax knew the Gantharians hated him, but that didn't matter, since he considered them ultimately inferior. Ruling by fear among his subordinates, he made sure he was at the top of the food chain.

"Trax. I can't say I'm pleased to see you. I thought you were dead and, honestly, seeing you alive disturbs me deeply. Your crimes against the Gantharian people, and others, are hardly surprising, but it still pains me that we come from the same womb." Andreia stepped closer and looked down at him with hard, amber eyes. "Your latest crime, stealing davic crystals and indulging in slavery—"

"Slavery?" Trax thundered. The coughing spell that followed annoyed him, but he pushed through it. "I have not enslaved anybody."

"You took a young woman and stuck her in an oxygenizer chamber.

She would have suffocated in there, drowned, if her friend hadn't saved her."

"That was no woman. That was a damn android. A *machine*." Trax had no idea why he bothered to defend himself. Honestly, it wouldn't have mattered to him if the android had been human.

"No. A human brain and spinal column in a BNSL body."

"Liar." Beads of perspiration formed on his forehead. No doubt he was sweating profusely all over, like he always did when he experienced stress. "I don't know what this is supposed to accomplish—"

"Closure," a husky voice said behind Andreia. "Hello, M'Aldovar."

Admiral Rae Jacelon, Protector of the Realm, circled Trax's sister and stood before him. He remembered nearly killing her, and also what that had led to. He hated her passionately. She had a strong presence that would've been formidable had she been on the right side of this conflict. Like Judge Beqq, her hair was red, but more of a fiery auburn, and it suited her well, despite her cold stare.

"How's your neck?" Trax said slowly, deliberately hinting at the damage he had done to her carotid artery. Seeing her in a pool of blood had been most satisfying. Such a retro battlefield experience.

"How is *yours*?" Kellen O'Dal, Protector of the Realm and guardian to the heir to the Gantharian throne, walked up to Admiral Jacelon. Her SC uniform only seemed to add to her stunning blond looks. "I thought I'd killed you. Guess I did snap it fairly well, though, since the finest Onotharian doctors couldn't patch you up."

"I did live. And I did rise in the ranks. I gained power."

"And used it for your own gain. How noble." Kellen's voice oozed sarcasm. "Now we can continue to fight the good fight for Gantharat, knowing that the likes of you and your entire crew are where you belong. In a cage."

"I have standards that need to be met." He was beginning to realize that he was going to prison. His rank would afford him decent accommodations, but he was used to utter luxury. How would he tolerate "decent"?

"Your medical needs will be tended to," Ewan Jacelon said calmly. "Regarding anything else, you will have to yield to the regular conditions of our maximum-security planetoid prisons." He smiled coldly. "And an MSPP facility is not exactly like an Imidestrian resort."

Anger rose so quickly within Trax, his mouth filled with bile. Swallowing it, he said, "You will not get away with this. You will not! My government—my family has connections all the way up to the chairmen of Onotharat."

"I think we've said all we came to say," Rae Jacelon said lightly. "Dinner, was it? In the officers' mess hall?"

"I believe so." Kellen O'Dal put her arm around Rae's shoulders. "I'm starving."

As the group of people who came to gloat left the room one by one, eventually only one person, apart from the security officer and a medic, remained. Andreia walked up to him, regarding him with a sad, wistful look.

"This will probably mean nothing to you," she said, raising a hand and briefly touching his cheek. "When we were very young, and played together like children do, you were always the leader, always the one in charge, and I was happy to follow like the adoring sister I was. I can't quite say when everything changed, but gradually it all became very clear how different we are and how fundamentally opposed our values are." She drew a trembling breath and Trax wanted to take the opportunity to say something scornful, but she forestalled him. "I guess we're the opposite sides of a medal. You are very much our parents' son, loyal to our old, malevolently governed world. I'm the individualist, the freethinker who empathizes with and is loyal to the world we grew up in, Gantharat. The sad thing is, documents exist that prove this never had to happen. Gantharat was ready to share its resources with Onotharat, just as Gantharat had opened its intergalactic borders to allow limitless immigration.

"If the Onotharian government and its chairmen hadn't been so greedy for political power and so afraid to lose face, Gantharat would have continued to flourish and been able to sustain two worlds. Worlds that once were sister planets!" Andreia blinked against tears.

Trax found it hard to speak, his breathing labored.

"Know this, brother," Andreia said, her voice now low and menacing. "Gantharat will be great again. Onotharat and its hardcore leaders will never dupe it into trusting them. Perhaps, in time, new generations with less ambitious motives will reign and we can find a way back. As long as people of your kind are in charge, I don't see that happening." Her smile turned scornful. "At least we don't have to worry about you popping up like rotting seed."

"Don't count on it, sister," Trax muttered, but his voice held no power, no energy.

"Oh, but I do. Once you are in SC hands, they will keep you locked away and it will be up to you to see the errors of your way and make a change. Other people have. Weiss Kyakh, for instance. I'm afraid I gave up hope for you a long time ago. Our parents corrupted you, and you willingly let them."

"H'rea deasavh!" Trax cursed in Gantharian without thinking.

Andreia laughed. "My thoughts exactly. Now I'm late for lunch. Good-bye."

Trax sat motionless, like he usually did, and watched the medic and security officers punch in commands to disconnect his chair from the bulkhead power source. They wheeled him to a different door, which led to a transport corridor and directly to the brig hospital wing. As the staff helped him into bed and attached his life-support apparatus to the wall unit, he closed his eyes. He had thought his life was over when Kellen O'Dal nearly killed him. He'd proved himself and everybody else wrong. This time, he was even less optimistic, despite his bravado earlier.

He had no way out of this mess.

Chapter Thirty-four

"Bigger than our quarters about the *Salaceos*." Madisyn tucked her hands behind her back, lacing her fingers.

"I would imagine the broom closets onboard the *Brilliance* are bigger than our old quarters." Weiss motioned for Madisyn to sit down. "I hope you really are all right about sharing. I don't think Dr. Meyer would have let you out of the infirmary if you were left to your own devices."

"I got that much, and a long lecture what I can and cannot do in the upcoming weeks."

"Anything I need to know about?" Weiss winked, but managed to look just as nervous as Madisyn felt.

"Plenty of sustenance and rest, combined with light physical training."

"Huh. She told me the same thing. How about that?" Weiss motioned toward the couch. "Please, sit. Want something to drink?"

"Water, please." Madisyn wasn't really thirsty, but she needed to stall. She had longed to have Weiss to herself, but now that she did, she was ridiculously close to panicking.

"Here you go," Weiss said, interrupting Madisyn's thoughts as she handed her a glass of water.

"Thanks." Clinging to the glass, Madisyn took a deep breath.

"What's wrong, Madi?" Weiss sat down next to her, looking concerned.

"I'm fine. I mean, I'm a bit nervous, but I'm all right." Having Weiss call her Madi actually helped. "I—I've missed talking with you. Just the two of us."

"So have I." Weiss moved closer. "All right if I hold you, Madi? I nearly lost you."

"You saved me." Madisyn acted without hesitation, wrapping her arms around Weiss's neck.

Weiss pulled her closer, up on her lap.

"I'm too heavy," Madisyn said breathlessly.

"You're perfect." Weiss buried her face against Madisyn. "You feel wonderful."

"Oh." Madisyn began to tremble at the tone of reverence and something more in Weiss's voice. Desire?

"So soft." Weiss pressed her lips against Madisyn's jawline, tracing it as she clearly headed for her mouth. *Yes, definitely desire.*

The arousal echoing within Madisyn, she turned her head and caught Weiss's lips with her own. Pulling the clasp from Weiss's hair, she freed it and pushed her fingers through it. Touching Weiss like this, tousling her hair, was all she needed to see the Weiss she'd come to know aboard Podmer's ship.

"Oh, Madi, I love you so much. I can't believe I'm holding you, or that you're allowing me to hold you. You hated me." Weiss pulled back a little. "Perhaps part of you still does."

"I don't." Madisyn knew this was complicated and their only chance at mutual happiness was if she remained totally honest. "I did at first, once you told me of your past. After a while I had to force myself to hate you. I felt I owed it to my parents. Even before you saved my life, I knew I didn't hate you."

"And now?" It was Weiss's turn to tremble.

"I don't hate you. I love you." Madisyn looked into the eyes of the one person who had been the first one to regard her as human, even before Madisyn told her the truth. "I love you."

"I have a lot to atone for." Weiss drew a shaky breath. "I owe the people I robbed, hurt, or killed, to not waver from this path. I need to keep doing this."

"So do I." Madisyn curled up, snuggling closer. "We make an awesome team, don't you think, Weiss?"

"We do." Weiss slid down along the backrest of the couch, pulling Madisyn with her. "Right now, there is something far less unselfish on my mind, though. I need you." She slid her hands under Madisyn's SC-issue shirt. "I want to feel you against me, with no barrier between us, physical or emotional."

"Then undress me." Madisyn raised her arms above her head, allowing Weiss to remove her shirt.

"Stars and skies, you're beautiful."

"So are you." Madisyn tore open Weiss's buttoned uniform jacket. "Oh. So are you." She pushed her hands in under the retrospun tank top. "And you feel amazing." She cupped Weiss's breasts, caressing them greedily, making Weiss give an uncharacteristic whimper.

"Damn." Weiss rolled them over, pushing the tank top up above Madisyn's breasts, immediately lowering her mouth to one of her nipples. The searing pleasure showed Madisyn beyond any doubt that her body functioned perfectly. Moisture dampened her underwear and she gasped as she held Weiss closer.

"Make me yours," Madisyn whispered feverishly. "Show me."

Weiss tugged at Madisyn's pants, pulling them off as she caressed her with steady, soft hands. "What is it you want me to show you?"

Arching under the hands of the woman she loved, Madisyn couldn't take her eyes off the sight of a half-naked, passionate Weiss. "Show me that I'm humanoid."

"Madi," Weiss removed the last of her own clothes in a frenzy. "You are. You are."

"Show me that I'm still me."

"You are!" Weiss pressed her body in between Madisyn's legs. Spreading them willingly, Madisyn felt Weiss's damp sex press into her own. Her own moisture mixed with her lover's, and the heat between them, around them, seemed to eradicate the years of desperate loneliness.

Placing one hand between them, Weiss caressed Madisyn, at the same time undulating against her busy fingers. As Madisyn felt impossible heat emanate from inside her belly and between her thighs, she wrapped her legs around Weiss. It was when she felt Weiss's rapid, strong heartbeat against her own chest that she knew.

She was Madisyn Pimm, loving and caring humanoid, who in turn was fully capable of loving Weiss and caring for her. She was real and she was still here.

EPILOGUE

Four months later

Kellen O'Dal stood with Rae behind the prince as he rose from the gilded throne. Armeo, a mere thirteen years old, wore white and gold, the traditional Gantharian O'Saral Royale colors. Tradition also dictated that he would make his first appearance before the Gantharian people on the stairs leading up to the royal palace gates. Granted, the palace was still in ruins and it was doubtful if it would be possible to rebuild it to its former glory. Many Gantharians wanted to, but the Gantharian funds would be better spent on more pressing matters: hospitals and schools, to start with.

Glancing to her left, Kellen saw Rae regard the crowd with narrow eyes. Not a gan'thet master, Rae wasn't dressed in the Ruby Red suit but in a form-fitting black version, which Rae had found a bit too revealing, but succumbed to when she viewed images of previous protectors. Kellen had never seen her look more commanding than she did now with the black leather-like cape billowing behind her.

To Rae's left stood Ewan and Dahlia, wearing their respective uniforms as admiral and chief diplomat. Dahlia was one of the negotiators who had worked tirelessly with the Gantharian interim government, and she was also Armeo's grandmother. In addition to being his grandfather, Ewan was the highest-ranking SC military presence at Gantharat. On the other side of Kellen were three representatives of the M'Aido family from Onotharat, distant relatives of Armeo's Onotharian father.

Behind them, dressed in civilian festive attire, Andreia M'Aldovar sat next to Roshan O'Landha in the first row of white chairs, both representing the leadership of the former resistance movement. Mikael O'Landha, Roshan's father who had suffered for more than twenty-five years on an Onotharian asteroid prison before his rescue, sat in a hover chair next to his daughter. Behind them, distinguished guests and friends from the Supreme Constellations and Gantharat sat in row after row. Kellen had greeted them all personally and was pleased to see, sitting beside Owena and Leanne, Dwyn and Emeron, who'd helped save Dahlia when M'Aldovar kidnapped her. To everybody's joy, the de Vies family had traveled from Earth. Dorinda, their daughter and Armeo's best friend, had been instrumental in helping Armeo cope when both his guardians were deployed. Next to them stood Madisyn Pimm and Weiss Kyakh, who had shortened the Onotharian war effort by years when they prevented Trax from obtaining davic crystals.

"And now to another historic event," the official Gantharian speaker said, raising his hands. "We have regained an O'Saral Royale to take the throne, but that is not all. Today, for the first time in more than a hundred years, a member of the royal family will initiate a new line of protectors."

Murmurs erupted in the crowd and the cheering grew louder as Ayahliss stepped forward and knelt before Armeo. In danger of choking up, Kellen forced herself to think of the scene from last night when Ayahliss and Armeo had "practiced" and eventually ended up giggling on the floor, much to the chagrin of the newly appointed court officials. Kellen, who knew how nervous Ayahliss was about the ceremony, thought it was good to get all potential nervous giggles out of the way.

Ayahliss looked up at Armeo as he extended his right hand to his new marshal of the realm, a young man whose grandfather and father had held the position before him. The marshal handed over a deep red cape lined with silver threads. Armeo took it and reverently held it for a moment before he addressed Ayahliss and the several hundred thousand people who filled the big field outside the ruins and the streets of Ganath.

"People of Gantharat." His young voice echoed through the city via the sound system. "I am honored to initiate a new member of the royal court. Almost thirty years ago, we lost most of our protectors when the occupation commenced that left Gantharat in the shadows for decades. We now know that greedy, corrupt leaders, not the majority of the Onotharian people, wanted them destroyed. I stand before you as your prince, but also as an Onotharian, and that is how we must proceed as a nation. We must remember that the Onotharian people still suffer on a depleted planet, and despite the way the occupiers have mismanaged it, Gantharat is still very rich in natural resources. We can afford to share with those who have less."

Kellen monitored the reaction to Armeo's words. They were his own, drafted over weeks and only slightly edited by his grandmother. Most of the people looked adoringly at the young O'Saral Royale, but a few frowned. The hatred toward the Onotharians ran deep with some.

"It is my pleasure that my first official duty is a positive one. My friend Ayahliss, who has proved herself as a member of the resistance and as an unofficial member of my security detail, has completed her training. She will today receive the Ruby Red Cape of the Silver Order, the second-highest rank among protectors."

Armeo let the cape billow in the wind and then placed it around Ayahliss's shoulders. He gave her his hand and she rose to stand in front of him.

"Prince Armeo," she said, "I am now your protector and will serve as such. You and your family will be mine to keep safe, and I will do so with pride and self-sacrifice." Ayahliss turned and bowed to the cheering public. She smiled broadly, walked over to Judge Beqq, who waited among the dignitaries, and kissed her. The judge had accepted a position as head negotiator and supreme judge on Gantharat earlier in the week.

Armeo looked relieved as he sat down on his renovated throne. He glanced over at Kellen and Rae, who gave him a discreet nod of approval. Kellen suppressed a smile at her blatant disregard for protocol.

❖

The large villa, built inside the old palace walls by Gantharian masons and carpenters over the last four months, easily hosted the festivities for two hundred guests. Outside, five hundred more celebrated the return of the last O'Saral Royale. The three protectors were on duty overseeing the security arrangements, aided by their friends.

In the ballroom, Ayahliss danced with Amereena Beqq, surrounded by dignitaries from the closest sectors. Rae stood watching, a glass of water in her left hand, the right resting on her holster.

"Never quite relaxed around him, are you, Rae?" a male voice said. Marco Thorosac, leader of the Supreme Constellations, and his wife joined Rae at the far end of the dance floor.

"He's my responsibility, and my son," Rae said politely.

"I didn't mean to criticize. On the contrary. You're perfect for this job."

"As a protector? Doubtful. I'm horrible with the rods and will never earn my Ruby Red suit and cape." Rae shrugged.

"Perhaps not, but you will make a very good fleet admiral for the new Gantharian space fleet."

"What?" Rae spun so fast she spilt water on her shoes.

"Marco," his wife said, admonishing him. "I told you to pick a better time and place to ask her."

"I'm stunned." Rae looked at her father, who approached them, smiling broadly. "Dad. You knew about this."

"I did."

"As did I," Kellen said from behind her. "Since this afternoon. Ewan made me promise not to say anything."

"I'm speechless." Rae looked around her, at the dancing people, the son of her heart, Kellen, whom she loved more than life itself, and her parents. "And I accept."

"Splendid." Councilman Thorosac beamed. "This deserves a toast. Gantharian champagne." He motioned for a waiter with a large tray of champagne flutes.

Soon they all stood in a large circle, and Rae looked at them all as she toasted family, friends, colleagues, and subordinates who had all had a role in the liberation of Gantharat in general, and in her and Kellen's life in particular. Other faces, the images of the individuals who had fought them every step of the way, lingered in her mind, but only to remind her why they needed to remain cautious. Hox M'Ekar was imprisoned, as was Trax M'Aldovar. Most of the Onotharian oppressors had gone into exile—some on Onotharat, others on home worlds farther away.

"I have another toast to make," Kellen said, interrupting Rae's thoughts. "To my wife, Rae, who dared to put her life and career on the line and marry a strange Gantharian woman and…love her…" Kellen swallowed hard, but crystal blue tears ran down her cheeks. "And love her and the boy she brought to the Gamma VI space station."

"To Rae!" The voices around her echoed as they all raised their glasses. Rae returned the toast, but focused only on Kellen. She raised her free hand and wiped away the tears.

"To Kellen," Rae whispered, out of earshot. "Who dared to love her captor and trust her with her heart."

The music began again, and this time, knowing their subordinates were in control of security, Rae bowed before Kellen and asked her to dance.

About the Author

Gun Brooke resides in the countryside in Sweden with her very patient family. A retired neonatal intensive care nurse, she now writes full time, only rarely taking a break to create Web sites for herself or others and to do computer graphics. Gun writes both romances and sci-fi.

Visit Gun online at http://www.gbrooke-fiction.com
Facebook: http://www.facebook.com/gunbach
Twitter: http://twitter.com/redheadgrrl1960
Tumblr: http://gunbrooke.tumblr.com/
Email: gun.brooke@gmail.com

Bold Strokes
BOOKS
WEBSTORE
PRINT AND EBOOKS
Romance
Mystery
Intrigue
MATINEE BOOKS
LIBERTY
EDITION
BOLD
STROKES
BOOKS
Adventure
victory
EDITIONS
AEROS
e
BOOKS
Erotica
Fantasy
Sci-Fi
http://www.boldstrokesbooks.com